"What we did last night was definitely not nice..."

Garrett discreetly drew his fingers down the length of Tiffany's spine before cupping her bottom through her dress.

Tiffany shivered at the touch.

Now she wished they were anywhere but here in this crowd. The way Garrett talked to her, the way he'd been looking at her since their eyes had met at the head of the aisle told her that he wanted more.

So did she.

"On the contrary, I think the things we did were *very* nice."

"If you thought that was *nice,* then maybe I need to work harder at living up to my badass bodyguard image," he said, and the look he sent her made her wonder what bad-boy secrets Garrett might be hiding.

She was dying to find out, but it was supposed to be only that one time. Just one night.

"I suppose I could give you another chance to show me how bad you are," she said, playing it cool even as her heart beat faster at the thought of being with Garrett again.

He stepped a little closer.

"Oh, I can be very bad...."

Blaze

Dear Reader,

Bodyguard Garrett Berringer—suave and sexy as all get-out—jumped from the page for me from the moment he appeared in *Mine Until Morning*. A widower who's waiting for his heart to heal, Garrett just needed to meet the right heroine.

When Garrett ends up as a reluctant groomsman in his friend's wedding, paired with bridesmaid Tiffany Walker, he falls head over heels—right into her bed. Their hot weekend affair should've lasted only a night or two, but Tiffany, a private eye in training, clearly needs Garrett to be her unofficial bodyguard as she tries to solve a dangerous crime. Garrett makes sure that he guards Tiffany *very* closely.

As they tour the City by the Bay and solve the crime, they also fall in love. It was a great story to write, and I hope you enjoy it. The best part is that there are two more Berringer brothers who have to find their perfect matches, so keep an eye out for Ely's and Chance's books in December and January. Drop me an email or catch me on Facebook to let me know what you think!

Happy reading,

Samantha Hunter

Samantha Hunter

YOURS FOR THE NIGHT
&
VIRTUALLY PERFECT

HARLEQUIN®

entertain, enrich, inspire™

ISBN-13: 978-0-373-79724-0

YOURS FOR THE NIGHT

Copyright © 2012 by Harlequin Books S.A.

The publisher acknowledges the copyright holder of the individual works as follows:

YOURS FOR THE NIGHT
Copyright © 2012 by Samantha Hunter

VIRTUALLY PERFECT
Copyright © 2004 by Samantha Hunter

Recycling programs for this product may not exist in your area.

www.Harlequin.com

Printed in U.S.A.

CONTENTS

ABOUT THE AUTHOR

Samantha Hunter lives in Syracuse, New York, where she writes full-time for Harlequin Books. When she's not plotting her next story, Sam likes to work in her garden, quilt, cook, read and spend time with her husband and their dogs. Most days you can find Sam chatting on the Harlequin Blaze boards at Harlequin.com, or you can check out what's new, enter contests or drop her a note at her website, www.samanthahunter.com.

Books by Samantha Hunter

To get the inside scoop on Harlequin Blaze and its talented writers, be sure to check out blazeauthors.com.

All backlist available in ebook. Don't miss any of our special offers. Write to us at the following address for information on our newest releases.

Harlequin Reader Service
U.S.: 3010 Walden Ave., P.O. Box 1325, Buffalo, NY 14269
Canadian: P.O. Box 609, Fort Erie, Ont. L2A 5X3

YOURS FOR THE NIGHT

Thanks to Jamie S for her help with my questions about rooftop access and other geographic nuggets of information about San Francisco. You were so helpful!

Thanks to Selena Blake and Donna Cummings for beta reading and then reading again. And again.

Many thanks to my editors and friends who offered patience and encouragement during a difficult time when this book was being written; you are appreciated every day.

And for my parents, who are deeply missed.

1

THE FULL-ON chaos of San Francisco's Union Square on Friday night surrounded Garrett Berringer as he walked down the concrete steps of the Westin St. Francis. A warm November breeze blew through the city, and he hadn't bothered with a coat. People hurried by as he stood, taking it all in.

The flight from Philadelphia had been uneventful and long. Tonight, there was time to relax before spending all of Saturday at a friend's wedding. Ed was an old friend from college, and he'd been one of the ushers at Garrett's wedding.

A trolley packed with tourists rolled by. The grinding sound of the wheels on the tracks was much louder than he'd imagined, and not nearly as romantic as it came across in the movies. Across the street, people in the square were setting up for a weekend art festival. Onlookers milled around, standing in line at a small café located in the center of the square by the bronze statue of the Goddess of Victory.

Garrett's eye was drawn to two huge painted hearts that were poised on either side of the square, one beneath a towering palm tree. The palm trees, he'd read, were not native to the city, but brought in and planted at significant cost. The hearts were the city's ornamental symbol.

A young couple embraced in front of one of the hearts while someone snapped a picture of them. Garrett's heart experienced a slight pinch. He hadn't left his heart in San Francisco, but part of it was back on the east coast, where his late wife, Lainey, had died—or rather, where she had been killed. They'd been married for six years when it happened, and now she'd been gone equally long. A strange kind of circle, he thought. They'd married young, their future full of so much promise, all destroyed in one instant.

Lainey, a junior state prosecutor, had been working her first big case—a murder trial against a local gang member. She'd been so excited about it all. After earning her guilty verdict, she'd been on her way to meet Garrett and his family for a celebration. However, the brother of the convicted killer had waited for her to leave court, following her in his SUV.

All prosecutors received threats now and then, but there had been none during the trial. There was no reason to think she was in specific danger. Or so Garrett told himself, thousands of times when agonizing about not having picked her up that day. The crash would still have happened, but so many times he'd wished he'd been with her.

The gang member's brother had broad-sided her at full speed, killing her instantly. Garrett supposed he'd hoped to make it look like an accident, hoping to walk away, but he'd been seriously injured as well. Garrett waited until he was released from the hospital and testified at his trial. Both brothers ended up convicted to life sentences. Garrett had attended their trials and planned to attend any probation hearings to make sure they never went free.

Suddenly, the palm trees, the people, the colorful hearts, all made him a little homesick for life back east. He'd thought he'd wanted to leave it all behind. Cold, dark days and the impending holiday. Only seven days away, Thanksgiving was always a stark reminder in itself. The crash had happened a few days before the holiday. Had he really thought he could outrun the memory by traveling across the country, changing the scenery?

Turning away from the couple and the hearts, he stepped out to cross traffic. He'd let his grief go, thankful for what he'd once had with his young wife, but sometimes he wondered if he would ever meet anyone as right for him as Lainey had been. In six years, he'd had no significant *click* with any woman he spent time with. Sex, a few dates, but no click.

He'd met her when he was studying business management in college; he also had a minor in criminal justice. He'd been thinking about following in her footsteps and attending law school. After her death, he'd thrown himself into creating the bodyguard business—Berringer Bodyguards—with his brother Jonas, who had quit the Philadelphia police force around the same time. He couldn't save Lainey, but he had saved many others since.

Garrett had always enjoyed that he and Lainey had similar sensibilities and goals, the same appreciation for organization and a quiet life. They were both practical thinkers and rarely fought. Those were qualities that now made him feel antiquated, even at a youthful thirty-six years old. Stepping back, a young man with orange hair zipped by him on a skateboard, and Garrett smiled at the timing.

Garrett hadn't taken time away from the business since the funeral, as his brothers frequently pointed out. Who needed time off? What was he going to do with it? He had weekends and evenings to fish, spend some time with family. He was a simple, basic man.

Finally, though, vacation was thrust upon him whether

he wanted it or not. Jonas had taken off on a holiday trip with his new wife, Tessa. They'd barely returned from their honeymoon when they were off again with her father to spend a few weeks in Europe over the Thanksgiving holiday.

Garrett couldn't be more thrilled for his brother, but some parts of the wedding had been difficult. Dancing with Tessa in her gorgeous dress made him recall dancing with Lainey on their special day, and he'd been happy to escape afterward. He knew his real fear, down deep, was wondering if there ever would be anyone else for him again. Maybe he'd had his shot at happiness.

If so, he'd live with that. He would do it all over again, even if it ended the same way, he assured himself.

About to gently decline flowers from a street person attempting a sale, he gave in and bought the thatch of daisies that looked like they had seen better days, too, then stood looking down at them, feeling ridiculous.

What the heck was he going to do with a bunch of daisies?

Chance, his youngest brother, had been itching to go on a survivalist training trip that was only offered for the month of November. Their parents were off to Florida, their first year as "snowbirds," escaping the cold winter to live in the Florida sun. Ely had taken off with a bunch of old military friends for a wild vacation somewhere, so they'd decided to close the business through the New Year.

When Garrett had gotten the invitation to the wedding, it seemed like a better choice than haunting around Philly with too much time on his hands or following his parents to Florida.

He walked down a few blocks and turned left, remembering the general directions the concierge had given him to get to Chinatown. The daisies swung at his side, gripped tightly in his hand, all but forgotten as he walked on, pondering his evening.

Later he could grab some dinner and go back to his room to read or look through brochures and maps, planning for what he'd do over the next month.

As he passed small shops loaded with all kinds of Asian items, he saw a beautiful, hand-carved garden statue that he knew Tessa would love for the window of the soaps and lotions shop that she owned back in Philly. A late wedding present, as he hadn't been sure what to buy at the time. This would be perfect. Garrett turned into the store to ask about it when his cell phone rang.

"Garrett," he answered absently, still studying the ornate fountain, looking for a price tag.

"Gar, my man! You're here?"

It was Ed, and Garrett smiled at his friend's familiar, boisterous tone. "Yep. Walking through Chinatown as we speak. How are you doing on your last night as a single man?"

"Happy to leave it behind," Ed said. "I can't wait for you to meet Isabel."

"I'm looking forward to it."

"You have plans for tonight?"

"Nothing much. Just unwinding from the flight and hanging out."

"Um, would you be interested in coming to the rehearsal dinner?"

Garrett squinted, looking down at the daisies, which were starting to look a little wilted. How to gracefully decline?

Ed was only being polite since Garrett was in town alone, he was sure. Garrett had often encountered the same from well-meaning friends since becoming a widower. He appreciated the intention, though it was unnecessary. He didn't mind being alone; he'd more or less gotten used to it.

"Isn't that for people in the wedding party?" he hedged, pointing out the obvious.

"Um, well, that's kind of the other reason I'm calling. I need a favor."

"Sure, shoot." Garrett offered, assuming it might be a simple thing, like picking up more film.

"Isabel's cousin, one of our ushers, has food poisoning. It's bad, and he's in the hospital for the next few days."

"Sorry to hear it."

"Thanks. But we're down one usher the night before the wedding…"

Garrett's warning bells rang a second too late.

"…and we were hoping you could take his place."

Words deserted him for the moment, so Ed quickly filled in the silence.

"I know. I didn't ask you to stand up for us in the first place because I didn't want to make you feel obligated to come out here. And I know things are busy, with the business, and everything else."

Garrett knew "everything else" was the fact that he was a widower.

"I completely understand if you can't do it, bud. I'm happy that you're even here."

Garrett took a deep breath, releasing it. "It's just, I… well, I don't have a tux, right? Or, anything…" he finished lamely, knowing his goose was cooked. How could he say no when Ed needed him?

"Not a problem. Jimmy's around your size, if I recall, and his tux could probably be fit to you pretty quickly, if we can get to the tailor early tomorrow."

"Oh, well, that's good, then," he said with false brightness, running a hand through his hair and wishing he could think of some way to get out of this, but he couldn't. He'd been totally caught off guard.

"I'll owe you, Gar. Isabel was freaking out. I told her two girls could be escorted by one of the other ushers, but she was upset about pictures being out of balance or whatever," Ed said, the familiar male tone making Garrett smile.

He remembered how frantic Lainey had been in the days before their wedding, too, even though theirs had been a small one. Things like how pictures looked or what people wore were important, at least to the brides. He sighed, accepting his fate.

"It's my pleasure. How do I get there?"

"I have a car on its way to pick you up outside the hotel."

Garrett had to laugh out loud at Ed's characteristic brashness. "I'll be there, but your driver will have to wait for me to change. I'm not exactly dressed for a rehearsal dinner at the moment."

"It's pretty casual tonight, so don't worry about that. Just hop in and come. In fact, if you let me know where you are, I'll have them come to you."

"Thanks, Ed." He clicked the phone off after telling him the name of the shop. Maybe it wouldn't be so bad, Garrett thought, trying to convince himself while keeping an eye out for the car and kissing his restful night alone goodbye.

TIFFANY WALKER LOOKED at her watch and tried to avoid wrinkling her dress too badly as she twisted to focus her 35-millimeter lens on the hotel window. The camera was eleven years old—a high-school graduation gift—from when she was sure she wanted to study to be a professional photographer. It was a high-quality piece of equipment that she had, at the time, imagined using to frame brilliant nature shots that would appear in national magazines, or maybe using it among the throng of photographers on a fashion runway.

Never in a million years had she imagined using it to get the money shot of a cheating spouse at a seedy hotel in a San Francisco neighborhood she didn't normally visit. This was her third attempt before her client had threatened not to pay if she didn't come up with something Mrs. Hooper could use to nail her philandering husband. At this point, all she had were pictures of Mr. Hooper entering the hotel, and the length of a female arm holding the door open for him. Not very incriminating.

The pay was minimal; what Tiffany was more worried about was the ding to her fledgling reputation as a private investigator. It was competitive, and there were dozens of P.I.s more experienced than she was in the area. She'd found one agency so overbooked that they'd decided to throw her the few bones they tossed out. She'd only gotten her license the month before, after completing her online certification, and this was her second job.

Much like the bent trajectory of her photography ambitions, this wasn't exactly what she wanted to do as a private investigator—she wanted to solve cases, murders and other important, life-changing crimes. But everyone had to start somewhere.

Marcus Hooper was definitely cheating on his wife. Tiffany had seen him come to this hotel several times now, and had seen a woman's hand on the door as she let Marcus in. But after that, they were out of view. The woman never stepped outside the door. What Tiffany knew and what she could prove were two different things. She'd taken all of the makes of cars and plate numbers from the lot, looking for repeats that she might track down to the woman in the room, but she must have taken a cab—a theory Tiffany was currently pursuing. Unsuccessfully. Cab companies were difficult to penetrate, let alone getting any one particular cabbie to talk. But she didn't need to know who the woman was—all she needed to do was catch Mr. Hooper in a compromising moment. Let him explain who it was to his wife and her lawyer.

Looking at her watch again, Tiffany groaned in frustration. The rehearsal dinner was tonight, and she had to be on time. As the lights clicked off up in Marcus's hotel room, she mentally calculated how long she had to spend on wedding responsibilities. No more than three hours.

If she was lucky, maybe Marcus would be here longer than that, and she could come back and finish the job. Maybe it was time to get a little more creative, pretend to be room service—wait, no, this place didn't have room service. But she could come up with some ruse to get him to open that door, and if she was standing right there, maybe she could get the shot and run.

It was risky, but she had to make this work. Good detectives did whatever they had to do to get the job done. She couldn't fail, not again.

She also couldn't risk anyone asking her why she was late to the dinner—or why she had been late to work a few times this week, and why she completely forgot her brother's birthday party Wednesday night.

No one knew about her new profession. Tiffany hadn't wanted to share until she knew she was going to meet with success. After a string of brilliant failures in life, her family very likely wouldn't support this new venture and she couldn't blame them.

So she led a double life. By day, she worked in her parents' jewelry store, making the rent and convincing them that she was a reliable adult. At night, she parked here in the lot of the Fall Inn and waited to get photos of a cheating spouse.

Putting the camera down safely on the car seat and starting the engine, she drove out of the lot and toward Sausalito, where the dinner was being held. A short while later she arrived and was only a teeny bit late.

Smoothing the front of her dress, she grabbed a champagne cocktail from the tray that a server carried past her as she entered the reception room, spotting the table where her party congregated. It was going to take a few more fizzy peach drinks to make it through this evening, though she'd only allow herself one, since she still had work to do.

Her worlds had almost collided earlier. One of the employees who worked the afternoon shift at Jarvis Jewelry —the jewelry store owned by her family and named after her grandfather, Jarvis Walker—had a personal emergency that left Tiffany on her own to run the counter, finish the weekly inventory and close up the store. Her parents were off for the weekend on a purchasing trip they couldn't cancel, and Tiffany was left in charge. She almost hadn't done it all, changed her clothes and gotten ready for the party before heading out to catch Marcus after he left his job, following him to the hotel. He went there Monday, Wednesday and Friday, like clockwork.

She'd have thought a cheating husband might be a little less predictable, but he'd followed the same routine each time. She could have called her younger brother to cover the store, but Nick was neck-deep in his MBA program at Berkeley, and he spent weekends up to his ears in books. He would take over Jarvis's someday—with her blessing— but for the moment, she was perfectly competent to watch over the place. Or at least, that was what she was trying to prove to her parents. Also, Nick might have questions. He was a little too perceptive sometimes. *Maybe he should be the detective,* she thought with a sigh.

She didn't mind working at the store; she needed a paycheck and it settled some of her parents' worries that their eldest daughter was never going to be successful at anything. Sometimes Tiffany wondered about that, too.

Turning her thoughts back to the wedding, she wondered why they even needed to rehearse. How hard could it be to walk down an aisle and stand still for fifteen minutes while her friend got married? It was the first wedding she'd been in, and it had all been a lot of fuss, though fun at times. It was slightly less fun being paired up with Jimmy, Isabel's brother. He was a nice enough guy, harmless, really, though he could find any excuse imaginable to touch her.

During a dance at the engagement party, he'd snuck his hands down to her backside before they were halfway through the song. She'd been taking some local self-defense classes to be prepared for any trouble she might confront in her investigations. Also on the sly, she was learning to shoot, though she didn't own a gun yet. She traveled to a rural shooting range in Point Reyes once a week for lessons, far away enough that word could not get back to her family.

Still, neither skill would help her deal with the bride's touchy-feely brother.

Finishing off her cocktail she took her seat at the table, the chair next to hers still empty.

"Tiff, you made it!" Isabel chirped, dashing around the table as fast as her high heels would allow, wrapping Tiffany in a perfumed hug. Isabel had been her friend since fourth grade, and Tiffany was really happy for her. She only wished her good pal could have matched her up with anyone but her little brother.

Then again, Jimmy was a safe bet for Tiffany being able to keep her resolution to swear off men for a while—there was no way she'd consider getting involved with him at all.

"I told you I would," Tiffany said. She had even called to let them know she'd be a few minutes late.

"I know, but, well, you know how things go with you sometimes," her friend said with no malice at all, hugging her again.

Tiffany did know. She was, after all, Tiffany the Impetuous. Tiffany the Spontaneous. Nick had called her "Froggy" for years because she had something of a reputation for leaping before she looked. Hopping from one thing to another. She'd always defended her adventurous spirit, championed spontaneity, but looking thirty in the face was even making her wonder if she'd ever find her real path in life.

She had a college degree in English, but didn't want to teach or write. So, she had set out into the world to find her bliss.

Among a litany of boring or dead-end jobs was her stint as a flight attendant, which she had liked, but she hadn't been able to handle the rude passengers.

Then there was the time she started her own dog-walking business, which was a booming industry in the Bay area, but after one bad bite, she was reluctant to carry on with that enterprise.

The capstone was emptying her savings to go into business with a friend who had started an adventure-tourism company. She'd become a local hiking guide. It sounded fun—until she had gotten lost in Yosemite overnight with eight tourists. Luckily, everyone was fine, and Paul was good at *his* part of the job. The business hadn't been running long enough to see much profit, so he couldn't buy her half out now, but swore he would. She trusted him, but it still left her broke. Adventurous as she was, she was more of a city girl.

And then there was Brice.

Everyone she knew had told her Brice was a bad bet, but she had refused to listen. He'd been charming, sweet, sexy—and a crook. He'd emailed her to ask her to dinner one night, and when she got home—after being stood up—everything she owned was gone. Stolen. He'd cleaned her out. That would never have happened to any of her favorite fictional detectives. Well, maybe to Veronica Mars, who had suffered worse.

The cops said they couldn't do a thing about it because she'd given him a key and legally, he lived in the apartment. There was no way she could prove anything he had taken was hers as she hadn't kept receipts, many of the items bought years before.

It was a hard lesson learned. She needed to focus, to be responsible. The first step had been taking a responsible job. The next was staying away from men until she could trust her judgment again. Still, she needed to pursue her dreams, but she was going to do it in a more sensible—and low-key—way. Work at the store—familiar but boring—and make her parents happy. Being in the wedding with Jimmy made Isabel happy, and it certainly made Jimmy happy. Tiffany would be happy if she could just get that picture of Marcus for his wife.

"Where's Jimmy?" she asked, looking down at the empty seat.

"Oh, I was so busy I forgot to call and tell you. Jim got severe food poisoning. He's in the hospital."

"That's awful! Will he be okay?" Tiffany didn't like Jimmy all that much, but still didn't wish him that kind of suffering.

"He'll be fine, but he was really sick."

"So he won't be in the wedding?"

"No, he can't be," Isabel said sadly.

"Um, do I have to do this alone?"

Somehow that suddenly made her more nervous than fending off Jimmy's octopus hands for a few hours.

"I wasn't sure what we were going to do, but Ed said he has a friend in town who will take Jim's place. He's on his way here."

"Oh. A stranger?" Tiffany said, wary but intrigued.

"He's a friend of Ed's from college. He's here from Philadelphia. I asked Ed what he looked like, but you know how guys are. He just said 'tall,'" Isabel said, lowering her voice to mimic her husband-to-be, laughing.

Tiffany smiled, intent on being a good sport. "I'm sure he'll be great if he's a friend of Ed's."

"Probably. Maybe it will be more fun for you. I know you weren't crazy about being paired up with Jimmy, but he's always had a crush on you. I just couldn't say no when he asked me," Isabel said by way of apology.

"Hey, Jimmy's a great guy. I'm just too old for him," Tiffany said, an excuse that had saved her from having to be fixed up with Mr. Hands before.

"Please, this is me you're talking to," Isabel said with a grin. "You know my parents would love you to go out with him, but I completely get it. He can be…pushy, I know. No worries," she said, hugging Tiffany again.

"Thanks, Iz," she said, meaning it.

Tiffany smiled at the other attendants who were already sitting, and she joined them as Isabel returned to the other side of the table to sit with Ed. She was glad she'd made it in time for dinner. Her stomach was growling; she hadn't had a chance to eat anything since breakfast.

She focused on the first course that a server placed before her and picked up her fork, ready to dig in when she heard her name again.

"*Pssst,* Tiff! *Psssst!*"

She looked up, zeroing in on Isabel, who was urgently gesturing toward the entrance to the restaurant.

Tiffany looked, curious what Isabel could be so excited about. Then she saw him.

She was sure the man making a beeline for their table was an actor, a celebrity she'd seen before but couldn't place. Tall and confident, he moved with a powerful, smooth stride, seemingly oblivious to his own dangerous good looks.

Then Tiffany finally realized why Isabel was so worked up.

It wasn't a celebrity-spotting, but the new usher.

She whipped back around to look at the bride-to-be, mouthing "Is *that* him?" across the table. Isabel nodded enthusiastically.

Mary, the matron of honor, who was sitting directly across from Tiffany sent her the thumbs-up, wiggling her eyebrows.

The new guy walked around the other side of the table to where Ed was sitting, and that was when Tiffany saw the somewhat battered spray of flowers he was holding. They had certainly seen better days, and she discreetly covered a smile at how they sort of moved with his hand, like an extension of his arm, losing a few petals every time he did so.

The two men shook hands warmly. Ed introduced Isabel to his friend as everyone watched, and she also gave the new guy a hug.

He was even more impressive up close, weary flowers and all.

"Do we all get to hug him?" Mary, Isabel's cousin, asked out loud, grinning, causing all of them to chuckle. Her husband laughed, too, shaking his head ruefully. Mary was often the comic relief, which had been a blessing at long dress fittings and times of other wedding stress.

Ed declared, "Sure!" and introduced his incredibly sexy friend as Garrett Berringer from Philadelphia, the new usher who was generous enough to stand in for Jimmy at the last minute.

It was lust at first sight for Tiffany.

She barely remembered her own name by the time he came to her chair; their eyes met first, sending a zing of excitement down to her toes.

"Hi, I'm Garrett."

His deep, gravelly voice had her rapt. When he smiled, his hazel eyes were friendly, but guarded. She got the impression that he was going along with the party, but perhaps not as social as he was pretending to be. It made him even more intriguing to her.

"Tiffany Walker," she said, trying to sound as casual as everyone else, though her breath caught a little as she put out her hand.

"Not a hugger?" he asked, his eyes warming slightly as his large hand encompassed hers and didn't let go right away.

The group at the table started chanting "hug, hug, hug," and Tiffany rolled her eyes at them. Garrett laughed, leaning in for a quick, polite hug before taking his seat. For the brief second he held her against him, everything inside of her melted, and her temperature went way, way up.

"Who are those mums for?" she asked, eyeing the desperate blooms.

"Mums?"

She pointed at the bouquet.

"Oh, I thought they were daisies," he said. "I bought them from a street person, and ended up sort of carrying them around. I almost forgot I had them," he said with a slight smile that made her toes wiggle. He was hot and sweet. Sweet-hot. Her favorite flavor.

"I see. Here, they don't travel well," she said, taking them from his hand, planting them in her water glass.

They made small talk as they ate, but Tiffany's imagination was working the whole time, wondering what he would look like out of his suit or half-covered by the new sheets she had just bought for her bed. Even the flowers perked up considerably as they sat and chatted over dinner, seeming to reflect her mood.

"Can I get you another drink?"

Tiffany blinked, taking in his sensual lips, a strong chin, slightly crooked nose and those tawny eyes. Like a lion's.

"Did you break your nose?" she asked, oblivious to the non sequitur.

He nodded, a slight smile tugging at the edge of those lips. "Yeah. Once or twice," he admitted. "My brothers and I all have. We played a lot of sports, and our work puts us in the way of fists now and then. Gives my mother fits."

"There are more at home like you?" Tiffany said, and heard Mary snort from across the table.

"Three more, actually, though my brother Jonas just got married."

"Congratulations," Tiffany said.

She thought maybe she'd noticed his gaze dip discreetly to her bodice, which showed a little more cleavage than she normally exposed, but her push-up bra was the only thing not in the laundry. She counted that as a lucky thing and sat up straighter.

"Can I get you another drink?" he repeated.

She shook her head with a smile, silently damning Marcus Hooper.

"So no, then?" There was a flicker of disappointment

in Garrett's eyes, thrilling her. He wanted to spend time with her, as well. If only.

"Maybe something non-alcoholic. I don't want to teeter down the aisle at the rehearsal," she joked.

"Don't worry, I'll keep you on course," he said, standing and offering her his arm, his words wiping her brain clear of any thoughts at all.

She stood, slipping her arm through his. It was old-fashioned gallantry, and she liked it.

She looked back to the activity around the table. "Oh, it must be time to get over to the church. It's not too far from here. I have my car if you need a ride," she offered, and then bit her lip, wondering if she wasn't leaping into spontaneous mode again.

"That would be great. To tell you the truth, I am a little out of my element here. I've never been in any wedding but my own and my brother's."

"Yeah, sure. No problem," she said breezily, all of her lusty thoughts spiraling right down the drain at his mention of being married. She looked down quickly and saw no ring.

Oh, great. Of course there had to be a catch. He'd been too perfect, but he was just one of *those*. A guy who took his ring off when he was out of town, though she didn't even see a tan mark from it. She didn't need to be a detective to figure out his game; she only needed to be female. She'd definitely seen a spark of answering lust in his eyes, but that only meant Tiffany was going for the record in being a loser-magnet.

She was stuck offering him a ride, so they walked out, joining the others. Tiffany might be Ms. Spontaneous, but that didn't include fooling around with married men. She had a few rules she wasn't willing to break. In spite of all of her promises to herself, she'd been ready to throw caution to the wind to spend some sexy one-on-one time with Garrett Berringer.

Now she didn't have to worry about that. Controlling herself around him would be no problem at all.

2

GARRETT SURVIVED THE rehearsal and in the end, he was glad he'd agreed to help Ed out. Mostly because of *her*.

Distracted from any sad memories by the woman he'd walked down the aisle with, he watched Tiffany look at the clock for what might have been the hundredth time in an hour. She appeared to be in a hurry to leave, saying goodbye to Isabel, from what he could tell.

Ed was in party mode the night before his wedding, and they'd all decided to go out for a round of drinks and some dancing after the church. Garrett had planned to go, hoping that he might get to know Tiffany a bit more. It had been a long time since his first thought upon meeting a woman was, *how do I get her into bed?*

She'd seemed responsive enough at dinner, flirting with him, unless he was seriously out of touch. Then, mysteriously, her attitude had cooled down considerably, inexplicably. Conversation on the drive to the church was limited to brief, general topics. She didn't laugh at his jokes, and she didn't meet his eyes once. Her posture was rigid as they had linked arms to walk down the aisle during the rehearsal.

And she hadn't stopped looking at her watch since

they'd gotten there. Was she in that much of a hurry to get away from him?

So what had he done to turn her into the ice queen? And how could he reverse that trend? He wasn't used to this, feeling unsettled, unsure of what to do next. Berringer Bodyguards was his main focus, and he liked it that way. He knew what to do there, and he did it well. The business was gaining more prestige—especially since his brother had married a U.S. senator's daughter—and it took even more of his time and energy.

But he wasn't there right now. He was here, watching Tiffany, whom he'd only known for a grand total of four hours. Less than that if you counted only the time they'd spoken directly to each other.

The rings on her fingers sparkled as he watched her talk, her graceful hands accenting her conversation. He knew in his gut that she would be as expressive in bed. He liked the loosely tied knot of long auburn hair at the nape of her neck and he wanted to untie it. Let it fall down over her shoulders, his fingers. He liked the scooped back of her dress, how it revealed the contours of her shoulders and neck. He liked the idea of planting kisses there.

A fling suddenly sounded like a very appealing addition to his vacation itinerary, but he wasn't sure she would agree. And now she was leaving, before he could find out what he had done to offend her. Watching her kiss Isabel's cheek and head to the door, he found himself following her out.

"Hey, Tiffany, hold on a second," he called to her, watching her pause and turn, her shoulders sinking a little as she seemed to accept her fate.

What the hell had he done to cause this reaction?

"So are you going to tell me what I did?" he asked,

looking directly into her gorgeous green eyes. Directness was usually best.

"I don't know what you mean," she said testily. "And I need to go," she said, clearly agitated and wanting to leave.

"Hmm. Did you know that while it's commonly thought that people who don't make eye contact are unreliable, in truth, someone who is lying will go out of their way to make eye contact, trying to convince you they are being honest?"

He saw irritation flash in her eyes, and her cheeks warmed, making her even prettier.

"Are you saying I'm a liar?" she asked, and tried to break away, but he held her fast. "Funny, I thought the same about you."

"When did I lie to you? We've only known each other for a few hours."

She glared at him, facing off in the middle of the small parking lot, until she sighed and shook her head.

"Look, drop it. I don't get involved with married men."

"That's a good policy, but I'm not married."

"Really? Here's an FYI—just because you don't wear your ring doesn't mean you're not married. Thanks but no thanks," she said, storming away, back stiff, nose turned up.

He thought she was amazingly cute, even though he had no idea what she was talking about.

"Wait," he said as he hurried up to follow her. "I'm *not* married. Who told you I was married?" he asked.

"You. You said you've only been in two weddings, your brother's and your *own*." She punctuated the last two words with an accusing finger poked into his chest.

"Ohhhh." He was used to everyone around him know-ing, and saw how she would have jumped to that conclusion. "I'm sorry. I *was* married. My wife died several years ago."

She gave him an even dirtier look. "Right. Listen, I get that you want to hook up while you're out of town, but I'm not interested. And it's pretty awful to say your wife died just to get some other woman to—"

Garrett reached into his back pocket, pulling out his wallet, sliding out a memorial card with Lainey's picture, and her dates of birth and death.

"This *was* my wife, Elaine," he said softly, showing Tiffany. "And this is her obit," he added, flipping the picture over where the funeral home had printed a lovely quote that he had selected at the time. He watched Tiffany read the back of the card, as if convincing herself it was real. Garrett knew what it said by heart: Elaine Elizabeth Berringer. Born May 20, 1978. Died November 15, 2006. *Remember two kisses, the first and the last.*

Tiffany stared at the picture for several long minutes, flipping it over in her hands, and when she looked back up at him, her eyes had welled.

Damn, now he'd made her cry.

"Don't cry, please," he said, almost desperately, taking the picture back and slipping it into his wallet. "I just wanted you to know I wasn't lying. Completely understandable how you would misinterpret what I said earlier," he added, and put his hands firmly on her shoulders, making her look at him.

Obviously he didn't quite have the way with women that he used to. "I'm sorry for making you cry, too," he added for good measure.

"No. I'm the one who's sorry. I always do this, leap to conclusions, leap into relationships, leap into trouble... I just tend to...*leap*. And what I said was horrible, considering. I am *so* sorry," she repeated. "She was lovely."

Garrett's heart softened even more. "Yes, she was. But it was a long time ago," he added, experiencing a little kick of surprise at how easily the words fell from his lips, accompanied by a tiny sting of guilt. He'd never before tried to push Lainey's memory away.

"How long were you married?" she asked.

"Six years," he said. "I put this in my pocket at the funeral. It took me two years to clear a lot of her things out of the house, three years to take my ring off... I guess I thought I should keep something of her with me."

Tiffany smiled a little. "That's sweet, and sad."

Garrett frowned. First Tiffany thought he was a player trying to have an out-of-town fling behind his wife's back, then he'd called her a liar and made her cry. Now she thought he was clinging to the memory of his long-dead wife.

When he'd lost Lainey, it was as if Garrett had died, too. He would wake up, move, breathe, eat because of the demands of his body and because he knew his family worried about him. They grieved, too, and he didn't want to cause them any more pain.

Gradually, it got easier, better. The business had saved him. His brothers, his family, had saved him. His heart had scarred over sufficiently that he could go on. But he hadn't really *moved* on.

Meeting Tiffany made his blood move again, coursing through him with new vigor. He was excited for the first time in a long time, his heart doing more now than just keeping him alive.

And he *was* alive. He'd never known that fact more keenly than when he looked down into Tiffany's face, her beautiful green eyes still a little blurry with tears.

Garrett pulled her closer, experimenting, operating on instinct and sheer male desire. It coursed through his blood like a river that had been held back for too long. He could only think of one way to convince Tiffany that he was very much living in the present, not the past.

He kissed her.

It was as simple as that.

Or so he thought, until her arms crept around his neck and that lovely, lush, curvy body pressed into his and she was kissing him back.

"Yeah, just like that," he breathed against her mouth, and dove back in, plundering the inside of her mouth with his tongue. Suddenly starving, he couldn't taste or touch enough of her.

Walking her back, he pressed her up against the car, loving how she kissed him as hungrily and desperately as he did her. He moved his hands over full breasts that strained the tantalizingly thin material of her dress. Her hands stroked his back, and then went down to his butt, her fingers gripping him and pulling his hardness closer into the soft cushion of her hip.

She sighed into his mouth. It was such a pure, uninhibited sound of pleasure that he wanted to lift up her dress and take her right there. Garrett—known amongst his family and friends for his level-headedness, his deeply ingrained sense of responsibility and self-control—was ready to get as deep inside this woman as he could, here and now.

Voices behind him reminded him they were still in an all-too-public place for that. He backed away slightly, clearing his throat.

"I don't usually, I mean, I shouldn't have—" she said. Her tone was husky, breathless, turning him on even more.

"Come back to my room with me," he interrupted, kissing her again, unable to get enough of how she melted into him. "Please," he added, doing what he had been fantasizing about and sliding his hand up to her neck, releasing her hair from its knot.

As it fell down around her shoulders, her eyes darkened as they held his, but she shook her head.

"I have to go. I have…work."

Work? At this time of the evening?

"Skip it."

"I can't," she said, pushing gently away.

"Then meet me later."

She stared at him long and hard, and shook her head again. "I don't know how long I'll be."

"I don't care. Here's my hotel and room number. I'll wait."

She nodded, clearly torn, which gave him hope. Then she got in her car, drove away, leaving him standing, watching, and hoping that she'd take him up on his offer.

Otherwise, it was going to be a very long night.

TIFFANY KNEW SHE was doing it again as she rode in the elevator all the way up to his room. It was only an hour after she'd left him, but Marcus's car was gone, the room empty. She'd knocked on the door, hoping that the woman he'd been meeting might answer, and maybe she could get a lead that way, but there had been no answer.

Her second detective job was a bust, and rather than go home and be depressed at her failure for the rest of the night, she decided to let Garrett take her mind off things.

Tiffany was being impulsive. She wasn't thinking about consequences or complications.

But what was the harm? Garrett was in town for the wedding, and people hooked up at weddings all the time, right? So she had a little fling with an usher over the weekend. So what? Then he would go back to the east coast, and she would go back to her life as it was. No one would be the wiser.

Everything would be fine.

Besides, his kiss had been *soooo* good.

Walking down to his room, she steeled herself once more to knock on her second hotel room door of the evening, and hoped for better results this time.

What if he had changed his mind?

He opened the door, looking delicious in loose jeans, a T-shirt and bare feet. His smile and the warmth that flooded his eyes told her he was glad to see her. He held a book in his hands—he'd been reading, apparently. She loved that he read.

"Hi," she said, suddenly feeling a bit self-conscious.

"Hi. That didn't take long," he said.

"Yeah, I managed to finish quicker than usual," she said, not intending to tell him what had really happened.

"I'm glad you came," he said, standing aside to let her in, and massive doubt assailed her.

After what she'd been through with Brice, and after what she'd seen even in her short stint as a detective, was this smart? Meeting a man she barely knew at his hotel room, and no one even knew she was here?

Rationality prevailed; Garrett was not Brice. Or Marcus Hooper. He was a good friend of Ed's, and lowlifes didn't usually rent suites in upscale hotels.

"You okay?" he asked.

She broke out in a smile, feeling strange. "Yeah, sorry. I just don't normally, um, well…do this kind of thing."

He smiled, too. "Yeah, me either. And if you want, we could just go down to the bar for a drink, and talk. That would be fine," he said, making her relax even more.

"No, I'm fine," she said, meaning it and walking inside,

giving a low whistle as she took in the huge room. She'd noticed it was a suite, but this was living in style, for sure.

"I splurged since I was going to be here for a month. I didn't always want to be eating out, or cramped up in a little room."

"Makes sense," she said.

"I didn't think it would be quite this luxurious, but it is pretty nice, I agree."

A large chandelier sparkled in the light, and Tiffany was transfixed on that for a moment.

The suite had three rooms and a kitchenette, including the main living area, a large master bedroom and bath. The small kitchenette was tucked into the side of the main room, and on the other side, tall windows revealed a fantastic view of Union Square and the San Francisco skyline. Tiffany crossed to the window, drawing back the curtain.

"I never get tired of looking at this city," she said in awe.

Garrett walked up behind her, placing his hands on her shoulders and looking at the view with her. "It is pretty spectacular. I can't wait to get to know it better. And you. I'd like to get to know you better, too," he said, his voice soft and low.

"What would you like to know?" she said, her voice huskier than usual. His touch seemed to do that.

"Let me make you a drink—I was having a bourbon. You want one?"

"That would be nice," she said, turning as he crossed to the bar where a bottle of expensive whiskey had apparently just been opened. "Neat, please."

He smiled. "A woman after my own heart."

"I overheard you telling Mary's husband you're a bodyguard?"

"Yeah. It's a family business. I started it, and then my

three brothers joined in," he said, handing her a glass and tipping the edge of his against hers before taking another sip.

"So how many more like you are there at home?" she said, making him smile.

"Three more, though I'm the oldest."

"And you're all bodyguards? Pretty exciting work."

"Sometimes," he agreed as they crossed to the sofa and sat. "Sometimes it can be boring."

Tiffany found that hard to believe. Let him do a twelve-hour shift showing diamonds to socialites if he wanted to know about boring.

"What do you do?" he asked.

"I work for our family business, too. A small jewelry store downtown."

"How long?"

"Just a few months now. It pays well, and I do like shiny things," she said, laughing and looking at the chandelier again, and then at her own rings. She'd worn a few of her favorite rings, and a bracelet, and she really did love how they added a special something to the moment. "Love of jewels runs in the family. My mom even named me and my sisters after jewelry."

"Ah. Tiffany's. And your sisters are?"

"Ruby and Jewel."

"So there are more like you at home?" he said, echoing her tone, making her laugh. He was way too charming.

She smiled. "Two more, both married. And our youngest brother Nick."

"It sounds like you enjoy the work."

"It's okay. It pays the bills for now and helps out my parents, and I've been able to replace all the stuff I lost, but I want to move on to something better soon," she said vaguely, toying with the idea of telling him she really wanted to be a detective.

What if he laughed? Worse, what if he told someone at the wedding? Better to let that stay a secret, she decided, though the urge to tell *someone* was eating at her.

Garrett frowned. "Lost? Did you have an earthquake?"

She smiled. "Well, we do have those here, but in this case it was because of a robbery."

His face became very serious then, and he looked her in the eye. "You weren't hurt?"

"No, I wasn't even home. But I did have to replace everything I had, right down to the toaster."

"I didn't think toasters were hot on the black market," he said.

"Yeah, me, either."

"No insurance?"

"Unfortunately no," she said, expecting him to offer the same look of surprise and recrimination that others did when she revealed her lapse in personal responsibility, but he just nodded sympathetically. No way was she going to let him know it had been her former boyfriend who had ripped her off. She might as well wear a T-shirt that said I Have Poor Judgment.

"That sucks" was all he said, his tone nothing but sympathetic.

"Yeah, it did," she said, and took a sip of her drink, though the smooth whiskey didn't even touch the heat caused by the way his fingers were suddenly stroking the back of her neck, ever so gently. She swallowed hard, the touch making her glad she was sitting as she was sure her knees would not work if she was upright.

He slid closer, put his drink on the coffee table in front of him, and then hers.

"That's nice bourbon," she said, turning to face him slightly.

"It is, but I'm betting it will taste better on you," he said, sliding his hand around her neck and pulling her close for a deep kiss. Tiffany was pretty sure she forgot to breathe, and was okay with that. He pulled back, obviously feeling the same way.

"Okay?"

"Better than," she said, desperately wanting more.

This is a good thing, she thought as he nibbled at her neck, his thumb moving over her nipple in a way that made her knees tremble.

"Oh," she moaned, thinking everything was more than fine as Garrett slid a hand up inside her skirt, brushing his knuckles along the very damp material of her thong. She turned more fully to him, her hands gripping his shoulders.

"Don't stop." Her eyes met his as he dipped his hand inside the thin strip of material.

"Whatever you want," he promised against her lips, his fingers finding the very swollen, sensitive pearl of her clit and stroking her to a quick, sharp orgasm that had her clinging to him, riding it out.

"I want everything," she said against his ear, sliding her hand down the front of his jeans and massaging him through the material. "And I want it without all of these clothes in the way."

His nostrils flared as he kissed her hard, pressing her up against a cushion. Tiffany had to almost pinch herself to believe she was here with this movie star of a man, doing these wonderful things with him. It wasn't as if her previous boyfriends hadn't been good-looking, but they weren't anything close to Garrett.

Garrett was older than any of the other men she had known, and she wondered how old he was, exactly. Not that it mattered. She liked it. From what he'd said of his wife, Tiffany estimated Garrett was somewhere in his mid-thirties.

She couldn't imagine the hell he must have gone through losing his wife, but it had given him a kind of quiet integrity that shot his innate sexiness through the roof. Strong-chinned and broad-shouldered, classiness exuded from his posture, from his sure movements. Combined with the experience that he had in life—and the fact that he had so intensely loved and lost—it was all enough to make a girl go for it, just like she was doing now.

Things were heating up fast, and they wasted no time getting rid of each others' clothing. The lights were on, and she fought the urge to cover up as he took her in, that serious gaze studying every inch of her.

It was erotic but disconcerting to have a man look at her like this. When Tiffany looked at herself that closely in the mirror, she wasn't always pleased with what she found, noting all of her faults. Compared to what she saw in magazines, her breasts were too round and too heavy. Going bra-less hadn't been an option for her since she turned fifteen.

Though she ran almost every day, chugging up and down the steep hills of the city, her thighs never slimmed down as much as she wanted. Lately, she'd gotten a little hippy from the darned croissants that came from the bakery across the street from the jewelry store. Right now, she wished she had more willpower, except when it came to Garrett of course.

"You're gorgeous. Sexy as hell," he said, his Adam's apple bobbing as he swallowed hard, not taking his eyes off her.

The way he said it, the hungry expression on his face—as if he wanted to eat her whole—made it easy to believe him. His ready erection hardened even more, proof of his desire.

"Thank you," she said, feeling slightly shy, but a whole lot turned on. "You, too."

She wished she had something more clever, sexier, to say, but he didn't give her time to think about it, pulling her flush against him.

Oh. He felt really, *really* good, she thought hazily, every inch of their hot skin in contact, everything soft about her and hard about him meeting up perfectly.

"I love when you do that," he said as he lowered to explore her breasts with his lips. He seemed to like them a lot, she thought with a soft smile.

"When I do what?" she gasped as he sucked a nipple in between his lips, rubbing his tongue against it in a way that zoomed all the blood in her head straight south.

"Sigh. I love how you sigh…" he said hoarsely.

"Oh, good, because you're making me do that a lot," she said, but her sighs turned into moans as he drew harder on one breast and then the other, paying homage to that part of her anatomy for a good, long time until other parts were screaming for attention, too.

That would have to wait, she thought. Curling her fingers into the soft hair at the back of his neck, she gently tugged him upwards.

"My turn," she said, planting a hand on his chest and pushing him gently back against the sofa. He stretched out before her, and for a few minutes all she wanted to do was look at him.

"Whatever you want," he said again, bending his arms to fold his hands behind his head, as if he were a fantasy buffet set out for her pleasure.

Which she supposed he was.

Dark hair fell over his forehead, mussed by her hands, and his eyes were like hot, melted caramel as he looked back at her. His was an athlete's build, muscled but toned, not bulky. He had a little bit of hair on his chest, but not a lot. She followed the silky path of it leading down to his groin to take in the sights there, too. The vision of strong, muscular thighs made her tighten. Everything about him was perfect. She bit her lip, trying to decide where to start first.

She straddled his thighs, the touch of his skin next to hers making her close her eyes again for a moment in sheer bliss. Reaching down to wrap her hand around him, she drew her fingers over the head of his cock and then down along the shaft, seeing what he liked. Tiffany continued to touch, exploring down underneath the root of his cock and back up the length of him again. He groaned in pleasure, arching a little into her touch, as if wanting more. His muscles stood out in relief as he did so, making him even more spectacular, so she did it again.

"You're a tease," he said, his breath shorter, but he didn't sound upset about the fact.

"Maybe a bit," she admitted coyly. "Just getting to know you better."

"By all means, get to know me as well as you like," he said.

Their eyes met and she didn't look away as she planted her hands on the back of the sofa, on either side of his shoulders.

"I suppose we should get the disclaimers out of the way first, huh?" she said and told him what he needed to know, delighted to discover that they were both as healthy and protected as could be.

Kissing her way down his chest, and then pausing to lick the crown of his shaft before taking him in her mouth, she was gratified by his intense response as he groaned loudly. Out of the corner of her eye, she saw his fingers curl into the upholstery. Nice.

A low moan shuddered through his body as she enjoyed learning every inch of him with her lips and tongue.

When she knew he was close, she stopped and moved to kiss the inside of his thigh, nipping him there, feeling him jerk in response.

"That's enough, you siren," he growled playfully, rising up to standing, and carrying her to the bed where he towered over her.

"You're wicked," he accused, his eyes hot, jaw tense as he reached for the box of condoms he'd bought on the way back to the room.

"You have no idea," she said, wanting to play up the fantasy as he sheathed himself. They'd agreed that a little extra protection never hurt. Tiffany also secretly liked the extra texture a condom could provide—and they typically made men last longer. She so wanted this to last.

Touching her hands to her breasts, the look on his face as he watched encouraged her to do more, his cock nudging the entrance to her body and then slipping inside as their eyes met. She arched to take more of him, sighing again as he pushed deeper.

He took it slow, the fullness of him gradually filling her completely. She gasped when he was planted completely inside, her fingers grasping his shoulders as he lowered down to kiss her.

"Wow, that's good," he said, the words choked from him, as if he was also feeling the unbearable pressure that held back pleasure she could only guess at; the heat and need to move stalled only by the amazing feeling of fullness that she didn't want to lose just yet.

"Better than good," she managed to agree, her body accommodating him, adjusting to him as he pulled back slowly, then thrust forward again, making her cry out, lifting her hips up to meet his rhythm.

Heat suffused the space between and around them as their movements became more focused and intense. Wordless, he pulled her legs up around his hips, fastening her to him even tighter, and rocking against her clit so that she felt herself tipping quickly over the edge.

"Yes, yes," Tiffany panted as she gripped his shoulders, losing track of everything but the release that seemed to be building through her whole body.

When he kissed her, his tongue doing to her mouth what his cock did inside her body, her mind blanked, her body clenching and trembling as they groaned into each other, never breaking the kiss and not slowing their movements until the last ripple of climax had faded.

The heat they'd generated left them sweaty, tired and, Tiffany thought, more satisfied than she could ever remember being in her life. Garrett rolled to his side, but brought her with him, his arms still around her.

It was impossibly sweet and made her feel all kinds of things you weren't supposed to feel for a guy you were having a wedding hook-up with.

"That was…" he started to say.

"Yeah, it was," she agreed, interrupting, and not wanting to talk about it. Her body could still feel him, his touch, inside and out. The heat from release pulsed through her blood, like embers of a strong fire still simmering under the spent coals. She liked—too much—how his arms wrapped around her.

This was dangerous. Her impulsive heart wasn't listening to her newly logical brain, and she didn't need to be a detective to figure out that she could fall hard for Garrett, given the chance. Her body had its own agenda altogether.

She discovered this as she started lazily sliding the arch of her foot up and down the hard column of his ankle and shin. They were both spent, but she felt his semi-erection twitch against her hip, as if wanting more.

Unbelievably, she wanted more.

She kissed him once and pulled gently away, sitting up, taking the sheet with her.

"Where are you going?" he asked, frowning.

"Shower and home. I guess. Wedding in the morning, remember?" she said with a smile, wanting nothing more than to go back to bed with him for the rest of the night.

But she was going to be smart—and strong—for once in her life.

"Yeah, I guess you're right," he said, sounding disappointed, which floated her heart and weakened her resolve. He was disappointed that she was leaving, and she took a moment to soak that up. Some guys she had been with couldn't wait to get her out the door after the good part was over.

He nodded, yawning. "I am a little jet-lagged after the flight and then getting recruited into the wedding. And I have to be there extra early to get the tux refitted before we're good to go."

It was a credible excuse for both of them, and one she was thankful for. Sort of.

"Do you mind if I use your shower?" she asked, cutting to the chase.

She took one last, long look and wondered if she wasn't completely crazy for not crawling right back into that bed and having her way with him again.

"Not at all. Do you mind if I join you?" he asked, his eyes telling her he had more in mind than washing up.

Tiffany nodded, unable to repress her enthusiasm for the idea.

"I'd like that."

She still planned to leave afterward—to stay strong—but she wasn't stupid.

3

TIFFANY HAD NEVER enjoyed a wedding more. Several people asked her what was different about her—had she colored her hair? Changed her make-up?

She couldn't tell them the reason for her extra shine was having been well and truly done and done again by Garrett, who stood with Ed and the other men by the side of the altar. Even when all other eyes were on Isabel—and rightly so—Tiffany could feel Garrett's on her. It made it hard to breathe, wanting him so much. She'd never been quite this fully in lust before.

They'd barely said five words since arriving at the church, since she'd spent all of her time with the bride and other attendants, and he was with Ed and his groomsmen. As they all walked out the door in a shower of birdseed and flower petals, guests and the bridal party milled around and chatted as the photographer grabbed them for photo-taking opportunities. The park was lovely, with the Golden Gate towering majestically in the background, its red towers grand against a pure blue sky.

"The weather is just perfect," Tiffany said, tipping her

face up to the sun and smiling at the bright fall sky. "It's like a picture."

"It's a beautiful day," Garrett agreed, handsome as sin in his classic tux, which made him even more celebrity-like. "The wedding was very nice, too."

"You know, in that tux you look more like a spy than a bodyguard," Tiffany commented, tapping her chin as she assessed him playfully. "You're too refined to be a body-guard. Aren't they supposed to be bruisers who have tattoos and wear leather? You're so nice," she teased with a smile.

He laughed out loud. "I think you're confusing body-guards with bouncers, but are you saying I'm not a tough guy?"

"Not at all. I bet you are tough. I paid close attention to every muscle under that suit last night," she said, sending him a flirty look. "If you recall."

He grinned, rocking back on his heels. "Oh, I do. So you should also know that I'm not all that refined or polite, and what we did last night was definitely not *nice,*" he said silk-ily, reaching to discreetly draw his fingers down the length of her spine before cupping her bottom through her dress.

Tiffany shivered at the touch. She hadn't slept a moment after returning home, instead reliving every single second since she'd met Garrett—especially the ones at his hotel room. It had been hard to get out of bed, and nearly impossible to focus on the wedding, but somehow, she'd managed to do what she had to.

Now, she wished they were anywhere but here in this crowd. The way Garrett talked to her, the way he'd been looking at her since their eyes had met at the head of the aisle told her that he wanted more.

So did she.

"On the contrary, I think the things we did were *very* nice," she argued under her breath, enjoying the secret repartee as they smiled at other wedding guests who walked by.

"If you thought that was *nice,* then maybe I need to work harder at living up to my badass bodyguard image," he said, and the look he sent her made her wonder what bad-boy secrets Garrett might be hiding.

She was dying to find out, but it was only supposed to be that one time. Just one night.

But that wasn't exactly realistic, was it? They were, for all intents and purposes, each others' wedding date. He was here out of town, not knowing many other people; she couldn't just ditch him, after all. The wedding was kind of like a vacation weekend; their little fling could last until the wedding was over, and then they would be, too.

Tiffany's skin was warm even though there was a cool breeze, and she turned to face him.

"I suppose I could give you another chance to show me how bad you are," she said, playing it cool even as her heart beat a little faster at the thought of being with Garrett again.

He stepped closer. "Oh, I can be very bad," he promised, just as suave.

"Prove it," she breathed.

She so very, very much wanted to know, but she didn't expect it when he slid an arm around her waist and scooped her next to him, taking them both around the other side of the tall shrubs into a small, secluded grotto.

Large boulders had been arranged with smaller, sculpted rocks into a secluded sitting area that was fragrant with lush flowers and a garden that made the spot seem as if it were truly an escape from the hustle and bustle of the world. The air was slightly cooler in the shaded spot, but Garrett's lips were hot as they captured hers in a kiss that was anything but polite.

His tongue tangled with hers as he slipped his fingers beneath the low scoop of her neckline to play with a nipple as the other was bunching itself in the skirt of her dress, lifting it up.

"Garrett, everyone is right over—"

He moved his mouth to her ear, nipped her earlobe and ordered, "I know. Be quiet. Not a sound. They could hear," he cautioned.

Her breath caught at his tone, apprehension erased when he kissed her until objecting was not on her mind at all.

As his hands made their way along the garters she wore, his very appreciative, guttural curse told her he enjoyed the sexy discovery. Tiffany was pretty sure she'd never been so turned on when his hand slipped into the lace scrap of panties she wore. She held her breath in anticipation of his touch, but then, to her surprise, he looped his hand through and tore them from her with a single pull.

"Gar—" His name came out on a squeak, but he gave her a warning look. She pressed her lips shut, unsure what he was going to do next, but wanting desperately to find out.

She watched as he took the lace from under her dress, and pushed the scrap into his pants pocket before dropping to his knees and pushing her skirt up enough that he could see her.

"Beautiful," he murmured, running his fingers under the strap of the garter again. Tiffany reached out to brace her hand on the rocky wall of the grotto behind her. She expected to feel his fingers on her, but she drew in a sharp breath when he parted her thighs and the warmth of his tongue slid along the soft, sensitive skin of her sex.

Biting her lip to keep from moaning out loud, she peeked toward the corner of the grotto, and jerked away, her skirt falling into place as she heard voices and saw two bridesmaids walking around the edge of the shrubs.

Garrett must have seen as well and pretended to be looking for something on the ground as the two approached.

"Ah, there it is," he said with satisfaction, standing and putting what had to be nothing in his pocket.

Tiffany tried to get her breathing under control, her entire body hot with the fires he had kindled.

"Tiffany! We were looking for you. The photographer needs you. Both of you," Mary said, and then paused. Looking back and forth from Garrett to Tiffany for a few seconds, she smiled wickedly.

"But I'm sure he can wait for five more minutes," Mary said with a chuckle, still grinning back at Tiffany as the women left the grotto.

Tiffany groaned to herself, her cheeks warm. Mary wouldn't say anything, but she had definitely been able to tell that Tiffany and Garrett weren't sharing friendly conversation.

"That was close," she whispered.

"It certainly was...but all the more exciting for it," he whispered back, winking at her as he held his arm out for her to take. She did, appreciative of the small gesture.

"Every time I reach into my pocket today, I'll have these to touch, and every time I look at you, we'll both know how I got them and that you are naked underneath that dress. Just let me know if you want me to finish what we started."

She sucked in a deep breath, trying to control the

surge of lust that ran through her at the thought of that happening. Words abandoned her. The wedding reception hall held endless possibilities. Lounges, coat rooms, closets.

She shoved a playful elbow into his side, her cheeks warming though she loved every second of it. The next half hour was taken up with yet more picture-taking, but Tiffany had a hard time taking her eyes off Garrett. As they filed into limos and headed to the reception hall, she sat close to him, another couple she didn't know as well sitting opposite and deep in their own conversation.

Leaning in close, Garrett whispered in her ear, "Was that bad enough for you?"

"It was a start," she said primly, smoothing the skirt of her dress, and feeling deliciously naughty about being bare underneath.

"A start," he repeated lightly, looking at her warmly. "I like the sound of that."

Everything about him turned her on. Still, she argued with herself.

"So much for not being impulsive," she mumbled to herself more than him.

"What?"

More time with Garrett sounded like everything she wanted, and while it was true that in the past, she'd jumped into relationships without laying down rules, or knowing what was coming, this she was going into with her eyes wide open, right?

No, she had to stick to her guns.

"I really like you, but—"

"Don't worry Tiffany," he said easily. "I didn't mean to imply I was looking for anything more than enjoying what's left of our wedding fling," he added, close to her ear, his tongue flicking the lobe and making her breath catch.

"Oh. Then yes. Absolutely," she said, breathlessly.

She wanted as much of Garrett as she could get in the time they had left. But like Cinderella, when this party was over, so were they.

GARRETT WOKE UP late, turning over in a tangle of flowered sheets that smelled like lavender and Tiffany.

They had ended up back at her place this time. He punched down into a soft, luxuriously full pillow, coming awake slowly and thinking he had not had that much fun at a wedding, ever. Not even his own, he realized with a pang of guilt.

His wedding to Lainey had been beautiful, elegant and quiet. There hadn't been the raucous partying that had followed yesterday's event. Normally Garrett might have found it not quite his speed, but with Tiffany sparkling at his side—and her panties in his pocket—he'd joined in and had a great time.

They'd had an even better time back here, too.

Rolling over, it didn't take long to see that he was alone in the big, soft bed, and there was a note on her pillow. She'd said she didn't have to work on Sundays, but apparently there was some kind of crisis and she was needed at the store she managed.

Garrett—last night was wonderful. (Oh, and the coat room was pretty amazing, too.) I'd hoped we could have breakfast together, but there's a problem at work. Help yourself to anything to eat, or there is a nice place on the corner. Thanks for…everything. ☺ Tiff.

He couldn't help a tiny pang of disappointment. While they both agreed that this was a sex-only, weekend-only thing—a wedding hook-up, as she called it—he'd hoped to spend some time with her this morning. They might be temporary, but he liked Tiffany. He would have enjoyed taking her to breakfast, or talking over coffee, but it didn't look like that was going to happen. He'd slept so hard that he hadn't heard her phone or heard her leave, also unusual. Normally, he was a very light sleeper.

He smiled to himself. Tiffany had a way of wearing a guy out. He made his way to the shower, grimacing as remembered the only clothing he had to put back on was the tux, which he also had to return to Ed at some point. He didn't like not seeing Tiffany again—not even to say goodbye. She had certainly helped him enjoy the first days—and nights—of his vacation more than he ever thought he would.

After his shower, he dressed and headed for the front door, though curiosity got the best of him as he walked through the main rooms of the apartment. He couldn't say he'd noticed much about the decor the night before as they had stumbled in and headed directly for bed.

Her bedroom had been airy and feminine; the rest of the house was more classic, with clean lines to the furniture and southwestern tones and touches adding color to an otherwise modestly decorated room.

Out here, there were shelves full of books—every mystery and suspense series he could remember reading or knowing about, including all of the original Sherlock Holmes collection—and some he'd never heard of. She had a DVD collection that was just as impressive, with everything from *Veronica Mars* to *Monk*. On a reading desk where a pink laptop sat was a miniature action figure of Sherlock Holmes.

Tiffany was a mystery junkie. Somehow he would have pegged her for more of a romance reader. Garrett liked to read, though he tended to read broadly—fiction and nonfiction, popular and more obscure literary books as well as plays and essays. He enjoyed a good suspense novel now and then, and had even read one of his mother's romances once, as she had dared him to do it. It was pretty good, actually.

But not a single clinching couple graced Tiffany's shelves. It was all guns and shadowy figures running into the night on her book covers.

Given her light, effervescent personality, it was all a surprise. Tiffany's fun-loving, sexy demeanor didn't suggest someone who liked to sit in the deep leather chairs by the heavy bookcases and read about grisly murder in dark alleys.

But he liked the contrast; it showed him there was more to her than met the eye. Maybe that's why she intrigued him. The discovery deepened the nudge of regret about not seeing her again, but they'd both had a good time, and that was that. Now he had the rest of his vacation to enjoy.

Sherlock was standing on an ornate business card with her name on it, Tiffany A. Walker, Assitant Manager, Jarvis Jewelry, complete with phone and address. An idea formed. Maybe he could stop by, see her and just get a coffee, if she had time, and say a proper goodbye. It seemed like the right thing to do. He would call after he got back to the hotel and changed, and hopefully she would be up for it.

Outside, he hailed a taxi out on the quiet Sunday morning street and headed back to the hotel, contemplating his next adventure. He was pretty sure nothing was going to be as adventurous as being with Tiffany, he thought, an edge of loneliness cutting through his otherwise happy mood.

As the cab took him across the bridge and back downtown to the hotel, Garrett noticed runners and groups of tourists taking their Sunday walk over the bay via the bridge.

"How far is it to walk over and back on the bridge?" he asked the driver. Maybe he'd put on his running clothes, grab his camera and start his vacation by running the length of the most famous bridge in the U.S., with the exception of The Brooklyn Bridge, which he had also run across.

"A little less than two miles, point-to-point, but watch out for the bikers, they can come up on you fast sometimes," the cabbie warned, and Garrett nodded.

"Sounds like a nice way to spend a Sunday," he replied.

For the rest of the way back, the cabbie chatted with him, giving him some good ideas for things to do around the city, off the beaten track. Sights that he would find interesting like the Moraga Steps—a neighborhood stairway that went up a hillside, with one hundred and sixty-three steps that were redone with art tiles by local residents to beautify the neighborhood. There was also the Bison Paddock in Golden Gate Park, which he thought he might visit after his run.

More enthusiastic about setting out on his own for the day, Garrett paid the fare and thanked the man for his suggestions with a generous tip before heading into the hotel to change.

As he changed and got set up for what he needed for his excursion, he looked down to check the time and found he hadn't put on his watch. It was still on Tiffany's night stand, by her bed, where he had taken it off the night before. He'd been so distracted by their nocturnal fun, and then with the unfamiliar morning routine after waking up in her bed, that he'd completely forgotten to put it back on.

It was his grandfather's watch, one his father had given him on his eighteenth birthday. Garrett had to get that watch back, and smiled at having a good excuse to see Tiffany again. Pulling the card from his wallet, he looked at the number at the bottom and dialed.

TIFFANY WAS READY to pull her hair out by the roots as she watched the police poking around her shop. She was exhausted, frustrated beyond the telling of it and wishing so much that she could have one thing in her life that didn't blow up in her face. Maybe this was karmic payback for her breaking her vow not to be impulsive this past weekend, but she couldn't bring herself to regret any of it.

Garrett had been worth it.

Too bad a promising final morning with him had been cut short by business, an emergency call from the police: Jarvis Jewelry had been robbed. Her family business, started by her great-grandfather, Jarvis Walker, had suffered the only robbery in their history, and it had happened on her watch.

Tiffany looked like hell and she felt like it, too. Yanking on a pair of black yoga pants, a black T-shirt, sneakers and a sweater, she didn't exactly look like a retail manager as she encountered the swarm of police, none of whom wanted to tell her anything. She asked questions, smart ones, she thought, but was met with silence. Worse, they seemed to think she could be a suspect. It looked like an inside job, they said, and then proceeded to ask her scores of demanding questions.

She knew why. This wasn't an ordinary, random break-in. There had been a series of robberies that had been plaguing jewelry stores from San Jose to the entire Bay area, and they had been the most recent victims, even though the cops wouldn't confirm that.

The wedding covered her during the daytime hours, but the robbery had happened after that. She didn't relish having the police find Garrett at his hotel to confirm he had spent the night with her. How embarrassing. As if it wasn't bad enough to walk out on the guy in the middle of the night and not even see him for breakfast—and potentially more lovely sex—the cops would ask him if he was her alibi.

"Ma'am, we will need the contact information for the man you claim to have spent the night with, and we need it now," a severe-looking officer said again. She frowned up at him, but then sighed. He was only doing his job.

"Can't you at least tell me what was stolen? If you have any leads? I need to call my parents. They are the owners, and the insurance, and—"

"You can do that after we confirm your alibi."

"Fine," she said through her teeth. "He's staying at the Westin St. Francis, and his name is—"

She was interrupted by Chumbawamba singing "Tubthumping." Saved by the ring tone, she thought, not recognizing the number as she answered.

"Ma'am," the officer interrupted testily, but she glared at him and answered.

"Hello?"

"Tiffany, it's Garrett."

"Um, hi, how—"

"I grabbed one of your business cards when I left this morning. I hope you don't mind," he said before he continued. "Anyway, I left my watch at your place. It's a special watch, a gift. I was wondering if there might be a time I could meet you to pick it up?"

"I—um, of course, but listen, I need a favor, too, if you have a minute," she said hesitantly, peeking up at the officer, who was looking increasingly suspicious.

"What's that?"

"I need you to talk to the police, right now," she said quickly, giving the phone to the officer before Garrett could ask anything else.

"Here. He's on the phone," she said to the officer, her cheeks warming again. Hopefully the officer wouldn't want details.

The cop took the phone and spoke to Garrett, his expression relaxing somewhat as he did, and he stopped looking down at her so accusingly.

"I'll need you to come down and sign a statement to that effect, if you can, Mr. Berringer," he said politely, before handing the phone back to Tiffany.

"Your boyfriend wants to talk to you," he said, before he strolled away.

"He's not my—" she tried to correct, but the cop was already gone. She looked at the phone, taking a deep breath.

"Garrett?"

"Hey. So what's going on that you need an alibi, not that I mind providing one. Are you okay?"

He sounded so concerned, it touched her. Not many guys would be this cool about being dragged into something like this, at least none of the ones she'd known. She'd followed every single protocol for closing up Friday night before she had left, and she related every detail to Garrett on the phone, needing to tell someone.

"Tiffany, this is not your fault, okay?" he said calmly. "There's no way you could predict being robbed. What did the police say?"

"They haven't told me anything much yet. They were too busy thinking I might've been in on it. All I know is that they think it was an inside job," she said. "It's very likely this is one of the serial robberies that's plagued the city lately, though they haven't confirmed that."

"Robberies?"

"Four other stores have been robbed in the last six weeks. Each appeared to be an inside job, but all of the employees have been cleared. The thieves only take a few select items, usually very high-end stuff," she said, and then realization dawned. She'd been so upset about the officers not telling her anything that it hadn't registered until right now.

"Oh, no," she said more to herself than to Garrett.

"What? What's happening?"

"We only have one thing in the store that these thieves would be after," she said urgently, standing up and pushing past a few other police officials to find the detective in charge. "But no one was even supposed to know about it."

"I'll be there in a few minutes. Can you wait for me?"

She paused. He was coming to her store?

Irrationally, she looked down at her clothes. She hadn't put on fresh make-up from the night before, and her hair… she didn't even want to think about her hair. The way the officer who had been interviewing her kept staring was proof enough that she was less than put together at the moment.

But the idea of having him there with her was a nice one.

"Okay, I'll wait for you," she said.

She heard him say something, probably to the cab driver.

"You're in a cab already?"

"I was already in one, coming back from your place. I'm not far away, the driver says. I'll be there in two minutes," he referred back to her.

"Oh. Okay. I'll be out front."

Garrett arrived in what seemed like only seconds later. As he crossed the sidewalk to her, he didn't even seem to notice her less than polished appearance. He took her in his arms for a hard hug and then looked down at her.

"Are you okay?"

She nodded. "I am, but I'll be better when I know the vault wasn't breached."

But in her gut, she knew what was coming. This was no ordinary robbery. Garrett nodded, his mouth flattening, and his arm staying on her shoulder, supportive.

"Let's go do that, then," he said.

They went in and walked directly up to the detective in charge, who turned his attention to Garrett as if working on some invisible male radar that told one man in charge that another alpha male had entered his territory.

"Detective Ramsey, I need to know what was stolen— did they get into the vault?" Tiffany asked, straightening to her full five-seven.

The detective's eyes met hers, and then moved to Garrett.

"Detective Ramsey, SFPD North. And you are?"

"I'm Garrett Berringer, a friend of Ms. Walker's."

"Why did you think it was an inside job? *Is* this one of the serial robberies?" Tiffany asked boldly on the heels of Garrett's introduction. She put a hand on the detective's arm, refocusing his attention on her. "Did they get into the vault?"

He stared for a second before offering a curt nod. "Yeah, they did."

Tiffany closed her eyes, fighting to stay composed.

"The diamonds. They're gone?"

"The vault is empty. Can you elaborate about what was in it? What diamonds?" the detective asked.

Tiffany took a deep breath. At this point, it didn't matter if it was her fault or not. Everything her parents had worked for was on the line. The loss was just too great. She'd let her family down, big-time.

"A special collection of very rare pink diamonds," she said weakly. "They were being set into rings for the daughter of an Argentine political official, and we were holding them before they went to the gem cutter. My parents acquired them in Spain, and they were our biggest find."

Both men were silent as she shared that news. What she didn't add was that her parents had taken a sizable business loan against the store to build the new vault and purchase the rare gems, hoping to enter a new level of sales, since local sales were down. They had leveraged their equity in the store, and the insurance alone could do them in if it didn't pay out.

"What were they worth?" Ramsey asked.

"Pink diamonds of this quality are relatively rare, and the market demand is high. These were exceptional, priced at about one million dollars per carat."

"And how many carats?"

"There were two one-carat diamonds in the vault, and one half-carat rock. They'd been appraised, certified and were due to be sent to a gem cutter this week. We've kept it all very low-key."

"So someone had to know they would be gone soon, and that they had to strike now," Garrett added.

"The only ones who know are my parents, the Argentines and myself."

Detective Ramsey looked at Tiffany with a considering gaze that told her she might not be completely off the hook. Just because she had an alibi didn't mean she didn't have accomplices. She read enough mystery novels to know that. She also knew police, overworked and stressed by pressures to solve many crimes, often took the most obvious route to solve the problem.

"If you can catalog the rest of your inventory to let me know if you're missing anything else, I would appreciate that, Ms. Walker," the detective said.

"Of course."

"And in case we need you, don't plan any trips out of town any time soon, okay?"

Tiffany stiffened at the hint of accusation; her heart was slamming inside her chest. "Of course," she said calmly, proud of herself for that much.

"How could someone do that without a blast being heard, or triggering alarms?" Garrett asked, stepping forward.

"No blast. That we can tell, they just walked in and emptied it out. They obviously knew that the diamonds were there. Someone had the codes, the combinations and the door was left open. It's what ultimately set off the alarm, though they were long gone by then, which is why it has to be an inside job. Who has those codes?"

"Only my parents and I do. That's it."

"Is the lock digital?" Garrett asked.

She nodded.

"It could have been hacked. Do you have a computer forensics team?"

Detective Ramsey eyed him speculatively, reassessing him as more than "a friend."

"The lock is on a non-networked circuit, separate from the system that notifies the security team of a breach," Tiffany said miserably.

"It still could have been hacked on-site," Garrett said. "In which case, they have to have someone very good with technology on their team, and I'd think that gives you a place to start. There can't be too many jewel-thief hackers in the world," he added.

"That's a good theory," the detective said, pinching his chin.

"I have some contacts you could use. People who might know who could do that kind of work," Garrett said, explaining about Berringer Bodyguards.

The two men started talking as if she wasn't even there, and Tiffany was tempted to scream to make sure she was. On one hand, she was fascinated by what Garrett knew, and thankful for the help he offered; on the other, she had been effectively cut out of the conversation.

When they were done, Detective Ramsey turned to her. "I'll need you to check the inventory, and an officer will take your statement," he said, and she nodded, about to say something as he turned away.

"Well, nice to know he acknowledges my existence," she grumped, crossing her arms across her middle.

"Most of those guys aren't too chatty, not in the middle of an investigation, anyway," Garrett said, opening his smartphone. "Don't take it personally."

"I'm not supposed to take it personally that he thinks I was involved?"

"I think we all know you weren't, but it's their job to suspect everyone, dust out every corner."

Tiffany took a deep breath, calming her agitation. She knew that was true. Detection 101—no one was above suspicion.

"You're right. I guess I'm just tired and touchy."

"Perfectly understandable. Tiffany?" Garrett prompted, looking concerned.

"Sorry, just zoned out for a second. I'd better get this inventory done," she said with a sigh.

"Okay. I'm going to make a few phone calls. Let me know when you're done. Don't worry, we'll figure this out."

"You don't have to wait. I could be a while," she said, wondering if he meant "we" as him and herself, or him and the police. Tiffany felt disgruntled and out of the loop.

"No problem. Let's grab something to eat after this and talk," he said, and leaned in to kiss her cheek almost absently before going back to his phone.

Well, okay then. It wasn't that she didn't want to see Garrett after this was done, and she could use a meal but... she just felt dismissed. *You go take care of the inventory and just don't worry your pretty head about anything else,* she thought crankily, knowing she was probably being unfair, but it was how she felt.

She was a detective, but she didn't feel much like one at the moment. At the moment, she was the assistant manager of the jewelry store, and she *did* need to do the inventory, so she focused her attention on that for the next hour or so. When she was done, she sought out Ramsey and told the detective what he needed to know, and what they had expected all along.

In spite of the several very lovely and expensive pieces

in the cases, the only things missing were the diamonds. That was exactly like the other robberies, as much as she knew about them, anyway. The only other thing was that all of the paperwork, the certifications, bills of sale, everything that had come with the diamonds, was also missing, having even been wiped off of the computers. Someone knew exactly what they were looking for, and now they had no records of ever owning the diamonds at all, which was going to make settling the insurance even more difficult. Tiffany understood why it seemed very much like an inside job, because who else would know exactly where to find all of this material, the computer passwords, and be so thorough?

Making her way to the back office, she sat down at the desk, discouraged and exhausted, and let her head fall down on her arms. She only intended to rest her eyes for a minute....

4

GARRETT FOUND TIFFANY at her desk in the back office. The police were gone, though tape remained around the entrance, indicating it was still an active crime scene. He'd given his official statement clearing Tiffany of any suspicion, and had spent almost the entire time on the phone tracking down any information he could.

Unfortunately, there wasn't much anyone knew; the police were doing a good job of keeping it quiet. Some criminals thrived on attention and notoriety, but these guys were more likely professionals who didn't want to draw much attention; they didn't vandalize, kill or do anything that left much evidence behind or that would create a public outcry. They were smart.

However, Garrett had called a friend in London who specialized in art theft. Berringer had provided security for several of his museum's pieces as they were being moved from D.C. to London. Daniel might know something that even the police wouldn't.

He'd kept that contact to himself, sharing only a few others with Detective Ramsey, who was still fairly tight-lipped, even given Garrett's help. Like he'd told Tiffany, Garrett didn't take it personally. The guy had a job to do

and was obviously under a lot of pressure with these robberies.

These thieves could be difficult to catch, Garrett
thought regretfully. Time was of the essence; the black
market moved fast. Or, if there was no news underground,
then they could be sitting on them until things calmed
down, he supposed. Or they simply could have been sold
directly to a private buyer and once the diamonds were
cut, no one would know where they came from.

There were a lot of possibilities, but often these kinds
of items—fine art, jewels—were never recovered. Often,
they were found in the homes of wealthy, private collectors decades later, if at all.

Knocking lightly on the door, he heard Tiffany talking. She must be on the phone, and he cracked the door,
intending to let her know he was there.

She paced behind the desk, pushing her hands through
already messy hair, looking and sounding as if she were
on her last nerve.

"I'm sorry, Mrs. Hooper. I know. I told you my fee
wasn't refundable, but obviously you don't have to pay me
the balance since I didn't get the shot. I could try again, if
you want. In fact, how about this? I'll give it another week,
and you don't have to pay me at all, okay? I just want to
finish the job for you," Tiffany said.

Garrett frowned. Finish the job? What on earth could
she be talking about? Mentally noting the name Hooper,
his mind flickered over the possibility that Tiffany was
lying about the thefts—was she involved?

But nothing in this conversation sounded jewelry-
related. What kinds of "shots"? It sounded like Tiff was
moonlighting in some capacity, and Garrett thought back
to the night of the rehearsal, when she had been so anx-

iously following the time, and had to dash off "to work" before coming back to meet him.

He paused, wondering what Tiffany was up to. She'd mentioned a fee—a payoff of some sort?

"Thanks, Mrs. Hooper. I promise I won't give up until the job is done. On my dime."

She sounded a bit more relieved, and Garrett frowned, not having meant to eavesdrop, and feeling itchy about it. He heard her hang up, and opened the door up completely.

"Hey, Tiffany," he said gradually, and she spun around, looking guilty, tired and anxious.

The guilty part concerned him.

"How long were you standing there?"

"Just for a second. I knocked, and then realized you were on the phone."

She became extremely guarded. "You were listening?"

"I overheard some, yes," he said. He wasn't going to lie to her. "But it's none of my business, and I didn't mean to eavesdrop."

"But you did."

"Yeah. Do you want to tell me what's going on?"

"No."

"Okay, then."

She nodded faintly, blinking her pretty, catlike eyes and stretching her arms up over her head in a way that drew her shirt tight and garnered Garrett's interest.

"I saw you come back here about a half hour ago, so I thought I would check and see how you were doing. The police are gone, and you're in the clear."

"Thanks," she said, still maintaining her distance, but he was unable to stand there and watch her stretch and fidget around for one more second without touching her. He knew Tiffany wasn't involved in the robberies, and whatever he had overheard probably had a completely innocent explanation—which, again, was none of his business. He crossed the space between them, pulling her up close to melt the ice that had formed in between them.

"Oh, no, don't," she said, surprising him with a hand planted right to his chest, pushing him away.

It wasn't the reaction he expected. "Why?" he asked, stepping back.

"I need a shower, to brush my teeth and put on some decent clothes. All living creatures—especially you—should keep at least a three-foot perimeter from me until I do."

Garrett laughed, a mix of relief and humor at her revelation. She *was* looking a bit rumpled at the moment, especially her hair after pushing her hands through it, but he couldn't say he cared. She still looked cute and sexy to him.

"Listen, it's almost dinnertime. My hotel is closer than your place. Come back with me, clean up and we'll get some food and talk. Sound good?"

Her eyes warmed, and then she looked away. Not a good sign.

"I can't. I have to call my parents about the robbery and…do some other stuff."

"You're exhausted. No way am I letting you drive." Reaching out to cup her chin with his fingers, he stared into her eyes.

She stiffened. "I'm perfectly able to take care of myself, thanks."

"Ouch."

Her shoulders sagged. "I just have things to do, Garrett, and there's no point in dragging this out." She pointed a hand between him and herself, indicating "you and me." "You have a vacation to get to, and I have to—"

"I get it, Tiffany," he said, relenting. He was disappointed, and a bit concerned, but he wouldn't push. "But listen, I need to get my watch back from you. Let me drive you back. I'll get the watch and leave. Okay?"

Her beautiful mouth pursed as she considered, and then she nodded. "I am pretty tired. I'd forgotten about the watch."

"That's okay. You have a lot on your mind."

"Just let me set the vault again—not that it matters, I guess—and then I can close up," she said, leaving to go deal with the vault.

Garrett eyed the cell phone that she left on the desk, and paused. He was about to cross a line, and he knew it. But his instincts were still prickling about that phone call, and he worried that Tiffany was in some kind of trouble.

Picking up the phone, he checked the numbers on the incoming calls, saw the name Sally Hooper, and quickly memorized it. Garrett was pretty sure that Tiffany wasn't involved with the jewel thieves, but she might have unwittingly given up information she didn't realize others could have used to get inside the store. Or maybe he was wrong about her.

Putting the phone back on the desk, he took out his own, and dialed the number.

"Hello?" a very cranky, but sophisticated-sounding female voice answered.

"Hello, Mrs. Hooper?"

"Yes?"

"My name is Gary Iverson, and I was told that Tiffany Walker had done some work for you?"

"Are you a lawyer? Are you working for my husband?" The woman's voice went up a notch.

"No, no, I'm thinking about hiring Ms. Walker myself, and I was just wondering if you could give her a reference. She said you'd be happy to," he offered congenially.

"Well, so much for her services being confidential," the

woman said waspishly, making Garrett cringe inwardly. He wasn't helping Tiffany win rave reviews, but it sounded like the woman wasn't exactly thrilled with her in the first place.

"She didn't say a word about what work she was doing for you, just that you were a reference."

"Huh. Well, she's a nice enough girl, but out of her league, in my opinion. But she was willing to do the job cheap, and I thought, what the hell, I'd give her a chance. But to be honest, I don't think she's going to be able to pull it off. She's too sweet for this line of work."

The woman said *sweet* like it was a character fault.

"Thank you. The work I'm thinking about assigning her is quite important, and I don't want to lose money."

"Oh, well, then, I would tell you to find a professional investigator. It's probably going to cost you, but I wish I had now. Though if she can get some pictures of that lousy, cheating husband of mine, I'll call you back and give her a glowing review," the woman said with a harsh laugh.

Garrett was stunned silent, then murmured a thanks and hung up the phone just as Tiffany entered the office.

"Okay, all done. All I need to do is set the alarm and lock the door behind us, and we're out of here."

Garrett blinked, looking at her more closely.

Tiffany? A private investigator?

He had a hard time getting his mind around it, and then thought about all of the mystery novels in her apartment. Then he remembered the camera and notebooks he'd seen on the backseat of her car when they'd driven to the rehearsal dinner, and suddenly it all made sense.

So that's why she'd been in a hurry to leave that night— she was doing surveillance on Sally Hooper's lousy, cheating husband. Not very successfully, apparently.

"Earth to Garrett?" She waved a hand in front of his face, and he smiled, snapping to.

"Right. Sorry. Let's go," he said, planting his fingers lightly at the curve of her back as they left, his mind still processing the fact that Tiffany was moonlighting as a P.I.

On the trip back to her place, they didn't talk much, as she seemed to nod off easily, snapping herself awake only to nod off again. It was the right move not to let her drive.

He thought about bringing it up—telling her that he knew—but couldn't imagine it would go over too well that he had snooped on her phone and into her personal business.

At the same time, he couldn't help but be concerned. P.I.s did some nasty, dangerous work. Tiffany might think it was like her mystery novels, but tracking down guys cheating on their wives wasn't a safe enterprise. According to Mrs. Hooper, Tiffany was new to this—very new— and so her risks were even higher.

Pulling into a parking space at her building, he looked over to find her passed out, head propped against the window. He'd decide how to handle this, but for the moment, he just had to get her up to her apartment.

"Tiff? Wake up," he said, shaking her gently.

She opened her eyes blearily, only to land her head back on the car window again with a soft *thunk*. She didn't even seem to notice.

Garrett got out, fishing her key out of her bag, and grabbed the notebook and camera from the backseat before pulling her up into his arms.

"Wassha doin'?" she asked tiredly, pushing away a bit.

"Getting you to your apartment," he said, unable to resist planting a kiss on her forehead. She *was* sweet. "Go back to sleep. I've got you."

She muttered something that sounded like "perfectly

able to walk on my own," and he grinned as she snuggled down, snoring again in seconds.

Cuddled up against him, Tiffany didn't look at all like a tough private investigator or a sophisticated jewelry store manager. She looked soft. Vulnerable. Like she needed someone to watch her back.

Garrett figured he was the man to do it.

MONDAY MORNING, TIFFANY WOKE UP in a panic, not even remembering having fallen asleep, but as soon as her vision cleared, she realized she was snug in her own bed.

In her underwear. Her clothes were tossed in the basket in the corner, and a glance at the alarm clock showed it was just after dawn, soft sunlight just starting to filter through the curtains.

Garrett. Her mind went back to the last minutes they spent together, leaving the store, and she had let him drive. She'd passed out in the car, completely exhausted. He must have brought her up to her place. Undressed her.

Too bad he hadn't stayed and joined her, she thought, casting a look at the empty side of the bed.

But no, there'd be no more of that.

Grabbing a robe, she slid out of bed, wondering if he had perhaps fallen asleep in the front room. There had been some tension between them at the store, especially when she realized he'd heard her on the phone with Mrs. Hooper.

Tiffany stopped in her tracks, covering her face with her hands. Marcus Hooper. She should have been at the hotel last night, having missed the shot on Saturday night. Even if Marcus didn't typically meet his lover on Sundays, Tiffany had promised Sally Hooper that she would catch the woman's husband in the act, and that meant staking out the Fall Inn every night until Tiffany got the evidence she needed.

Too bad there wouldn't be more than the nominal fee she'd asked for up front, but it was more about getting the job done at this point.

Proceeding to the living room, she discovered it was empty, and felt a pang of disappointment.

Well, what did she expect?

She'd more or less told Garrett they were done, and he had said he'd take her home, get his watch and leave. Apparently, he'd kept his word.

While showering, she refocused away from Garrett and the day before. That was the past, and she had enough to worry about in her present. She still hadn't talked to her parents, and the store had to stay closed until an insurance investigator came in and concluded his work. Though it was clearly a theft, because of the possible insider element, they had to do their own investigation to check out any possibility of insurance fraud.

That would take a couple of days, and so there were customers to contact as well. Her parents in Italy would be awake now, and Tiffany headed to the kitchen, letting her hair air-dry as she started some coffee. She'd need the fortification of caffeine to deliver this news to her parents.

As she did so she saw a manila envelope on her small kitchen table, placed underneath her camera and notebook. Anxiety gripped her. Had Garrett gone through her things? Discovered her other job?

How dare he? She fumed, but put a cap on her anger. He might have just pulled the stuff up from the car, worried it might be stolen.

Moving her camera, she saw the writing on the front in a strong, male scrawl: *Tiff, this is for you. Garrett.*

Short and sweet, and she ripped open the envelope, wondering what in the world he could have left for her. She gasped when she pulled out several clear, damning shots of Marcus Hooper and a dark-haired woman, *in flagrante delicto,* seeming completely unaware of the camera. The images were centered between two dark edges—the curtain, she realized.

Garrett must have walked right up to the window and snapped the shots through a gap in the curtain.

Tiffany shook her head, looking through a stack of pictures, finding ones of Marcus leaving the room, getting into his car, the sign and hotel clearly in the picture with him.

More than enough for Mrs. Hooper to secure her alimony check.

Tiffany noticed that Garrett had not included individual pictures of the woman he was with, and in fact, had only taken pictures that more or less obscured her facial features.

Wow.

A small slip of white paper slipped from the envelope to the floor, and Tiffany bent to grab it, seeing Garrett's handwriting again: *Give these to Mrs. Hooper and tell her to pay you the full fee. She'll be able to afford it. Garrett.*

Tiffany set the pictures and the note down, coffee forgotten as she absorbed what he had done. What he had done—not her.

Why would he do it? Because it was more than obvious that she couldn't get the work done? Or just because he was a nice guy, trying to help her out?

So why wasn't she happier about it?

Because she wanted to get the job done—not have it done for her. Whether Garrett was trying to be helpful or not, he'd interfered where he shouldn't have.

She would give these pictures to Mrs. Hooper—how could she not? But she wouldn't accept any money for them. She hadn't been the one who had taken them, and

Tiffany didn't feel like she deserved to be paid for work she hadn't done.

More glum than ever, she poured some coffee and dialed her parents' number, bracing herself to give them the bad news.

As expected, they were stunned, but immediately more concerned about everyone's safety.

"We're all fine. Like the others, the robbery was at night, and there wasn't even any damage to the store or the vault. It's like someone just walked in, helped themselves and then walked right back out again."

"I just can't believe it," her mother said. "And you're absolutely positive you locked everything up?"

In the wake of Garrett's obvious vote of lack of confidence in her ability to do her work, she bridled at the same from her parents.

"I followed the routine to the letter," she responded stiffly, feeling tears burning behind her eyes. "Four other stores have been robbed the same way, remember," she said a tad defensively. "They couldn't all have left the door open, and neither did I."

"Honey, calm down. We weren't criticizing you, it's all just so upsetting. What did the police say? Do they have any leads?"

"None they would share. They are investigating everyone, and the insurance investigator will be there tomorrow."

"This isn't good," her father said, the concern clear in his tone. "We should cancel the current deals here and come back before we make any new acquisitions. If they don't solve this, the insurance could use this as a reason not to pay out, and we'll have to pay the Argentines out of our own pocket."

"I know. Though I can't imagine why they think we

would do this…" she said. "I wish I could find a way to make this easier for you guys."

"Don't worry, Tiff. We'll be home in two days, and we'll handle it. You're doing the best you can," her mom said, and Tiffany knew they didn't mean it, but somehow, the doubt underlying her mother's tone dug at her.

How could she prove to them that she wasn't completely unreliable? The robbery wasn't her fault, but it had happened when she had been left in charge. How could she ever make it up to them if this cost them Jarvis's?

As they said their goodbyes, a thought formed.

Maybe Garrett had done her a favor after all. Not that she liked him sneaking around behind her back, but he had gotten the Hooper case off her schedule, and with the store closed, now she was completely free for a few days.

Free to do a little poking around of her own, into the robberies. If she could solve that case, it would be a huge feather in her cap. It would prove she could hold her own as a private investigator and it would save her parents' store.

It would prove to Tiffany herself that this really was the thing she was meant to do. The police didn't seem to be turning up much, and she was an insider—she could approach the other store owners as one of their own and see if there was anything she could find that would provide some stronger clues.

As she grabbed more coffee, excitement replaced the glum feeling that had colored her morning. At her computer, she began searching and reading everything she could about the robberies. She started with the names of the stores that had been robbed, and found out as much as she could about the people who ran them. There wasn't much, but if she worked off of what she had here, she could find more leads to follow.

She murmured, "The game is afoot," grinning. And as

she turned her full attention to the task, a plan coming together in her mind, she sent a silent thank-you to Garrett. With his photos, he'd inadvertently taught her an important lesson: she had to get out of the car, figuratively speaking. He hadn't sat back, waiting for a shot, he'd walked up to the window and taken one.

That was how she had to start thinking if she wanted to make it in this business.

Instead of sitting in the parking lot of the Fall Inn, she'd be spending her time and energy on a *real case,* and she'd get as up-close and personal as she had to to do it.

5

TIFFANY WAS DRESSED and headed out to her car by lunchtime, her mission clear in her head. She was wired. She planned to meet Mrs. Hooper and give her the pictures before heading to the first store that had been robbed. Mrs. Hooper seemed surprised at the quick turnaround, and offered to pay, but Tiffany declined, apologizing for it taking so long, and feeling her professional points go up. Mrs. Hooper promised to recommend her if she ever knew anyone who needed a private eye.

That alone made Tiffany's morning, and she set out to start her investigation of the robberies with new zeal. She shook her head at her own slowness in realizing that she couldn't just sit around waiting for the world to hand her jobs. Crimes were all over the place; she wanted to solve them. And hopefully, eventually, people would want to pay her for the work.

While she had been pouring over whatever she could find in regard to the jewel thefts, her mind had wandered back to Garrett, and a few times she had been tempted to call him. She still wasn't sure if she wanted to thank him or be angry with him, but if he hadn't interfered, she wouldn't have had this epiphany.

So maybe it was best to just leave it at that.

It wasn't real, what they'd had. It was a weekend fling that had found extra time by chance, and that was all.

In addition to her robbery research, combing over newspaper articles and making lists of people she could contact as well as people who could be the common touch points for access at the stores, she'd given in to doing a little research on Garrett Berringer as well. Unable to resist, Tiffany had also looked up Elaine Berringer on the internet, and what she found told her it had been the right decision to walk away.

Garrett's late wife was beautiful in a classic, understated manner, with long, straight brown hair that she'd often clipped back in the pictures Tiffany found. She was slim, serious-looking, though the smiles they both wore in a wedding photo that was posted on Ed's Facebook page told Tiffany all she needed to know. Garrett had loved his wife, and when you loved once like that, did it ever happen again?

She was just a fling.

Ouch.

And Elaine—Lainey—had been more than beautiful. Accomplished, graduating at the top of her class, having published regularly in legal journals and working as a consultant to several high-profile companies, her intellectual credits were impressive. She had been a budding prosecutor on her first big case when she had been killed, tragically, by the brother of a man she had just helped convict.

Tiffany couldn't imagine the pain Garrett must have suffered. She didn't want to.

But there wasn't even a comparison between Garrett's late wife and herself. Garrett had obviously only been interested in her for one reason. Even though her interest had been the same in him, it still hurt a little. It became clear that there was no way she could ever compete with the memory of Lainey Berringer. Not that she had ever intended to, but it did inspire her to investigate this case even more than before. Tiffany was tired of never measuring up, and she wanted to change that, starting now. Lainey had been accomplished in her career; Tiffany didn't even have one—yet. If she wanted this to work, it was up to her. Starting now.

With a renewed sense of purpose, she mentally reviewed her research again, thinking about the auction sites she'd discovered, looking for anything that seemed suspicious. That offered her first clue: she had to know what was stolen at the other stores before she could attempt to find it. The police hadn't shared any information with the media about that, and they certainly hadn't shared it with her. In fact, they had told her emphatically not to reveal what had been stolen from Jarvis's.

She knew only the names of the stores from the police blotter, and she planned to visit each of them today. They were all small stores, like theirs, that functioned on a foundation of trust and reputation, much like a bank. Surely the other stores were in similar financial binds as Jarvis's, having to cover their expenses while waiting for the investigation to conclude before the insurance would pay out.

If she could find the diamonds, or at least find some clues that she could take to the police, before her parents got back, maybe they would all stand a fighting chance.

Crossing the Bay Bridge, Tiffany headed south to San Jose, where the first store had been robbed. After talking to management there, she'd circle through Menlo Park, Berkeley and back to the city. It would make for a long day, but at least she felt like she was *doing* something. And who knew what she would find; she had to start somewhere. Spotting the exit for San Jose, she pulled away from the main highway and followed her GPS's directions to her first destination.

The store was smaller than her family's, dealing more in vintage gems and jewelry, and Tiffany spent several minutes rapt with the beauty of some of the old pieces, loving their classic design and the original settings. These old pieces were about glamour and class, not the flash that was so often the focus these days. There was a green opal necklace she would give her right arm for, but it was totally out of her price range.

"Would you like to try it on?" the clerk asked, and Tiffany smiled, knowing the move. Trying it on was one step closer to a sale, but as there was no way she could afford it, she wasn't in any danger of caving to that.

"I'd love to," she accepted happily as the clerk retrieved the necklace from the case and attached it around her neck.

Tiffany looked in the mirror on the counter and sighed.

"It's lovely. The orange fire is so intense. I've never seen opals quite as color-saturated as these. They're almost brilliant," she commented, leaning to the light.

She'd have to take it off to get a better look, but there were no blind spots—a bad thing in an opal, where the color dulled or disappeared when looking at it directly. She assumed there would be no real defects in these beauties.

Seduced by the small, iridescent teardrops that hung daintily around her throat, Tiffany found herself mentally calculating the sums left in her savings and credit card balances, but regrettably shook her head.

"Maybe someday. Thanks for letting me try it on," she said, taking the necklace off and handing it back to the clerk.

"Those stones are gorgeous, aren't they?" a male voice asked from behind her, and Tiffany turned to find a handsome young man watching her admiringly.

"They are."

"You wear them well. They complement your hair and skin tone, also lovely," he said suavely, and Tiffany found herself smiling. He was probably five years younger than she was, but he had adopted the mannerisms of Clark Gable, she thought with a grin. And he managed to pull it off.

"You must be Armando," she said, recognizing his face from the collection of family pictures at the front of the store. His grandfather owned the store, but he was the manager. He reminded her of her younger brother, and was sure he wouldn't care for the comparison. "I'm Tiffany Walker."

"So nice to meet you," he said. "What can I do for you?"

Tiffany explained that her family owned Jarvis's, and had also just been robbed. "I was sorry to see your store mentioned in the paper as the first one in the recent series of thefts. Do you mind me asking what was stolen?" she asked, getting right to the point.

"We were asked not to talk about it by the police, and for insurance reasons, you understand," Armando responded. "Why do you ask?"

"I'm just…reaching out, trying to find any information I can that might shed some light on what's going on. Maybe if we all shared with each other, we might find some connection, something the police could use—"

"I am not sure that is a good idea." The young man started to walk away, and Tiffany put her hand on his arm. She hoped she could use some female charm on him the way female TV detectives did all the time.

"I'm just another family business owner, like you. If this situation isn't resolved, my family could lose Jarvis's," she risked revealing. "The police don't seem to be coming up with much, and so I hoped perhaps we could all at least talk to each other, and maybe try to work together to see what we might come up with."

Armando softened, and his eyes were warm on hers as he took her hand from his arm and sandwiched it between his.

"Certainly. There is a café across the street. Let me buy you lunch, and we can talk. Though I don't know if there's much I can tell you that would help. We lost several pieces that had been set aside to go to auction," he explained, opening the door for her as they emerged out onto the sunny sidewalk. "My grandfather despairs of ever getting them back. They have already been sold, most likely."

"To go to auction?" Tiffany repeated Armando's words. They sometimes bought jewels at auctions, but rarely sold them there.

"We sell many antique and vintage pieces that special collectors, museums and other buyers are interested in. More of our overall revenue comes from those sales than walk-ins at the store, though we do a good business there, too. Vintage is in these days," Armando said as a waitress who obviously knew him well—and liked him—took them to a table.

The woman noted their orders, but smiled particularly warmly at Armando.

"What kinds of things were you sending to be auctioned off?"

"It was a Hollywood collection my grandfather managed to buy from a private collector in L.A.—some jewelry used in old movies. In this case, three pieces all worn by Marlene Dietrich in her films," he said with a sigh.

"I thought that movies used costume jewelry, or paste?"

"Most do, but some pieces were owned by the actors or actresses, so even those are collectible, but others were loaned by jewelry stores for use in the films. These were real and had their own, intrinsic value, but are even more valuable for the film history."

Tiffany sagged, suddenly not hungry. "It's very sad to lose that history as well as the jewelry itself," she said.

"You understand, then," Armando said, flirting with her again.

They talked more as they ate, and while Tiffany was glad she'd come and learned more about this aspect of the industry, there were no common denominators between the thefts at this point. Entirely different security, vaults and items stolen.

"Do you think it's a job-for-hire of some sort? Perhaps someone is targeting our special collections specifically for some reason?" she asked as they left the café.

"It's possible. Many collectors would have liked the pieces that were stolen, but doubtful in your case—how many private owners would want uncut, unset pink diamonds?"

Tiffany wondered that, too. Was there any chance the robberies weren't related? Everyone was only assuming they had been carried out by the same thieves.

"Well, thank you so much, Armando. If I find out anything, I'll be sure to let you know."

Armando smiled and took a step closer. "Perhaps you could let me know over dinner. Next weekend, perhaps?"

Tiffany smiled, though she had no interest at all in seeing Armando again. Her mind was still on a particular bodyguard who made Armando, for all of his polish, look like he was playing dress-up.

"I'm sorry, but I'm involved with someone at the moment," she said, lying to let him down gently.

"I should have known," he said with regret and a smile, far too charming for his own good. She imagined he was a successful salesman, though.

"Thank you, again," she said, getting into her car. She drove off, mentally going over all that they had discussed when a connection she hadn't seen earlier occurred to her.

Armando had mentioned that his grandfather was thinking about selling the business, sales being down in general. Armando was urging him not to do so because it was his dream to run the store. As in the case of Jarvis's, the robbery had potentially cost them far more than the insurance might cover.

How could someone know about the financial status of each business? The robberies put both stores in financial jeopardy—but why would someone want that? Or was that even a factor?

Tiffany hit the gas a touch harder, eager to arrive at the next store to see if her theory held. Seconds later, she noticed a car behind her. She remembered seeing it from the restaurant window, and had not thought twice. But the SUV had pulled away from its spot on the curb almost as soon as she had.

She shook off the paranoia as she pulled into a gas station. There was no way the SUV was following her. Was it?

As a P.I., she needed to follow her instincts, and years of living in a large city had taught her not to ignore hers when she felt there was something dangerous nearby.

The car still hung by the corner as she put gas in the car and tried not to look.

Tense, and reluctant to get on the road again until she knew that she wasn't in trouble, Tiffany decided to take the bull by the horns. In the small convenience store, she paid for her gasoline and bought a sample-sized can of hair spray. Putting it in her pocket, she asked where the restroom was, and made her way to the back, but slipped by the ladies' room and found the rear exit instead.

She'd circle around the back of the few businesses between here and the corner to approach the SUV from behind. Then she could at least find out if anyone was in it, or she could grab the license plate and note any distinguishing marks, just in case.

Making her way carefully to the spot, she realized the car was empty, which relieved her paranoia and made her feel a little foolish. Still, she took down the plate number and noticed it was a rental, with a San Francisco parking tag on the dash.

So whoever it was had come here from the city, just as she had. Typing it all into a message app on her phone, she took a deep breath and thought to return to the gas station.

Emerging from the restroom area, she headed toward the door just as she saw the shape of someone by her car. Tiffany froze. A man. He'd been standing, but then ducked down as if looking under her car, but she'd only caught sight of his shoulder and the side of his head before the column of the gas pump obscured her view.

Her heart slammed in her chest as she walked toward the door, spying the clerk, the camera very clearly placed at the entrance, and the other customers getting gas— surely no one would try to hurt her or even steal her car here in broad daylight?

Rounding the pump, she jumped out of her skin as she nearly ran directly into whoever it was that was skulking by her car. His solid mass was like hitting a wall as strong fingers closed around her upper arms to steady her.

Looking up, she couldn't have been more surprised.

Garrett.

"WHAT ARE *YOU* doing here? Did you *follow* me? What's going on?" Tiffany asked the questions in rapid succession, shaking like a leaf under his hands where he still held her.

He'd frightened her. Garrett hadn't quite believed his

eyes when he saw her emerge from the jewelry store. Just as he parked his rental, he'd watched her go into the café with some pretty guy who smiled way too much. Then, when he'd gone into the store himself and spoken to the clerk, he found out that guy was the manager.

What was Tiffany up to? He had some questions of his own, but for now, he wanted to calm her down. They were drawing attention.

"I'm sorry," he said sincerely. "I didn't mean to frighten you."

Her eyes narrowed. "Are you some kind of weird stalker now, following me around because we spent a few nights together? How long were you watching me?"

Her voice rose, drawing the attention of a few people nearby, two guys in particular who stopped and watched them closely.

"I am *not* stalking you. It was simple coincidence. I was going to the jewelry store and saw you walk out with the manager. I was curious and concerned, so I waited and followed you back here. I guess my tailing skills are a little rusty," he said with a grin, hoping to lighten the tension between them. "What were you doing down here?"

"It's none of your business what I do, and you have no right to follow me anywhere. You scared the life out of me," she said, taking a step back, her arms still wrapped protectively around her middle.

Garrett hated that he had scared her so much; it wasn't his intention at all. Why did he always seem to make the wrong move with this woman?

"I said I'm sorry. I really had no intention to follow you, or to scare you. But I am curious why you were at that store."

She started to open her mouth, and then closed it again, pinning him with an intent look. "Really? Maybe Armando is a friend. Maybe we're lovers. What business is it of yours? A better question is why were *you* there?"

Garrett knew from watching her with Armando that they were not lovers—not that the younger man wouldn't be open to it. But she had a fair point, that it was more unusual for him to be there than her.

"I thought I would track down a few leads on the robberies, see what I could find out. I went in, talked to the clerk for a few minutes while you were in the café, and she didn't know much, so I came back out."

"And waited to follow me. Why are you investigating my case? Aren't you supposed to be gone on your vacation?"

Garrett blinked at her aggressiveness. "Your case? What am I missing here?"

Before she could answer, someone else spoke.

"Is there a problem here? Is this guy bugging you?" a voice interrupted, and they turned to find one of the men who had been watching them, eyeing Garrett closely.

"No problem," Garrett said. Tiffany said nothing, but just glared.

"It looks like the lady doesn't agree," the guy said, waving his friend forward to join them. "Maybe you should be on your way."

Garrett sized the guy up. He wasn't small, but there was no way he was leaving Tiffany alone here. A second man joined them, and Garrett tried appealing to them on a different level.

"We're just friends having a disagreement. I don't intend her any harm."

"Then you won't mind leaving," the second guy said.

"Actually, I do mind leaving," Garrett said, giving the guy a look that reinforced the fact, pulling up to his full height.

Sensing that things were heating up, Tiffany stepped in.

"I'm sure he doesn't mean me any harm, guys, I was just angry—"

"Maybe you should let us handle this," the second guy said, sliding an appreciative look over Tiffany. "And you can thank us later."

"I think you should leave us alone, or I'll call the police and let *them* handle it," Tiffany said, pulling her phone from her pocket.

The first guy who'd approached them put his hands up, backing off. "Hey, we were just trying to help."

"Thanks, but I can handle him myself," she said, giving both men a look that carried more steel than Garrett would have given her credit for. The men backed away, the second one throwing out a curse at them as the men disappeared down the street.

"You handled that well. Kept your cool," Garrett said approvingly.

The look she threw him wasn't a friendly one. "Gee, thanks for admitting that I might be able to take care of myself, but I don't need you sticking your nose in, like you did with Marcus."

Garrett paused. He wasn't sure how she would react to his reading through her notes, but he hadn't been able to sleep and decided to go see what he could see. As it turned out, he'd had lucky timing, and saw Hooper going into the hotel with his date. It hadn't taken long to grab some shots through a partially closed curtain and leave. In truth, he hadn't liked the idea of Tiffany hanging out in that neighborhood, and it made him feel better to finish the job for her.

Now, staring into her stormy green eyes, he realized the error.

"Tiff, I wasn't trying to—"

"What? Act like I couldn't handle it? That I can't do this job? That it's too tough for a girl like me?"

"Not exactly that, no. I was just hoping to do you a favor, as Mrs. Hooper sounded angry, and, well, yes, I will admit I didn't think it was safe for you to be hanging out in that parking lot night after night."

"Private investigators have to be in dangerous situations sometimes, Garrett. Like I need to tell you that? I was fine. I can handle myself."

Garrett didn't want to burst her bubble, but he just wasn't sure.

"Did you deliver the pictures?"

"Yes. She was very pleased."

"Did she pay you?"

"She offered. I declined. *I* didn't finish the job, not that I told her that. She promised to refer me to friends, if she had the chance."

Garrett shook his head. "Let me tell you something, Tiff—"

"No, let me tell *you* something. You had no right to go sniffing around in my things. You had no right to do any of this just because we slept together."

Garrett noticed more curious interest from people getting gas, and smiled to one guy, waving him off.

"You're right. I was wrong. I'm sorry," he said, trying to calm her down. "But what about this? Why are you investigating these robberies on your own?"

"Because it's what I want to do, and because I had to tell my parents what happened on the phone this morning and hear the worry in their voices. I can solve this case, or at least I can try." She sighed, whispering, "I have to do something."

"This is a lot different than getting pictures of cheating husbands, Tiffany—and that's dangerous enough—

cheating husbands can get pretty angry. But these thieves are professionals. That's a whole new ballgame."

She clenched her jaw, and made him want to kiss her until she relaxed it. "I'm talking to people, Garrett. That's all. Nothing dangerous about that."

He supposed she was right. Maybe. His protective instincts, and his worry about her getting in over her head, warred with the realization that she was an adult who could make her own decisions. But maybe there was another way to come at it.

"Did you find out anything interesting?" he asked.

Her expression told him that she wasn't in a sharing mood.

"Why don't you let me buy you lunch?" he offered.

"I already had lunch—as you know—since you were watching us."

He rocked back on his heels. "Right. You and Mario Lanza."

"I thought he was more like a young Clark Gable," she retorted with a slight smile. She knew that he was just a bit jealous, he realized. And he was. He'd hated sitting there, watching from the car during their lunch. Business was the last thing on that guy's mind, and it bothered Garrett, though he certainly had no claim on Tiffany.

She sighed, shaking her head. "Garrett, go enjoy your vacation, okay? This isn't your problem."

"Are you visiting more stores today?"

"You're like a dog with a bone, I swear. And I don't like being the bone," she said testily.

"Just let me tag along and make sure that you're okay. I won't interfere, but just in case something happens, I'll be there."

"Garrett—"

"Listen, Tiffany, I've seen a lot of seemingly harmless

situations go bad. I've seen people get hurt and worse. Believe me, the worst mistake you can make is thinking you have everything under control."

"I'm sure—"

"What if these robberies are an inside job? What if one employee at one establishment is involved, and you are poking around, asking questions? You could hit a nerve. It's hard to predict what people will do in that situation. Let me be your bodyguard for the day. I'm good at this. I can stay out of the way, but make sure you're safe. And if you find anything, we'll take it to the police, and then I'll go my merry way, okay?"

She bit her lip in the fashion that always drew his attention to her lips, and Garrett experienced a split second of doubting his own motives. He was being honest—he did worry that something could go wrong—it happened all the time. If something happened to her, he wouldn't be able to forgive himself. But in all honesty, he also still wanted Tiffany. Still wanted to be around her.

"Okay, fine," she said, though clearly unhappy. "I guess it can't hurt."

He smiled. "Thanks. Where to next?"

She gave him the list of stores she was planning to visit, and he typed them into his smartphone. He'd map the routes into his GPS in case he lost her.

She smiled slightly, the tension seeming to ease between them. "Thanks for having my back, Garrett. And thank you, I suppose, for Marcus, as well. It ticked me off at first, but I learned a lot from what you did there. In fact, it inspired me to take this case on," she said.

Not exactly what he had intended, but at least she was less angry with him.

"But you know, next time, don't go behind my back to

do it," she continued. "Not that there would be a next time, but you know what I mean," she added.

She was so pretty; he couldn't stop looking at her. It was all he could do not to kiss her. Damn. But she appeared to be waiting for a response, and he cleared his throat, shaking himself out of his thoughts.

"You're right. Let me buy you dinner after you're done, and make it up to you? And we can talk about the—your—case?"

She laughed lightly, her head tilting back like it sometimes did when he was inside her, when she was letting go, falling apart for him.

"Dinner would be nice. And maybe I can show you some of the city after dark," she said, peeking up at him through her lashes.

"I'd like that," he said. He liked the sound of that a lot.

"But first we have work to do," she said, all business again as she walked around to the other side of her car.

We have work to do, she'd said. He liked the sound of that, too.

6

"THIS IS EXACTLY like I imagined it," Garrett said, taking in the quiet streets of Russian Hill as he walked arm-in-arm with Tiffany toward the Spanish tapas restaurant she said was her absolute favorite.

Trolleys rolled by, stuffed to the brim with tourists and locals out enjoying the nightlife. While walking the hills was a workout, Garrett was glad to stroll along the pretty, blue-grey lit streets with Tiffany rather than being in the middle of the crush.

This neighborhood, which was residential with a spattering of boutiques, small businesses and restaurants, was completely different from the crazy urban vibe of downtown. The architecture was classic, clean and charming, the soft colors on the building fronts accented by almost golden street lighting.

Garrett felt like he had just walked onto the set of *Monk*. It was blissfully quiet compared to Union Square; a few people walked with their grocery bags or their dogs, and a few other couples passed by, wrapped up in each other. Laughing groups of diners emerged from small restaurant entryways.

"It is one of the nicest sections, certainly. And very expensive to live here. Lombard Street isn't far away. We can walk down there after dinner and do the tourist thing," Tiffany said, sounding happy and satisfied, and much more relaxed than she had been earlier in the day.

"Here we are," Tiffany announced as they arrived at the top of the hill, stopping at a corner restaurant that specialized in tapas, or "small plates." Garrett hadn't been to a place that specialized in the appetizer-like entrées for quite some time. The dining area was small, and sitting at one table was actually more like sitting with six other people, as they were all so close together. But it wasn't crowded so much as companionable.

A large, boisterous man who appeared to be the owner greeted Tiffany and then Garrett, and obviously knew her well, asking how her parents were doing.

"They're good, Gio. They're off on a buying trip right now," Tiffany said, not mentioning the robbery.

"You have this table by the window, so that passersby can see how beautiful you are tonight," the older man said, winking at Tiffany.

"Thank you. You're such a charmer," Tiffany said, her cheeks pink from the compliment.

"I'll pick you a nice wine that you will like. Perfect with tonight's specials," Gio announced happily, and then went to greet more people at the door.

"He's been a friend of my father's for decades. They both started up their businesses around the same time," she explained to Garrett. "The whole family is like that. And they're all amazing cooks, too."

"We have some family friends back in Philly who own an Italian place down in the old neighborhood and it beats anything the food magazines recommend, but not too many people know about it," Garrett responded.

"Why not?"

"Fishtown has a somewhat mixed reputation, especially for tourists. To us, it's just home, you know? But it's kind of run-down in places, there's some crime and it's off the beaten track. But overall, it's a wonderful spot. Real Philly. Tourists wouldn't find the restaurant listed in most tourist guides, but it's a local favorite."

Tiffany grinned. "When you talk about your city, your accent gets stronger."

"What accent? I don't have an accent," he said in a more heavily accented tone, laughing.

Philadelphians had accents that reflected a mélange of ethnic influences, and he knew his strengthened when he was at ease, with friends, or when he was intense about something. He was glad Tiffany liked it.

"It's sexy," she said, and Garrett felt his heart catch. She had a way of knocking him off guard with comments like that. He wasn't used to it—Lainey had always been more reserved—but he liked it.

"Tiffany, how nice to see you," a voice interrupted them, and Garrett looked up to see a balding, older man approach the table with a smile aimed at Tiffany. "Are your parents back yet?"

"Hello, Arthur, no, not yet. Wednesday," she said with a smile as he took both of her hands in his for a friendly greeting. "Arthur Hayden, this is Garrett Berringer, a friend from out of town. Garrett, Arthur is our main appraiser. He's worked with us and most stores around town forever."

"Ha, I'm not that old," the man said, shaking Garrett's hand as well. "Welcome to our city. And Tiffany, please tell your parents to call me when they're in. I was so sorry to hear about what happened at the store," he said in a soft, covert tone.

"How did you know?" Tiffany asked, knowing he was talking about the robbery.

"The police called to confirm the appraisal of the diamonds. How infuriating, to think of such beautiful gems in the hands of such barbarians," he said, his cheeks darkening with anger.

"I know, Arthur. Hopefully they will catch them."

"Indeed. The police warned me to observe utmost confidentiality, as if I need to be told that in my business, but I had to say how sorry I was to hear it when I saw you here."

"I understand. I appreciate you saying so. I know Mom and Dad will, too."

"Well, you have a wonderful night, and don't forget to tell your parents to call," Arthur said to the both of them.

"He was upset," Garrett noted.

"He's been part of the scene around here for at least twenty years. You need something reliably and fairly appraised, he's the man you see. He takes his work very seriously," she said.

Gio returned to the table with the wine and waited until they both tasted and praised it. He took their orders, promising to add some of the specials he knew they'd want to try—on the house—and left them alone again.

"So what's it like being a bodyguard? And you said you run the agency with your brothers?"

Garrett nodded. "I started it up after Lainey died. My brother Jonas was a Philadelphia cop then, but he left the force and joined up with me. Ely was in the Marines at the time, but when he got home he wanted in, and Chance, the youngest, followed suit. Before we knew it, we were all in it together."

"You must all get along very well. Not many families could work together like that."

"We do, most of the time. When I started it up, I actually didn't imagine it being a family business. It was a lark. I figured I'd contract guys to work for me, and I would just manage the business, but it went this other way and I love it. My brothers were made for this work. They excel at it."

"You're proud of them," she said with a smile, sipping her wine.

"I am. They're good men. Jonas just got married. He met his wife on an assignment, actually."

"Very romantic," Tiffany commented. "Falling in love with your bodyguard."

Garrett laughed. "Ha, it wasn't like the movie, I'll tell you that. It was kind of a mess. Jonas lost his eyesight—"

"No! He's blind? How?"

"Protecting Tessa. It was a temporary loss, but it brought them back together. And while their relationship wasn't easy, they are happy now. Hard times for a while, though."

"The path of true love never runs easy?"

"Sometimes it does, I think, but Jonas isn't an easy guy."

"And the others? Ely and Chance?"

"Ely is kind of a mess at the moment. I guess we didn't recognize how hard it was for him to adjust coming back from Afghanistan. Then he got duped by a woman he really cared for—found out she was engaged after he was already building the picket fences in his head."

"That's awful."

"Yeah. He's been unpredictable ever since. Great on the job, always a professional, but his personal life...well, I'd probably rather not know. And Chance. As long as he's jumping off of something high or dodging bullets, he's happy. I can't see him ever settling down. There's probably not a woman who'd be able to put up with his antics, but he's never short of companionship, and seems happy enough."

"And you? What makes you happy?"

The deep scarlet of the wine in his glass drew his attention as he paused, staring into it before he took a slow sip, contemplating the question.

"That should be an easy question, shouldn't it?" he finally said, though he didn't really have any clue for how to answer it.

"Maybe not. Sometimes the things I think will make me happy don't…and then something I didn't count on, like this weekend with you, makes me very happy," she said simply.

Garrett smiled, relieved that she understood. "Exactly. I was going to say that I'm happy when things are going smoothly in life, no bumps, but that wasn't quite right. I like excitement, too, and the unexpected. More so now than I used to, even. And this weekend was definitely unexpected, in the best possible way," he said, holding her gaze and lifting his glass to meet hers.

"I like to shake things up a little, too. I need variety, to be up and moving, not just caught in one place all the time."

"Like in your family's store?"

"Exactly. I've been trying to find my calling, my niche, and so far, no luck. I have a feeling though…about this…." she drifted off, and he watched as she visibly held herself back from talking about her new venture.

"About being a P.I.? A good feeling?"

"The best," she said, her eyes shining. "I haven't had much experience, and I'm still figuring things out, but even these low-level jobs are more fun than any other job I could imagine. I want to learn more, be better at it. Become a real investigator."

"You will. It just takes time. Experience."

"I have been trying to get that. I took an online course

to get my license, and I have been taking self-defense and shooting lessons. I talk with whoever will talk to me, in the business, I mean, though they can be very cagey. It's a competitive business. But you taught me a great lesson today."

"What was that, exactly?"

"When you took that picture of Marcus, you just walked up to the window and took it—you didn't wait for the shot. You got out of the car and went after it. I should have done that, so, really, I think I was angry with myself more than with you," she said. "But now I know. I have to go after what I want, to show people I'm serious about this." Her words came out in a rush.

Garrett listened closely. "Who do you have to show that you're serious?"

Their food arrived, and after several minutes of complimenting the variety of goodies and filling their plates, Tiffany responded.

"My family, mostly. I can't blame them for having their doubts. I've had kind of a bad string of employment ventures, and now this happening at the store…"

"The robbery is hardly your fault," Garrett interjected.

"I know, but it just sort of adds to my pile of work-related disasters. Not to mention the personal ones," she mumbled before taking a forkful of some delectable-looking roast. Garrett did the same, and they ate, doing nothing more than complimenting the food for the next few minutes.

"It's why they can't know about this. Not yet. My parents would have a fit. They've been so happy with me at the store, doing something 'normal,'" she said, using air quotes around the last word. "I don't think they'd be very happy about me learning to be an investigator."

"They don't know?" Garrett asked, surprised.

"No, and they can't. Unless I manage to do something that could show them I can really do this, like solving this case, or at least finding something instrumental in solving it. I just can't bear to worry them any more than I have already, or to feel their disappointment," she confessed, putting her fork down.

"They probably have more faith in you than you imagine," Garrett said, hoping that was the case. He couldn't keep that kind of secret from his own family; they were all so close. Sure, they had their moments, their disagreements, but his parents had always been supportive of anything their sons wanted to pursue, succeed or fail.

"Maybe, but they certainly don't need any more worries, considering recent events," she said.

"You mentioned sisters? And a brother?" Garrett asked, curious about her family now.

"Yes. Ruby is the oldest, married, two kids. She's very much an earth child. She lives on a farm with her husband and they grow a lot of their own food, grapes for wine, that kind of thing. Jewel is the youngest next to Nick, and she's more of a hell-raiser, but smart as a whip. She and her partner just started a practice in the city."

"Practice?"

"Architects. Both of them."

"Husband and wife architects. Ambitious," Garrett commented.

"Close. Jewel's partner is Gracie."

"Oh, my mistake," said Garrett, surprised but not at all put off.

"My real question is, if you wanted to distract me from thinking about the case, you couldn't do any better than asking about my sisters?" she asked mischievously, and Garrett had to stop from jumping out of his chair when her foot suddenly slid along the inside of his thigh.

"Uh, um, well," he said, clearing his throat as he reached down to stop the upward progress of her foot.

She laughed, withdrawing her toes.

"Sorry, couldn't resist."

He looked into her eyes, and wished the restaurant weren't such a crowded place. "Don't resist too much," he said and meant it.

Desire blazed in her eyes, but then she took a breath and shook her head.

"Actually, would you mind if we talked about the case? About my discussions with people at the stores today? I wouldn't mind bouncing some ideas off of someone, and since you're the only person who knows what I'm up to..."

Garrett was happy to have any reason to spend more time with Tiffany; in fact, he was going to try to convince her to let him help her with this investigation. It was too dangerous for a novice to be poking her nose into something like this on her own. How he would convince her, well...he had several notions about that, but first things first.

"I'd like that. But why don't we just enjoy tonight, and we can talk about the case tomorrow?" he said, signaling for the check.

"Tomorrow?" she echoed as they left, emerging out into the cool night air.

Garrett paused to take in Tiffany as her hair blew softly around her face, her scent surrounding him. He was tired of resisting and pulled her over to the side of the walk and into his arms for the kiss he had been thinking about for hours.

She didn't resist, either, wrapping her arms around his neck and drawing him closer. Of all the things he enjoyed about Tiffany, it was how she let herself go, especially in this way.

She tasted spicy, like the wine and the food. And suddenly, he was a lot less interested in talking about anything, only deepening the kiss and tightening his arms as she melted into him.

"Garrett, why are you doing this?" she asked breathlessly as she broke the kiss, placing her hands on his chest between them.

"Because I like being with you. I want you. I think you want me, too. Isn't that reason enough?"

She looked past him toward the bay, as if fighting with herself, not knowing the answer.

"Nothing can come of this," she said, and he knew she was losing that fight.

"Let's not worry about what's coming. Let's just enjoy tonight," he said coaxingly, tipping her chin up so that their eyes met.

"Okay," she said with a slight shake of her head, though she was smiling.

"Okay," he said back, taking her hand as they strolled down the romantically lit streets back to his hotel.

TIFFANY HAD ARGUED with herself all the way back to the hotel, listing all of the reasons why this was a bad idea.

One fact trumped all of the common sense in the world: she wanted Garrett. Wanted more time with him, wanted to be with him, wanted to know as much as she could about him. She'd made plenty of bad decisions in her life, but she couldn't for the life of her convince herself that he was one of them. Even if what they had was temporary, it was good.

When they were in the room, she stood by the window taking in the night views of the city. Her life felt like a fantasy. For the moment, everything else fell away.

She didn't hear him come up behind her, his arms coming around her waist to splay over her middle. The heat from his touch burned through the light material of her blouse, and she was glad she'd put on some of her sexier lingerie that morning.

"You're like a cat," she said breathlessly. "I didn't even hear you move."

"You seemed deep in thought," he whispered in her ear, pressing against her but leaving his hands where they were. Her breasts already felt sensitive and heavy, wanting his touch.

All she had to do was ask, or take his hands in hers and show him what she wanted. But the anticipation, drawing out this indulgence was sweet, too.

Dropping her head back to his chest, she angled to look up toward him, but before she said a word, his mouth captured hers in a long, soft kiss. Linking her arm up around his neck, she deepened it, whispering against his mouth that she wanted more. Much more.

He pulled the material of her blouse from the waist of her skirt, undoing the buttons so slowly that she almost couldn't stand it. When his palms finally covered her aching flesh and encountered the lacy material she wore, he stopped.

"What's this?" he whispered against her lips.

"Want me to show you?"

He nodded, and she looked out at the darkening skyline. "Shut the lights, or dim them, would you?" she asked. She wanted her show to be for Garrett, not for the entire city.

"Sure," he agreed, and dimmed them low enough that she felt more secure letting the blouse slip from her shoulders. She still didn't face him, but watched him in the reflection of the darkened window.

"Turn around," he said softly.

She did, and saw him unbuttoning his own shirt, exposing an expanse of taut, muscular torso that made her mouth dry.

She met his gaze as she released the clasp at the front of the bra. It fell from her shoulders and to the floor in a silky puddle. He took off his belt.

She took her time sliding the zipper on the side of her skirt down, in concert with him unzipping his slacks. She shimmied out of hers as he kicked off his shoes and stepped out of his.

He was already hard, visible through the close fit of the black boxer briefs he wore.

Feeling even more daring, she turned back to face the window. They were high up, facing away from the main street, with the lights dimmed. She supposed someone could see, if they were looking, but she was willing to risk it for the thrill that raced through her at the possible exposure.

Sliding her thumbs under the lacy edge of her panties, she eased them down, making sure Garrett received a nice show as she bent and pulled them away from her ankle, tossing them back toward him. She was rewarded with an audible groan.

Planting her hands on the window, she stared down at the busy street and bent slightly, looking back at him over her shoulder.

"I think I'll leave the heels on," she said with a naughty wink.

His boxers were removed quickly as he joined her, hot and hard behind her, his hands sliding up over her thighs, covering her butt and then drifting up her spine before he reached around to cover her breasts. As he played and tweaked her already hard nipples, she groaned, too.

"Now, Garrett. Right here," she said, her voice quavering. She kept looking down, letting the height and the sparkling lights of the city swim before her eyes as he nudged her thighs farther apart with his own. He thrust forward, hard and deep, making her gasp at the sudden sensation of being so quickly and completely filled.

Leaning in, he planted his hands over hers flat on the glass of the window, winding their fingers together as he kissed her shoulder, nuzzled her neck. She turned her face to reach his kiss as he started to move. Bracing herself against his thrusts, she broke the kiss as her head fell forward, her breath bursting in short, hot bursts.

"Yes, more," she commanded, hardly recognizing the throaty, sexual tone of her own voice as she widened her stance for him.

His fingers tightened on hers as he pumped harder into her, their bodies finding a furious rhythm together as her fingers grasped his. Everything inside of her tightened, the pressure unbearable until it all spilled over, her release flooding her body on waves of orgasm that left her shaking. Garrett picked up the pace, his arm looping around her waist to hold her there as he rode her even harder.

"Again, sweetheart, go over with me," he panted against her ear before nipping at the base of her neck and planting hot kisses along the tender skin beneath her ear.

She wouldn't have thought she was able, but his words and the delicious friction of his cock, which became harder and fuller as he approached his own breaking point, pushed her over again, even more intensely than the first time. The soaking pleasure of it nearly doubled her over his arm as he groaned through his own climax. She was limp from the waves of pleasure that weakened her until he brought her back up against him, into his arms.

He was shaking. She could feel it, and it amazed her. How much he gave, and how much he took; she'd never experienced anything like this with any man. It made her glad she had decided to go for it, and a little worried it would never happen again.

He swept her up into his arms, making her laugh weakly, though she didn't mind at all as he carried her over to the large sofa where he pulled her down on top of him. She sighed as his arms closed around her.

"You're going to kill me, Tiff," he said affectionately, his hand stroking her hair, the other placed loosely on her bare bottom.

"Same here," she said with a tired smile. "But what a way to go."

"I'm glad you came back with me," he said against her hair.

"Me, too."

They lay in silence for a few minutes, letting the quiet after the storm wash over them, and Garrett stroked her hair in a way that made her never want to get off this couch, ever.

"You said something earlier, about having had some professional problems, but you also mentioned some personal ones. What did you mean?" he asked.

Tiffany opened her eyes, the semi-drugged, sex-saturated coma she'd been slipping into clearing fast. Pushing up, she folded her hands under her chin on his chest, looking into his handsome face. Would he think less of her if she told him?

She didn't want to risk it, but Garrett had been so open with her about his own past, she didn't feel right shutting the door on his question.

Tiffany related to him the various problems she'd had recently, including being ripped off by her former boyfriend, Brice.

"He stole from you? And the police wouldn't do anything about it?" Garrett repeated, pushing up to a sitting position and taking her with him. His expression was serious now, and his eyes held a little bit of an edge that made him look dangerous.

A shiver of arousal traveled down her spine. Garrett was a nice man—a caring man—but he could be dangerous. When protecting someone he loved, or even someone he was hired to protect, she had no doubt he could do whatever the job required.

"My sisters seemed to pick up from the start that Brice was trouble, but I didn't listen. I jump in and get involved, and then it always comes back and bites me in the ass."

"Maybe because you have a very delectable ass," Garrett said, his hand running over her knee and thigh, stroking lightly. "But it's not your fault you met a loser. It happens to everyone at some point, and you learned from the experience. That's the best you can hope for," he said. Then his lovely mouth turned down for a second. "I only wish I'd known you then. I wouldn't have gone as easy on him as the police did," he said in a tone that nearly made her jump him on the spot.

"Thank you," she said sincerely as she faced him, sitting cross-legged in a style that provided him a very interesting view. He noticed, his eyes darkening with renewed interest. "But seriously, I'm really trying to make some better decisions. More responsible decisions, fewer impulsive ones," she said, catching her breath as his fingers drifted closer to the crux of her thighs.

"Really? What category do I fall into?" he asked as his hand slipped down in between and stroked her already slick flesh, making her whimper in response.

"Impulsive," she managed on a short breath as he stroked and explored. "But in the very, very good way," she added.

He laughed, sliding a finger, then two, inside as he

rubbed his thumb against her swollen clit. She started to untangle her legs, to stretch out, but he stopped her.

"No, like this. Don't move…I want to watch you come," he said huskily.

He didn't have long to wait as she flooded into his hand seconds later, her fingers digging into his arm as she rocked against his fingers, crying out his name.

"I don't think I can get enough of that," he murmured, easing her back against the cushions as he slid his hands down under her beautiful ass and buried himself inside of her.

She framed his face with her hands, watching him, too. Wanting to see. He didn't make her wait long, either, coming after a few hard pumps against her, collapsing back over her with a heavy sigh of satisfaction.

She missed him when he withdrew, and that worried her. Could she ever get enough of Garrett? Probably not.

But whatever they could have right now was going to have to be enough.

7

GARRETT KNEW PRECISELY when Tiffany had slipped from his arms early that morning, covertly watching her grab her notebooks from her bag and head to the front room.

She didn't get dressed; wasn't leaving. He relaxed back into the mattress, exhausted but more invigorated than he had been in years.

They'd made love in every way they could for most of the night, as if unable to stop touching, stop tasting, in case this was all they'd have. But the more they had, the more they seemed to want.

For him, anyway.

He was adult enough to know he was getting in deep. This was different, and it was powerful. There hadn't been a woman in six years that he hadn't been able to walk away from, until now.

At the same time, he knew it couldn't work. He wasn't about to uproot Berringer Bodyguards and move to the west coast. More than that, Tiffany's new revelation about her dream job disturbed him. Not just because she was new to it, or because she might be getting in over her head.

Garrett knew he couldn't go through again what he went through with Lainey. He had underestimated the dangers

associated with his late wife's work, and he was clear on
the dangers associated with being a private investigator.
She'd told him that she was taking self-defense, learning
to shoot—required skills for an investigator, but that was
for good reason. Tiffany would always be walking into
dangerous situations—an idea that didn't seem to put her
off one bit.

But it did put Garrett off. Not enough to walk away right
now, but as much as he liked her, wanted her, he couldn't
face a future with another woman who worked in a job
that could take her away from him.

It was a blatant contradiction, he knew, given his own
line of work, but he couldn't help how he felt. For him, for
his brothers, putting themselves between a bullet and a client was their way of life; he knew the score. But Tiffany
was different. He couldn't help but think she was still not
quite in touch with the gritty reality of real investigative
work, much of which was tedious as well as dangerous. It
was often nothing like what she read in her mystery novels, but it clearly excited her.

Her zest for life and her spontaneity were addictive. He
hated that she saw her impulsive nature as a negative, or
thought that that she had to hide it from anyone, especially
her family, or that she had to change. He wouldn't ask her
to change, even if it meant they couldn't pursue anything
beyond what they had right now.

He didn't love Tiffany. But he could. Maybe.

So he would just make sure that didn't happen.

Feeling he had the issue settled in his mind, he swung
his legs over the side of the bed, about to call for room
service to order breakfast for them both when his cell
phone rang.

Picking it up, he saw Daniel's name showing, his museum contact in London.

"Daniel, how the heck are you?" Garrett answered heartily. He and Dan had become friends over the years of doing museum business.

"Getting better-looking every day, I'll tell ya. I practically have to fight the women off," Dan answered in the normally cheerful, heavy English accent that Garrett would often imitate in fun.

James Bond, Dan was not. The pale, lanky, tall Brit whose suits were often too loose and who usually was pasted to his BlackBerry was probably telling the absolute truth, however. Women loved him. When he and Garrett hit the pubs, Dan never went home alone.

"Well, that's good to hear."

"I could give you some pointers, if you'd like," Dan teased.

"I'm good, thanks," Garrett said dryly, looking at the tangled sheets he'd just crawled out of. "More than good, in fact," he added, not realizing he'd said it out loud.

"Oh! That sounds like a tale to be told. You've met someone, and have called to share all of the dirty details?" Daniel said, laughing.

"No, actually, I called to get your perspective on a ring of jewel thefts we've had here in the U.S.," Garrett said, turning more serious as he explained the situation to his friend.

"This is exciting. A good, old-fashioned jewel theft rather than the coarse snatch-and-grabs or violent robberies we see too often these days," Daniel said with relish.

"Well, it's not too exciting for the stores that were robbed. These aren't major stores we're talking about. They're all small, family businesses, and they could end up in serious financial jeopardy if the insurance won't pay out," Garrett said.

"Ah, that is a damned shame," Daniel said on a sigh.

"Can you give me a list of what was taken, from whom it was acquired and where it was going, that kind of thing? I can do some poking around. Not my usual area, gems and things of that sort," he said with a note of caution.

"Except that these are items that could interest collectors, I think, and I know you know people who might have more information," Garrett pushed a bit.

"That I do. Send me the complete list, and I'll get back to you in a day or two?"

"The sooner the better. And thanks, Daniel. I owe you dinner when I see you next," Garrett said.

"At least that," Daniel said with a laugh. "I'm glad to do it, and especially if it's going to help this new woman who has you sounding more cheery. Will be in touch," Daniel said, and hung up, leaving Garrett looking at the phone.

He hadn't said a word about knowing Tiffany, or that her store had been robbed. But that was why he'd called Daniel—he was scary perceptive, and very good at his job. The people he knew, particularly in London's underground, or at Interpol, might dig up something interesting, as jewel thefts on this level were often international in scope. As Daniel mentioned, most were crude hold-ups, street criminals or drug addicts looking to score. This was a whole other class altogether, which comforted Garrett to some extent in terms of Tiffany's involvement.

Chances were, she wouldn't turn up much, but he'd keep looking to see what he could find on his end.

Ordering breakfast and taking a quick shower, he walked out to the main room to find her curled up on the couch in one of the suite's white terry robes, hunkered over her notes and her phone.

"Morning, gorgeous," Garrett said, leaning down to take her lips in a light morning kiss that deepened quickly until she pulled away as her notes nearly fell from her lap to the floor and she lurched to save them.

"Good morning," she said brightly, smiling up at him with bright energy. He wanted to get rid of the notebooks and the robe, and say good morning properly, but breakfast would be delivered soon, so he simply sat down on the sofa across from her.

"You rolled out of bed early."

"I know, I'm sorry. I hope I didn't wake you. But I had so much stuff from the interviews rolling around in my head, and I wanted to get up and start going over things, and do some brainstorming."

"Brainstorming?"

"Yes, it's one of the techniques I learned in the online class. We take all of the things we know, the facts, around particular aspects of the case, and you jot them down and then try to write down whatever each one makes you think about…. It helps open up ideas or connections you might not see otherwise."

Garrett nodded. "And did you find anything interesting?"

"Nothing I hadn't already thought of. All of the stores had different items stolen, though all very high-end pieces that few people knew were there. All are small, family businesses who can't afford the loss, and all look like inside jobs. There's no commonality among the vaults or the security systems, nor the time of installation."

"Hmm."

"Yeah. I thought that maybe the stores had been bugged? So the thieves could have overheard people discussing the security, but that doesn't apply in our case. My father changes the vault combination daily, and he never says it out loud. He always writes it down in a journal he keeps at our house, not on the store premises. The only commonality is that all of the stores had either taken out recent loans or are paying off some sort of improvements, like my father buying the new vault, but all of the loans come from different lending institutions," she added. "Still, the debt puts them in precarious financial circumstances. That's one common problem, but it doesn't really point to anything in terms of who the thieves are."

A knock on the door interrupted them, and Garrett rose to answer it, letting in two waiters rolling trays full of various breakfast foods. He was starving after the evening's activity, and he assumed Tiffany would be hungry as well.

He kept to himself that he was secretly somewhat relieved that she wasn't finding much so far in her investigation. This was heavy-duty stuff for a fledgling investigator.

"Come on, eat. I ordered enough food for six," he said, cajoling, and she got up from the sofa to join him with a grin.

"I'm pretty hungry, thanks," she said. "If we were at my place, I could have made you breakfast."

Garrett grabbed a plate and piled on some pancakes, offering Tiffany some as well as some fruit and bacon.

"I'd like that," he said and saw her pause as she reached for some butter before covering her pancakes in syrup.

"Yeah, I would, too," she said tentatively before moving to sit at the small table by the window.

He joined her, and they ate in companionable silence for a while, enjoying the view of the city in the soft morning light. A bit of fog hung over the tops of the buildings, but the sun was evident beyond it.

"I can't think of anything better than to spend more time with you, Tiffany. No strings. I have to go back to Philly in a few weeks, and you have your commitments. But we could enjoy what we've got now, and I could help you with your investigation, or at least provide some back-up," he said.

"Garrett, I don't know," she started, but he didn't intend to let her get far in her protests.

"Did I hinder your interviews at all yesterday?"

"No, you didn't. I didn't even see you. At the third stop, I thought maybe you had given up and gone back to the city."

He smiled. "I was there. I was even inside the store for a while when you were talking to the manager."

Her eyes widened in surprise. "You did not. I didn't see you at all."

He shrugged. "I'm good at what I do. I can be as visible or as invisible as you want me to be."

"I should do this on my own. You've helped enough. How can I ever know if I can cut it if I'm always depending on someone else?"

"You are doing it on your own. I'm just the muscle," he said with a smile, biting into a ripe piece of cantaloupe. "You're the brains of the operation, *sweethot,* and you got some nice gams, too," he teased in a noir detective tone that made her laugh.

"Thanks, but you know what I mean."

"I do. And you know what, a lot of investigators will work with someone else, a partner, hired security, depending on the job. Police even depend on backup, Tiff. It's not a weakness. It's being smart and careful."

"What will I tell my parents? They're home tomorrow, and the store will be open again, and how do I explain you?"

Garrett laughed. "Tell them I'm your vacation fling," he said.

"Yeah, that will inspire faith in them that I'm a responsible adult," she responded, rolling her eyes.

"You're a completely responsible adult, making decisions in your own life, and one way or another, they have to respect that—whether it's about the men you sleep with or the work you choose, whether they agree or not. You should just be up-front with them."

"I know. I just feel so…lacking, compared to my siblings. I'd like to have a success under my belt before I tell them what I've been doing."

Garrett leaned across the table. "You aren't lacking anything, Tiffany, and don't let anyone tell you otherwise."

Her cheeks bloomed with pleasure at his words, and she smiled at him. "You're great for my ego, you know."

"Good."

Having polished off her food, she took her coffee and went back to the sofa, grabbing her notes.

"There has to be something here I'm missing, some lead to follow."

Garrett watched her brow furrow in concentration, and enjoyed seeing her so sucked into her work. He finished his breakfast, letting her concentrate as she sketched out more little bubbles and lines between her ideas in the notebook.

"Wait…wait a minute," she said, more to herself than to him, and looked up. "Can I use your laptop for a second?"

"Sure." He grabbed it for her, and watched her peck at the keys quickly and surely until she was bouncing with excitement.

"Are you afraid of heights, Garrett?"

He gave her a quizzical look. "Nope. Why?"

She popped up from the chair, her eyes glowing with excitement. "I think I might have just found a possible lead. We're going to have to get up on some rooftops, though, to see for sure."

"Rooftops?"

"Yes. Don't you see? All of the doors were left open at the stores that were robbed, and that set off the security alarms, but too late. But we only assumed they had come in that way. I just remembered a mystery I read where a killer was finding access into apartment buildings through the roof. And a website I remembered gave stats for several high-value jewelry thefts that were accomplished when thieves accessed the properties from the roof using the buildings' ventilation systems to access the apartments. No doors were ever opened, but the vents were easily opened and closed, so no one thought of them right away. Sound familiar?" she asked excitedly.

Garrett stared in surprise. She really had tripped on to something. A possibility, at least.

"The site said that sometimes security wasn't triggered by rooftop entry. Doors and windows were wired for intrusion, but not ceilings or walls. There were cases where the thieves were still in the building, or on the roof, even as the police arrived and the thieves still got away."

"No one checked the roof?"

"No one asked about it. No one thought about them coming in from the top."

Garrett picked up on her excitement, and felt the buzz of a possible lead with her new idea. "We should tell the police, let them check it out."

"I want to do that first, at least at our store, and talk to my father and the other store owners about the security system. I never asked them about their roofs. I don't want to give Detective Ramsey useless information," she said, humming with so much excitement she was almost bouncing in place.

"Okay, then, let's go," Garrett said. "I guess I'm on board as your bodyguard?"

She bit her lip hesitantly, and then grinned. "Sure. You're hired."

TIFFANY SMILED AS she watched Garrett assess the slim access ladder that clung to the back of their building. It was only three stories up, not much at all.

"My brother and I used to climb up there all the time when we were at the store. Our parents would be furious, but we liked going up on the roof to play. The ladder is safe, you just have to watch your step. Although, if you're squeamish…"

Garrett smirked, crossing his arms. "Where you go, I go."

Tiffany nodded vaguely as she noticed something else at the base of the ladder.

"Look. Someone was here, there are footprints," she said, taking out the small digital camera she'd carried with her and snapping several shots.

"Well, like you said, could be anyone. Kids, maintenance workers, whoever."

"I just have a feeling…." she said, grasping the rungs of the ladder and stepping carefully over the spot she had photographed, not disturbing the prints that were there, and started to climb.

She was keenly aware of Garrett behind her, but she didn't look back, paying attention to her foot and hand placement until they reached the top and she was up over the edge.

Sweeping her gaze over the surface of the flat, rectangular roof, disappointment hit her first. Nothing obvious jumped out to suggest anyone had been up here. What had she expected? That the thieves would have left a gaping hole in the roof?

She checked the edges first, looking for any evidence left behind, and worked her way inward, toward the large ventilation unit where Garrett joined her, examining the edges and kneeling down behind it.

"Here," he said, and she moved quickly to join him.

"See," he said, indicating something on the surface. "New roof tar. They covered their tracks."

"It just looks like someone patched the roof."

"Yep. Have you had any leaks or any repairs?"

"No," she said, her excitement lifting again. "And I texted Dad. He said there is no wiring in the ceilings except for the sprinklers, but if they had a building plan, they could have worked around those."

"Looks like you've found a solid lead, Tiff," Garrett said, giving her an admiring look that made her feel amazing. "Let's call Ramsey."

"I will, I promise. But let me call the other store owners first and have them check their properties as well. Then it will carry even more weight."

Garrett nodded, walking to the edge of the rooftop to admire the view while Tiffany made her calls. A few minutes later, she had left messages or talked to the other store managers, and found out, at least, that they all did have rooftop access to their buildings. They would get back to her if they found anything. She joined Garrett where he still stood, looking out over the street.

"It's so exciting! I can't believe I might have found such an important lead," she said, and popped up on her toes to kiss him quickly.

His arm slipped around her shoulders, not letting her off the hook quite so easily as he lengthened the kiss by several delicious minutes. Tiffany didn't mind, not one bit, and celebrated her breakthrough by enthusiastically responding.

"Hey, we're kind of all alone up here," he whispered against her mouth.

"Except for all of the people sitting or standing by the windows in all of these buildings towering around us," she pointed out.

"Ah, right. I noticed some people have their rooftops set up like decks, with chairs, tables and grills, and there's even a huge rooftop garden over there." He pointed to a patch of green a few buildings down.

"People make the most of rooftops in most cities, I think, lacking yards and such, but it's a big thing here. There are a lot of rooftop businesses, bars, restaurants, even public spaces like parks where you can go sit, have a cup of coffee and enjoy a different view of the city. I always thought it would be fun to have a rooftop patio, but my apartment only has its small balcony. The roof is off-limits to residents."

"Interesting. I'd like to see some of those if we get a chance. They could be similar things in Philly, but I'm not aware of it. My only interest in rooftops, generally, has been for security purposes," he said. "So, what next?"

"I'll call Detective Ramsey, and maybe he can meet us here. Then...I guess I'll start researching other rooftop jewel thefts that might have happened elsewhere, and see what I can find. I also have to check with the insurance investigator who is coming by. I left a key for him with the business next door, just in case, but I would like to be there when he is. Other than that, I guess I'm free until my parents are home tomorrow. Maybe we can do another quick sight-seeing tour," she offered. "Coit Tower is beautiful, and we can walk back down Telegraph Hill to the waterfront."

Before he could answer, her phone rang again, and she saw it was Armando, the manager she had had lunch with the day before.

"Tiffany, you were right—our roof also shows evidence of a new patch. I saw it when I went up there one morning, but thought my grandfather had simply ordered a repair. However, there is no record in our ledgers of paying for a roof repair," Armando said darkly, clearly not happy about the discovery. "I can't believe the police missed this. I have called our local department already to come investigate, though no doubt any lingering evidence has been washed away in the rains since," he said in disgust.

"Thank you, Armando. You're probably right, but this is important. What is the name of the detective investigating your robbery? I am going to call the police, now, too, and I will let them know so that they can get in touch."

After scribbling down the name, Tiffany hung up.

"His roof showed recent patching as well. He's called the police, so I should call Ramsey right now," she said, carried away by the moment, and eager to tell the detective about the lead *she* had found.

After she did that, she took a breath, facing Garrett again. "He's on his way—he sounded doubtful at first, but then I told him about the other stores, and he definitely got more interested. He'll meet us downstairs, and send an evidence team up here. I guess they might have to open up the roof again to see how the thieves got from here to there."

Tiffany chewed her lip, thinking as they made their way back down to the ground again, once more careful to not disrupt the footprints, but then she froze.

"Oh, no!"

"What?" Garrett said, frowning.

"I was so busy thinking about the footprint that I didn't

even think about fingerprints on the ladder, and now ours are all over them!" she said, shaking her head in disgust.

"Hmm. I didn't think of that, either, but chances are that these guys are too good to have not worn gloves through the whole operation, and very likely those boot prints you found are the only evidence left behind. The cops can still check for prints, and filter ours out, but I bet there aren't any. These thieves are too professional to be that sloppy."

"I can't wait to hear what they find out from the boot print!" she said excitedly.

"Maybe nothing, maybe a lot—the guy's size, weight, shoe size, possibly the kind of shoe and where it came from. It could lead to something, who knows? What matters is that you're the one who found it," he said, placing his hands on her shoulders.

"Yeah, I did, didn't I?" she said proudly.

"You sure did," he said as they walked around the building and Tiffany let them inside the store. The phone on the desk was blinking with messages, probably from customers and who knew who else.

"I should check those, just to make sure it's nothing urgent," she said apologetically.

"No problem. I'll keep an eye out for Ramsey, and I have a few calls to make as well," he said.

Tiffany listened to the messages and took notes for her parents, as most of it was business they would have to respond to as well as a message from the insurance investigator that he had already come the afternoon before, and would contact them with his site report as soon as possible. He would also want to interview them for filing the final version, of course.

"That was fast," Tiffany said, feeling a bit guilty about not being at the store to talk to the guy when he was there, but if she hadn't been out talking to the other managers the afternoon before, she might never have come to the realization about the rooftop entry, so maybe it evened out.

"They're here," Garrett alerted her, and she looked up to see Detective Ramsey exiting his car at the front of the store.

Taking a deep breath so she could be as calm and collected as possible, she welcomed the detective inside although his attention immediately went to Garrett.

"You found something?"

"Tiffany did," Garrett replied smoothly, gesturing toward her, which the detective followed.

"And how is it that you tripped onto this idea of the rooftop entry?" the detective asked, still clearly doubtful.

"I was rechecking a few things, and while I was brainstorming—"

"Brainstorming?" Ramsey echoed.

"Yes, while I was brainstorming ideas about the case—"

"Wait. Why would you be—"

"Are you going to let me finish what I'm saying, or are you going to keep interrupting me?" Tiffany asked tartly, and saw Garrett hide a smile behind a discreet clearing of his throat.

The detective blew out a breath. "Okay, sorry."

"I remembered a book I read where someone had broken into buildings through the roof. It seemed possible, so we took a chance and checked it out. Someone has been up there. There are footprints at the base of the ladder, and a fresh patch where the roof was cut through recently," she said, her excitement mounting.

Ramsey definitely looked interested now.

"What makes you think it's not just a repair?"

"My father owns this building, and so any repair would have shown up on the books. Also, one of the other stores that was robbed also has a patched roof where there was no repair scheduled. Don't you see? This is how they get in—security usually covers the entrances, windows, but not the walls or the roof."

Detective Ramsey said nothing, but turned away, flipping his phone open and muttering a few things into it before turning back to them.

"I have some lab guys on the way to check it out. We'll need your prints to eliminate them from the scene. We're probably going to have to cut the roof open again," he cautioned.

"That's fine," Tiffany agreed. She knew her parents would want this solved, even at the cost of a roof repair.

"So, my other question is, why would you be talking to the other stores? And why would they be giving you information when they were told to keep quiet?" Ramsey asked, pinning her with a look, hands on his hips.

Tiffany figured she had to come clean, and so she reached into her purse, pulling out her wallet and her small California P.I. license.

"I'm a private investigator. I thought maybe I could help, since you weren't, um, coming up with much," she said, trying to be tactful about it.

"You're a P.I.?" Ramsey said in surprise, looking her up and down.

"Well, I'm new, and—"

"And she's doing a hell of a job, wouldn't you say, Detective?" Garrett broke in, taking the wallet back and giving it to Tiffany.

"I have to admit, it's a good lead. My team should be here shortly. Stick around. I might have more questions. I'm going to call for a warrant to grab any local camera footage that could be directed at that alley. We already checked out the door, but didn't get much there, so hopefully this will turn up something," he said. And then to

Tiffany, "This is good, but I'm going to ask you to stop looking into this now. We'll take it from here," he told her in a tone that brooked no arguments before exiting-out the door.

"Cameras," Tiffany said aloud. "I didn't even think of that. But he can't tell me to stop investigating—can he?" she said, looking at Garrett.

"You've given him a lot. Let's see what they can shake out now, with their resources, and just back off a little," Garrett said, much to her disappointment. "You want the police to work with you, not to see you as a thorn in their side. TV might make that out to be entertaining, but if you really want to do this for a living, you have to learn to compromise sometimes," he said.

She knew he was right, but this was all so invigorating, she didn't want to bow out now, just when things were getting good.

"This whole private investigator thing is kind of a turn-on," he said teasingly, walking her backward against one of the glass cases, and burying his face in her neck, nibbling there until little sparks were flying all over her skin.

"Garrett, the police are right outside, they could come in. We can't," she said as he tugged her T-shirt free and ran his hand up underneath.

"They're out back, up on the roof. We have some time. Maybe we could go back in the office, for some privacy," he suggested.

His hardness against her stomach was very, very enticing.

"Maybe, if we were fast…and quiet," she agreed, sliding her hand down the front of him and swallowing his moan in a kiss.

Things were heating up considerably when a voice cut through their heated clinch.

"Tiffany?" a familiar voice, somewhat outraged, asked.

Tiffany knew that voice. As Garrett backed away, she peeked out around his shoulder, her face red as she hoped she could melt into the carpet out of mortification. Her parents were staring at them, eyes wide and full of disbelief.

"You're back a day early," Tiffany said weakly, stating the obvious.

"We got lucky on standby. We were so worried about you, and what was going on here," her father said. Then, scrutinizing Garrett, he asked in a more steely tone,"What *is* going on here?"

Tiffany took a deep breath, putting distance between herself and Garrett and she knew she was smiling too brightly, but she couldn't seem to unclench her jaw.

"Dad, Mom, this is Garrett Berringer. Garrett, these are my parents, Robert and Laura Walker," she said, glancing up at Garrett who seemed very pale.

"Mr. and Mrs. Walker, so nice to meet you," he said with calmness that she admired. Tiffany shared his relief when they both spotted Detective Ramsey in the doorway.

Tiffany discreetly pushed the edge of her shirt back inside of her jeans—a move her mother noted with a disapproving look—and turned her attention to Ramsey.

The cavalry, she thought.

8

"YOU DEFINITELY FOUND something up on the roof," the detective said, and Tiffany held his gaze, avoiding her parents' stare.

"You found some evidence?" she asked anxiously.

"Nothing concrete yet, but this is a good lead. They certainly knew the building and cut through precisely at a spot where access to a ventilation shaft allowed them to slip down into an upper hallway undetected. I can't believe we didn't think of it," the detective admitted sheepishly. "I'll give credit where it's due. If you hadn't started your own inv—"

"It was just one of those crazy ideas," Tiffany interrupted him, sliding a look at her parents. "Garrett and I noticed a fresh patch on the roof, and I realized it was how the robbers probably got in," she said quickly to fill in her parents, who looked a bit dazed.

"The roof? What were you doing up on the roof?" her father asked.

"I was just showing Garrett the view," she said, giving the confused detective a look that she hoped he knew not to mention her contributions to the cause.

"Right, well, we've dusted for prints, and nothing there,

and we've taken a cast of the boot print, though it looks like a standard work boot, so that might not lead to much," the detective said.

"So you don't think this will break the case?" Tiffany asked, disappointment coloring her tone.

"You never know. We can learn a lot from that cut in, the materials they used, the tools… It could lead to something, but it will be a few days until we know anything. And *we* can talk to the other store owners," he said, giving her a similar look back that she knew meant "keep your nose out."

Tiffany frowned in frustration. She'd found her first big lead, and her hands were being tied. She understood what Garrett said, that she needed to cultivate a positive relationship with the police department—P.I.s in books and on TV were always asking police counterparts for help—so she would try, but it would be difficult. If she'd found this lead, she might be able to find even more if she kept trying.

As if reading her mind, Garrett discreetly, barely shook his head in the negative, and she looked up to find the detective staring at her as well. Were both men reading her mind?

She rolled her eyes. "Well, we'll all be anxious to know what you find. I'm glad this could help," she said, trying not to sound as disappointed as she felt.

"Our guys will cover up the roof and tape the scene off once they're done—no more climbing up there for now, if you don't mind. We'll be in touch if we find anything new," Ramsey said with a smile that encouraged Tiffany somewhat. Maybe he'd be willing to at least keep her in the loop.

Momentarily distracted by the talk of the investigation, she faced her parents again once the detective had gone.

Oh, right. For a few seconds she had been able to block out the fact that her mom and dad had caught their daughter up against one of the jewelry cases with a man's hand in her shirt.

The silence between the four of them weighed heavily for a few seconds until Tiffany shook off the awkwardness. She was an adult, not a teenager. Her parents had caught her in a slightly embarrassing situation, but she was determined to forget it and walked forward to hug them both.

"I'm so happy you're home, though I wish I had better news," she said. "The insurance investigator has been here, so we can open tomorrow. He says he'll want to talk to us all, as well, before he finalizes his report," she said, jumping right to business.

Her father wasn't so willing to overlook the tall, handsome man standing a few feet behind her, though he kissed her on the forehead as he always did before turning his attention back to Garrett.

"And you are?"

"Dad, I told you," Tiffany said, stepping back, hoping her mother would help, though she received only a raised eyebrow from Laura Walker. "Garrett is a friend. We met at Ed's wedding. He and Ed have been friends forever, and we stood up together in the wedding party," Tiffany explained quickly. "Garrett's here from Philadelphia. He's a bodyguard there. I mean, he runs a bodyguard business… with his family," she added, fumbling and knowing she sounded like a babbling idiot.

Garrett stepped forward, holding his hand out.

"Pleased to meet you, sir, Mrs. Walker," he said with a friendly glance in her mom's direction. He was cool and confident, as always. "Tiffany has hit the basics. We met at the wedding, and she's been showing me around the city for a few days," Garrett said.

"She's been showing you more than the city, looked like to me," her father muttered, and Tiffany gasped.

"Dad!"

"That was uncalled for, Robert," her mother added.

"But you're right, we were being indiscreet. I apologize for that," Tiffany said sincerely, and her father's face softened.

"I'm sorry, too, honey. It's just been a heck of a few days," her father said, nodding and shaking Garrett's hand in return. Though he was still clearly sizing up Tiffany's new male interest.

Her mom was giving Garrett the once-over as well, and covertly winked to Tiffany from behind her father's back. Tiffany stifled a smile, and saw Garrett do the same.

"Call me Robert. So you're a bodyguard?"

"Part of the time. My brothers and I run a personal security business back in Philly, and we take on a variety of tasks in the scope of the business," Garrett supplied.

"That so? Sounds like dangerous work."

"Not so much when we get it right," Garrett said with a smile.

Robert laughed. "Yes, well, that makes sense. Is it a large company? Are you good at what you do?" her father fished without compunction. Tiffany nearly interjected, but Garrett didn't seem to mind answering.

"We work hard," he said diplomatically. "Like a lot of small businesses, we started out with small clients, personal security. Now we provide protection for several high-profile government officials, some museums, financial institutions, as well as working a few cases with the FBI," Garrett said without sounding like he was bragging. "It helps that it's just my brothers and myself. We work well together."

"Plans to expand?"

"No, I don't think so. We'd prefer to keep it a family venture."

Her father practically glowed with approval, and Tiffany was surprised to learn about the scope of Garrett's business as well. She probably looked as impressed as her parents did. For some reason, she hadn't realized that a bodyguard business would be so varied, but then again, she hadn't asked, had she?

"So, what do you make of this mess?" her father asked Garrett.

Garrett shook his head. "I'm not much of a detective, but it certainly looks like a professional job to me. Tiffany has actually come up with the best lead so far, as Detective Ramsey mentioned," Garrett said, smiling in her direction.

"How'd you manage to think of that, pumpkin?" her father asked.

"I, um, well, you know how I like to read mysteries, Dad," she said hesitantly. "And when I saw the fresh patch on the roof, and knew that no repairs had been ordered, it wasn't too hard to put two and two together," she offered.

"Good for you, honey," her mother said. "That was a good catch. Now maybe the insurance won't balk at covering the loss, if they have more proof that it wasn't anyone working here," she said, her miff at the idea clear.

"It's still hard to explain how they had the combination to the vault, and how they knew where to look for all of the paperwork, or how they even knew the diamonds were here," Tiffany said, not wanting to be the bearer of bad news, but she didn't want her parents having false hope, either.

"You're right, but this is just all so awful," Laura said, the strain showing on her face in a way that made Tiffany's heart twist. She couldn't stand how this had to be tearing her parents up inside. It made her want to forget her budding relationship with the SFPD and get back on the case to solve it as soon as possible.

Her mom put her hand on her father's back like she often did when she worried about him being overly stressed; her father was healthy, but he had high blood pressure, and this couldn't be helping matters any.

"Your father wouldn't care about the business as long as no one was hurt," she said.

Robert frowned. "I can't help but kick myself for wanting to expand. Building that vault, taking on higher-profile purchases... None of this would have happened if—"

"Dad, don't even think that way. None of this is your fault, or our fault. It's some nasty, greedy thieves and *we* are going to catch them!" Tiffany said fiercely, her resolve solidifying.

She felt Garrett's hand on her shoulder, as well, squeezing.

Her parents noticed, too, though they didn't seem to disapprove this time.

"I hope so, honey," her father said, sounding worn out. "I forgot how tough jet lag can be," he said, changing the subject with a laugh. "How long are you here for, Garrett?" he added, and Tiffany rolled her eyes at her father's lack of subtlety, though Garrett didn't seem to mind at all.

"A little less than a month now. I'll go home just before Christmas week," he said.

"Oh. That's all, then?"

"I'm afraid so," Garrett said.

"Well, you'll have to join us for Thanksgiving, if you don't already have plans," Tiffany's mom offered, and Tiffany was dizzy with how quickly her parents seemed to have warmed up to Garrett.

"Mom, I'm sure Garrett already—" She tried to beg off, saving him the trouble. She didn't want her parents thinking this thing between her and Garrett was more serious than it was, or pinning any romantic hopes on him.

"I'd love to, Mrs. Walker—"

"Call me Laura," her mother said with a warm smile.

"Of course, Laura. I appreciate your hospitality. I'd love to come if it's not too much more work," he said graciously.

Tiffany hadn't seen that coming. What was he up to?

"That's wonderful!" her mother declared. "It's no more work to have one more at the table. We'll cook as much as always. There's always room for a friend of Tiffany's."

Tiffany blinked in amazement at her parents and almost said *Since when?* but stifled the remark. She couldn't blame them for not exactly warming to her past boyfriends.

"So what are you two up to for the next few days?" her mother asked. "Garrett said you were showing him around the city?"

"Um, yes, we've only managed to get to the waterfront, Lombard Street and walking Russian Hill. There's been so much going on, with the wedding, the store and everything," Tiffany said. "If we're reopening the store, I'll be working tomorrow morning so—"

"Oh, don't worry about that. There are a few priority orders your father and I can handle, but with the holiday only two days away, and us being exhausted from the trip, I think we'll stay closed and re-open on Friday for Black Friday, but you should take some time off, Tiffany. Show Garrett around. Perhaps take a trip up into Napa or to Point Reyes," her mother urged, and Tiffany wanted to ask which aliens had kidnapped her parents and sent these imposters.

"Um, but Black Friday is always so busy, I should really—"

"Nonsense. You have a guest from out of town—you don't just leave him hanging and without anyone to show him around," her father said. "Nick said he'd work Friday. He's home for the weekend, and needs a break from his studies. You've been pulling long shifts, and with the break-in, you need to have some fun,"

Tiffany looked at her parents like she hadn't seen them before, but nodded. "Okay," she said, unable to argue with their generosity, whatever the source. She wasn't going to turn down the free time to spend with Garrett, or to work on the case.

"Why don't you two move along? The day is still early, and there's a lot you could do. We're going to catch up here, call that investigator and some of the clients who need an immediate response, and then we're heading home to rest," her mother said, practically pushing Tiffany and Garrett outside the door.

"Come at noon on Thursday, if that's not too early. We make a day of it. Cooking, the parade, football... Dinner is at four, but we'll have lunch, too, so come hungry," Laura said to Garrett before she closed the door on them both with a happy wave.

Tiffany covered her face. "Oh, God. I am so sorry."

Garrett peeled her hands off. "What for?"

"They have never been like that with any of the other guys I've dated. They think we're... They *like* you."

"I liked them, too. They seem like nice, solid people."

"You don't get it. They think we're more than we are... you know...more than a fling."

Garrett pursed his lips thoughtfully. "I don't think so— they know I'm just here for a month."

"Hmm, they've never acted like that before," Tiffany said. "I don't want them thinking I finally snagged a good one, and then they'll be so disappointed."

Garrett laughed. "Tiffany, are you worried I'll break your parents' hearts?"

She had to smile. She knew she was being absurd, but her parents had really thrown her off. "I suppose you're right. It was just so weird. And I didn't expect you to want to come to dinner on Thursday," she said frankly.

"Would you rather I didn't?"

"No, I'd love it," she said. "I just didn't expect it."

"Listen, I have no plans, and it made your mother happy. It gave her something to focus on rather than the problems with the store."

Tiffany's heart flipped in her chest. Oh, dear. For all of the fantastic sex and support Garrett had offered, for him to be so considerate of her parents moved her deeply.

"You are a good man."

"They're good people. So are you," he said.

"I guess I have time to show you around a bit now… and maybe time for some other things, too," she said flirtatiously, getting into the holiday mood.

She had time off, a wonderful man to be with and she'd found a solid lead in her first case today. Thanksgiving was two days away, but she had a lot to be grateful for already. Who knew what the next few days could bring?

"What would you like to do first?" she asked, game for anything.

His smile told her before he even spoke. "Finish what we started in there, for one," he said, leaning down to kiss her ear lightly, the slight touch setting quick little fires inside of her.

"I think we can do that," she said breathlessly, his response making her very thankful indeed as they hurried to her car and drove back to his room to do just that.

"THIS IS INCREDIBLE," Garrett said as they drove slowly along the bumpy, winding road that traveled along the rural edge of the Point Reyes National Seashore. "I can't believe there are cattle ranches here. Cows, right by the ocean," he said, grinning like a kid at a peaceful, pretty

Holstein that watched them drive by. Tall grass leaned with the coastal breeze all the way to the edge of the water, and they'd only seen three other cars.

Tiffany laughed. "That's the third time you've said that," she said.

He smiled at her, liking the way she'd wrapped a colorful scarf over her hair as he'd traded in the SUV and rented a convertible for the drive up the coast. It seemed like the thing to do in California, driving along the ocean.

"You look like Grace Kelly in *To Catch a Thief,* with that scarf and the sunglasses," he said. "Very sexy."

"'I've never caught a jewel thief before. It's stimulating. It's like...well, it's like...'" she quoted from the movie.

"'Like sitting in a hot tub?'" he filled in, completing the quote.

"Seems oddly appropriate, don't you think?" she asked with a smile. "I love that movie."

"Me, too."

"We should rent it and watch it before you leave."

"Sounds good," he agreed.

Garrett loved old movies, but that one was a particular favorite. He enjoyed that Tiffany knew it well enough to quote from. He'd never met a woman who shared that particular pleasure with him. Not even Lainey. Old movies had either put her to sleep or made her fidget restlessly through the entire show.

"So how did all of these ranches end up here?" he asked, still fascinated by the seemingly endless expanse of grazing land that went on for miles, the Pacific visible on the other side. There was a house or a drive every here and there, the ranches all named alphabetically: "the D ranch" or "the H ranch."

They'd driven up beautiful highways lined with redwoods the way the east coast highways were lined with maples and pines, but these seemed so much more exotic. After walking along one windy beach, they'd had lunch in the small town of Point Reyes Station. The cook at the only bar/pizza joint in the small town had snipped the herbs from gardens that surrounded a patio where they sat in the sun. It was some of the best pizza Garrett had ever had. Maybe that was because he was hungry from the coastal air. Or maybe being with Tiffany stimulated all of his appetites.

"This area is generally known as the pastoral zone. I always mean to come here more often, but then never get the chance," she said.

"It's a bit of a drive."

"But worth it. I love getting out of the city, closer to nature. Early settlers came to the area, mainly through the gold rush, I think, and discovered the area was very suited to raising dairy cows. There were several disputes and the land changed hands over decades, but it's part of the National Parks Service now as historic landscape, though obviously the ranches are still active. I think they even give tours of some of the ranches. We could look into that, if you want," she offered.

"Nah, that's okay. I just like driving by, though I would like to learn more about how they got here. It's just gorgeous. East coast beaches are beautiful in a different way—with sprawling dunes and long, sandy stretches. And we have dairy farms, obviously, but this is really something to see."

"There's a ranger station where we can probably get more information," she said as they drove to the parking lot at the headlands. "It's a short walk, but then we have to scale over three-hundred steps down to the lighthouse. Are you up for it?"

"Totally. Can work off that pizza," he said with a grin.

"I think we're good in the exercise department," she said with a wink, making him laugh as they got out of the car.

Garrett took in the rugged landscape and clear sky as they walked to the visitor's center.

"We're lucky it's clear and not too windy today. The last time I came up here, the fog was so thick you couldn't even see the parking lot. They closed down and turned everyone away."

"I guess that would indicate why the lighthouse is so important, with all of these rocks and cliffs, too," Garrett said.

They poked around the visitors' center for a while, looking at displays and talking to the rangers on duty, and then headed off for their walk to the lighthouse.

Smiling red-faced tourists passed them and heaved heavy breaths on their way back up the hundreds of steps as Garrett and Tiffany went down. The straight slope of steps allowing them to get down the rock face toward the water and the lighthouse wasn't very wide, and it was a little intimidating from the top. Though the steps were as walkable as possible, this wasn't the place to take a tumble, Garrett thought, keeping Tiffany's hand securely in his.

Down at the bottom, his legs felt like jelly, though he wasn't going to admit it. Tiffany's scarf had come off in the car; her hair whipped around her face in the wind. She looked as wild and untamed as the landscape around them. He clicked a picture of her staring out over the fence toward the water when she wasn't looking, and then admired the lovely, candid photo. It would be a treasured keepsake for the future, he thought, when they parted ways.

"Look!" she said, pointing enthusiastically to where a few deer sat in the grass, munching peacefully, and a falcon flew overhead.

The rock formations alone caught Garrett's attention, and he took several pictures with his phone, sending them off to his family with a click of a few buttons. His brothers had harassed him for weeks to go, and had made bets that he probably wouldn't do much sight-seeing once he was here, but would probably hole up in his room and work.

If only they knew what he was doing in his hotel room, they'd see how wrong they were. But this was proof that he was actually out and enjoying the sights.

Seconds later, his phone buzzed with the alert for an incoming text message.

Who's the hottie? his brother Ely asked with an emoticon representing an evil grin.

Garrett rolled his eyes and realized he had sent the picture of Tiffany along with the more scenic ones.

Whoops.

Just another tourist, he replied, not wanting to get into a discussion about Tiffany via text.

Yeah, right. Another evil grin. Hope you're having a good time with the redhead, and if you're not, go ask her out. Now.

Garrett flipped his phone shut, not about to encourage his brother's antics.

"What's funny?" Tiffany asked him, and he realized he'd been smiling.

"Nothing, just my brother. I sent him a few pictures to prove I'd gotten out of my hotel room," he said. "He was being a goof."

"Which one?"

"Ely."

"The Marine."

"Yeah," Garrett said, slinging his arm around her as they moved toward the area near the lighthouse and stared out at sea. A few other people who had been milling around started back up the steps, and others gathered for a short tour that was guided by a ranger.

Garrett didn't really want to join the group; he was content here with Tiffany. As the other folks moved out of sight, following the ranger as he took them on the tour, Garrett turned her to him and enjoyed her mouth under his for several long, delicious moments.

"You keep that up and my knees will be spaghetti— I won't be able to walk back up the stairs," she said, her hands fisted into his jacket. He found that incredibly sexy. Of course, he found just about everything about Tiffany sexy.

"Maybe we should wait until we get back to the car then, and go explore one of those deserted beach roads we saw on our way here," he suggested against her ear, and felt her shiver against him.

"Sounds good to me," she agreed.

They walked around a little more, hand-in-hand, though Garrett didn't pay as much attention to the scenery as he did to the woman who was with him.

Making their way back up the steps took some effort, but he was fueled by his motivation to get Tiffany alone for a while. Had he ever been this hungry for a woman?

Back in the car, they wound their way down to Drake's Beach, a low-lying beach beyond the ranch lands. A flat stretch of sand that extended beyond the parking lot met pounding surf, and one side of the lot was protected by the towering cliffs of the headlands. On the other side, docks and some bath houses were empty except for a few surfers out on the water. Garrett pulled the car over to the edge of the lot by the sandy cliffs and faced Tiffany.

"It's been a while since I made out in a car. A long while," he added with a slanted grin.

She smiled in the sexiest way, and leaned in close. "And I bet you didn't do half the things then that we can do now," she said.

Anything else was eclipsed in the hot kiss she laid on him, and Garrett didn't care what he did to his back in the cramped confines of the convertible, he was having her here one way or the other. The fog was falling around the beach, and the waves crashed the shore. Her sighs became moans as he pressed his hands against her breasts, and returned her kiss with equal fervor.

He took a breath, signaling to her to hold on for a second as he tested how far back his seat would go—far enough.

"Come here," he said, beckoning her to cover him.

Her cheeks were flushed with wind and arousal, and she didn't take her eyes off of his as she levered over him and pushed up his shirt, loosening his belt.

"You are so beautiful," he said, watching as she released his erection, and drew her hand over him a few times, making him groan with need.

"You really need to get out of those jeans," he said raggedly.

"You're bossy," she said with a grin. "Maybe I'm in charge this time."

Garrett's eyebrows flew up at her saucy tone, and it made him even harder when he saw what she had in mind.

Stripping her shirt off—she wore nothing underneath—she covered her own breasts for him to watch, before lowering down and not breaking eye contact as she took him into her mouth.

Garrett's entire body went taut as she dragged her nails along his thigh, the wet heat of her mouth encompassing him over and over as he looked up at the gray sky.

His mind glazed over with intense pleasure as she worked him, breaking the intimate kiss to let him know how good he tasted, how much she loved doing this for him. He found her breast with his hand, squeezing and fondling her, pulling at her nipples until she mewled against him, as turned on as he was.

"Tiffany, please," he huffed, at the edge of his control. "Join me, honey."

She looked up at him, lips rosy, gaze hot. "I think I'm good right here. Just don't stop touching me," she said, and lowered over him again, sucking even harder, taking him deeper. He worked her breasts as she did, feeling her shudder over him and gasp. That did it. He bucked up against her as a blissful climax gripped him and didn't let go for several long minutes.

She sat up, and he did too, readjusting himself as she put her shirt on and snuggled up against him as they looked out over the water.

They didn't say anything. What was there to say? No words would do justice to what they'd shared. The beach was deserted now, even the surfers coming in and leaving as more fog poured in over the water.

"We should get back," she said softly.

Garrett nodded as they parted with one more kiss and buckled up their belts.

On the way back, she nodded off as he drove, snoring just a little, lashes softly swept against her cheek. Garrett smiled, overwhelming tenderness suffusing him as he snuck a glance over at her.

It was just a fling, he reminded himself.

But it was starting to feel like so much more.

9

TIFFANY OPENED HER eyes to the sight of a pale concrete wall staring back at her through the windshield.

The back of her building, she recognized sleepily, still waking up. All of the fresh air and exercise had lulled her into a deep nap.

"We're back," Garrett said, and she turned to see him smiling at her in the sweetest way.

"Oh, my God," she said. "I can't believe I just passed out like that."

She was afraid to check her appearance in the mirror and see what she looked like after being windswept, and then mussed by Garrett's hands. Not to mention having had her head propped on the window for most of the drive back. Pulling the visor down, the mirror confirmed her worst imaginings. Flat on one side, crazy tangled on the other.

"I'm a mess," she said, fussing with her hair and trying to make it at least somewhat normal again.

"You're beautiful," he said, completely serious. And ran his hand over her hair to stop her from fussing, drawing her in close for a kiss. "Let me wake you up."

"I'll be fine," she said, smiling as she remembered how

passionately he'd responded to her back at the beach. She licked her lips a little, remembering his taste.

"You turn me inside out when you do that," he said with a similar heated look. He got out of the car and crossed to her side, opening her door.

"You're such a gentleman."

"Sometimes," he said, his eyes lingering on her lips in a non-gentlemanly way.

They barely made it up the stairs of her older, elevator-less apartment building, stopping on every floor for kisses that became progressively hotter.

By the time they got into the apartment, she didn't care about her hair or anything else. Clothes flew all over the living room as they made their way to the shower, and she turned the hot water on, letting it pour over them both.

Garrett grabbed the shampoo on the shelf at the back of the counter and soaped up his hands. Standing behind her, he buried his fingers in her hair, washing each strand with such decadent thoroughness that Tiffany sighed. She leaned against him as he soaped up again and ran his hands over the rest of her.

When his hands moved down to the apex of her thighs, she opened for him—he had to wash everywhere, right?—and let him soap her into a frothy orgasm that made her want to scream.

Then it was her turn, and she grabbed the soap, taking charge. Maybe that was the new theme in her life—she was taking charge. No more sitting back and waiting for things to happen. She made them happen.

Garrett seemed to pick up on her mood, and didn't mind one bit as she returned the favor, washing him completely with her hands, letting her fingers travel over him in intimate exploration until he was trembling under her touch.

When he tried to take control again, she planted a hand

on his chest, stopping him as the water rinsed them clean. Hitting the stopper with her toe, she grinned. This shower had just become a bath.

"Sit," she commanded, and watched him lower carefully into the accumulating water.

Standing over him, she took him in, her gaze lingering on the thick erection that beckoned her.

"You going to join me?" he asked, his eyes hot.

"Oh, yes," she whispered, lowering to his lap where she could wrap her legs around his back, taking him inside. They both groaned as the hot water swirled around them and she planted her hands on his shoulders, finding a rhythm that drove them both to shuddering satisfaction before the water got too deep.

She reached blindly behind him, shutting off the water and then relaxing with her forehead against his.

"I can't seem to get enough of this. What must you think of me?" she asked lightly, but truly, she had never been as sexually driven to be with any other man she'd known. Never like this.

"I think I feel exactly the same way," he said, claiming her lips in a kiss that made her willing to let him be in charge again for as long as he wanted to be.

But a shiver worked over her as the hot water drained, and she pulled away.

"Dinner? We can order out. Then you can help me make pies for tomorrow."

"Is that some euphemism for more sex?" he asked with hopeful eyes.

"No, I mean making pies—for dinner at my parents' house."

"Ah, I thought that's what you might mean," he said ruefully, making her laugh.

As they dried off, Tiffany became more thoughtful.

This day had been perfect. No crimes, no worries about when it would be over—but those things lurked just past the glow of perfection she'd enjoyed for the last few hours.

The store was still closed, her parents under threat of losing it. Garrett was still here only for a few weeks and would go home and this would all be over.

So, she would enjoy it while she could. Her new, take-charge self didn't mope.

"Nick came by to do some laundry last week, and left a few things I put in with my clothes. There are some clean shirts of his on the dryer, if you want," she offered.

His smile melted her from the inside out.

"Thanks. I'll go see. He won't mind?"

"He does his laundry here for free. He has no say in the matter," she said, laughing.

Tiffany padded into her own room to find some clean underwear and clothes, settling on some sexy lingerie under a pair of jean shorts and a tank—it would be hot in the kitchen if they were baking, after all.

She spotted Garrett's cell phone on the floor where it had likely been thrown in their crazy hurry to get naked. She picked the cell up for him, noting the message that had just come in a few minutes ago from some guy named Daniel, the "re" saying the message referred to the jewel thefts.

Frowning, and hearing Garrett in the kitchen, she hit the enter button to see the full text.

Gar, tried to call, no answer. Off to Shanghai tonight. Did pick up some buzz on thefts... Chk out a fence, Freddie, who runs a billiards hall in the Tenderloin. What kind of name for a neighborhood is that? Never got it. Anyway, good luck with it. D

Tiffany stared at the message, and felt the hairs on the back of her neck stand up. Garrett was looking into the thefts, obviously using connections to get leads he was not about to share with her.

Quietly furious, she knew exactly what she was going to do and hit Delete on the message, setting the phone on the dresser before she changed from her shorts into jeans and grabbed a jacket from the chair. Hesitating for a moment, she opened another drawer and took out her gun, slipping it inside her coat. She was only intending to go and see what she could see—she wasn't about to confront anyone or do anything foolish.

Garrett helping her with Marcus Hooper was one thing, but trying to steal her investigation out from under her was a whole other issue.

Halfway through the living room, Garrett stopped her.

"Hey, where are you going?"

She smiled, facing him and hoping the seething anger she felt inside didn't show.

"I forgot Dad loves peach pie—and I only bought apples. I have pumpkin, but I really can't show up tomorrow without peach pie," she said with a laugh.

"I'll come with you," he said, grabbing his jacket from the sofa where it had been tossed on the way in the door.

"No, really, the market is right down the street—I'll have to hurry to catch them before they close, but I'll be back in just a few. Why don't you start peeling the apples? Don't forget to put them in some lemon water so they don't turn brown," she said, even crossing the room to give him a quick, happy kiss.

He smiled. "Okay, sure."

She turned, smiling. That would teach him to try to investigate her case behind her back.

GARRETT DIDN'T FEEL right letting Tiffany go without him, and he was sure it had been a mistake a half hour later when she wasn't back yet.

He went to the bedroom and found his phone, intending to call her, when he noticed a new message on the screen.

At first he thought it might be Tiffany, but it was from Daniel. The message was short, a one-liner:

One more thing, this guy is dangerous... Go prepared. D

Garrett stared at the mysterious message, which seemed like either a partial message that hadn't come through, or an afterthought.

Clicking through his texts to see what he'd missed, he noted a message in his trash—Garrett never left files in his trash folder. If he wanted them gone, he deleted them entirely.

Opening it, he found another message from Daniel, and read it, noting the time—and realizing with increased agitation what had happened.

Tiffany had seen his phone, and Daniel's first message, then she had deleted it and was probably off searching the Tenderloin—one of San Francisco's tougher neighborhoods—on her own.

It explained the weird vibe she was giving off before she left.

Peach pie his ass. How could she head out into something like this alone?

Out on the sidewalk, he hailed a cab and asked for directions to the Tenderloin District.

"Anywhere you want in particular?" the cabbie asked.

"Looking for a pool hall run by a guy named Freddie?"

The cabbie shook his head. "Lotsa bars, pool places down there. You got a name of the place?"

"No, just drop me off in the area, and I'll find it."

The man looked at him speculatively, as if wondering about the wisdom of dropping him off in the district at night, but Garrett didn't want to waste time.

"Go."

"You must really need to play some pool," the cabbie said, and headed off.

It didn't take long, and when the cabbie dropped him off in the busy neighborhood past the theater district, Garrett was more frustrated than anything. She could be anywhere, out here, alone at night. Dialing her number, she didn't answer. Not that he expected her to.

What the hell had gotten into her?

Garrett started scanning the streets. Homeless people gathered, some approaching, along with some more dangerous-looking guys, but they sized him up and seemed to pick up the vibe that told them he'd be more trouble than they counted on.

Walking into a bar that advertised billiards on the front sign, he signaled the bartender and ordered a beer. When the guy delivered it, Garrett asked, "I'm looking for a guy named Freddie. You know him? Runs a pool place down here."

"Lotsa places like that down here, sorry," the bartender said, taking his money and turning away.

Garrett could only hope Tiffany had similar bad luck. He had to find her.

Then it hit him—he had a tracking application on his own phone—a slick mobile spy app—that an FBI friend had turned him on to. It was promoted to families as a way to keep track of children and family members—or cheating spouses—but was easily used for more nefarious purposes, he thought.

When he and Tiffany had been using her phone for

navigation earlier in the day, he had told her about it, and saw her upload the app from an online market as they spoke—no doubt for her private investigation aspirations. If he could link into it, maybe he could access the app and find her location on his phone.

His beer completely ignored, he opened the application on his own phone, sending a text to hers that should activate the tracker, asking for her coordinates. Hopefully she wouldn't notice or shut him down. In what seemed to take forever, finally a little red light appeared on the map of the street about two blocks over from where he was right now.

"Gotcha," he said and bolted out the door.

Two streets over, things got a little darker and a little rougher. Garrett kept a sharp eye out for Tiffany as he followed the tiny red dot. He was getting closer, noting that she'd stopped and had been stationary for several minutes.

Had she found Freddie?

Toward that end of the street, there weren't any pool halls, and Garrett had a bad feeling.

He was almost right next to her, and looked around, unable to see her amid the passersby and groups of less than desirable people gathered on the dark edges of the street. A young guy in a hoodie approached him, and Garrett became very alert.

"Hey, you lookin' for something to be thankful for?" the kid—no more than seventeen—asked. He opened his jacket to show off an array of drug paraphernalia.

"No, thanks."

"Maybe a lady to share the holiday with?" he suggested, and Garrett rolled his eyes until he noticed a group of women—working girls, across the street.

"That's what I'm talkin' about," the young man said approvingly. "You pick the one—or how many you like—and

I'll tell you how much for a very happy Thanksgiving," the kid joked.

Garrett didn't believe his eyes when a slim redhead slid out from the throng of working girls, giving one of them some money and…a hug? Tiffany.

"You ready to make a deal?" the kid pushed.

Garrett was already halfway across the road when she saw him.

She clearly wasn't happy to see him, but waited, since she knew she wouldn't avoid him now.

"What are you doing?" he asked, breathless with relief to have found her.

"I told you. I was out looking for peaches," she said belligerently.

"Is that her name?" he asked, nodding back toward the hooker he'd seen her with.

"No, her name is Belle. She's very nice."

"Don't tell me, you were sharing recipes?"

"Something like that," she said, turning away. He caught up, walking beside her. She stopped again, facing him.

"Leave me alone, Garrett. How did you find me, anyway?" she asked, and then paused, shaking her head. "The tracking app."

"Works both ways."

"Good to know you don't mind hacking my phone. I'll be sure to remove that when I get home."

"Just as good to know you don't mind reading my messages, and deleting them," he countered.

She halted her step, caught.

"How'd you find that?"

"Daniel sent me a follow-up that made no sense, so I looked in my trash, and there it was. You know, your private investigation skills shouldn't involve snooping on the cell phones of people you know unless it's for a damned good reason," he said angrily.

"Really? Fine, it was unintentional, and what about you? Going behind my back to work on the case? Were you planning to share that information with me?"

His silence told her the answer before he said it.

"No, I wasn't."

She looked so stricken, he felt like an ass.

"It's too dangerous, Tiffany. Look where you are right now. Off by yourself, at night, on streets like this?"

Her jaw clenched. "I come down here all the time with my friends. Believe me, I've grown up in this city. I know how to take care of myself. You don't seem to accept that."

"I do, but you're still new at this, and these guys, these thieves and this Freddie character, they're professionals, Tiffany."

Her eyes widened. "And I'm not?"

Garrett swore under his breath. "No, not yet. Not like this."

Her eyes became glacial. "Get lost, Garrett. Leave me alone."

She turned and marched away.

He followed.

She spun around again. "I told you to leave me alone."

"Where are you going? What did you pay Belle back there for? A tip on Freddie?"

Tiffany glared.

"I could just go back and pay her double for the same info, or you could share and let me help you," he said, hoping to lessen the tension between them.

He didn't like her doing this, but it was clear she was determined, and so maybe the best he could hope for was that she would let him work with her, keep her safe.

She'd said she was impulsive, and now he was starting

to see the problem. But he also liked it. It was where her passion and her charm emanated from.

It could also get her in over her head in a situation like this.

"Please? Listen, I'm sorry that I was pursuing leads on the case without telling you, but I also wish you hadn't come out here without me. What if we work together?" he proposed. "Truce?"

She crossed her arms, peering at him suspiciously.

"Will you share any more information or leads you have with me? No more going behind my back?"

"As long as you don't take off into dangerous situations without me."

She looked away, appearing to consider it, and finally nodded.

"Fine."

He held out a hand. "Shake on it?" She grabbed his hand to shake it, and he pulled her up against him hard. "Or is this a better way to seal the deal?" he whispered against her lips before taking her mouth in a hot kiss that she tried to resist. At first. Though still piqued with him, eventually she softened, her fingers curling into his jacket.

A low wolf-whistle from an observer in the shadows broke them apart.

"I'm still taking that tracker app off my phone when I get back."

"Keep it. You might need it. I promise I won't use it again until I absolutely have to."

She nodded and then they broke apart, and continued walking.

"So you know where to find Freddie?" he asked.

"Possibly. He runs a place called The Dice down on Post."

"And your plan is to go there? Now?"

"No time like the present."

"And what were you planning to ask him? If he has fenced any pink diamonds lately?"

"Not exactly. I figured I would play some pool, and just see what was going on, if the guy is even there."

Garrett didn't respond. So, she wasn't completely off base, just doing some surveillance. She also seemed completely at ease walking down the troubled streets where they were approached every five minutes by someone. When they met Garrett's gaze, they usually took off.

"There's a lot of poor here. A lot of people packed into a city, period, with some sharp contrasts between unimaginable wealth and unthinkable poverty. It can be rough, but it's not too dangerous if you're aware, and maybe a bit sympathetic," she said.

Garrett thought she might be being a bit too generous as he noticed two men falling in behind.

Luckily, they found The Dice straight ahead and went inside.

Garrett, watching the window, saw the men walk by outside.

The place was clearly a gambling bar, games of chance as well as flat screens with numbers, races and sports playing in every corner. The bar was an OTB outlet—off track betting—and a licensed card club, though Garrett was sure that a few of the games being played—such as those using dice—were not legal. Legalizing gambling was a complicated issue in California like it was in many states, but there was no doubt that gaming brought in revenue for the city and the state, as well as for the bar owner.

It was busy for a Thanksgiving eve. No surprise. He'd worked a bar for a while in college, and Thanksgiving and Christmas Eves were often the busiest, when some people with families in for the holiday were looking to escape, and people without them were looking for company.

Busy was good, he thought, as they managed to not stand out too sharply, pushing through the crowd, which was incredibly diverse. Older, obviously wealthier patrons played along younger, less well-off folks.

"So what now?" he asked.

"Let's get a drink, play some pool," she said, spotting an empty table and heading to claim it.

He went to the bar, ordered two colas—they needed to stay sharp—and went back to join her. When she took off her jacket, clad in form-hugging jeans and a tank top, Tiffany garnered more than one interested look and bets started lining up on the side of the table as more than one man wanted to play with her.

When she leaned over to rack the balls, the view at the top of her tank top was a little too inviting. She smiled at a tall, dangerous-looking brute who needed to pick his tongue up from the floor. Garrett stepped between them, offering her her drink.

"Sorry, guys. First game is mine," he said, silently adding, *and so is the woman.* At least for tonight.

"You any good?" he asked, chalking the end of a cue.

"Not bad. I ran the rec room in college for extra money. I'd play when things were slow, and some of the regulars taught me their tricks of the trade. It's been a while, though," she said nonchalantly.

Garrett narrowed his eyes at her as she broke the balls, sending several into the pockets.

"Stripes," she said with a wink, almost cleaning the table on her first turn.

"Been a while," he said to her with great sarcasm. "Riiiight."

Garrett was no slouch at the game himself, spending

more than one Saturday night at the billiard halls in Philly with his brothers, one of their main methods of working off stress. Focusing, he managed to do just slightly better, but then scratched on the eight ball.

"Aw, too bad, lover. You never placed a bet, either. What are the stakes?" she asked mischievously, lining up her next-to-last shot.

Garrett was as entranced as the other men surrounding the table. Tiffany was playing the role of 100-percent minx and she did it very well.

He wanted to make sure no one else was getting ideas, and pulled her away from the table, up against him for a kiss, and then whispered in her ear, "Winner gets to pick when, how…and where."

She smiled broadly, knowing exactly what he meant.

"Sounds like a no-lose proposition to me," she said, cleanly winning the game in two shots.

Garrett hoped she planned to honor the bet.

He backed away, leaning against the wall and watching Tiffany as well as the general environment as she took two more guys for their money. They seemed to think it was worth it, bearing no grudge.

"My turn again?" he asked, noticing her staring toward the far end of the bar.

"What's caught your attention?" he asked, leaning in close so it would simply look like they were sharing a moment.

"Look who's sitting in the last seat. I almost didn't recognize him," she said.

Garrett followed her gaze and it took him a second, and then he realized it was the same man who had been at the restaurant they'd gone to on Russian Hill.

"Your appraiser."

"Arthur. Yeah. Kind of a funny coincidence, don't you think?"

Garrett wasn't sure. "The guy could just be here gambling or having a drink."

"Only one way to know for sure," she said, taking a breath and grabbing her jacket as well as her winnings.

Garrett reached out to stop her as she headed toward the bar, but missed as she disappeared into the throng of people. Pushing after her, he caught up just as she wedged her way up to the bar, ordering another coke.

When she turned to Arthur, her face was a study in surprise.

"Arthur! What a surprise seeing you here," she said.

"Tiffany? What are you doing here?" he said, his surprise evident.

"Playing some pool, winning some money," she said with a laugh and a drink. "The store was closed this week since the robbery, so I figured why not get out and have some fun, right?"

"Sure, I suppose," the man said, looking around nervously.

"I thought you normally spent the holiday with your family in New York?"

"I have a morning flight for the weekend," he offered.

Garrett was about to suggest to Tiffany that they go when a blonde in her late fifties sidled up to Arthur on the other side, catching his attention.

The man's nerves multiplied, Garrett noticed, his hands shaking. Interesting.

"Arthur, are you flirting with this young woman? I swear, I can't turn my back on this one," the blonde said, smiling at Tiffany, though the smile didn't reach her eyes.

"Oh, no, Freddie. Tiffany is just a…business friend."

This was Freddie? Garrett was caught off guard, and saw the same reaction on Tiffany's face, just for a second.

"You're the owner of this place?" Tiffany asked baldly, looking for confirmation.

"Yep. It's not much, but it's all mine," the woman said with the same fake smile.

"It's a lot of fun. You do a great job," Tiffany said, holding out her hand. "So you and Arthur are friends?" she said, fishing.

"Oh, we're a lot more than that, aren't we, baby?" the woman purred at Arthur, and Garrett thought the appraiser looked like he was about to have a heart attack, though he managed to mumble something vaguely flirtatious back.

"Actually, I'm on a break, and I was hoping to have some alone time with Arthur," Freddie said.

"Oh, sure," Tiffany replied. "Nice to meet you. Have a happy Thanksgiving," she added as Arthur slipped from the stool.

Garrett saw Tiffany snap several discreet shots of the couple with her cell phone as they disappeared into the back room.

Then, to his angst, she turned and followed them.

10

TIFFANY HADN'T BOUGHT Freddie's girlfriend routine for a minute. Arthur had seemed extremely stressed and not at all like he was sneaking off for a few kisses. More like he was being summoned by the executioner.

"Tiffany," Garrett whispered, grabbing her arm. "What are you doing?"

"I need to see what they're up to. Arthur wasn't too happy about going in there with her, and what if he needs help?"

"Listen, Daniel sent me a follow-up text telling me to come armed because this Freddie is a dangerous person. We're not armed and who knows what's going on back there?"

"I am," she said.

"What?"

"Armed," she whispered, opening her purse to show him.

Seeing his face, she rolled her eyes. "Don't worry. I'm licensed to carry concealed and I have been taking lessons."

"Have you actually shot at anyone, ever?"

She looked away. "Not *at* anyone. Just at a target, but

ideally, I won't have to. I just want to see if we can hear what's going on," she said. "I need more than a picture of Arthur here to convince Detective Ramsey that Arthur might be the inside man," she said, her hand twisting the knob.

"Wait. Let me," Garrett said, running a hand backward through his hair and pushing in front of her, his back to the door, his hand on the knob. "Hit me," he said.

"What?"

"Hit me. In the face, hard as you can," he instructed, his gaze 100 percent serious.

"I am not going to hit you."

"You said you're taking self-defense lessons. Show me what you've got, hotshot," he teased, his eyes challenging her. "Or in your self-defense classes, like your gun classes, do you just pretend to hit someone?"

Tiffany knew he was goading her, but it worked. She doubted she could hit hard enough to cause him any damage anyway. Gearing herself up for it, she was shocked when he grabbed her, his hands roaming right down to her backside and groping in front of anyone who was looking on that side of the bar.

"Hit me," he said again, squeezing a butt cheek.

As he got even more daring with his hands, she didn't have to be urged again, offering him an elbow to the gut to get some distance between them, and then following up with a punch to his face, as hard as she could.

She heard his grunt as he stumbled backward, and discovered he had loosened the doorknob, crashing back through the door, onto his back in a dimly lit hallway.

A man dressed in a black suit guarded a door at the end of the hall, and stepped forward, his hand on his hip.

Garrett lay on the ground, holding his face, and Tiffany wanted to kneel down, feeling terrible, making sure he was okay. But then he winked at her, and she knew she hadn't damaged him too terribly.

"That will teach you to grope me in public like that!" she said with outrage, playing along.

"Is that an invitation to grope you in private?" he asked, wincing as he made his way to his feet, and turned to eye the man in the black suit. "Sorry, buddy, but the lady has a mean left cross. Is that the men's room?" he said, slurring his speech to give the idea of having drank too much, and heading toward the closed door at the end of the hall.

The man stopped him with a firm hand to the chest. "Out" was all he said, nodding to the doorway which Garrett had crashed through.

Garrett looked at Tiffany, and nodded to the guard. "Sure. Sorry," he said, and staggered crookedly back to the door, closing it behind them.

"Are you okay? I'm so sorry," she said, examining his face. Patrons of the bar were only mildly interested in the drama, probably seeing similar on a regular basis, and returning to their fun and games.

"I'm fine, but ouch," he said, touching his cheek again.

"Yeah, tell me. It was like hitting a rock wall," she said, flexing sore fingers. "I guess Arthur is on his own. I suppose we could wait to see if he comes out."

"Better idea," Garrett said. "Come on."

He took her hand and they emerged back on to the street, where he pulled her down an alley along the side of the building.

"Um, Garrett, where are we going?"

"To check for any windows along that side of the building. The room they went into should be somewhere around…here," he said, locating a tiny casement window that was propped open slightly.

"Oh, I can hear them," Tiffany said, though she couldn't

see much through the tiny window, meant for ventilation more than light.

"You've got a ways to go with your debt, Artie, and double-crossing us was not a good idea," Freddie said.

"You said you'd count my percentage as five percent—the last take alone should have covered my debt," Arthur said, clearly outraged. "I had to do something to get more."

"Bad choice," Freddie said in a hissing tone.

"I think you may have just stumbled upon motive," Garrett whispered.

Tiffany nodded, straining to listen. No more words, but sounds of a scuffle, a low moan.

"You're going to tell us everything, Artie, one way or another."

The polished appraiser she and her family had known for such a long time hardly seemed like an "Artie," Tiffany thought, but obviously Arthur's polish was hiding a damaged finish. And he was in quite a bit of trouble, by the sounds of it.

"We have to help him—he's in real trouble," she said, just when something made a noise in the alley behind them, and Tiffany saw a shadow move.

"There's nothing we can do now, not without blowing—"

Suddenly, out of the dark, a man rushed at them, swinging something. Unable to stop herself, Tiffany shrieked, ducking as something swished by her ear, and she tried to see who was coming at them, and hoped it wasn't more than one.

No such luck. Someone grabbed her arm painfully, and she yelped, but Garrett was clearly busy taking care of the first assailant.

Hard to make out who was who, all she heard were grunt and groans, the sounds of fists hitting bodies.

Her own captor was dragging her back, and she managed to fumble in her bag, grabbing her gun.

"Let me go or I'll shoot," she said, only to be met with a grunt as she lost her shoe.

Aiming upward, she closed her eyes and pulled the trigger, the blast firing and echoing in the alley. Everything seemed to take movement—her captor, shouting in surprise, dropped her on the spot. She landed hard on the damp alley floor. Some voices somewhere shouted, and other indiscernible noises surrounded her. God, where was Garrett?

Getting to her feet, she walked gingerly, taking a mini-flashlight that was supposed to have the power of a full Maglite from her purse, holding it in one hand, her gun still in the other. The small flashlight lived up to its promise, illuminating the alley at least ten feet in front of her, and she located her shoe, thankfully. When someone grabbed her arm, she shrieked again, and a hand went over her mouth.

"Shhh, it's just me, Garrett. Let's get the hell out of here," he said, and she whimpered in relief that it was him, and that he was safe. Making their way out to the street behind them, they waved down a rare taxi and slid in the back.

"Oh, my God, I was petrified," she said, settling in as she looked at him in the low light of the taxi, giving the driver directions back to her house. "Are you okay?"

"I'm fine, but you scared the life out of me when I heard the gunshot," he said.

He was dirty, his face bruised, probably from where she had hit him, but he'd obviously had more of a scuffle with their assailants, now bearing a torn shirt and a bloody cut near his brow.

She lifted her hands to touch it. "You're hurt," she said.

He touched the spot, seeming mildly surprised. "Didn't even feel it."

She couldn't stop staring at him. He was so damned sexy, even now, covered in alley dirt, bruises and blood. Maybe even more so. He was raw male, his eyes still dark with aggression from the fight.

"You should come up, let me clean that up for you," she said, surprised at the sexiness of her own voice.

"I probably should," he agreed. "Then what?"

She smiled, leaning in to kiss him. "Then we have to make pies."

TIFFANY HAD HAD some strange days in her life, but the last twenty-four hours topped them. She'd chased down Freddie, had the skirmish in the alley and then baked pies with Garrett until the wee hours of the morning. The range of activities left them both exhausted—and bruised. Garrett's rough-and-tumble look, including the cut by his brow and the bruise where she'd hit him, just made him even sexier.

Maybe he was tired, too, or something had gotten to him, because he'd been more distant, quieter, since they returned from The Dice. Maybe she was just imagining it, as she was awfully worn out herself. She didn't know him well enough to know his moods, really, regardless of how intimate they'd been. They'd known each other less than a week, and since they had crawled out of bed that morning, he felt more distant than ever.

Waking up late, she didn't have too much time to think about it, getting dressed to go to her parents' house. She spotted numerous bruises of her own, probably from the alley.

It was going to be hard to explain all that without either telling a complete lie or the whole truth. By the time they arrived there, she'd made up her mind.

"Listen," she said, placing a hand on Garrett's arm before they walked in. "I think I have to tell my family that I'm doing this private investigation thing. You were right. And I don't want to lie to them anymore, which will be really difficult considering we look like we just got into a brawl," she said.

Garrett nodded, but she read the apprehension in his face. "You know, this sounds like it's a family discussion, and a family event. Maybe you should drop me back at the hotel," he said, but she cut him off.

"I will, if you want, but I'd love the moral support, and basically, my mother will kill me if you don't show up," she said with a smile. "And, I think they have already spotted us from the window. Honestly, the bruises are going to be tough to explain otherwise," she said, not wanting him to think she was trying to involve him in her family issues.

"Makes sense, and good for you for deciding to tell them," he said, smiling and giving her hand a squeeze. It meant a lot, as she was beginning to wonder why he had been so aloof all morning.

Tiffany braced herself as they walked into her parents' house carrying the pies that they had made together. It turned out Garrett was no stranger to the kitchen, and they had had a lot of fun, tired as they were.

"You made it!" her mother declared happily as they entered the living room to the sound of the TV blaring the Macy's Parade, the aroma of turkey and other delicious items wafting in from the kitchen.

Then her mom stopped short, and her father's greeting was cut off, too, as they both took in the bruise on her arm as she handed over the pies.

"What happened?" her sister Ruby asked, crossing the room and getting right to the point. "Are you okay?"

Ruby eyed Garrett accusingly, and Tiffany frowned.

"Ruby, back off, this isn't Garrett's fault."

"That had better not be the case," her father said, clearly outraged as he studied her face and then pulled her in for a hard hug. "No one hurts my baby."

"Please, stop. As you can see, Garrett took the worst of it, and part of that was completely my fault," she said.

"Especially this bruise right here," he said with a smile, touching his lip where she had smacked him, obviously trying to lighten the mood.

"Anyway, if you want to sit, I can tell you all what happened," she said, and looked at her family, who were all looking back at her. "Now's as good a time as ever," she said.

"What do you mean?" her mother asked.

Her family members were clearly apprehensive, but Tiffany sat on the sofa and accepted the soda someone handed her.

"I've made a career decision," she said.

"Another one?" Jewel asked, but with a smile that took the sting out.

"I've been working on another career track while I was at the store…something I wasn't sure about, so I didn't want to tell you until I knew it was going to be the thing for me, but I really think it is."

"Just spit it out already," Ruby said.

"I've been training to be a private investigator. I've only had a few cases, but I really love it, and I think I could be good at it. I've been checking into the jewelry store robberies, and, well, we had a bit of a scuffle down in the Tenderloin last night, hence the bumps and bruises," she said.

Her mother turned a little pale, in contrast to her father's face going red as he looked at Garrett in disbelief.

"What kind of bodyguard are you? Letting her go down there after dark?"

Tiffany bit back a groan. "Dad, please. First of all, Garrett didn't even know I went. I found a lead, and I went on my own. He tracked me down there, to help. We had some trouble, but it was okay. I can handle myself. That's one of the things I'm learning," she said.

She held her breath, letting it sink in. Her family was silent, staring at her in blank surprise. Still, Tiffany was bolstered by Garrett's hand enclosing hers tightly.

"I know you all don't know me from Adam, but I work with a lot of P.I.s. Tiffany is new to this, but I think she'll be very good at it," Garrett added, much to her appreciation.

"This just takes the cake," her brother Nick said. "Getting lost in Yosemite was one thing, and then the deal with Brice, but now you've been hurt and you're getting in fights downtown at night? You are *not* serious about this?"

"Very," Tiffany said, holding her brother's gaze. "It's not a lark. I got my license, and I've been training in self-defense, marksmanship and working basic cases. I came up with real clues that have helped the police work the robbery, and I might have some more."

"But, honey…this is all so…unsavory. For a woman. Isn't this a man's profession?" her father asked, drawing a marked glare from her mother.

"Three of the P.I.s we work with in Philadelphia are women," Garrett broke in again. "Women make logical connections that men often don't, and they are also often better at getting people to talk to them. They're also really good shots."

"You have a gun?" her mother asked, shocked.

"It's not your sister who's putting herself in front of bullets or being assaulted," Nick said before she could respond to her mother, glaring at Garrett.

"Actually, Garrett and his brothers spend their time in

dangerous situations all the time. They're bodyguards, so shows how much you know, Nick. Anyway, this isn't up for a vote. I like it. I think I could be good at it. It's what I really, really want to do, and I was hoping you would be supportive of that," she said, almost pleading. "I'll be stopping my work at the store to do this full-time, once we're past the holidays. I know you need the extra help there right now."

Tiffany didn't often rock the boat with her family, but it was as good of a compromise as she could offer. This time, she had to make them see that being a P.I. was her calling. She felt it in her bones, and as she told them, all doubt faded away. It was another step in her taking-the-bull-by-the-horns lifestyle.

"Honey, we're all just worried. This is very new, and you were hurt, and you are talking about dealing with some dangerous people," her mother said, breeching the gap. "It doesn't mean we don't want to support you, but we also don't want anything happening to you."

"Bad things happen to people every day, Mom. We never know what's going to take place on any given day. Maybe, if I learn to do this job well, I can help a few less bad things happen in the world, you know? And learning to protect myself is part of the bargain. I won't always have my own personal bodyguard," she said with a grin, but as she realized the truth of her words, it stung a little.

"But can't you…look into cases on the side, and still work at the store, where things are more stable?" her mom asked.

"I know it's a risk, but I need to do it. I need to put one hundred percent of my time into this if I want to be good at it and really make a go of it. I can't do it part-time. In fact, if I had been training more regularly, I might not have had such a struggle in that alley last night."

"Alley?" Ruby said, her tone rising several notes.

"Um, yeah. But, anyway. That's most of it. I didn't want to tell you until I was sure, and I am. I have to do this."

They all continued to stare, making her wonder if she was talking gibberish. Even Garrett was looking at her, his brow furrowed in concentration, as if trying to absorb what she'd said.

"I think it's wonderful," her younger sister Jewel finally spoke up, coming forward with a hug. "I can't wait to tell my friends that my big sister is a private investigator."

Tiffany laughed. "Thanks."

"Okay, for today, it's a holiday," her mother said, clearly wanting to set this aside for later, and Tiffany was fine with that, having said her piece. "Dinner will be ready at four, and until then, there is a lunch buffet in the kitchen, a boccie game in progress in the backyard and the parade running, so let's just enjoy Thanksgiving," she said. "And be thankful that Tiffany is safe, and that she's found a career she's obviously excited about."

Tiffany felt her eyes sting slightly at her mother's approval.

"Thanks, Mom."

Everyone seemed more than willing to return to the normal holiday groove, and Tiffany collapsed back into the sofa. She was glad to have revealed her secret, but wondering how it would all pan out.

"You okay?" Garrett asked.

"Yeah. I guess. Though the pressure is on now, isn't it? If I fail at this—"

"You won't," he said, slanting a slight smile in her direction, but he didn't touch her again.

She hated that.

"It was brave to tell them all, and the right thing to do," he added.

"Thanks. And thanks for backing me up."

"I only spoke the truth. So what now?"

"I beat you in boccie and then we eat way too much?" she suggested.

"Sounds like a plan," he said.

Tiffany was still picking up a strange vibe from Garrett, and noticed that while they joined her family in fun and games out in the yard, and he sat next to her at dinner, he barely touched her, and when he did, only in the most casual of ways. She planned to ask him about it later, when they were in private.

Maybe he was just being discreet around her family, but they were an affectionate bunch, and after they had caught them making out in the jewelry store, Tiffany figured they knew the score.

It was something else, but she didn't want to pry. As they enjoyed the day, and stuffed themselves with her mother's amazing food, she let it be.

For now.

11

GARRET HAD THOROUGHLY enjoyed the day; Tiffany's family was wonderful, but by the end of it, he needed some time alone.

He needed to think and to sort out what he was feeling. When he asked Tiffany to drop him back at his hotel—bag of Thanksgiving leftovers that her mother had packed for him, and all—he should have explained to her why. She'd asked him if anything was wrong, but he wasn't even sure what to say, so instead he just kissed her and tried not to let his body's demands take over. He couldn't get enough of her, and that was part of the problem.

Moreover, shortly before waking up that morning, Tiffany curled sweetly into his side, and it occurred to him it was the first time in six years he hadn't set aside the day Lainey died. He usually spent it alone, remembering their time together. In fact, he hadn't thought of her at all in the past few days with Tiffany.

He'd spent the morning of the anniversary of his late wife's death with Tiffany at the shore, and then going home to make love to her.

Always the anniversary of her death had been a day that marked the years passing more for him than any other holiday or anniversary, but this year, his mind had been elsewhere.

All of his focus had been on Tiffany, who smiled at him even as her eyes were full of questions—and maybe a little hurt—as she parked in front of the hotel.

Tiffany, whom he had known less than a full week.

Who made love like a goddess, and who had a decent left cross.

Who had been bruised in a scuffle in an alley less than twenty-four hours before. What if he hadn't been there? What if both men had come at her?

The thought froze him to the marrow.

"Whatcha thinkin' about?" she asked as he hesitated before getting out of the car. He swallowed hard, looking at her, emotions a tangle inside.

"You."

She smiled. "Oh. Want me to park the car and come up?"

Garrett wanted nothing more, but...

How could he fall this hard for someone he'd known less than a week, and for someone with whom he had no future unless he uprooted his life, or she uprooted hers? Someone who was going to be putting her life in danger on a regular basis?

And maybe that was the root of it—could he be with her and not fear every single moment going through what he'd been through with Lainey?

It wasn't a decision that he could make based on a short-term affair.

"I was just thinking about how well your family took the news. And how things could have gone much, much worse."

She nodded slowly. "Guess I'd better get on those self-defense lessons," she said with a smile.

He didn't respond. What he wanted to tell her was to find a different profession. Something safe, where she didn't need weapons or self-defense, or end up in alleys or pool halls in shady sides of town.

He wanted to at least explore the option of having more with Tiffany, but he couldn't do that, not if she was putting herself in danger every day.

He couldn't lose her like he'd lost Lainey. He couldn't go through that again. It wasn't fair, and it didn't qualify him as an enlightened male, but the fear in his gut dictated his common sense. He wouldn't always be there to protect her.

"What's this about? What's going on? Is this just because you're worried about what happened last night?" she pushed, clued into his mood.

"No…. Yes, in part. I remembered this morning, that this was the first time I'd forgotten. About my late wife, the anniversary of her death."

Garrett was unable to get a fix on his feelings or thoughts. He didn't know how to deal with this. He'd always lived his life in a straight line. College, work, marriage, starting the business. Losing Lainey had thrown him a curve, but he'd thought that he had gotten back on his feet.

Tiffany had him thinking in circles.

"Oh. Oh, my God," she said on a hushed tone. "I'm so sorry. But that has to be a natural thing, a progression. You shouldn't feel guilty—"

"I don't feel guilty, which is part of the problem," he said, trying to express what was going on inside, and doing a poor job of it.

"Then what is it?"

"I don't know. Just…" He shook his head, unable to find words to express it all.

She put a hand on his arm. "I get it. You lost your wife

this week, six years ago. You feel responsible for that, in part, not being able to save her, and you're transferring those feelings to me, after what happened in the alley last night," she said, carefully measuring her words. "But I'm not her."

"I know that," he said, not wanting her to think that he was thinking about his late wife when he was with her. When he was with Tiffany, he didn't think about anything else. She was everything he needed.

In the stretch of silence, she nodded stiffly.

"I am tired, actually. It's probably not a bad idea for us to rest up tonight," she said softly.

Garrett knew something had changed, shifted between them. He'd messed up somewhere, but he wasn't sure how to fix it. Being married, and then out of commission for a long while, had left him out of practice on how to handle the more complex parts of a relationship.

Everything with Lainey had been easy because he hadn't known anything back then. They'd learned together. Additionally, he hadn't seen all of the things that he now knew were out in the world, things he saw as a bodyguard. He hadn't known what it was like to lose someone he loved.

Now he knew, and it changed everything.

"Okay," he said, leaning over to give her a long, soft kiss. "I'll talk to you tomorrow?"

She nodded, sort of, but didn't answer. He wanted to kiss her until they both forgot all of the problems and complications, and could lose themselves in each other again, for the rest of the night. But that wasn't the answer, as much as he wanted it.

What was between them was uncertain right now.

He was uncertain. It wasn't fair to either of them to keep fanning the fire.

From the sidewalk, he watched her drive away. Up in

his room, he stowed the leftovers in the fridge, shucked his clothes and grabbed a bottle of scotch he'd left on the bar.

He was tired, but sleep was a million miles away for most of the night. All he could think about was Tiffany in her bed—and in his heart.

And what the heck he was going to do about it.

TIFFANY WAS BARELY able to hold back tears until she shut the door behind her, finally home, and they all came pouring forth. The pain in her temple was nothing compared to the sharp ache that Garrett's words had triggered.

His simple response that he wasn't confusing her with his late wife told Tiffany exactly what she needed to know. She'd wondered what was bothering him, and why he hadn't been entirely himself all day, and now she knew.

So what? It wasn't as if they had ever said they were anything more than a fling, but during several moments of their week, she'd thought, maybe…

She could have sworn by the look on his face when he'd found her downtown that something special was happening for him, too. Underneath the anger had been concern, passion. Caring. Things on which to build something more.

Or so she thought. She should have known better.

Well, she'd known in her head, but perhaps her heart had started to hope…

Big, big mistake.

Clearly, he was upset about what happened to her, but it all still came down to losing his wife—that was the real trauma that haunted him. The worst part was, Tiffany couldn't even be angry with him for that. How could she be upset with a man who loved so deeply and still suffered so much for the woman he'd lost?

Except that she was here with him now, and she wanted

more. More than a fling, more than sex. And Garrett was still stuck in the past as she was moving into her future.

It was so typical for her to have found the man she could fall in love with, and he was completely devoted to his late wife. They'd obviously had a relationship that this silly fling could not measure up to.

Wiping tears away and reaching for some tissues, she pulled herself together. She had to toughen up if she ever expected to be a good investigator. She'd already seen evidence of how love went wrong through her camera lens—take Marcus and Sally Hooper for example—and in her own life.

"Love leaves you a jam every time," she said to herself in her best Philip Marlowe.

Staring at the ceiling, she got hold of herself and set her hurt aside. There was nothing she could do about that. But she could do something about the case.

Refocus and get to work. Knowing that a man they had considered something of a family friend, with whom they had done business for years, made it even more personal. That made her particularly determined to figure out what was going on. She needed some hard evidence; she couldn't just go to Detective Ramsey with her suspicions.

Arthur Hayden appeared to have some gambling debts that he was working off—perhaps by sharing inside information with jewel thieves—but until she had proof, there was nothing the police could do anyway.

She looked at the clock. This might be her only chance to find out what Arthur Hayden was up to. At the bar, he'd said that he was heading to New York that morning; which meant no one was home in his apartment.

If she was going to find anything incriminating, it would be in the small apartment above the office where he ran his appraisal business.

Hopping up from the bed, she changed into a pair of dark jeans and a dark sweater, tying her hair back and grabbing a set of lock picks she'd bought and hadn't yet had the chance to use—not on a real lock, anyway.

Arthur was gone, and she could have the run of his apartment and his office to try to find some evidence. Something that would be damning enough to take to Detective Ramsey, who could then bring him in for questioning, and hopefully solve the case.

Tiffany opted to leave her gun at home—she didn't feel comfortable enough with it yet, and took some pepper spray instead, along with a flashlight and her phone.

Everything a girl needed for a break-in.

She'd been to Arthur's office many times over the years. She was glad to see how quiet the street was in the Lower Haight neighborhood where the office and his apartment were located. Only a few people were out for late-night walks with their dogs.

Parking her car down the street from his address, she walked to the back and to her dismay, she had completely forgotten about the touchpad alarm system that protected the property. So much for trying out her lock-pick set.

Not giving up, Tiffany searched around the base of the building for an open basement window, but they all appeared secure with cinder block. Then it hit her, and she smiled.

The roof.

She couldn't cut through the rooftop, like the jewelers did, but these were residential buildings and might have doorway access or a roof hatch that she could get through. A friend of hers did that all the time when she locked herself out of her apartment. It was dirty, and there might be a drop to the floor, depending on where the hatch led, but it was worth a try.

Ambling up the fire escape, she made it to the roof in seconds and gasped in surprise. It was lovely. Arthur and his neighbors had all planted rooftop gardens on the tops of their buildings and stepping over into the greenery was a nice surprise. Flowers bloomed around her, and small topiary trees in pots gave her some cover as she took a breath of cool air, looking up and smiling at the starry sky, standing amid the plants.

She wished Garrett was here, sharing the stars and the adventure with her, but she supposed technically she would be involving him in a crime, so maybe it was better he was back at the hotel. Tiffany had the idea he didn't much approve of her taking chances, but she had to get the evidence somehow, and she couldn't just walk up to Arthur and ask for it.

The roof did have a hatch, cleverly camouflaged behind several pots of thick gardenias, though it was locked.

She hoped it didn't have security, but there was no way to tell. She'd find out soon enough. Pulling out her pick set and flashlight, she messed with the lock, and while doing so, reminded herself to invest in some mini bolt cutters she'd seen for sale. The gardenias were pungent, and she had to stifle several sneezes as she worked, but the locks were stubborn.

"Don't bother," Arthur said from behind her, making her fall backward in shock.

"Those locks are unbreakable, unless you can saw or somehow burn them off. I'm not stupid."

Caught.

Tiffany supposed there was no way to talk her way out of this one.

"I know you were involved in the robberies," she said, deciding to confront Arthur head-on. He was a man, but an older man not much larger than she was, and she could probably fight him if she had to, especially since he didn't seem to have a weapon.

"You're right, I was," he said regretfully, shaking his head and walking back to sit in an ornate cast-iron chair.

Hardly threatening.

Tiffany got up cautiously, sliding her hand into her pocket and closing her fingers around the pepper spray just in case.

"Why?" she asked, staying on her feet, not getting too comfortable with Arthur's apparent acquiescence.

He sighed heavily, tilting his head back as if to address the starry sky instead of her.

"Money, of course. It started slow, after my wife died years ago. I would go out to the bar, to have some feeling of life around me. I eventually started playing some of the games, and sometimes I won. It was the most exhilarating thing I'd felt in a while, and before I knew it, I was hooked."

"And you got in too deep?"

"Well, legally, of course, the bars can't act like casinos—they can't hold your debt or winnings—but what Freddie does with some of her *special* customers is lend them advances to play. So it's more of a loan. I was okay for a while. I do well through my business, but with the recession, slower business, I got behind quickly."

"And who came up with the idea of robbing local stores to pay off your debt?"

His head coming forward again, he looked her in the eye now. "I did. I was desperate. They made some serious threats, not against me—I would have let him kill me if it would have ended it, but they don't get their money then. They knew about my family and friends. They have reach," he said. "Helping them seemed like the only option, and they promised no one would be hurt. No one *was* killed in the robberies," he said beseechingly. "No property was even damaged."

"No, but livelihoods and what people like my parents worked for their entire lives could be lost. Because of you," she said accusingly, not letting him off the hook.

"You're right. That's why I'm telling you this now. I can't live with this, and it's never going to stop. I thought maybe it would just be a few jobs, and when I saw the diamonds your parents had acquired, I thought that would be enough to end it for good."

"But they want to keep stringing you along," she added.

"Yes. With the interest they charge on the debt, I could be in this until I'm no longer useful to them, even though they have already been paid twice over. I knew I had to get out, and that you were doing some…investigating. It's a federal crime, what they're doing…. It crosses state lines. I can name names," he said eagerly.

"I know a police detective who can help," she said, nodding. "Do you know where the diamonds and the other items went?"

"I wasn't involved in any way except letting them know where the special items were, the worth, any inside knowledge I had of the stores, that kind of thing."

"Like that my parents were out of town that weekend, and I was running the store?"

"Yes, things like that. Vault makes, whatever details helped their team finish the job. After that, I have no idea what they do with the items," he said, his head hanging again. "I am so sorry."

"Arthur, we should go. It's probably not safe for us to be out here."

"They think I've gone to New York. I bought the tickets, went to the airport even, but then circled back here."

"Did you take your own car? A cab?" she asked nervously, looking around. It didn't seem right that Freddie would be okay with letting Arthur off the leash so easily.

"My own car," he said hesitantly. "I could tell no one followed me."

Right. Everyone who had watched a cop show thought they knew how to spot a tail, but Tiffany knew that it was harder to spot a professional than someone might think, and the people who were involved with Freddie were professionals.

"Let me call the detective I know, and he can meet us here," she said, thinking that would be a better plan.

Dialing Finn Ramsey's number, it went to message. Frustrated, she said, "Call me." And hung up.

Pacing on the roof, a few minutes later, she tried again. Still no message. He was either on a call or not answering his phone. Maybe he was off duty, but Finn didn't seem like the kind of guy to ignore his phone, no matter what.

"Okay, we're going to have to go. But we'll take the back way around, through yards, down to my car."

Arthur nodded, and they made their way down to the driveway at the base of the fire escape as quickly as they could. Tiffany just couldn't shake the feeling of unease, though it was probably because all of a sudden she was trying to get a prospective federal witness to safety.

The game definitely changed quickly in the P.I. business.

"This way," she said, and motioned to Arthur to follow her, which he did, but as they started to make their way through a space between the houses, she saw two dark figures coming toward them on the other side.

Turning, her pulse slamming, they headed back to the street, where there might at least be the safety of the streetlights and possible passersby, but no such luck.

Another man waited patiently at the end of the driveway, illuminated in streetlight. It was the same guy from the back of Freddie's club, and the way he held his hand under the front flap of his jacket told Tiffany all she needed to know.

She walked up to him, remaining calm. There was no choice.

"I don't suppose you'll believe we're just out for a Thanksgiving walk," she said pertly, making eye contact so the guy at least thought she wasn't afraid of him as she started to pull the pepper spray from her pocket.

"Not exactly," he said just as casually. "And I'd think twice about whatever it is you're retrieving from your pocket," he said as she heard the footsteps of the other two men coming up behind them.

Her fingers loosened from the spray can, and she pulled her hands out, showing empty fingers.

The thug reached forward, pulling the pepper spray out of her pocket.

"Nasty stuff," he said, frowning. "I'd rather be shot."

She didn't agree, but to each their own.

He checked her other pocket, taking her picks and her cell phone. Suddenly, it started ringing, and people were getting knocked down and then up again. The thug actually laughed at that.

"I love that song," he murmured, shutting the phone off and putting it in his pocket.

It had to be Ramsey. But with her phone off, now no one could track her signal, even if they thought to do so.

"Where are we going?" she asked, eyeing the car at the curb, and assuming if they were just supposed to be killed, it would have happened already.

"Freddie wants to talk. Get in the car," he said.

Tiffany nodded and let herself be ushered forward to the waiting vehicle. For the moment, all she could do was hope that she somehow managed to walk away from this alive.

12

GARRETT KNEW SOMETHING was wrong.

He'd tried to call Tiffany twice, but no response. Assuming she was mad at him, he'd gone over to her apartment, only to find no one answering the door.

So he picked the lock.

No one home, and nothing disturbed, but his gut told him something was off.

As he was searching through the place, he was relieved to find her gun still there, but it was obvious she had taken off somewhere.

Maybe to her parents' house?

He didn't want to worry her family without need, so he drove there himself, relieved to remember the way, and rode by the house, but her car wasn't there.

It was just then that his phone rang.

Middle of the night and it was Ramsey. Not good.

"What happened? Is Tiffany okay?" he asked without preamble as he answered, his mind zipping over all of the possibilities. He never should have let her out of his sight, though nothing had been amiss when he dropped her off—at least, aside of the personal tension between them.

He'd been unable to settle down and absolutely unable

to sleep. He'd missed Tiffany so much after coming back to the hotel by himself that he knew he'd been an ass worrying about being with her because of her profession.

His brother Jonas confirmed as much in far more colorful language when Garrett had called him to make sure he wasn't nuts for falling for a woman he'd only known a week.

Jonas, who was usually brusque and blunt, often painfully so, though he had softened more since meeting and marrying Tessa, had said something that had shaken Garrett to his core.

It can all be gone in a minute, Gar, and you know that better than any of us. So why waste time? Why second-guess it?

It was all Garrett needed to tip him over into admitting his feelings for Tiffany—at least to himself. So when he'd called and couldn't find her, he had an awful feeling that he might have missed his chance.

That couldn't happen. He wouldn't let it.

"I was about to ask you that," Ramsey said just as tersely, shaking Garrett out of his reverie. "I got two calls from her a half hour ago, but I was in the shower. I noticed the messages as soon as I got out, called back, no answer. Seems off. She sounded…intense."

"What did she say?"

"Just to call her back, that it was important."

"Can you track her cell signal?"

"Already tried. Phone is off. So I take it you don't know where she is?"

"No. Not at home, not at her parents or with me. How about her car's GPS?"

"Working on that now. Waiting on a call."

"I'll be at the station in twenty minutes," Garrett

said, hanging up and focusing on driving the unfamiliar highways.

It was closer to thirty by the time he pulled up into the police station lot, and he ran into Ramsey on the steps.

"We have her car located down on a street in the Lower Haight," he said. Unfortunately, that meant next to nothing to Garrett.

Almost. "Wait. Where is Pierce Street?"

Ramset stopped in his tracks. "That's in Lower Haight. Why? What's there?"

"The business for the appraiser the Walkers use for their store," Garrett said, filling Ramsey in on their adventure at the bar the night before.

"And you didn't bring this directly to me because?"

"There's no proof he's involved, or any of them. Just what we could guess from what we saw, which wasn't much, aside of what my contact had to say. We know Hayden had some involvement with them, but there's no overt connection to the robberies. It's all circumstantial," Garrett said, feeling more annoyed with himself by the minute. It was circumstantial—which meant the next step should have been obvious to him, but he was so wrapped up in his emotions for Tiffany, he hadn't been thinking about the case.

"She probably went down there to get some kind of proof," Ramsey said, speeding up.

"Yeah, that would sound about right. Arthur said something about being out of town for the holiday. Maybe she's just in his place and turned her phone off to keep quiet," Garrett said hopefully, but he didn't believe it. His instincts told him something was very wrong.

"I lost my first partner in a shooting, you know," Ramsey said as they fell into silence.

"Pardon?"

"None of my business, but you've only been in town a week," he said, shrugging one shoulder. "Wondered if this was a permanent thing."

Garrett tried to keep up. What the heck was Ramsey getting at?

"What's that got to do with your partner?"

"You have that look. Who'd you lose?"

Garrett decided to play along, just to see where it was going. "My wife. Six years ago."

"Ah. Sorry. That's bad."

"Yeah."

"My partner, that was a little more than eight years ago," Ramsey responded, breaking his thoughts. "We were both new detectives. She was hot," he said with a smile and a whistle. "It's not a good thing to get involved with someone you work with, but you know how it is. We did anyway. I couldn't keep my hands off her, fell hard. Young love," he said whimsically, but Garrett could still detect the note of pain lingering under his tone.

"What happened?"

"Routine drug bust. Sometimes I still find myself going over it in my head, how it could have happened. How we missed it. Uniforms brought in a guy, higher than a kite. He'd been searched, cuffed, but he had a gun shoved down inside his boot and he shot her right where she sat at her desk. He didn't care about her in particular, he just started shooting randomly. We were talking about where to grab lunch when, suddenly, she was just gone."

Garrett felt his stomach turn. He knew there were no words that could adequately respond to such a horror. Jonas's words came back to him full-force, making him crazy to find Tiffany. Where could she be?

"My wife was a prosecutor on her first big case. We were meeting for dinner to celebrate. The guy she put away, his brother had been following her. Plowed his SUV into her side of the car at an intersection. She was DOS," Garrett said, just as mechanically. Dead on scene.

Ramsey cursed. "So, you'd never do that again, huh? I mean, if you met her again, you'd never make the same mistake twice."

"What?" Garrett asked.

"Your wife. If you met her, would you do it again, knowing the result?"

Garrett didn't say a word.

"I asked myself that a lot. But I have to tell you, after the worst of it passed, I had a lot of good memories that outweighed that bad one. I wouldn't have wanted to miss it, my time with her. I missed it and I want it again. You know, the passion, the sex...and the rest of it, too."

"So is this your way of telling me I'm making a mistake if I walk away?" Garrett said, turning to look at the detective as they hit a red light.

"Nah. It's my way of letting you know that after an appropriate amount of time, maybe a week or so, when Tiffany's really pissed at you and feeling lonely, maybe a little vulnerable, I'm going to ask her out," Ramsey said, and laughed. "So if you plan to change your mind, I suggest you do it fast."

If it wouldn't have risked both of them getting killed, Garrett would have hit the guy. So all of this to let Garrett know he was interested in Tiffany? What a guy.

He had no doubt the detective meant it. He'd seen how Ramsey looked at Tiffany, and why not? He was right. They were both here, and had made a connection, one that could easily be built through the commonalities in their work.

Ramsey would show her the ropes, help her along, while touching her, kissing her, taking her to bed....

No way in hell.

"I would," Garrett said under his breath.

"What?"

"I'd do it again. With my wife. I wouldn't have wanted to miss those years that went before, even knowing how it was afterward."

He didn't want to miss the years he might have with Tiffany, either. The past week had been amazing, and he wanted more. Much more. He didn't need to say it; he could tell Ramsey knew what he was thinking by the broad, tell-tale grin on the detective's face.

"I hope it works out. But if it doesn't, don't worry, I'll still be here to pick up the pieces."

"Go to hell," Garrett responded, but without any punch as they approached Freddie's.

"The Waller station is just a few blocks over. I'm calling for some backup, just in case," Ramsey said. "I have a feeling about this," he said more to himself than Garrett.

Garrett agreed, and it was all he could do to stay in the car. The lights were on in the back rooms of The Dice, for one thing, and it was the middle of the night. He supposed there could be some other explanation, but he knew Tiffany was in there. He could feel it.

Two more cars pulled up behind them a few minutes later, and Ramsey looked at him. "Stay in the car."

"Yeah, I don't think so." Garrett gave him a look, and Ramsey sighed, tossing him a Kevlar vest from the back-seat.

"Fine, but try to stay out of the way," he said, signaling to the other cars where four more officers appeared.

Surrounding the building, they found the doors locked, no surprise, and so Garrett brought them around to the window in the alley he and Tiffany had look through before.

Tiffany and Arthur were both sitting in chairs facing Freddie and a tall guy with a gun.

Ramsey lowered his voice, telling as much to the cops out front, giving them permission to enter the premises in whatever way they needed to.

However, as he did so, he saw Freddie motion to Tiffany and Arthur to stand—they were apparently leaving, the armed guy ushering them out.

As Arthur stood, he limped, and turned to reach for the chair—it was obvious they had worked him over pretty well to get whatever they needed from him.

Garrett's heart was in his throat as he couldn't see anything but Tiffany's back. Had they hit her, too?

His own fist clenched.

"If she's hurt..."

"Down, boy. We'll end this shortly," Ramsey said, a hand on his shoulder as they got up and took position. "I don't think they'd risk more than roughing them up on the premises, so it's good we got here before they took them away. Let's go."

As they rounded the front of the building and Ramsey joined the other officers, Garrett stayed to the back, at the corner of the building, as instructed. It killed him to hold back, but he wasn't armed, and he had to trust Ramsey to do his job now.

As the officers got through the door, sending silent signals to each other for how to proceed, everyone froze as two shots rang out. Silence was broken, shouts filling the air as the police stormed forward and Garrett bolted from his spot right after them, hoping they weren't too late.

TIFFANY GROANED IN pain, rolling on the floor. She flailed and kicked at anything around her, feeling contact with something, someone, but not able to concentrate on the voices around her. The fiery pain on her skin was distracting her from everything else.

She knew, when Arthur had told Freddie that he was going to expose them, that time was running out if she didn't do something. Desperate, she managed to stumble forward into the thug—Edward, as Freddie called him affectionately—and pickpocket her pepper spray. As he paused, she used it—and the stuff went everywhere. It certainly blinded Edward, and shots rang out, but she had no idea where they hit. The last thing she saw was everyone dropping, including herself, Arthur and Freddie. Multiple cries of discomfort immediately rose along with a whole lot of other noise.

When someone grabbed her shoulders, she fought back, assuming it was Edward, but then the scent—what she could smell through her irritated nasal passages—told her differently.

"Garrett?"

"Pepper spray!" someone yelled, and then warned everyone not to rub their eyes, which was torture.

The next thing Tiffany felt was someone gently wiping down her face with a cooling, soothing cloth, and she sighed, trying to open her eyes, which still burned.

"Take it easy. You really sprayed that stuff around, it will be airborne for a while," Garrett said, coughing as he ushered her out into breathable air.

Opening her blurry eyes, she saw figures milling around, and heard more sirens. More wet wipes were pushed into her hands, and she didn't hesitate to use them, feeling the effects of the secondary exposure to the spray diminish considerably, though her eyes continued to burn and water, as did her nose.

"I never used that stuff before. I had no idea it did that," she said.

"Only because you didn't aim straight," Ramsey said with a smile in his voice, then a cough. "You kind of sprayed the whole hallway."

"I did aim for Edward, but I wanted to get Freddie, too, and then I lost my balance," she explained. Her finger had been on the spray pump the whole time.

"You managed to take them all down peacefully just as we went in, so good job, Walker," Ramsey said.

"How did you know I was here?"

"Tracked your car to Arthur's street, and Garrett filled me in from there."

"I went to your place, your parents', looking for you," Garrett said, his tone reflecting a depth of emotion that might have made her cry if her eyes weren't already tearing like mad. "I couldn't find you, and it was the worst day of my life. Then we tracked you here, and I saw you in there..." he said, pulling her in for a tight embrace.

"Ah, get a room before I have to arrest you for gross displays of public affection," Ramsey teased. "Then I'll need you both down to the station for your statements as soon as possible."

"Finn... Detective Ramsey," she amended, given the scene, and all of the officers nearby. "Arthur Hayden talked to me tonight. He wants to be a federal witness. He says he can name names as to the jewel thieves, and everyone involved," she said.

"Really? You never fail to surprise, Tiffany. We'll make sure he's taken care of. EMTs are on their way over to check you out. One of the uniforms can take you back when you're done. Don't argue," Ramsey said as she opened her mouth to do just that, and then he turned back to business.

"You were looking for me?" she asked Garrett. "Why?"

"We can talk about that later. Let the EMTs check you over now," he said gently. "Then I'll take you home."

She did as he asked, letting the technicians poke and prod, thoroughly checking her out, but except for the remnants of discomfort from the spray, which were rapidly subsiding, she was fine. Arthur had taken a beating, though, the poor guy, and that had been hard to watch. She told Garrett about it, her voice cracking.

"I hope I never have to see anyone treat another person like that again. It was awful. I thought they were going to kill him right there," she said as the EMT told her she was fine, gave her some advice for taking care of her eyes, and left. "Maybe I'm not cut out for this work after all."

Garrett tipped her chin up, kissed her.

"You're fantastic. You closed this case with a bang, sweetheart," he said. "For your first case, this is pretty impressive stuff."

"Yeah? Even though I pepper-sprayed myself and everyone around me?"

"Especially because of that. You thought on your feet, you kept everyone alive and took the bad guys down. Though I'd prefer you didn't get so close to them if you can avoid it."

"Yeah, I'd like that, too. It was scary."

"Good."

"How so? I'm not supposed to be afraid. What kind of fraidy-cat P.I. am I going to be?"

"Fear keeps you safe. Makes you aware and helped you get out of this situation alive. Go with that."

It was what she needed to hear, and the tears that poured out now were from everything bottled up inside as she wrapped her arms around his neck and let it all out.

"So I can cry like this and still be a P.I.?"

"Absolutely, but only with me," he said gruffly, handing her another tissue from the stack the EMT left.

Tiffany didn't know what to make of that, and didn't want to ask here on the street, police and other personnel still all around them.

"I'd love to get cleaned up. And I'm starving. I have a ton of leftovers at the house—want to come share them with me?"

"I can't think of a better Thanksgiving meal...." he said, and went to find their ride.

Tiffany's head was swimming with the events of the night, the way it all ended, and most specifically, what Garrett had meant when he said he needed her. That he had gone looking for her.

Her heart was almost too afraid to hope, but after what she had gone through that evening, she knew she was at least going to take her chance to tell him how she felt. What she hoped for. If it was thrown back at her, well, those were the breaks.

They were quiet in the squad car on the way back to her apartment, except that Garrett didn't stop touching her for a moment. Not for a second.

"Ramsey said they'd get your car and have it brought back here," Garrett told her on their way up the stairs.

"That was nice of him," she said, glad to be home. She was exhausted, sore and starving. Her eyes and skin felt almost normal, just a little irritation remained, and she sighed contentedly as she stepped back into her apartment.

She had to admit, it felt a whole lot better with Garrett here with her than being alone, as she had been earlier.

The look on his face told her they had to talk, but she took a deep breath, needing time to decompress.

"I have to get in the shower. If you want to heat up the leftovers, they're in the fridge," she said, not quite making eye contact as she busied herself with winding her fingers together.

"You take your time. I'll handle the food," he said, leaning in to tip his forehead against hers, their noses just touching, before he left to do just that.

Tiffany did take her time. She followed the EMTs instructions to a tee, and emerged cleaner, fresher and unable to stall for one more second.

All the time, she wondered what Garrett wanted to say. She knew what she wanted to tell him, but suspected that what he was going to say was going to hurt a lot more than the pepper spray.

At least he was going to be honest with her, she told herself, and she respected that.

Right.

Putting on her most comfortable yoga pants and a soft sweatshirt and fuzzy slippers, she didn't figure she needed to dress up for leftovers and being let down gently at four in the morning.

Padding out to the front room, she blinked in surprise.

The coffee table in front of her big leather couch was set with a pretty linen that she recognized as her grandmother's—Garrett must have looked for it in the kitchen cupboards. There were candles, plates and wine glasses with a bottle of chilled champagne that she had been given last New Year's as a gift, but had never opened. She'd almost forgotten it was in the refrigerator, as she hadn't had anything to celebrate in a while.

Garrett came in, carrying two plates heaped with turkey, stuffing, mashed potatoes, gravy and cranberry sauce, and her mother's secret recipe butternut squash.

Tiffany's mouth watered for the food, and for the man carrying it. He looked delicious as well, his button-up shirt casually undone at the top, his jeans fitting just right as she let her eyes travel the length of him down to his bare feet. Even the man's feet were sexy, she thought.

"Hungry?"

"Definitely," she said, willing to put food before any conversation for the moment. Back at the scene at the bar, she'd felt far braver about telling Garrett that she was falling for him. Now, she just shoveled in the Thanksgiving goodies and watched as he poured the champagne.

Garrett Berringer sure knew how to break up with someone in style, she thought.

He handed her a glass. "To the conclusion of your first big case, and to many future ones," he said.

She smiled, accepting the praise. "Thanks. Though no more pepper spray, ever."

He laughed, and they finished their plates, talking about nothing more than how wonderful the food was, and in truth, after her close call, Tiffany thought it was probably the best food she had ever had in her life. She'd be sure to tell her mother tomorrow, but would leave out the bit about the close call.

"You okay?"

"Yes, thank you. Much better."

"Pie?"

While she welcomed the chance to delay the inevitable a bit longer through food consumption, it was probably better to get this over with. Then she'd have the pie to herself. Comfort pie.

"No, I'm full. That was even better than when we had it at dinner earlier," she said, trying to sound casual.

"It was. Being captured by bad guys will kick up the appetite," he said with a smile. "Among other things."

She blinked as he took her hand, wrapping it in both of his. He was so warm and strong; she loved when he touched her.

"Like what?" she asked, holding her breath.

"Like getting your head on straight. When I left you earlier, I know things were…awkward."

She sighed. "I know the score, Garrett. I know that—"

"You don't know how crazy I was when I couldn't get to you tonight, or how my heart almost stopped when I heard those gunshots," he interrupted. The look in his eyes robbed her of any doubts.

"I can guess. I know how hard it must be, given what you've been through, and reliving everything from before," she started, her heart squeezing. She wasn't sure she could bring herself to think about how much he still loved his late wife.

"No, that wasn't it. That might have been the case when I dropped you off. I was worried if I could do it again, if I could risk losing someone again…especially given your work. I told myself I couldn't, that it would be a mistake to set myself up for that kind of pain again," he admitted, breaking her heart a little more, but she was determined to do the right thing.

"I know. I understand. I can only imagine how awful—"

"But then I was pacing around my hotel room, alone. Lonely. I've been lonely a lot, and I thought I had gotten used to it, until I met you. You made me feel alive again," he said, tightening his hold on her hand.

She heard the past tense, and braced herself for what was coming next.

"And I realized that while I could lose you, or you could lose me, it was a stupid reason to not be together right now. I was miserable thinking about being without you, and no matter what the future holds, I want to have every single moment with you that we can have."

She blinked, unsure she'd heard what she thought she heard. "You mean, for the rest of your vacation?"

He shook his head. "No, for the rest of my life, if it works out that way. I don't want to put that kind of pressure on you, but I'm so in love with you, Tiffany, it hurts," he said roughly, and Tiffany stared, unbelieving.

Had she come home, fallen into bed, now dreaming? Was she in a hospital somewhere, unconscious, imagining this?

"You love me?"

"Totally and utterly. I know it's only been a week, but I know. I know what I feel, and I know I'd be miserable without you. And whatever time you need to make up your mind, that's fine, I just needed to tell you—"

"I love you, too," she said on a gulp of breath. "Totally and utterly."

It was his turn to stare, clearly astounded, and she laughed out loud, pushing up onto her feet to fall forward, tackling him, bunny slippers and all.

"I love you, Garrett. I want every exciting second together we can have. Family, crime-fighting, whatever… All of it. With you," she said, making sure he understood.

"Oh, honey, that and more. Much, much more," he said, his tone a promise as he wrapped strong arms around her and took her mouth in a kiss so consuming her entire body felt on fire for the second time that evening, though this time was a lot better than before.

"I've always wondered what it would be like to live in a place that has real winter," she mused as he worked his strong hands under her shirt. "Maybe I'll get to find out in time for Christmas."

He pulled back, looking at her closely. "Are you sure? You want to uproot away from here, come back east?"

"Do you think Berringer Bodyguards might be able to hook me up with some cases? Have some connections you could ask for a few favors for a new P.I. in the area?" she angled with a smile, undoing his buttons as well.

"Absolutely. But I can stay here for as long as you like, so you could be sure."

"I'm sure. Christmas in Philadelphia sounds wonderful," she said, unsnapping his jeans with a naughty wink.

"And this is the best Thanksgiving ever," he said, sliding the shirt up over her head.

As Tiffany explored him with her hands and her lips, thoughts of their future together swirling around in her mind, she was very, very grateful indeed.

Epilogue

ELY BERRINGER HELD his breath, slicing forward through the strong current of the Caribbean waters as he pushed through his twenty-fifth lap along the beach where he was staying. One of his buddies still enlisted in the U.S. Marines was on a long tour in Iraq, and had offered the small, remote beach house in Antigua to his friends whenever they needed it.

Ely had needed it. Away from the touristy areas, the small house had few amenities, no close neighbors and challenging waters right outside the door. It was perfect.

Completing ten more laps, he finally started to feel the loose-limbed, warm exhaustion in his muscles that he sought every morning. He'd run later, after he did some fishing. He liked to catch his own dinner.

He'd followed that routine for the last ten days, without fail, and finally some of the restlessness that had sent him here in the first place was starting to ease. He'd slept through the night before, a rare luxury.

Emerging from the water, he paused, surprised to find a few bikini-clad women standing on the beach—his beach—watching in admiration.

"You ladies lost?" he asked as he grabbed a towel from a branch, wiping the salty water from his face.

"We saw the truck and thought Adam might be here," one said, stepping forward and holding out a hand. She was gorgeous—perfectly tanned, curvy in all the right places, and nearly spilling out of the scant bikini she wore. "We have an open invitation."

"Sorry, he's lending me the place for a while. He won't be back around for at least another six months."

"Don't apologize," she said, smiling as she took him in. "We're not at all disappointed."

Ely smiled faintly; the offer was clear in her tone.

But he wasn't interested. Burned by love, sex—or whatever else you wanted to call it—twice inside of one month, he needed time to think, to get his head straight.

"Sorry, I have plans already. But I'll tell him you came by," he said with a nod, turning his back and heading to the house before they could say anything else.

He was here to avoid distractions, and those ladies were born to distract. When he'd come home from Afghanistan a few years earlier, he thought he knew what he wanted. To be back with his family, and hopefully to find someone, get married and to start a family of his own. That was what he was supposed to want, right?

Finding out that the woman he thought he could have that with was already engaged—after she slept with him— had been the first error. Ely had never cheated on anyone—anything—in his entire life, and nothing had made him feel lower than finding another man's ring in the desk drawer after he climbed out of bed with the woman who was supposed to be wearing it.

Falling into bed with the next woman who crossed his path had been the second error. A bigger one, since she was also the best friend of his new sister-in-law, Tessa.

Lydia Hamilton was the goth, tattooed temptress who ran the business next door to Tessa's. Ely had fallen into her bed within hours of meeting her and lost himself there in ways that he had never done before.

Ways that included satin ropes, handcuffs and letting Lydia see a part of himself that *he* hadn't even known existed. He had liked it, but he'd also been…exposed. Made vulnerable in ways that he hadn't ever done before. And unable to get it out of his head, until he'd figured out why.

He'd been thinking about things all wrong. Looking at relationships as long-term commitments, possibly getting married, settling down.

Why was he so eager to tie himself down? Lydia was a free agent, living her life that way, and that's what had really affected him. So, he was turning over a new leaf, leading his life the way he wanted. Just as soon as he could figure out what that was.

But the one thing he knew was that he wasn't getting involved in any long-term commitments anymore. Not until he was good and ready—ideally many years down the road.

Pulling on shorts and a shirt, he grabbed his fishing gear when his cell phone chimed—unusual, as he didn't often have enough signal for calls here. It was Tessa. He clicked in, immediately concerned—Tessa would have no reason to call him unless Jonas wasn't able to for some reason. Though his brother had gotten his sight back a few months ago, and was hale and hardy as far as they knew, they all worried about a relapse, though the doctors said it wasn't likely. Still, brain injuries were unpredictable.

"Tessa, what's wrong?" he answered.

The connection was scratchy. He could hear her speaking, somewhat, and roamed the house, stepping outside onto the patio hoping for more reception.

"Tessa, I can't make everything out.... Give me the key words," he said, agitated that he couldn't hear her. For the first time, his self-imposed isolation didn't seem like such a great idea.

"Something wrong...worried...your *help*."

Ely growled at the phone, the message so broken up that was all he could get, but he hoped Tessa could hear him even if he couldn't make out all of her words. He had enough to know he was needed back home.

"I'll be on a plane tonight," he said, and cut the connection.

Putting his fishing gear back, he dressed, packed his bag and headed toward town to the airport. Vacation time was over.

* * * * *

VIRTUALLY PERFECT

Many thanks to Cara Summers, from whom
I've learned so much. Your insight and good humor
added so much joy to the writing of this book!

For my husband, Mike: technical consultant,
brainstorming partner and the love of my life.
You're everything to me.

1

NORMALLY, RAINE COVINGTON would've enjoyed a stroll on a snowy evening. Though Salem was renowned to tourists as "Witch City" for its gruesome persecution of women and men accused of witchcraft, the town had more than the history of its witch trials and occult legends to offer. It was a quaint New England coastal town, but in many ways it was also a developing metropolis.

She'd always felt comforted by the homey, narrow streets and historic Federal-style homes huddled up against each other. Right now, however, she couldn't enjoy any of it. She was too preoccupied figuring out some way to escape Jerry Donnelly who was by her side, nudging into her suggestively from time to time. She clenched her jaw, didn't say a word and walked a little faster.

Jerry was a freelance graphic artist she'd met at an office lunch given in appreciation of freelance workers. He'd seemed nice enough then. Yeah, *nice*—they were all "nice" until they were trying to slide their hand up your leg under the dinner table. He had beachboy-blond hair and soft, brown eyes that gave him an innocent look that she'd found attractive. It hadn't taken much time alone with him to discover that he was anything but.

When he'd suggested dessert-to-go so they could enjoy it in more interesting ways, she officially called time and asked to go home. Who the heck suggested something like that two hours after meeting someone on a first date? Well, apparently Jerry did. And she had the feeling he didn't take rejection easily.

They were finally here. On the sidewalk in front of her house. The porch light warmed the step, and she gazed at the brick-red door wistfully—escape was so close at hand. Jerry moved closer, going in for the kill, and Raine, trying to avoid a confrontation, did the only thing she could think of.

"Oh, God!" She doubled at the waist and held her stomach hard, contorting her face in what she hoped looked like a very painful expression. Startled, Jerry stepped back.

"Um…uh…what? What's the matter?"

She threw a little heavy breathing into the mix, and winced up at him, backing away slowly. He started to follow, but she held a hand out, motioning him to stay away as she inched toward the porch.

"Oh, Jerry, I'm so sorry, but I have to get inside quick. Something bad… Stomach cramps… Night!"

"But you seemed fine a moment ago…."

His voice trailed off behind her. Without a glance back, Raine closed the door behind her with a blustery sigh of relief, leaning back against it as if the devil himself were on the other side. It wasn't her most elegant escape, but at least it had worked.

Resting her head against the door, she let the emotions roll over her. Annoyance, relief—and, ah, there it was— disappointment. Her familiar friend. All she wanted was some good company, a little romance, and, if she was lucky, halfway-decent sex. When it came to men, those things were getting increasingly hard to find.

There was only one man whom she missed when she

didn't get to see him after so much as a single day. Only one who popped up in her thoughts and made her smile, and who didn't disappoint.

Rider.

Not even bothering to change, she grabbed her laptop and plopped down on the sofa, a soft shiver of anticipation taking the edge off an otherwise miserable night. The screen glowed, and she tapped at the keyboard, hoping she hadn't missed him.

She hadn't! He was there! He saw her log on immediately. She smiled wider, watching his words appear across the screen. He had been waiting. For her.

"Hey, beautiful, I thought you might not be by tonight. Working late?"

"No, was just out for a while."

"Hot date?"

"No. Boring, boring night."

She lied, not knowing exactly why she didn't want to tell him she had been out with someone.

"Nilla, maybe it's time to spice it up a little."

"I think we have been quite spicy enough lately."

Nilla—her pseudonym. She hadn't been able to think of anything else when she had registered on the site, and had been eating vanilla cookies at the time. So much for her creativity.

"Oh, I don't know. Depends on your taste. I like things a little on the hot side."

She grinned, her fingers racing over the keyboard.

"Hold on, tiger. Let me get a glass of wine and change into something more...comfortable. I'll be right back."

Jumping up off the sofa, she headed into the bedroom to change. She had been talking with Rider—not his real name, of course—online for a little more than a month. They had met online at RomanceMUD, an interactive virtual world. She'd been researching internet romances for her most recent column in *Real Woman* magazine, which was just hitting its stride as one of the leading women's magazines in the U.S.

Over the last decade, she had literally grown with the magazine, which had recently relocated to a bigger and more prestigious building overlooking Salem Harbor to house its ever-expanding staff, now topping two hundred. She'd started as a freelance writer right out of college. The job had really just fallen into her lap and she took it for some income while figuring out what to do next. Then as more and more magazine pieces came her way, she discovered a knack for writing; she loved the work. Eventually she was hired for a permanent position.

She was the head writer for the Lifestyles beat, which covered everything from raising children to fashion. She provided editorial input and was deeply involved in planning each issue's content. She hired freelancers for most of the articles, but the core element of the section was her relationships column. It had begun as an advice-type column and had blossomed into longer pieces of social commentary. She wrote about all kinds of relationship issues, including friends, siblings, marriage, sex, same-sex families and working parents.

Pouring herself a glass of merlot, she thought about how

some things never changed: jealously, passion, misunderstanding, loneliness.

Since more and more readers were writing in with questions about internet romance, she'd pitched a series of columns exploring love and sex on the internet—and here she was right smack in the middle of it herself.

She had started off the series by writing about internet dating services that had emerged over the past two or three years. Plenty of people used the formal services, but since the majority of her readers had "just met" someone online, she'd been wandering through chat rooms and virtual erotic playgrounds to see what she found "out there."

Raine had joined the RomanceMUD site on impulse, and there she'd met Rider. They'd clicked immediately. With him, she felt that little hint of something special she had been missing with the men she'd dated.

Padding back to the sofa, she sat, lugged her laptop up close to her and stared at the screen. What was he doing right now? What was he thinking?

She was coming to understand more and more about what attracted women to men on the Net. She and Rider talked about everything. They shared intimate fantasies without the disappointments and expectations that often plagued relationships. He could be intense and romantic, and he was always amazingly sexy. It was a compelling combination.

She was sure that in real life, Rider, like all men, probably left the toilet seat up and his beard shavings in the sink. He would make promises he didn't keep and would glaze over when you talked about things that mattered to you. Online, she didn't have to worry about any of that. If she wanted to, she could just hit the off button and he would be gone. The perfect man.

He had started out being part of her research project. An experiment. But things had changed, and she felt that they were becoming, well, close. They talked every night, long discussions that kept her up into the morning hours. She was starting to feel as if she knew him, and he her.

Their online talks were always varied. Sometimes it was casual conversation; sometimes it was very *intimate* conversation. At first it was awkward, writing out her innermost feelings on her laptop's screen. But then it became more like they were weaving their own little world. As if she was the heroine in her own romance novel. She didn't have the chance—or the nerve—to be as bold, funny or daring in real life as she could be online. But here, all inhibitions were lifted without risk. What could be better? She shook her head briskly, shaking herself out of her thoughts, and typed.

"Hey, sorry I took so long. I'm back. So, have you thought about joining up with another game?"

"No, I think I am done with that for now—this was just a whim to keep me amused while work was slow. I think I would rather take a dip into reality for a while. How about you?"

Grunting in annoyance, she had hoped he would drop the issue, as she'd obviously ignored it several times before. Another infuriating male trait—if it wasn't what they wanted to hear, they refused to get the message when it was offered loud and clear.

Rider had been hinting about taking things to the next step, referring to real life a little too often, and she wasn't big on that idea. However, she knew from her previous research and interviews that this was also the key moment that came about in every internet romance: should we or shouldn't we? Fish or cut bait. And she had no idea what to do.

"Still there, Nilla?"

She typed a smile into existence for him.

"Yes, I'm still here. Just caught up in thought. Sorry."

She watched the words appear on the screen that glowed in the darkness of her room.

"What are you thinking about?"

"About being a 'whim that has kept you amused while you have been at work.' I think my ego just dropped a few notches."

"The game was a whim to keep me amused at work. You are something else entirely."

"Oh, and what would that be?"

Nilla held her breath as she sat back, sorry she had asked that question, but it had just flown from her fingertips.

I smooth your hair from your face, and look in your eyes. I slip my hands up the back of your shirt, and rub your bare shoulder blades, then pull you closer to me. "I don't know, I am still trying to get a handle on it myself. But it's something special. I'm intrigued by you. That doesn't happen too often, for me at least."

Raine sighed and closed her eyes. She never would have believed it if she hadn't experienced it herself. It was amazing how erotic, how amazingly vivid the words could be, typed across the screen. There was no sound, yet she could hear each word as if he was whispering it in her ear.

She felt her back arch a little as if she really was being pulled closer to him, and she imagined she could feel his warm breath on her face. Then again, maybe she had just gone without real sex for so long, lame as it usually was, that she was like tinder to a spark—even a virtual one.

JACK SAT BACK and waited to see how she would respond to his request. *C'mon, Nilla, sweetheart, talk to me.* He couldn't get over the effect this woman had on him. He was hypnotized. He hadn't understood why for weeks he would rather be here, sitting on his sofa with a beer and a hard-on, typing pages and pages of conversation, having virtual sex and whatever else they came up with, instead of going out and bringing home a real live woman who could do more than just get him completely hot and then leave him to take care of it by himself.

He was getting impatient with the whole situation; it wasn't his usual style. Nothing about this was his usual style. He wasn't a party animal but he'd had a healthy social life that had gone to the dogs lately. He liked to go out, meet women, hang with his friends and have a good time. He hadn't been with anyone exclusive in a while, but maybe that was because he was spending way too much time sitting in front of his laptop. His pal Greg had called him to go out twice in the last two weeks, and he had made excuses. He said he had to work, when the truth was he really didn't want to miss time with Nilla.

He muttered to himself, "I must be crazy. Getting desperate in my old age." Of course, thirty-four wasn't exactly ancient. The lines appearing on the screen erased his thoughts.

I am sighing as I press into you. I pick up your shirt at its edges, peel it up over your skin, up over your head, and nestle my face against your chest, sucking on your skin, biting you lightly.

Jack sighed, feeling a surge of arousal. Hey, he was human. Having a woman say things like that was the next best thing to being there. The next best thing. But not the best thing. He ignored the doubt that was chipping away at him, and started to respond in kind, when another line appeared, and then another...

I slide my hands down your stomach and wrap my fingers around your erection, squeezing and stroking, loving the feel of you in my hand. "Rider, I want you.... I want to make you crazy...."

He felt his heart pound and shook his head, surprised that this was affecting him so deeply. He had been using online networks before most people knew networks existed. His dad had helped him build his own computer, and he'd "talked" to people on the old, slow FIDOnet bulletin boards in the eighties when he was just a kid.

He had literally grown up with the internet, and it had always been a part of his life—but it had never, ever, been like this. This was a whole new world, a different kind of reality. His jaw clenched as he pounded out the words to her.

"You've made me crazy every night, and a good part of every day, for weeks now. I want you to make me crazy for real, Nilla. I want to do the same to you."

Nothing. The cursor hung like heavy silence between them.

"Hmm, Rider. Are you okay? You don't seem like yourself tonight."

Jack shook his head and ran his hands over his face. It was all he could do not to track her down in real life. During the day, he would think of her, something they'd shared, something she'd said, and feel immediately aroused, which wasn't always convenient. When he wasn't losing sleep, he dreamed of her at night. Of knowing her. Finding her.

He was an internet security expert. He certainly had the skills to find her, to get past the pseudonym and find out who she really was. Hell, at his level of expertise, locating her wouldn't even be a challenge. Even though they used generic emails with pseudonyms, it was a simple matter of finding her network address, locating her service provider and making some phone calls.

What most people didn't understand in the miraculous age of the internet was that the most common method of hacking wasn't done with computers, but by finding out the information you needed the old-fashioned way: talking to people who could tell you what you needed to know.

Most people were afraid of putting their credit card number online, but didn't think twice about handing it over to a waiter who disappeared with it for five minutes. It never failed to amaze him, but those curious social and psychological traits made his work interesting. Computers, he knew, were all about the people sitting in front of them.

A few keystrokes, a few casual requests, and he could know who she was, where she lived and worked, and probably anything else he wanted to know, in just a few hours. But he wouldn't do it, though he damned his sense of ethics to hell. His job was to enforce the rules, not break them himself. Though he was desperately tempted.

"Nilla, baby, I am in knots. That's the problem. You tie me up."

"We could certainly try that, if you want."

Jack nearly broke into a sweat. She could do this to him just with the words. What would the reality be like? There was some kind of wild connection between them, though he didn't know how it happened, or what to do about it.

He reached down, slid his hand over his crotch, felt the stiffness pushing at the seam of his jeans and dropped his head back, the sharp edge of need burning through him. But this time, it just wasn't right. He was sitting on his sofa in the dark. Again. Alone.

No. No more of this.

This wasn't what he wanted, how he operated. It just wasn't enough anymore, not nearly enough. He sometimes felt as if he lived in front of the screen—it was where he worked, kept up on current events, had his morning coffee and sometimes his dinner—but he was damned if he was going to have his sex life there, too! He typed, impatiently this time.

"Nilla, I want to meet you. We need to meet. For real."

"Not a good idea. I could be fat, bald and seventy-five years old, for all you know."

He let out a heavy breath. She was trying to deflect him. Disappointment doused arousal as he realized she wasn't as avid to make that connection as he was.

"Nilla, we're two healthy adults who are driving each other crazy and then ending up in bed alone every night. I want to kiss you. I want to stop imagining and pretending. I want to see what color your eyes are. What's wrong with that?"

"I don't know, Rider. We don't know each other well enough. This is just a game. I like it this way."

"It stopped being a game a while ago. For me, anyway. Think about what we could be missing."

"Like I said, it could be all lies, Rider. How can we know? We are creating a kind of fiction here, right? That's what this place is for, not truth. But at least here we know that outright. Why do you want to complicate this?"

"Have you lied to me, Nilla?"

He held his breath for the few long seconds the screen remained blank.

"No, but I haven't told you the truth, either. You don't really know anything about me. Not really. I don't want you to know."

"What I know is that there is something in you that speaks to something in me. I know you are smart, funny and passionate. I know your politics and your beliefs, but I don't know the shape of your face, the scent of you, the sound of your voice. And I want to. I didn't go looking for this, for you, but now I can't settle for words on a screen."

"Hold on. This is getting too intense, Rider. I need to think."

Jack's shoulders slumped and he rubbed his tired eyes, shoving the computer back on the table. He wandered into the kitchen to get another beer. He had pushed the issue, and he was going to lose her. Though he felt ridiculous getting all worked up over a name on a screen, that idea really hurt.

RAINE CLOSED HER EYES and let out a frustrated sigh. Since they'd never even mentioned meeting in person, they'd openly shared their thoughts and feelings, developing a high level of intimacy fairly quickly, something she had never actually had happen in a so-called normal relationship. She wasn't sure she believed it could happen in a normal, real relationship.

She had never known a man could share this way, communicate feelings and thoughts the way Rider did. It certainly had never happened to her. If he was like this in real life... She blew out a breath and dropped her head back, amazed at the possibilities. But that was unlikely—this was fantasy. In real life, everything would be exposed, all the faults and awkwardness, all the things that got in the way.

She wished she could meet a man who would not leave her hopes in shambles, but she couldn't bring herself to believe he really existed. She steadied herself, and wrote carefully.

"Rider, you're right, this has been special. And if we meet, it might all just evaporate in a big cloud of disappointment. Here we can say, do, be anything we want. We get to be larger than life, but in real life we would probably just bore each other senseless. Or worse."

"I don't think so, Nilla. And what if we didn't? But so what if we did? What's to lose?"

"I don't know, Rider. I don't want to lose this. I enjoy what I've had. You. Here."

"Nilla, this is not real—we're just two strangers sitting in front of a computer every night, having to face being alone when the screen clicks off. I want to know you. I want you to know me, for real."

Raine felt a dark cloud of frustration descend around her as she read his next words.

"We have to meet, or I'm out. I'm done."

She gaped, the ultimatum slamming into her like a hard, cold wind.

"I have to think about it, Rider. Please, I have to think. I'll meet you here tomorrow night and we can talk about it some more, okay?" I kiss you softly, press my lips to yours. "Goodbye."

"Wait!... Don't go..."

She turned the computer off, ruthlessly cutting the connection.

Collapsing on the soft cushions, she groaned in frustration—this night was just not going well. She had always looked forward to these times with Rider. Meeting him had made her typically quiet evenings exciting.

Though physically it *was* difficult to be so consistently aroused by someone who could never be there to actually help you release those passions, for her it had been wonderful just to be able to *feel* them—to walk around basking in the glow of it, to dream of it at night, and to be blissfully unafraid of the pain or disappointment that inevitably followed when you dared those things in real life.

Though she didn't feel so great at the moment. It was distressing to realize that this wonderful interlude she had discovered and enjoyed was coming to an end. He wanted more, and she did not believe there could be more. She would not be meeting Rider the next evening, for talk or anything else. He would not stop pushing her, and she knew she would not hold out against him in the long run. And that would be an awful mistake.

She knew exactly what she had to do to get some distance on this situation, to grab control of it and put it behind her. First, she could never meet with him again, obviously. Next, she had to write about it. She had experienced internet romance, right? She had faced the tough decision, and she had made it. Now it was time to share what she had learned with her readers. Only then could she move on and forget all this. Hauling herself upright, she grabbed her laptop again. She opened a blank word-processing page and went to work.

2

"WELL, THIS ISN'T a bad start, but we need more."

Raine resisted the urge to roll her eyes, and stared at Duane, her managing editor, straight in the eye. She liked him, though grudgingly at times such as now.

"I need to add in the research, get some outside interviews. That should round it off. This is just the first draft, obviously."

Duane nodded and set the draft of the article she had been up nearly all night writing on the desk between them. She could've had his job if she had wanted it, but she liked being a writer. Duane was a good manager, and oddly, he seemed to enjoy it.

He was twenty-eight, almost four years younger than her, fresh out of graduate school, and on the job for a year. He was cute in a frat-boy kind of way, with shaggy, dark brown hair and bright blue eyes. Half the women in the building were gaga for him. Raine just couldn't work up that kind of enthusiasm, though she had come to respect him as an editor.

He had one of those low-key, soft-spoken, intensely focused personalities that could be deceptive at first. But when the chips were down, or when he wanted things to go his way, he would wield his will like a sword. So far, he'd kept the ship on course, and skillfully managed a diverse group of writers at the magazine. But at the moment, Raine wasn't in the mood to be managed.

"C'mon, Raine. You know as well as I do what you have to do here to make this article pop. The real meat of it is in the move from online to real life. You need to meet him. This is too good to pass up. See it through."

She just glared, and her voice was stiff and caustic when she spoke. "Is that an order? Just how far would you like me to take this, Duane?"

"I'm not saying you have to marry the guy, or do more than have a cup of coffee with him. But you have already invested all this time in establishing a connection with him, right? And how can you answer the questions that are facing readers if you haven't really put yourself in their place?" His eyes narrowed thoughtfully, and she resisted the urge to squirm under his gaze.

"This isn't a real romance, is it? You have chalked this up as research?"

She closed her eyes and thought of all she had left out of the draft—if only Duane knew the connections she had "established" with Rider. She'd left out most of the intimate material and had written up the experience as a light flirtation, a dalliance. She wasn't about to expose the reality—or herself—like that for the sake of a column. But deep down, she knew that Duane was right, and just for the moment, she hated him for it.

She nodded. "More or less. But he is a nice person, as far as I know, and you can't just play with people's feelings, Duane. He's not just a lab rat for the article."

Nodding again, Duane quirked an eyebrow.

"If the safety aspect of it is worrying you, we can help

with that. I don't expect you to go out and meet some creep by yourself."

"He's *not* a creep." She felt a headache fuzz her thoughts. "At least, I don't think so."

"Okay, but that's what we need to know. And what you need to find out." He picked up the draft and handed it back to her. "You pitched this, you make it work. Meet the guy, then take another stab at it. This could be a killer story, Raine, but you have to see it through."

"I THINK HE LOOKS LIKE Superman." Gwen sighed dreamily, watching a man who stared intently at a computer on a desk directly across from them.

Raine snorted and put sugar in her coffee. "That's Jackson Harris. I think everyone calls him Jack, though. He is the ultimate in computer gurus, from what Duane says. Been here about six months."

Raine didn't add that the new guy seemed to have taken a dislike to her on sight, for reasons she couldn't fathom. He seemed friendly enough with everyone else, but gave her the cold shoulder. The few times they'd crossed paths he hadn't even returned her hallway acknowledgments. So she'd stopped offering them. She only knew his name because he had been introduced to everyone upon his hiring.

"He's a computer geek—that would make him a lot more like Clark Kent, right?" Raine didn't bother holding back on the sarcasm.

Gwen stuck out her tongue. "Kent *was* Superman—and those dark glasses he always wore were so sexy. Anyway— that guy would look great in a tight blue bodysuit. How the heck did I miss him? This place is hiring one buff guy after another, first Duane, now Jack. I love working here."

"Please. Spare me."

Gwen just shrugged and continued to watch Jack work. "So what's the news on Jerry?"

Raine rolled her eyes and leaned back against the kitchen counter in the employees' lounge at the end of the hall. The staff often worked late hours, especially on a deadline. Having a full, stocked kitchen available was one of the luxuries that made the company worth working for.

"It was ridiculous. Terrible. He was like a dog in heat— it was crazy, I don't think I did anything to lead him on. In fact, quite the opposite."

"Yeah, the buzz is he wasn't all too happy about it, either. Did you guys argue?"

Raine expelled a disgusted breath. Word traveled fast. Jerry must not have bought the stomachache defense. Oh well.

"No, no arguing. But I was barely able to eat because I had to keep stopping him from mauling me under the table at the restaurant. He couldn't even hold a conversation. Everything—and I do mean *everything*—had to come back to sex. And it wasn't just talk, he has hands like an octopus. So, when we got back to my place, I pretended I had to throw up to escape the good-night grope. Or worse, him wanting to come in."

"Hey, that's a new one! I don't know if he bought your excuse though."

"Yeah, well, whatever. I have a whole repertoire of techniques to get away from men at the end of dates. I'll scratch that one off my list."

"Maybe you should be thinking about things to do to get them into bed at the end of dates."

Raine snorted. "All I would have to do to get Jerry into bed is breathe. There's no point."

Gwen's jaw dropped in shock. "Wow, you really have

forgotten, haven't you? Jerry aside, orgasms are the point, girlie!"

Raine sipped her coffee and muttered over the top of her cup, "Really? I've never known a man who thought so."

She turned and headed back to her office. Gwen followed, slipping into Raine's office before she could close the door.

"Gwen, really, I have work…"

"Whoa—hold on. Are you trying to say you have *never,* you know—that you haven't had…"

"An orgasm. Yes, I have. Plenty. Just not with a guy." She sighed. "They haven't got the faintest clue. I mean, I don't want to have to tell someone what to do. Women shouldn't have to come with an instruction booklet."

"You should use that line in a column. Clever." Gwen grinned.

"Yeah, right. Sometimes I wish I was a lesbian, maybe a woman would be better at it. That's my curse—I'm stuck with men."

Gwen sighed and dropped down in the cushy chair in the corner of the office, ignoring the impatient looks Raine was sending her way. When Gwen was intent on a visit, there just was no stopping her.

"Oh, now, it'll happen one of these days. But, geez, I can't believe you are, what…thirty-two?" She ignored the glare Raine shot at her. "And you haven't had one tiny tingle with a guy? I guess I can see why you don't want to bother anymore, but you know you have to keep on trying. Sitting at home in front of your computer certainly isn't going to help things any."

"I never should have told you about that. Let's just drop it. That whole thing is coming back to bite me in the butt now, big-time."

"Why? Are things going downhill? Is the prince turning into a frog?"

Raine sighed and knew Gwen would not go away, and she would not be able to get any work done until she dealt with it.

"No. I don't know. Rider's getting too pushy, so I ended it. I wanted it over with." She sat back, staring out the window at the dark gray clouds forming in the sky over the shops lining Pickering Wharf's crescent-shaped streets. "But Duane, in his ultimate wisdom, doesn't want it over with. He says the article won't fly unless I 'see it through.'"

She screwed up her eyes and did a shabby Duane imitation on the last three words. "But I don't want to see it through. I want to see it over."

"Why? The computer guy sounds hot from everything you've said."

"Yeah, well, he wants to meet, and I don't want to— end of story."

Gwen pursed her lips and considered that for a few seconds. "Maybe you should meet him."

"Are you in cahoots with Duane? Why on earth would I want to do that?"

"Maybe he would be the one to, you know…"

"Gwen, it can't all be about that. And most likely, it wouldn't happen. Hot online and hot in real life are two entirely different things. Besides, my luck isn't exactly good lately."

"How can you know that until you meet him? You two seem to have such chemistry. I talk to lots of people online, you know I have all my pagan discussion groups, and we have a good time, but it's not like anything you have been describing."

Raine sighed. "Well, yeah, I didn't count on it, it just

happened. If we meet, all of that chemistry could go up in smoke."

"So then, what do you have to lose?"

"Now you sound just like him."

"Well, you know, I don't think you should just dismiss it. You don't have to get serious, but you can, you know, just take him for a test drive, so to speak. All in the name of research." Gwen's naughty grin almost had Raine's own lips twitching.

"Not my style, Gwen, you know that. I'm tired of test drives. I think I am just going to take a break from men for a while."

"You have been on a break from men for about ten years, by the sound of it. You need a man—a real one—who can flip your lid, so…"

"…to speak, yeah, I got it, Gwen. Stop."

The warning tone made Gwen sigh and shake her head at Raine. Raine watched her pop up from the chair and felt a twinge of envy. Gwen was intelligent, quirky and an annoyingly eternal optimist.

As the main health and fitness writer for the magazine, Gwen had a body that wouldn't quit and a lively attitude that drew everyone to her. She and Raine should not have been compatible at all, but they'd become very close over the past few years. Gwen changed her hair color weekly; right now it was platinum-blond with some red and green streaks for the holidays. Thanksgiving had just passed and Christmas was only a month away. Gwen was all sparkly. Raine supposed Gwen made everyone who came into contact with her feel a little sparkly, too.

Today she was slinking around in snug black leggings and a fitted black sweater. She wore at least a dozen silver pentacle earrings and little jingle bells on the toes of her short, stylish boots. It didn't surprise Raine one bit that Gwen mixed her Wiccan jewelry with her Christmas decorations—Gwen celebrated everything—and at least the jingle let you know when she was coming.

Men tripped over each other when Gwen walked by, not that she noticed. "Love 'em and if it's good, love 'em some more and see what happens" was Gwen's philosophy. She just tripped through life and "trusted the universe"—as she was always advising Raine to do. And she was a good friend. Suddenly Raine felt like queen bitch. Expelling a heavy breath, she tried to make nice.

"Gwen, I'm sorry, I'm just frustrated with Duane and this whole article thing and I want to get it over with and—"

"No problem, sweetie. I have to get back to work, too. Oh, crikey—he's coming this way!"

"Who?"

"Clark!"

Raine puzzled for a moment and then saw Jack Harris appear in the doorway. He would make a lousy Clark Kent, was her first thought. His hair was not black, but more of a chestnutty auburn, and his eyes were not blue, but brown. He had a good build: tall, lanky, muscular and thin. Like a cowboy.

She frowned; he wasn't dressed for the office. True, the magazine had a fairly relaxed dress code, but Raine valued a professional appearance. Jack did not look very professional in tight jeans and a black cotton, button-up shirt. His hair was a little too long, curling around the collar a bit; he needed a haircut, she thought. No, he did not resemble Superman one single bit. He said something but she missed it, and blinked at him, returning to the moment.

"Hmm?"

"I need to look at your computer. It will only take a few minutes."

"Why?"

"Routine. We've set up a new security system and need to make sure everything is working."

"Well, okay." She rolled her eyes at Gwen, who was unabashedly checking out his butt as he walked into the office. As Raine passed by him to get to the other side of the desk, she couldn't help but notice that he smelled great, like sand and sea.

She looked up, and locked glances with him, then tilted her head a bit, narrowing her eyes and studying him intently. She froze on the spot. Something itched at the back of her mind but she couldn't reach it. Something familiar. His eyes cooled and took on an unfriendly edge that made him look decidedly un-Clark Kent like. He cleared his throat.

"Excuse me."

She raised a dismissive eyebrow and slid past, following Gwen out the door.

"God, isn't he *hot?*" Gwen gave a dramatic little demonstration of being weak in the knees as she walked down the hallway.

Raine blinked. "Jack? I guess. Though there *was* something about him… I think I have seen him somewhere, but I'm not sure."

"Well, it's a small town. You may have seen him around before and just not thought about it."

"Yeah, maybe. There was something about his eyes. I just can't figure out why he seemed vaguely familiar."

"Oh well, you'll remember. Anyway, okay, back to Rider—I think you should meet him, just for kicks."

Raine rubbed her temples. "Gwen, I think I am getting too old to do things just for kicks."

"You're thirty-two, not eighty. Not that being eighty should stop you, you know, if you were. Just imagine, if he is even *half* of how you described him online in the flesh—so to speak."

Raine could imagine. Imagination wasn't the problem; reality was the problem. It never lived up. But still, what if it did? How could she ever know if it was worth the risk? She heaved a sigh and looked back down the hall toward Duane's office. Even if she didn't want to meet Rider, she felt outvoted by people who wanted her to do it. But what did she *want*?

"I need to get back to work. I guess I have some major revisions to do on this article."

"Okay, well, but think more about meeting him, anyway—it could be the chance of a lifetime."

JACK SWORE PROFUSELY at the computer as he tapped keys and compared what he was seeing on Raine Covington's computer to what he was checking on his laptop. Something just wouldn't take and he couldn't figure out why. He changed the setting on the firewall—the device that kept the network safe—for this particular computer, and it would click off again the minute it rebooted. That just shouldn't be happening.

He was going to have to take a deeper look to find out what the bug was. It would take some time and digging. Usually this was the part of his job as Network Security Administrator that he liked best—prying open the mysteries of the wires, swimming down into the information flows, right into the nervous system of the machine, and figuring it out. He could get lost in there for hours, forget to eat, and not care.

But now he felt the pressure of time. The last thing he wanted was to spend more time in Raine Covington's office, so he would have to come in during the evening or on the weekend. It galled him how she had looked at him as if he were a bug on a microscope slide, and then dismissed him like one, too. It even bothered him that it galled him—everything about her was annoying.

He'd remembered her right away when he had seen her name on the employee list. She, apparently, did not recognize him. That was really not a surprise, but it was what rankled most, in spite of himself. Some things you carried with you, whether you liked it or not.

She'd barely noticed he was alive when they were in high school together, though he shouldn't take that too personally—that was how she was with everyone. He'd thought she was the most beautiful girl in school, but her personality was far from attractive.

Living in a mansion in an exclusive neighborhood in the Connecticut countryside outside Essex, she rarely socialized with anyone at the school, and in fact, looked miserable most of the time. She obviously detested coming to school with the common folk. It hadn't been a slum, for God's sake—Eaton Marsh was a well-respected private school.

He had first noticed her in their sophomore year. He had watched her, considered talking to her, practiced what he would say—had a mad crush on her. She was beautiful then; she was drop-dead gorgeous now. But she had the same imperious attitude—that had not changed.

His parents weren't anywhere near as wealthy as hers. They worked hard maintaining a small bed-and-breakfast in Essex, and it was a life they enjoyed. He had been raised in a home that was open to visitors nine months out of every year, and he'd loved it. His parents were warm, friendly people who'd encouraged him to interact with the visitors at the inn, who were often treated more like family than guests. Through those experiences, he had developed confidence and social skills that many young people lacked. None of it was enough to deal with the likes of Raine Covington, though.

But it was a small world, and now here they were again, and still, when she looked at him, she just saw through him as if he wasn't even there. At least he didn't have a crush on her anymore. Though he did feel a little rush of heat when she brushed past him—she was incredibly soft, and smelled like heaven. Flowers and citrus. He closed his eyes and shook his head. She may be a snob, but she was a gorgeous one.

"Is there a problem?"

He snapped his head up, eyes wide-open at her voice. She stood directly in front of the desk, watching him closely.

"A small one. I'll look into it later."

"From the way you were sitting there shaking your head, it looked like a lost cause."

He stared at her then, and he felt something pull deep down inside his stomach. Emotions crowded in, confusing him. How could he still want her after all these years? Because he wasn't blind, that's why. God, she was hot.

Idiot. He didn't want her—he didn't even know her. It was Nilla, his phantom online lover, who had his head, and his hormones, all worked up. Raine just happened to be there, a warm body for him to focus all his frustration on. Nothing more.

"Yeah, I guess you could say that."

"So it *is* serious? I have a lot of work on that computer— I can't afford for it to die on me. It's been acting up lately, so if you could see that whatever is wrong is fixed, that would help."

"It won't die on you," he said. "Just a minor security problem that has nothing to do with everyday functioning. We'll figure it out another time, but I will have to get back into your computer."

Her lips pursed, and he realized how much those delicate, arching eyebrows contributed to her expressions. At the moment telling him she was inconvenienced and displeased.

"I have an article due soon, I can't afford to have these problems keep coming up, and I will be working long hours in here—"

He cut her off, his voice cold. "Don't worry, I won't interrupt your very important work, Ms. Covington."

She couldn't miss the sarcasm, and she felt heat stain her cheeks. He was angry, and she had no idea why he should be. Maybe he was just having a bad day, or was generally rude. Maybe that's why they kept him in the basement, she thought with a little sneer. She wasn't sure she cared, but right now she wanted him out of her office.

"Fine. Thank you. That's all, then." She dismissed him curtly with those few words and went to move around her desk, when she ran into him again, directly on the spot she had bumped into him the first time. She made a mental note to move her desk over so she could widen that space.

Now he narrowed his eyes, pinning her with a glare. "If you want to be formal, *Mr.* Harris is acceptable, and if you want to be friendly—although I can't imagine it—then it's Jack. Jack Harris. But don't talk to me like I'm one of the servants of the manor, Ms. Covington."

He was taken aback to see those cool green eyes flare, and for a moment he was curious to see what would follow. Had he finally gotten a rise out of the cool Raine Covington? Then he saw the puzzlement, and the searching—it was amazing how you could see the mind functioning behind someone's eyes. She whispered his name, more to herself than him.

"Jack Harris." She shook herself, and blinked. "I'm sorry." She diverted her eyes, looking down. "I just thought maybe we had met before."

"No, I can safely say we've never met."

He had just watched her from afar; they never *had* actually spoken. Right now, this minute, he found himself closer to her than he ever had been, practically pressed up against her slim, soft form twice within an hour. He shifted a little, trying to slide by, and it just happened that his shoulder brushed one of the soft mounds under her sweater. He saw her eyes widen, and felt a little jab of heat himself. Looking down, he saw a nipple bud tightly beneath the soft material, and felt a masculine surge of satisfaction. Oh, yeah, she definitely noticed he was there.

"Um…" She was flustered, he noted, and trying to move past. Getting a grip, he ignored his moment of insanity and walked around to the front of the desk.

What had gotten into him? Sheesh, she would have him up on charges of sexual harassment, and she wouldn't be far off the mark. He also felt…guilty? Shaking his head again, he knew he had made the right decision about meeting Nilla or breaking it off. Now he was actually feeling guilty about having a response to another woman behind the back of his virtual lover? This was ridiculous. He had to get his life back. He had to have sex. With a real woman. Clearing his throat, he modulated his voice to be cool and professional.

"What kinds of other problems have you been having?"

"I came in on Monday, and for some reason, all my article files had been erased. I had backups of most of them, but it put me behind because—"

"Where did you have them stored?"

Bristling at his interruption, her eyes went glacial.

"I always keep my active folder on the desktop, so I can have quick access to it."

"Maybe you deleted your files by mistake. Folders and files don't usually delete themselves."

"No, they don't. But neither did I. Something happened, and they were gone."

He sighed. It was never anyone's fault when something happened to their computer. "Anything else?"

"Yes, last week I could barely get anything done. My computer kept freezing up, and was very slow. I had to keep shutting it down and restarting. Then it just snapped out of it and was fine."

"Sounds like minor stuff. Probably won't happen again. I'll send a tech up to look at it later."

With that, he gathered up his laptop and walked out of the office, leaving her feeling abruptly dismissed. Raine sat down in her chair and let out a breath it seemed she had been holding the entire time he had been in the office. What a strange conversation. Why did he dislike her so much? And why had her body leaped in response to such a casual, accidental touch? It was horribly embarrassing, especially with him.

She tried to forget it. Maybe he hadn't even noticed. He was in no small hurry to get out of her office, so she wouldn't have to worry about it again. Shaking off the uncomfortable feeling, she checked her inbox, and saw the email pop up on her screen. From Rider. No subject line. Opening it, she saw only one word.

Please.

The decision to meet Rider was becoming a vague possibility in her mind. She kept trying to push down the sense of anticipation, of hope that this time—this man—could be different, but it kept emerging, especially after talking to Gwen. How could she use this as research when she was so obviously losing her objectivity? What if he *was* just the way he was online? Could she do this? Should she? Her stomach fluttered thinking of it.

What if meeting him turned out to be a total bomb? What if he was crazy, or even worse, married? But in her gut she knew neither one would be true. He would be great. And she would be…well, she wasn't exactly chopped liver, but she also wasn't the adventure girl that she had come across as online. In fact, far from it.

But she had always thought, with the right man, someone whom she could open up with, someone who would care, maybe things could be different. Maybe *she* could be different. At the worst, the spark would fizzle when they actually met, and that would not be a tragedy.

All in all, she led a pretty normal, sane and sometimes boring life. Could she live up to the sexual fantasies they had shared online? Her sex life had ranged from mildly interesting to nonexistent.

But maybe it wouldn't even come to that. All she had to do was meet him. That was all.

Her readers had been sending her tons of similar questions and stories about their internet romances and how to handle them. And now here she was, like so many of her readers, wondering what to do. Take the chance? What was life without a little risk, right? How could she ever really know unless she took the leap? She would just control the risk, make sure things didn't go any direction she didn't want them to go. Maybe. Maybe she could risk it. One more time.

JACK SHOOK OFF his aggravation, catching a coffee at the cafeteria and heading back downstairs to the Batcave, as they affectionately referred to the subterranean floor of the office building.

He tried to ignore the anxiety of wondering what Nilla was doing at this very second, what she was wearing, if she was thinking of him, if she was considering making *them* a reality.

The incident with Raine only had his body more fired up, and he hoped something would happen soon, or he was going to have to dig into his address book, which he was loath to do. They were women he had dated, and whom he liked. He wouldn't feel right using one of them to work off the hots he had gotten from someone else. It was more likely he was facing several weeks of cold showers until he got over this.

Never again would he get involved in an online love affair. It was just too hard on the body. He slid a furtive glance at his email. He couldn't believe it, but his heart actually flipped when he saw an email from her. Sent only moments ago.

He stared at it for a few moments, then opened it. One word.

Okay.

Hot damn! He thought his face would split from grinning, and all of his aggravation was lost in a consuming sense of anticipation. He was caught unawares by the person standing behind him.

"Uh, sir? Sir?"

Jack spun around in his chair, realizing he probably looked as if he had won the lottery, and not really caring. One of his guys, Neal Scott, was standing in the doorway behind him. Taking a breath, he got his excitement under control and put his professional face on, though he couldn't quell the buzz of anticipation that was running through his blood.

"What's up, Neal? Sorry, I just, um, just got some good news."

"Oh, that's good, sir."

"Please don't call me sir, Neal. Jack is fine."

"Okay, um, sir, Jack. You asked me to stop by to look at the security bug you were dealing with."

Jack watched the young man in the office. Neal was a great worker, and a nice kid, if a little shy. Jack knew he was in his twenties, but there was just something about him that made him seem much younger. Neal kept to himself a lot, but Jack had been including him more, trying to draw him out a little, and it was working. Neal was loosening up a lot, and had even gone out with a bunch of them a few times.

Jack liked the kid and thought he could really be an asset to the company. Hell, Neal seemed to do nothing but work—he had been in his office most of the weekend, which Jack had seen when reviewing the security logs.

He was smarter than hell, too, but he didn't have much confidence, and was generally overlooked by management. So, Jack had been giving him some more challenging jobs, bringing him along slowly. He pulled a chair up and gestured for Neal to sit down.

"Yeah, take a look at this. It's been giving me a headache all day."

Neal squinted behind the thick, black-framed glasses he always wore and read the screen full of numbers and symbols quickly and with interest.

"Yeah. There. I see it. Might be a worm."

"I've tried to close it down about ten times, but it keeps popping open. You are a much slicker programmer than I am, can you work on it?"

"Yeah, sure."

Neal got up to leave and Jack shook his head.

"Hey, Neal. I see you were here all weekend?"

"Um, yeah." Neal creased his forehead and then pushed his glasses up.

"I appreciate initiative, and you're doing a great job—but don't get burnt out—there's more to life than work."

Neal nodded, and headed to the door.

Jack sat back and flipped the email from Nilla back on-screen, smiling broadly again. He knew he wouldn't be spending *his* weekend at work. With any luck, he would be spending it making a fantasy come true.

3

RAINE DASHED THROUGH her apartment door and almost dropped the pizza she'd grabbed on the way home. She was giddy with nerves. She didn't want to think about why the change in her decision to talk to Rider tonight had such an effect on her mood. After all, she was just going to talk to him. If anything didn't hit her right, she would call it quits and that would be that. She would remain in control of the situation.

Forgetting the pizza on the entry table, she made a beeline to her computer and logged on. Connection time was slow, and she jittered on the sofa, wiggling her fingers in the air over the keys, going crazy waiting for the screen to tell her she was ready to go. "C'mon, c'mon!... There, good!"

A few quick keystrokes and she was in. She looked at the list of players logged in, and his name was not there. Damn!

She fell back against the cushions, closed her eyes and let out a frustrated breath. It was only seven; it was early yet. She thought about the pizza, but wasn't hungry now. She put a hand over her eyes. Was she crazy? Maybe it was better this way; maybe she had made the wrong decision.

This could be her reprieve. Then she peeked through two fingers and sneaked a look at the screen, smiling widely.

"Wake up, hot stuff. You beat me here. Your email made my day." I kiss you warmly.

Raine watched the cursor blink, and felt as she typed that every line was rewriting her life in ways she couldn't even imagine. She hoped it was for the better.

I kiss you back. "You're pretty easy to please."

"Generally. But you seem particularly good at it."

Raine held her breath, and typed, before she could change her mind.

"We need to talk more about what we want out of this whole thing."

"Well, how can we know until we meet? Maybe nothing, maybe we end up married with five kids, who knows?"

Raine felt her jaw tense, and responded bluntly.

"You see, that's it, Rider. I don't want a house and five kids. I don't want anyone pushing me. That is why I'm not sure this is a good idea."

"Okay, well, I wasn't proposing marriage there, just saying that we can't possibly know what we want, or what this will be."

Raine pressed on, screwing up the courage to say what she really meant.

"Yes, we can—we can say what we want it to be, we can say what we will do, and what we won't—what things are possible, and what things are not. So there are no unreasonable expectations, and no one gets hurt."

"Okay, not getting hurt is good. So you want rules?"

"I suppose…sort of. Yes."

"What rules do you want?"

Raine considered, and typed slowly.

"All right. First of all, maybe both or either of us may not be interested right away. At that point, maybe we have a nice dinner and part ways."

"Okay, I'd say that's a given."

"And if we do like each other, if we are just as attracted as we are here, we can just let it be what it is—it doesn't have to get weighed down with all the emotional baggage, promises of forever."

"Nilla, are you saying you only want to have a no-strings relationship?"

"Are you saying that you wouldn't be interested in that?"

Jack sat back and thought. What was she offering him? No-strings sex if they hit it off? Or was she saying it could never lead to anything else? Something itched at the back of his mind, and he turned cautious.

"Nilla, are you married? Or involved in some way that would keep you from having a committed relationship with me?"

"Oh, no...no! Geez, Rider, do you think women can't pursue simple, uncomplicated lives? I am just saying, you and I can avoid messy emotional entanglements. Because we have met here, and we have already shared so much... I just think we should be clear about our expectations."

Jack considered that. He wasn't in love with her, he knew that. But he was intrigued by her, and he thought there was more than sex going on between them. Less than love, more than sex. Something in between. That seemed to be what she wanted. He wasn't going to look a gift horse in the mouth. He wasn't looking for commitment, either, though he was open to the possibilities.

"I think I understand. We can see if we are even attracted to each other, and go from there, gorgeous."

"You don't know if I am gorgeous or not. I could look like a frog."

That had crossed his mind. He didn't think so, but no matter what reptile, bird or fish she might resemble, if she could do half the things to him in real life that she could online, it would be worth finding out.

"Mmm. I like frogs. Especially their legs. Very tasty."

"Well, then, I suppose we have to talk about this, set something up?"

"I guess for starters, what is your real name, Nilla?"

"Let's not share too much here—we can find out names and those kinds of details when we meet. Tell me what you'll wear, so I can recognize you. We can meet at a restaurant or something. Plus, I may bring a friend, if you don't mind."

Jack felt a stab of disappointment, but realized she was going by the book, and he was glad for it. It was smarter not to share names just yet or share any physical details about herself. Anyone could easily locate you that way, or simply go about prying into your life.

"Sounds good. I'm thirty-four, about six foot, one-ninety, and I'll wear jeans, a brown leather jacket and a Red Sox cap. That's pretty much what I wear everywhere. Friends are fine. Maybe I'll bring one, too. Your turn."

Raine stared at the screen and felt her mouth go dry, her imagination filling in the rest of the details. So far, this was sounding very, *very* good. And he hadn't balked at meeting in a public place, or with friends—that was a good sign. Then she laughed.

"Okay, well. I just turned thirty-two last month. I don't know what I'll be wearing, but I'll put a rose in my hair, so you'll know me that way."

"When? Make it soon."

Raine smiled at the sexual intensity he could communicate in so few words, and began to feel a deep sense of anticipation soak into her, right to the bone.

"Yes, soon. But I don't even know where you live. Red Sox cap? Are you in the northeast?"

"Yep, live north of Boston. On the coast, just below Gloucester."

Raine practically fell over in shock. They were neighbors! She'd figured he was in the same time zone because they were always online at the same times, but she hadn't thought he would be that close. That could end up being either a very good—or a very bad—thing. For now she would go with it being good.

"Hey, looks like we're neighbors. I live in Salem, a bit of a drive, but not too far."

"Less than an hour's drive. I commute to work every day, so that is no problem at all. I can leave now, be there by ten."

Raine felt her heart pound and almost told him to come.

"Tempting as that is, I think we should wait. But this makes it more convenient, at least. I'm glad. I thought you might be far away."

"It wouldn't matter. I would come anyway."

Raine shivered and took the leap.

"How about this Saturday night, seven, at the bar in La Luna, on Pickering Wharf. It's a nice place but not too formal. Great food, if nothing else works out."

"Okay. Let's make it six—we'll have a drink before dinner."

Raine watched the words travel across the screen and could hardly believe it. They were going to meet, to really meet. *In person. For real.*

I stare into your luscious brown eyes. "Okay. So, in three days we'll know."

I pull you close to me. "It seems like forever. Are you sure you don't want me to drive up tonight?"

I run my fingers through your hair. "No, I am sorely tempted, but this is probably a better idea. And remember, it is just dinner—we can opt out at any time."

Jack knew it was the right thing, though he was so hot for her he could barely imagine not touching her, or making some of what they had shared a reality. But she was providing an out for him, too. Just in case. And when he got there, if things were good, who knew what could happen? He had a feeling about this; he was willing to just go with it.

"Agreed. Just dinner—unless you beg me to go back to your place and engage in illicit activities."

"You never know. Maybe it will be you doing the begging."

Jack smiled. Desire raced through his blood and flowed through his fingers out into the words.

"I'd beg for you, Nilla, you can count on it. I'd like to drop to my knees in front of you, kiss your feet, taste the skin on the back of your knee, and then work my way up, slowly, taste you, run my tongue over you until you come with my mouth on you, until we are both begging. And that's only the beginning."

"Um, I am not sure this is a good idea...."

Raine swallowed, and tried to focus as her breath became shallow. The hunger she had been feeling for weeks was suddenly a little frightening. This wasn't a game anymore; it was real. He was real. They were going to sit across a table from one another and have dinner and talk, and all that while they would both be remembering the secrets that had passed between them. She closed her eyes and tried to settle herself.

"Why not?"

"I don't think we should really discuss this, considering..."

"Nilla, tell me how you feel, how your body feels right now...."

Raine tried to think, and quell the heat pounding through her bloodstream. She wanted to back off, and knew she should, but sheer desire weakened her. She knew what she wanted, and reached down for the courage to ask him for it.

"Rider, your number. Give me your number."

"What?"

"Your phone number, Rider, tell me. I'll call you. I need to...hear you."

Jack was shocked speechless as he contemplated her request. No, not a request, a demand. The idea of actually talking to her stole his breath, and he didn't bother thinking about it, but just responded.

"Oh, yeah, sweetheart, yes. Here."

Jack typed in his cell phone number.

"I'll call you in a little while. I just want to shower and change out of my work clothes."

Work clothes? He smiled knowingly, pure masculine satisfaction pooling in his heart. She had come directly to find him. He acknowledged her message, and signed off.

His house was suddenly incredibly still and quiet, and he could hear his own heart pounding. The wind howled outside the windows, and minutes slowed down as if he was drugged, the feeling of waiting for the phone to ring weighing down on him. God, she had taken him by surprise.

She was changing. She was taking a shower. He closed his eyes and imagined the hot water running over her naked, soft skin. Then she would put on…what? His imagination nearly drove him mad. By the time the phone rang, he had imagined her in everything from black dominatrix leather to pink lace—and then in nothing at all. His mind went still. He pressed the talk button, and was relieved to discover his voice actually worked.

"Nilla."

Raine thought for sure she would pass out just hearing him say her name—well, her screen name, but the same difference. Low and smooth, it slid over her like hot lava, and she tried to sound calm in response.

"Hey, Rider."

Her voice was like whiskey, hot and golden. He closed his eyes and let it ease over him for a moment before speaking again.

"It's much like I imagined it would be."

"What's that?"

"Your voice." He settled more comfortably into the chair, and smiled into the phone. "When we talked online, sometimes I imagined I could hear you, but the real thing is a million times better."

Raine smiled. "It is. I love hearing you, too." She took a deep breath, trying to calm her nerves. "This is pretty intense."

"Something tells me it's about to get even more intense, Nilla."

Raine felt weird being called by her pseudonym, and almost caved to the temptation to tell him her real name, but held back. That could wait. For now, this was good. She laughed, and almost didn't recognize the husky, sexy sound of her own voice.

"Could be."

"Um, Nilla, not to be too cliché, but exactly what did you change into?"

She laughed. "Rider, are you *actually* asking me what I am wearing?"

He laughed, too, a warm, husky, *sexy* laugh.

"You bet I am. You can't leave a guy hanging like that and not expect him to go half-mad with wondering. Tell me, Nilla."

Raine looked down, and nervously smoothed her hand up and down over her thigh.

"It's no big deal…. Usually when I get home from work I shower and change into my comfortable clothes."

"Tell me about them."

Raine smiled, and shook her head. This was crazy. She had thought calling him might add the edge of reality and stem the passion that was quickly getting out of control online.

She couldn't have been more wrong. Voice to voice, they were spontaneously combusting. She took a breath, and spoke, feeling a little silly, but pressed on anyway, remembering that Nilla would have no problem responding to this request.

"Flannel pajama shorts and a top. Cushy socks. Not exactly Victoria's Secret, but soft, warm and comfortable."

Jack chuckled, intrigued by the thought of her cuddled in flannel, the cotton sliding against warm, soft skin, clean and smelling of soap and powder. The slight edge of shyness that came through her voice made him want to break through, to make her lose control and tell him what he wanted to hear.

"I wish I could smell you. I want to slide my hands along your skin, touching you. I want to know what secrets you are keeping under that flannel."

Raine felt rather than saw the flush work its way over her body, his voice setting off pins and needles of passion on her skin. She tried to speak normally, but her breath caught, betraying her response.

"Rider, I think we should just talk, we probably shouldn't…"

She could almost see his naughty grin as he spoke. "That's what makes it so much fun, Nilla. Forget the shoulds and shouldn'ts for a minute. Just relax. It's just me—Rider. Do something for me?"

"What?"

"Touch yourself—and tell me what you feel."

Okay, stop the bus!

She was not prepared for this! Nothing in thirty-two years prepared her for this onslaught of what she *wanted* to do, which was completely in conflict with what she didn't know if she even *could* do.

He was asking her to share something wildly new, and for her, something incredibly daring. It had been easy online. This was different. Way different. She closed her eyes, and couldn't think of a single way to respond. He spoke again.

"It's all right—we'll go at whatever pace you want. It's just that you are driving me crazy. The sound of your voice."

"Me? What did I do?"

"Nilla, don't you know? You turn me inside out." The words ground out of him and shocked her—frustration, desire and control that came across clearly in his voice made Raine feel a bit faint. "Just hearing your voice has me close to coming, all I would have to do is touch myself. God, Nilla, tell me you want me to."

Raine squeezed her eyes shut and almost dropped the phone, fumbling to catch it, and wished she had bought the speakerphone she had seen on sale a few weeks earlier. She was in a sexual twilight zone, nothing was real, and everything seemed to be magnified, every touch, every sound, every thought.

She pictured him as he existed in her imagination, sitting on the other end of the phone, needing her, wanting her. Fear and feminine power warred in her mind, and in her heart. She took a deep breath, and she let herself slide out of reality.

"Yes. Yes, Rider, I want you to touch yourself, to make yourself come. I want to help you, to be part of it."

Jack slid one hand under the thick cotton of his robe, and let his head fall back on the chair as he slid his fingers over his swollen penis, rubbing his thumb over the dew that had accumulated at the head. He squeezed, sucking in a sharp breath, slowing himself down before it was all over too fast.

"Tell me, Nilla, talk to me… I'm aching for you.…"

Raine turned off her light and quickly slid out of her clothes. She didn't—wouldn't—think about this. She just wanted to experience this moment of absolute letting go. She slipped back on her bed, not needing the covers. Her body was white-hot and ready to go. She felt awkward as she spoke, but just said what she felt.

"I'm naked, Rider, I took my clothes off, and I'm on top of my covers, thinking of you and what you are doing. I wish I was touching you. I wish I could wrap my hands around you. Slide my mouth over you. I want to taste you."

She heard no words in response, just a masculine groan of appreciation. Still a little unsure, but encouraged, she continued.

"I'm touching my knee, running my fingers over the hollows in the back. The skin there is smooth, and so amazingly sensitive…. Up the inside of my thigh… I'm so hot, Rider, I'm wet already…just thinking about you, what you are doing…."

"Jesus, Nilla, I want you, baby, please, I need this, don't stop…."

"Tell me what you want, Rider, tell me where you want me to touch, where you would touch me."

"Lick your fingers, make them wet, then run them over your stomach. Think of me kissing you there."

She did as he said, and arched up toward the little paths of fire that danced along her skin, imagining his touch.

The small, kittenish sigh that traveled across the line made him smile, and he refocused, running his hand over himself slowly, imagining her hands, and what they were doing, what he could make them do.

"Nilla, cup your breasts, your beautiful breasts. Are they aroused?"

"Oh yes, Rider…. Oh, that feels so good. I want to come…. Come with me…."

"Hey, not so fast," he purred into the phone, gaining

control from her loss of it. "We have time.... Roll over on your stomach, Nilla."

Almost drowning in swells of excitement, she mindlessly rolled over, and set the phone on the bed. She rested her head on the receiver, freeing her hands.

"There, Nilla?"

"Mmm-hmm."

"Good.... The blankets are so soft, so warm from the heat of your body. Imagine me, Nilla, behind you—I want to rub myself on you, slide my cock along where you're melting for me. Do that, Nilla, touch yourself there, and think of me pushing inside, sliding into your heat. I'm so hard, so damned hard for you. I wish I could be inside you, Nilla."

He was quickly losing the ability to talk at all, spurred on by her increasingly passionate sighs and moans. He heard her chanting his name into the phone, and pumped himself harder, faster, feeling the blood pool in his lower stomach, his body going taut as he neared the edge.

"Nilla, now... Stay with me.... I'm almost there, Nilla!"

She had never been so gloriously lost in her life, consumed by the voice on the phone, the hands on her body that barely seemed to be her own. She could only think of him, his voice, his hands, somehow at once bringing himself, and her, to pleasure, and she slid her fingers inside herself, finding the sensitive spot she knew would send her over, her cries filling the room and traveling over the line to touch him on the other side.

"Rider, yes... Oooooh! Oh, God..."

Jack nearly dropped the phone as he listened to her give in to the throes, his taut body bowing as he fell sharply into his own release.

Raine smiled, listening to his guttural, animal sounds, wishing she could see his face right at the most intimate moment. She basked in hearing him lost in his own orgasm as the pulsing warmth of hers receded. Lying in the darkness, spent, her heart pounding against the softness of the cover, she murmured gentle encouragements, just sounds. His breath was still labored, then slowed; he was saying her name into the phone over and over again. Her body cooled, and she pulled the covers up over her, turning onto her back. She couldn't stop smiling.

"Rider?"

"Mmm. Nilla. Not quite back yet, sweetheart."

She smiled, and kicked her feet on the bed a little, feeling amazing and powerful and feminine. Her body felt wired and relaxed simultaneously, and she couldn't believe she had just had phone sex—really, really amazing phone sex. She laughed delightedly, making him smile.

"What's so funny?"

"Nothing.... I just feel so incredible. That was so much fun—I have never done that before."

"Me, neither. You inspire me."

"Maybe we shouldn't meet, maybe we should just do this."

"No way, Nilla—no way are you getting out of this. Not now."

Jack lay back, eyes closed. His body was a mass of conflict, at once sated and yet begging for more—for her, for real. Three more days.

"Yeah. And if this thing works out, Nilla, as they say, you ain't seen nothin' yet."

4

Raine watched Gwen crease her forehead as she studied the tarot cards she'd laid out in front of her on the table. Gwen had arrived at the door to drag her out for lunch. Gwen's hair was freshly colored with purple highlights and glitter eye shadow to match. Raine was just happy the Goth days were over; she preferred Gwen colorful and upbeat.

They sat in high-backed booth seats at a favorite diner overlooking Salem's pedestrian mall, soup bowls and coffee cups pushed to the side while Gwen turned out cards. Raine looked out the partially fogged window, watching people scurrying in and out of shops, rushing to get their Christmas shopping done.

Everything was decorated and cheerful. The sun shone brightly off the snow, almost blinding her with the glare. She was meeting Rider tonight, and the brightness of the day seemed like a good omen.

Gwen insisted on doing tarot readings for her once a month. Raine never so much as read the astrology forecasts in the newspaper, but today she was grateful for the distraction. It was a day for new adventures, and Gwen had shown up with her cards, so now the two sat eating lunch and peering into Raine's immediate future. Raine munched her tuna sandwich absently and looked on.

"So, what's the verdict?"

"First, the Chariot—that figures—he is traveling to see you, that's kind of obvious. But the card is about being balanced, in control. It suggests a sense of purpose and direction. It's a strong card. Maybe a very confident man who knows what he wants, or could be you trying to control the situation, which isn't necessarily a bad thing, just something to think about. And—" she pointed to the next card "—then you have the Ace of Wands—kind of a sexy card, eh?"

Raine peered at the card that showed a club, or tree branch—a very *erotic*-looking tree branch—standing straight up against a sky, surrounded by ivy and flowers, and nodded. Really, it did look like an erection. Or maybe she just had penises on the brain. She shook her head.

"That one's usually about new beginnings, creativity and sexuality. Good sign for getting laid." Gwen grinned and pointed to the next card, which depicted a castle-type building with flames flying out of it, and people being tossed out of the windows into the crashing seas below.

"Hmm, this one might be a problem."

"Looks ominous." Raine wiggled her eyebrows dramatically.

"Can be, but it's more about life shaking us up, throwing us on our asses when we need it. There could be something really unexpected that will happen tonight. Could be good, or not so good. You had better just keep your radar sharp."

"For what? A sexy guy with a big stick and a nice car who is going to surprise me somehow?" Raine smiled naughtily, and Gwen gave a hearty laugh.

"Good one. Let's hope so. Now it gets interesting. This chick here—" she pointed to a picture of a woman standing blindfolded in the middle of a circle of swords "—the Eight of Swords, she is imprisoned by something—see how the swords do not circle her tightly? There are ways she could free herself if she wanted to. The blindfold suggests she may not be seeing things clearly."

"Or maybe it means he is going to blindfold me."

"I never looked at it that way. Hmm…and tie you up…"

"I was kidding, Gwen."

"Hey, I'm not judging—everyone is into their own thing." She ducked as Raine took a playful swat at her, and went on.

"But seriously, the cards can mean different things to different people—it's obvious what's on *your* mind." She grinned cheekily. "Okay, then you have these last three. The Devil is what challenges you—not the devil like hellfire and brimstone, but this card can be a lot of things— obsession, darkness, or being hounded or harassed in some way. The Two of Cups follows, a card signifying what you should strive for, a meeting of the minds, coming together, emotional healing. Finally, the Four of Wands is your destination card—where you could end up—a very nice, happy, successful card, celebrations and accomplishments. Maybe marriage. Kids, you know, the whole ten yards."

"Bite me, Gwen."

"Sorry, I couldn't help myself." She grinned, summing up. "So, the Tower and the Devil are still giving it all a pretty interesting slant, kind of intense—will be interesting to see what *that* is about, though sometimes it is nothing. I draw the Tower every month when I am PMSing." She pursed her lips and looked up at Raine.

"As for the rest, looks like maybe you have some bumps in the road, a few explosions along the way—hey! I wonder if the Tower could be about orgasms? You know, lightning striking? Like getting thrown from the heights and into the waves of passion? I never thought about that—I like it! That would kinda mesh with what you see in the eight."

"Well, it would be nice if you're right about the orgasms." Raine laughed and slid off the seat, thinking about her experience with Rider two nights before. She hadn't told Gwen about that. "But I need to think about what to wear. Come help me, okay?"

Grabbing the check, she went to the counter to pay. Gwen left the tip on the table and followed her out the door into the brisk, bright air. "Okay, what to wear? Exactly how crazy do you want to make him on the first date?"

RAINE SAT on a stool at the bar feeling jittery and unsure. She swirled the little plastic stick around in her Manhattan, her hands cold even though heat from the whiskey had worked its way through her bloodstream and softly smudged her eyes and cheeks.

It was a little after six—this wasn't a good sign. Maybe he had changed his mind, maybe he had arrived, seen her, and just left without a word—he might have considered fantasy a better deal than the reality. She made a point of turning her back to the door. She didn't want to know when. If.

She looked down at her boots, swinging her foot. The soft black leather caressed her calf. The gray wool skirt had seemed sensible and still sexy, warm enough for the weather, exposing just a little leg between midthigh where the top of the boot met her knee. The deep green cashmere sweater was nice but not revealing, at least not in the obvious sense, though it clung to curves in all the right places and had attracted more than one admiring look when she had slipped off her jacket at the door. Gwen said the color emphasized her eyes, making them look like crystal-clear jade.

Raine took Gwen seriously, which not everyone did, at least at first. But Gwen was smart, and she had style. The two women had a deep respect for each other and that had been the basis of their friendship almost from the start. Gwen was really the first close friend Raine had ever had, and Raine thought of her almost like a sister, though she never told Gwen that. She wasn't one for gushing her emotions all over the place. When it came to her own life, she was never quite sure where the lines were between people, what was allowed and what wasn't. So she tried to err on the safe side.

Raising her fingers to the small pink rosebud that was clipped into her hair, she tried not to look at her watch yet again. Her nerves settled, her hopes started to fade, and she felt a little like a fool. Ten more minutes, and she would go home and forget about this for good.

JACK CURSED the weather. The drive had been much nastier than he had anticipated. The winter storm that passed by the night before had cleared out to sea, but it had left the roads slick and dangerous. Everyone was trying to get somewhere for the weekend, and he was caught in one traffic jam after another.

His feet were freezing, and as much as he was looking forward to meeting Nilla—to put it mildly—he was very focused on getting warm. If getting warm with Nilla was in the cards, even better. But for the moment, he was so cold even thinking about that didn't warm him enough. A few miles back, a college student—driving too fast and too confidently for the conditions—had spun off the road into a snowbank, directly in front of him.

The kid was not hurt, but was not getting out of his predicament alone, so Jack climbed into snow up to his thighs to help dig the car out. He lost his beloved Red Sox cap in the wind, watching it whirl away into darkness. Jack sent the kid off again with a growling warning about driving more slowly before he killed someone else or himself.

Though he had managed to brush off most of the snow, his pants were still a little damp. He was tired, hungry, and he seriously needed a drink.

He spotted the restaurant and pulled into the first available parking space. The place was hopping, even at this early hour. He glanced at his watch. He was only fifteen minutes late, not too bad, all things considered. He took a deep breath and closed his eyes, glad to shut the engine off and concentrate on why he was here.

Reaching for the flowers he had brought with him, he shook off the agitation of the drive. His jacket was covered with salt and sludge, so he left it in the backseat and grabbed a fleece he had lying there.

The night was clear and cold, and his heart was thudding deeply in his chest as he approached the restaurant. This was it. In another minute he would be looking at, handing these flowers to—touching—the woman who had been the focus of his dreams, waking and sleeping, for the last month. He steadied his breathing and walked through the restaurant door.

He spotted her immediately, from the back. Seated at the bar, she was turned about three-quarters away from him, blond hair flowing down her back, a pink rosebud tucked sweetly behind her ear. Not white for purity, not red for passion, but something in between.

Jack watched quietly as she leaned forward and laughed quietly with the bartender, who was pouring her another drink. The soft line of her jaw entranced him, and he stared, losing all sense of time or place. He frowned for a moment, feeling a prick of recognition, but ignored it.

He forgot that he was cold, hungry and tired as he took

in the graceful curve of her neck, the slope of her shoulder and the way her hair tumbled down over the womanly shape of her back. He flexed his fingers, imagining wrapping his fingers into it, getting tangled in all those silken strands.

His mouth went dry as he followed the length of her body. She sat saucily on the stool, legs crossed at her very beautiful knees, the black leather boots offering only a hint of leg, making him lick his lips. Thank you, heaven.

The bartender walked away, leaving her with her drink, and he saw her look at her watch, and observed how her shoulders lifted and fell slightly in what must have been a sigh. Taking a deep breath for courage, he stepped forward, quickly covering the space between them.

He stopped and caught his breath when she suddenly spun around and slipped down off the stool, face-to-face with him. He stood stock-still, disbelieving, his brain and body frozen in shock. It was only a matter of seconds, but it seemed like seasons passed. She looked at him squarely.

"Oh. Jack. Hi."

She didn't appear shocked to see him, though she was less than thrilled, obviously. He realized she had no idea that he was there to see her. He didn't—couldn't—say anything. He watched her lean over, grab her purse, then her jacket. She looked miserable. She thought she'd been stood up.

Conflict raged as he realized his out—he could let her think that her date was not coming, and just walk away. But when he saw the disappointment in her face, he couldn't do it. Not that the alternative was going to get a much better response.

"Um…yeah…" He had never been so truly lost for what to say. It was a cruel trick of the universe that the woman he had been dreaming about, sharing such intimacies with—hell, getting off on the phone with—was *her*.

His brain still refused to process this new situation, but as she walked past him toward the door, he spontaneously reached out and grabbed her arm. She turned and looked at him, confused, and maybe a little peeved.

"Excuse me?"

There was only one way to deal with this, he figured. Jump right in. "I'm sorry I'm late." His slightly strangled voice did not sound like his own. He tried to smile, but it didn't quite work.

She looked at him as if he had lost his mind and removed his hand from her sleeve.

"Jack, I have no idea what you are talking about, but it looks like you have a date." She tilted her head at the flowers. "If you're late, you'd better get moving. Good night." She turned toward the door again.

He sighed, and took the leap. "You're right. I do have a date. With you. *Nilla*."

She stopped and turned slowly to face him. He watched disbelief, and then shock, cross her features. She had such an expressive face. Not saying anything, she just stared at him, her cheeks reddening. She dropped her purse, and looked as if she wanted to slap him.

"You! Is this some kind of joke?"

"No. No joke. I'm Rider, and you, apparently, are Nilla."

She just stared, and Jack took her elbow, steering her to the bar again, to sit.

"Let go of me!"

"Fine. This is not exactly what I expected, either, believe me."

She was still too horrified to really hear him or process what he was saying to her—this was the man she'd been sharing her intimate fantasies with? Jack, the guy from her office, was the mystery man she had phone sex with?

Her heart sank into a pit of humiliation. She had helped him have an orgasm over the phone the same day they had exchanged swipes just a few hours earlier in her office! How could this be? He must have known. He must have set her up somehow; this must be an office prank. Her fingers tightened painfully on the edge of the bar.

"Can I get you another drink? I could sure use one." His voice was resigned.

"I don't think so."

"Have it your way."

He signaled the bartender and ordered a brandy, and they both sat there silently, looking dumbfounded. When she spoke, her voice was accusing.

"Why aren't you wearing the clothes you said you would? The Red Sox hat, leather jacket? Were you trying to trick me?"

"Hardly. I had some trouble on the road, lost my hat and ruined my jacket. What do you take me for, anyway?"

"I don't know what to think about this. I mean you… We…"

He watched the emotions play over her face, and felt like a cad, even though he had not done anything wrong. He sipped his brandy, trying to think of what to do next.

"We have reservations. What do you say we make peace, laugh it off and go have dinner? We could at least talk about it. You have to admit, this is one hell of a coincidence."

"I'm going home." She got up, walked toward the door then outside. How could she stay? How could she let him see how devastated she was? She would not—*not*—let a single tear escape, though it seemed as if several thousand of them were threatening.

"Hey, you forgot this." He was there again, right beside her in the parking lot, and she slid a quick look to see him handing her purse over. She hadn't even realized she had dropped it. She reached out for it blindly, feeling the dam behind her eyes burst. She would not let him see her this way. She would never give him the satisfaction of knowing how much she had been looking forward to this. She hadn't even realized that herself.

Jack frowned. He was ready to go wallow in disappointment and beer for the rest of the evening, but the stiffness of her shoulders, the angle of her face—as if she couldn't even look at him—it was just too much.

He stepped around and took her shoulders in a firm grip, turning her toward him. The distressed sound she made concerned him, and he turned her face up to his, surprised to see fat tears streaming down her pale cheeks. She looked so sad it just about ripped his heart out.

She tried to turn away, but he wouldn't let her. He pulled her close against him and rocked her gently. She trembled in his arms, and he pulled back to look at her again, watching as snowflakes fell, melting with the tears that were staining her skin.

Even now, she was the most beautiful woman he had ever seen, and though he didn't want to acknowledge it, something tugged deep inside him. She was his lover, his Nilla, after all.

He spoke, his eyes glued to hers, his voice rough.

"I'm so sorry this is such a disappointment for you, Raine. Really. But it is just a coincidence. I promise. No tricks."

Puzzlement and distress mixed for a moment, and she couldn't take her eyes off his face. Then, realizing her position, she broke away and turned toward the car, but felt his hand on her arm again. Looking up, she saw his mouth set in a grim line, but his eyes were warm as they moved over her.

"C'mere. You can't drive in this condition."

Her eyes widened as she felt the warmth of his fingers stroke her damp cheek, and her mind seemed to disengage in response to the unexpected gentleness; her breath caught. He was very close—how did he get so close?—everything about him was hot, solid and male. His eyes were like magnets.

She heard him say her name as he moved in closer, but it was as if she was in a dream, frozen and unable to move. The flowers he had been carrying all this time fell onto the fresh blanket of snow at their feet. She knew this shouldn't be happening, though somehow it was. She shouldn't be allowing it to happen, but she had been waiting for so long.

His large hand had solidly planted itself on the small of her back, supporting her, pulling her in just a bit closer. Her eyes held to his, and she shivered, though she wasn't cold.

He said her name again, and tilted his forehead against hers, their bodies pressed close, snow swirling all around them. The hand that had been on her shoulder fell to his side and found her fingers, stroked them, then wrapped them in his. Pulling her palm up to lay flat against his chest, their hands pressed between them, he angled his head and lowered his lips to hers.

"Nilla."

She didn't breathe, didn't respond. He pressed his mouth on hers, then just rubbed gently back and forth, not so much an embrace as a greeting. He kissed each corner of her mouth, and she leaned toward him, seeking more. He pressed her closer, and she could feel the hardness of his chest and his heart pounding underneath the fleece.

Of its own volition, her other hand touched his face, passed gently over the heat emanating from his skin. He tested, lightly sliding his tongue along her lips, wetting them. Melting against him, she slid her fingers upward, burying them in his hair as his lips pursued the kiss, nibbling hers, sucking her lower lip into his mouth, teasing it with his tongue. She felt her knees weaken, and opened for him, giving him full access to explore the insides of her mouth, and heard him groan inside of her as the kiss turned scorching.

Never, in recent memory—hell, in her entire life—had she been kissed like this. It wasn't really even a kiss, it was too consuming to be called that sweet of a thing. Her body was burning and aroused just from the crushing of his lips on hers, the feel of his tongue teasing the roof of her mouth, the gentle scraping of his teeth on her lip. God, she was raw, and didn't realize how needy she was.

When he sought her tongue, wrapped his lips around it and sucked it into his mouth, she moaned as she felt herself go hot and slick, knotted and ready. His hands were wrapped in her hair and she lost herself in tasting him. They blended, pressing into each other, stumbling back against the car.

Jack hadn't intended to become so encompassed by the kiss; touch her just once, he had taunted himself, just to know what it would be like, just for a moment. Just to comfort. But by God she was sweet, the way her hands had fisted into his shirt beneath his jacket, and now how they splayed across his chest, fingering his nipple absently, sending waves of desire pulsing through him. He couldn't get deep enough into her mouth…. He wanted to drown in the honey he found there.

After all the time, all the talk, all the imagining, he was desperate for her as he had never been for anyone before in his life. They twisted again, dancing around each other as the snow fell in a thick curtain around them. He found himself pushed back against the car, her lips never leaving his as they switched positions.

She was demanding from him now, meeting fire with fire. He moaned into her mouth, and let her have him, let her have anything she wanted. He smiled and encouraged her as her hands moved down and closed firmly on his butt, grinding him against her until he was sure he was going to come.

He had never been this hot with a woman before, and didn't know it would be so intoxicating. He wanted to forget control and just be consumed. Her tongue lapped at his like a cat with milk, her fingers kneading him, and he wished he could feel more of her flesh against his. He breathed her name raggedly, dangerously close to the edge as she pressed her hip against his straining erection. He pulled back, his voice rough.

"Let's go."

"Where?" Her heart was pounding so hard she could barely hear him, and she stayed leaning into him, afraid her knees would not support her.

"Anywhere. Anywhere we can be alone."

5

WARINESS STARTED to edge into her mind, but he stemmed it, kissing her hard, then pulling her close, his mouth by her ear.

"Just for now, let's forget everything else. I want you. I want you *now*. We've waited too long. Thought about it too much. Just this once. Let's just take what we both want."

Beyond thought, Raine nodded, and fumbled for the keys in her purse, somehow managing with shaking hands to press the button that unlocked her car. He took the keys and opened the door.

"I can drive."

"Listen, you've had a few drinks and no food, and a shock to boot. Just tell me where."

She walked to the passenger's side, numb and on fire at the same time. Somewhere, deep inside her brain, she was thinking something wasn't quite right, and she shouldn't be doing this...should she? But the way he was looking at her when she slid into the car next to him blotted out reasonable thoughts. Never had a man looked at her in just that way—with that hungry, starving, I-want-to-eat-you-alive look that Jack was giving her now.

She wanted him, too. He was right. They had waited a

long time. In an urgent whisper, she told him how to drive to her place, and in a few minutes, like magic, they were there, and she was stepping out into the cold in front of her home.

Everything still had that dreamlike quality, and when he came around the car and took her hand, she closed her eyes, not wanting the spell to break. *Don't think too much—don't think at all—just let this happen.* She felt a sharp tug on her hand, and she was facing him, in front of her door. His voice was quiet, his eyes intense.

"I want you like hell. But I'll give you a chance to change your mind now. I'll go, if you want."

She looked him square in the eye, ignoring any voice in her head that told her one-night stands were not her thing. That she would have to work in the same office with this man on Monday. That she didn't even really know him.

"No. I...I want this, too. I've wondered if...what it would be like to really...know you."

He smiled, quick and sharp, and handed her the keys so she could open the door.

"Me, too." He watched her slip the key into the lock, and felt his breath catch as she opened the door. His body was tight with anticipation, and he could sense her next to him as they stepped into the darkness.

Before she could reach for the light on the table beside the entry, he moved quickly, pressing her back to the door and burying his face in her neck, inhaling her scent, biting the soft skin behind her ear. When she shivered, he couldn't help but moan against her soft, feverish skin.

He moved his lips gently from ear to cheek to lips again, sliding his mouth over hers while he unbuttoned her coat and slid it to the floor. His hands spanned her rib cage, molded her to him, and he bit her bottom lip, sliding his tongue across it before kissing her hungrily. He was so lost in the fog of lust they had created that he barely felt her pushing the coat off his shoulders, her voice husky and suggestive.

"Let's get more comfortable."

He nodded, and stepped away—sensed more than saw her move. Suddenly the light was on, and he briefly noted their surroundings. Comfortable. Homey. Warm. In his passion-fogged brain, something wasn't clicking. Looking around, he tried to figure it out as he picked up his coat and threw it over a chair. But this was not the time for thinking. When he saw her beckoning him in stocking feet, her hair mussed from his hands, her cheeks hot with desire, he could only stare and wonder if this was really happening. She stood next to a doorway across the room—her bedroom, he assumed—and smiled at him.

It was all the invitation he needed. Crossing the room, he framed her face in his hands and worked his mouth over hers until they were both so weak with need they stumbled into the dark room, barely paying attention to where they were going, stopping only when Raine felt the bed push against the back of her knees.

God, Jack felt so good. He smelled so good. She blocked all logical thought and concentrated only on the want, the ravenous need, that was burning within her. *More.* She must have more of him. All of him. Running her hands up under his shirt, she gloried in his hot, firm, male skin, working her hands through the hair on his chest and pushing his shirt up and over his head.

At some point, he worked his own hands up under her sweater, lifting it off, and she heard him moan in male appreciation as his hands moved back down and closed over her breasts, weighing the fullness of them in his hands, pinching the turgid nipples between his thumb and forefinger. She cried out in sheer pleasure as her knees buckled.

He caught her, lowering her gently to the bed. He stood in front of her, taking a moment to unbuckle his belt and slide off his pants, never letting his eyes leave hers.

Raine thought she would melt from the intensity of his gaze. He was beautiful…male, sculpted and just *beautiful*. His eyes were almost black with desire, and she felt the gush of passion between her legs as he stripped in front of her. Her eyes roved over him and lingered on his desperately erect penis. *Beautiful*. The word became a chant in her mind.

She sat up and touched him tentatively, running her hand over his hard length, and then leaned forward to kiss him in that very spot, darting her tongue out for a taste. His breath contracted sharply, and his hands were on her shoulders then, pushing her away gently.

She looked up, and he smiled down at her, his face ruddy with desire, his voice strained. "Do that and it will be over before we've begun. And one of us still has too many clothes on."

She stood, finding herself unbearably close to him, wrapped in the heat that was pulsing out from his body. As if they could not bear to be separate, not even slightly, they quickly disposed of the rest of her clothes, until she was naked in front of him, flesh to flesh. His eyes devoured her as hungrily as hers had him.

"You're like a goddess. You're not even real—you can't be." He touched her hair almost reverently, and she was lost. Sliding back, she sat up on the pillows. Feeling wanton and wanted, she lifted an arm over her head and let one bent knee fall to the side. His eyes fixed on the patch of sandy-blond hair and the wet, pink folds she exposed, and he licked his lips.

"I'm very real. Join me?"

"Oh, yeah."

Then he was next to her, and they wound around each other. Raine ran her hands down his back, exploring the muscles, gripping on to his rock-hard buttocks. She shifted to maneuver his cock between her thighs, then pressed him between them. Jack growled in pleasure, rubbing himself along the silky pocket of skin, and, bracing on one elbow, dipped to draw one breast into his mouth, suckling and teasing her until she was writhing and he could feel her nails digging into his back.

He felt her teeth on his shoulder, and sparks of pleasure sizzled in his brain. Sliding one hand down, he found the juncture of her sex and purred into her mouth as he touched her.

"You're so wet—like hot, wet silk…"

"Jack…please…I want you. Now."

She shifted again, bringing him up closer to where she needed him to be, wanting him inside, but he drew back, his breathing labored, sweat gleaming on his forehead.

"Protection…in my wallet…"

She smiled, and drew him back to her, opening her thighs and cradling him.

"All set." She patted her hip, and showed him the transparent birth control patch. "Don't worry."

He nodded and braced himself over her, rubbing the hot tip of his desire along her wetness, causing her to arch her back in response. She sought him, and he found her, enveloping himself in one deep thrust.

Her eyes widened with a shock of pleasure, and then closed again as small sighs of need escaped her lips. He fisted his hands into the sheets, remembering when he had made her come on the phone, how she had made those same noises then. Her quick pants and needy moans had driven him over the brink then, and they were threatening to this time, as well.

It had been a while, and he knew he wouldn't last long, but he wanted her to share the pleasure with him. Withdrawing slowly, he balanced back on his knees. Then, placing his hands underneath her hips, he pulled her up toward him, moving his hand between her legs. He rubbed her hot, tight nub expertly with his fingers while still shallowly thrusting into her.

Her face contorted in desire, and she pushed forward, trying to take him deeper. He moved up over her, wanting to be next to her when they both fell. Thrusting deeply, taking what they both needed, he increased the rhythm. Sliding his hands up behind her head and into her hair, he whispered to her as he felt his own peak close at hand.

"Come, Nilla, I want you to come with me...."

The dull ache of loss consumed her as she sensed her body's hesitation, an all-too-familiar sensation, and suddenly hot tears spilled out before she could stop them. Unable to stop his body's reaction though he detected the faint change in hers, he poured himself into her, searing pleasure wracking his body.

Catching his breath, he felt her tense beneath him, and lifted himself, shocked to see her crying, her face turned from his.

"Raine, did I hurt you? Jesus, oh, God...I'm so sorry...." He sat up, confused, and tried to gather her to him. She pushed farther to the other side of the bed, and he didn't know what to do.

Raine closed her eyes, humiliated. She was hurting, but not in the way he thought, so she struggled to speak. Her voice, when she spoke, was low and miserable, confirming his worst fears.

"No, no, you didn't hurt me."

He sat up and scooted to the other side of the bed so he

could see her. Her face was turned into the pillow. At a loss, he stroked her hair.

"Then what? What happened? Talk to me…."

She sighed and worked up the courage to meet his eyes. He was concerned, that was clear, so she sought to comfort him.

"It's no big deal, forget it. I'm sorry. I hope I didn't ruin it for you, at the end—" She stopped as she saw awareness dawn on his face, and her humiliation doubled.

"No, no, you didn't ruin anything." As he reached for her, she drew back.

"But it *is* a big deal, Raine. It's important that both of us find equal pleasure and we didn't—something happened there that chilled you—what? Was it something I did? Said?"

Raine sat up, and tugged the blanket up in front of her defensively. "It's nothing, okay? It's nothing you did. I just never come, not like that, so don't worry about it." She offered him a wan smile. "I'm just a little frustrated, that's all."

Jack watched her, her face masking hurt, her eyes shadowed. He remembered how pliant and hot she had been in his arms. This woman couldn't have orgasms? That was hard to believe.

"But that night on the phone, you…?"

Her cheeks went hot. "Yes, that was different."

He nodded slowly, understanding. "You just have problems experiencing orgasm with someone, with intercourse."

She felt like a fool, like a failure, but nodded. A big part of it, she knew, had been that he had not used her real name when he'd spoken to her, but she would burn in hell before she'd admit that to him. It took only that moment to break the spell, to cool the pleasure she was eagerly hoping to attain, just once, with someone who had excited her beyond knowing. But then again, she probably wouldn't have made it anyway—she never did.

She knew it was her long history of not knowing how to open up that was to blame, but she didn't know what to do about it. The thought made her even more miserable. All this time she'd hoped it was the fault of lousy lovers, but she couldn't say that was true of Jack. It was just her.

She practically jumped out of her skin when he shifted over and sat beside her, placing her head on his shoulder. She stiffened and resisted, but then gave in to the comfort of it. Why not?

His voice was gentle, but with some lightness.

"I wish you had told me that. You know, there are things we can do. That was a bit…rushed. I thought you were with me. I'm sorry."

She shook her head. "It was good. Really. I told you, I don't usually even get that excited. It's just me. Really, I'd rather drop it." Her voice took on an edge, but he didn't want to drop the subject, not yet.

"It's nothing to be ashamed of, Raine. A lot of women can't have orgasms that way, but they can have them other ways—have you ever tried?"

She shrugged noncommittally, and wondered why he just would not let the subject drop; the other men she had been with hadn't cared overmuch, but Jack seemed determined to pursue the issue. She tried to sit up, to get some distance, but his arm tightened around her, so she gave up the struggle and buried her face in his shoulder instead, to avoid that penetrating gaze. She sighed against his skin, her tongue darting out unconsciously to catch the salty taste of his skin on her lips.

"I haven't had any adventurous love affairs, sex has been fairly routine, I suppose. Nothing out of the ordinary."

"What has the ordinary been? Maybe we should try something a little *extra*ordinary?" Surprisingly, he felt a warm hum in his loins again, thinking of it. This woman seemed to inspire him.

"Um, no...I'm fine. Really. I think maybe we should just call it a night."

"Well, it's up to you, I suppose. You know what you want, right?"

He turned a little, his face in her hair, and ran his tongue along the shell of her ear, and felt her quiver. Sliding a hand up to her breast, Jack kneaded gently, then ran his tongue from the curve of her ear down to her jaw, hungering for her again. He captured her mouth before she could say anything, and kissed her deeply, seductively.

Raine felt herself float away on the kiss. While it still had the edge of passion—she could tell he wanted her again—he took his time, plundering deeper, not ending the kiss until they were both gasping for breath. He settled her back on the pillows, shifted over her, kissing her everywhere, his breath feathering her sensitive skin.

"But Raine...maybe you want me to do this? Just a little?" He caught her nipple in his teeth and flicked his tongue over it lightly. She whimpered and managed to speak.

"Maybe...a little."

She couldn't take much more. He'd had her in such a state of arousal the crash had been almost too much to take. But even if final completion was not a possibility, the way he made her feel along the way was too good to stop. She couldn't say no to how he was touching her. She gave herself over to him, he could do anything he wanted.

He ran his tongue over her stomach in the most erotic patterns, her supersensitive skin responding achingly to his light touch. Then he burned paths up and down her thighs as he stroked them.

"God, you're gorgeous. You are so much more than I ever imagined…. Remember when I wrote about doing this to you online? How I wanted to taste you?"

He moved up over her and looked. She was like an angel of desire, her skin flushed with passion, arms thrown to the side, hair tangled and splayed over the pillow. When he moved his hand up between her thighs to insert a finger, then two, into her heat, he was gratified to find she was still wet; she moaned and ground against him, and he sighed in awe. She was so responsive.

He kissed her breasts again, and feathered his lips down her stomach. Nudging her knees apart, he lay between them. He didn't rush, but lifted her leg, trailing his tongue along her instep, to her ankle, and then kissed her knees, tracing his tongue up the inside of her leg to the sensitive crease where hip met thigh, and kissed her there, biting lightly, feeling her strain and stretch underneath him.

"Is this the usual, Raine? The ordinary?"

She heard him, his voice hot and teasing, and she struggled for clarity against the onslaught of passion, and faintly shook her head from side to side. "Um, no…nothing usual about this."

"Good. Tell me if anything gets…boring. Tell me anything you want, just like you did online. I'm Rider, Raine— you can tell me anything." He grinned and bit her neatly on the thigh, and she cried out the "okay" that started as a whisper and ended in a moan.

Parting the flesh that concealed her clit, he rubbed his thumb over it and then took her in his mouth, sucking hard, then softly lapping his tongue over her, then stroking long, hot sweeps from that sensitive nub to her vagina with his tongue, gratified by her increased sounds of arousal, the tightening of her thighs on his shoulders. Backing off for a moment, he looked up at her, and felt desire rip through his own body, but he quelled it. This time was for her.

"Raine, touch yourself, sweetheart."

Her forehead creased. "Hmm?"

"Touch your breasts, Raine…. Do whatever feels right…. It's okay…anything is okay."

Raine was unsure about this request, but as he closed his mouth over her again and his tongue was making those long, hot trips back and forth along her most sensitive areas, she lifted her own hands to her breasts, and ran her palms lightly over her nipples, so hard and stiff they were almost sore, and arched her back reflexively.

The world hazed when he grabbed her cheeks in both hands, squeezed and opened her wider, penetrating her with his tongue, then running it up to suck on her clit again. The pressure built unbearably, and she couldn't think. Pulling sharply at her nipples, she was panting, willing her body to go where it needed to—she was *so* close. He was sucking her now, continuously, in a rhythm, without stopping, probing his fingers into her, seeking out her sweet spot. He growled his encouragement as he felt her body suddenly wrench in pleasure.

Raine was caught off guard by the sharp release of pressure, the pulsing heat that exploded and spread out through her limbs. A cry escaped her lips and she bucked against him, seeking more, experiencing every last second of it.

Jack smiled when he felt her muscles gently clasping his fingers. He nuzzled her encouragingly, his groan vibrating against her skin, until he felt her relax.

He maneuvered himself up next to her, watching her face. Her eyes were closed, and there was a faint sheen on her skin that seemed to make her glow. He touched her face, and she opened her eyes, looking at him in wonder and shyness. He smiled, and kissed her.

"Heya."

"Jack. God...that...was...definitely not...the ordinary." She touched his face. "Thank you."

He chuckled. "Be careful, you'll inflate my ego.... But I'm glad. I enjoyed that every bit as much as you did."

She frowned, reaching over to him. "You did?"

He laughed again, scooching down next to her, yanking up the blanket. "Oh, yeah. I, uh...when you came, it felt pretty good to me, too—but you'll have to change these sheets later, I'm afraid."

Raine smiled, exhausted in the best possible way, his admission making her feel womanly and wonderful.

"Stay."

"I don't have much choice, I think. We took your car."

But she was already asleep, and soon so was he.

RAINE WOKE FIRST, entangled in more ways than one.

Legs and arms were wound around each other, and the very handsome face of Jack Harris was facing her, close enough that she could feel his morning stubble on her cheek. He was beautiful—warm and lost in sleep. She stared at him, remembering. She found herself wanting to touch him, badly, but curled her hands into fists. As her mind cleared, she groaned, rubbing her face and wondering how she could have been so foolish.

Looking at him now, it was hard to imagine that the rude jerk in her office, a man she didn't even like, had just spent the night in her bed. Even worse, she had practically begged him for sex, and he had been the only man who had been able to...well... She remembered with a sigh, closed her eyes, and shook her head in a mix of regret and disbelief. She opened her eyes and looked at him again.

He was Rider. Her Rider. But he was also Jack. Jack, who obviously couldn't stand her.

Panic caught her breath. Could this really be a huge coincidence? How could she trust him? He was an internet expert—he could have set the whole thing up, right? What if he told the guys at the office? She would be a laughingstock. It was all too much to process. She needed to get out, to get away, but she didn't want to wake him. She couldn't handle that yet. She couldn't face him and see him gloat.

Quietly, little by little, she slid from the bed, hoping like anything that he didn't wake up until she could get dressed. She needed to be alone. She had made a very bad decision last night, and she was going to have to think about how to handle the consequences.

JACK WOKE TO HEAR the shower running, and was momentarily disoriented. Picking up the scent of perfume and sex from the sheets, he smiled, stretching like a big cat. Raine. Last night had been a shock, but not a disappointment. Well, to be completely honest, it had been a disappointment at first, but now it ranked as one of the best nights of his life.

He pushed up on the pillows, rubbed his face, and glanced at the clock. It was almost nine, but it was Sunday, so he was not in a rush to go anywhere. He wondered what Raine would want to do with the day. His smile was wicked as he considered what he would like to do with it, with her.

He swung his legs over the side of the bed, found his jeans and yanked them on. Nothing was as he thought it would be.

The house was small, a classic New England cottage. Raine had nice taste, he thought as he ran his hand over the solid wooden frame of the mission-style bed, the earthy tones of the unfinished wood blending beautifully with the rose-tinted walls, but the place was not exactly what he would have expected of the very wealthy. She had nice but not extravagant things. The rooms were comfortable, but hardly grand. Not at all what he would have imagined.

Flowers were peeking at him from wall vases she had installed in every room. Snow blew against the white three-over-three frames, making the place feel like a cocoon. Her bedroom dresser looked old, an antique no doubt, and the bedding was soft, good-quality cotton. He smiled, running a finger along the edge of a daisy on the pattern. It was all female, all soft and inviting. Like Raine.

So she was Nilla. His Nilla. Never in a million years would he have thought Raine Covington was even capable of the kind of charm that he found so attractive in Nilla, let alone the passion she had shared with him last night. It looked as if he was wrong.

Nothing he would have imagined about Raine Covington seemed right. She had been standoffish in high school, and she sure as hell was not all that likable at work. How could he have been so wrong about her? Thinking of her in his arms, and how he had been able to help her experience passion she didn't even think she was capable of achieving, made his toes curl. He glanced toward the bathroom where the shower had just turned off, and thought about joining her.

RAINE STOOD IN the shower, stalling, still not knowing how to handle the situation. How could she face Jack? She had clearly messed up. It just didn't pay to be impulsive; it never worked out for her. They had to work in the same office, and she would be lucky if he was just willing to forget about last night and keep his mouth shut.

She rubbed a towel almost violently over her hair

and had a brutal moment of honesty as she looked at her scrubbed face in the mirror. What really bothered her, down deep, was that he didn't even like her—he wasn't even really with her last night—while they had been making love, he had thought of her as Nilla, called her Nilla, not Raine. He was just living out a fantasy.

She had been able to live one out as well, she admitted. It was fantastic with him. When he had seduced her that second, wonderful time, when he had shown her what real, satisfying sex could be like with a man, it had moved her deeply. But now, in the cold morning light, the experience felt hollow and wrong. She had opened herself to him completely, and he had only seen her as a fantasy, not as Raine Covington, but as some figment of his imagination come to life.

She put a hand to her face, sinking against the edge of the vanity as she realized how she had let him take her over, she had been so eager for what he could give her. He was likely motivated by a mix of male ego and pity, and while neither was a particularly great option, she would prefer the first to the second, thanks very much!

Her hands worked themselves furiously through her hair, and she stopped, sighing in defeat, feeling tears sting behind her eyelids. It was just her lousy luck that the lover of her dreams was not the man of her dreams, nor she the woman of his. She spoke determinedly to her image, convincing herself of what she had to do.

"Remember, he wasn't making love to *you*. An idea of you, a version of you—yes—but not you. Keep that straight, and try to have a little dignity, in spite of the fact that you just made a tremendous fool of yourself. Try to keep it together, get him out the door quickly, and get through this. See it through."

Setting her shoulders back, she slipped on a mask of

calm that hid the hurt. It was something she was practiced at—a skill she had honed to perfection in the lonely, painful years of her youth.

She pulled on a robe and walked out into the bedroom. The little bit of cool she had maintained nearly slipped away completely as she saw him standing by her bedroom window holding a cup of coffee and looking magnificent dressed only in his jeans. She licked her lips and blinked hard, reining herself in.

"Um. Good morning." She sounded like a frog.

He turned and smiled. "It is. I made coffee. Hope you don't mind."

She took another step awkwardly into the room. "No, no, that's good, fine. Thank you."

He set the coffee down on the table, and crossed the room, the sleepy, sexy smell of his body slamming into her and blowing away her rehearsed calm as his arms came around her and he pushed his face into her neck, inhaling, and making her head spin.

"I missed you there when I woke up. When I heard the water running, I was going to come join you, but then you finished. Too bad…"

There was a warm suggestion in his voice that made Raine's knees weak, and she fought for control, keeping her body rigid, and put her hands lightly on his shoulders. Piling one mistake on top of another wasn't going to help, as much as her body was screaming for his. Using every ounce of strength she had, she applied gentle pressure, pushing him away.

Frowning, Jack loosened his arms, stepping back slightly, and looked into her face. She held herself stiffly near him, and didn't want to meet his eyes.

He thought, perhaps, that she was embarrassed. He had already figured that much of what he had assumed about her seemed not to be true, at least in what he'd experienced with her last night, and from what he could gather from her home. She probably wasn't used to taking a man home and, well, doing what they'd done.

He didn't know her, but he was willing to give it a try. Tilting her head up with his fingers, he made her face him and found her eyes dull and remote, the mouth that had been so hot under his was stretched tight. She wrenched her face away again and stepped back.

"Jack, this was obviously a mistake—we are just acting on ideas we got about each other on the Net. We don't even know each other."

His eyes narrowed, and he became cautious, hating the way the atmosphere in the small room had changed, had chilled. Confusion, hurt and anger rolled over him. He stepped forward and pressed her up against the wall with his body, holding her shoulders tightly, his gaze fierce, demanding something from her.

"I thought we had something starting here, Raine. What's going on?"

She shifted against him uncomfortably, a flush moving up her throat. She wasn't immune to him, that was for sure. She brought her chin up in that way that always set his teeth on edge, that imperious, arrogant tilt that drove him crazy, and she shook her head.

"Nothing is going on here, Jack. Nothing went on. This was just two strangers acting out a fantasy. It was a bad idea, especially since we have to work together. I would appreciate it if you would be, um, discreet."

Discreet? What the hell? She was lax under his hands, not resisting, not responding at all. She just looked him dead in the eye and told him to be discreet. It was somehow much more painful than if she had just told him to get the hell out.

"Well, what do you think, Raine? That I'm going to go post it on the internet? Go tell all the guys at the office I had a hell of a night with Raine Covington and they should give you a call?"

She slapped him then, and though he knew he had it coming, it didn't matter. Her eyes were fiery and hurt, but he suspected it was a hurt that was reflected in his own.

"I don't know, Jack. I suppose that is possible. That's the problem. I don't know. I don't know you well enough to trust you, and that's why last night was a mistake."

All of the warmth he had felt toward her slid away on a greasy slick of anger and regret. He looked hard into her eyes, finding it difficult to believe what she'd just said. But it was real, and he had to leave before he said something he would really regret. He didn't look at her as he found the rest of his clothes, his tone reflecting the iciness he felt.

"Well, then, just let me get dressed now that you have made up your mind about me, and I'll be out of your way."

"Your car..."

"Don't worry about it.... I'll walk back."

His tone cut off any comment she would have made, and she turned and left the room, not breathing until she reached the kitchen, feeling unsure as she sat at the small white table. She heard the door click quietly shut out in the living room, the soft sound more wrenching than a slam, and fought back tears.

She told herself it was better this way.

6

THE DAY WAS SUNNY, and Gwen was just as bright, bouncing into Raine's office Monday morning. She poised herself on the edge of the desk, leaned over, and in a conspiratorial whisper asked, "So, how'd it go? I want to know everything!"

Raine didn't even look up, and tried to sound as if she had no idea what Gwen was talking about. "Busy, Gwen, not now." Her curt tone would have made most people cringe, but Gwen, as Raine had learned, was generally unrebuffable.

"That bad, huh? Was he a complete toad?"

Raine sat back and put her hands on her temples, sighing. Gwen would not let this rest, she knew. As her closest—and her only—real friend, she didn't want to hurt Gwen's feelings, but it was an annoying part of the girlfriend relationship that you were expected to tell all each Monday. She never could quite get used to it, and since typically she didn't have much to tell, she just listened to Gwen's tales.

But Gwen was relentless, and she felt herself cave. Maybe it would be good to vent. She opened her eyes, only to find Gwen regarding her patiently.

"I want to hear all about Rider, and your weekend, and then I'll tell you about mine, too. I met a new guy. He's dreamy."

"Don't you ever work?"

"Tons, but I manage my time so I can hear all about your weekend on Monday mornings. I find this little storytelling session is good for motivating me to get out of bed on Mondays, it primes me for the day. So go ahead, prime me."

Raine had to smile. "I don't think you need any more priming, but okay. I'm not quite sure how to start. Let's just say this weekend was…unusual."

Gwen slid off the desk and into a chair in one lithe movement. "Ohhh…unusual is good! But details, I want details."

Raine sighed. "Okay. Well, good thing you are sitting down. Turns out Rider is someone I know. Someone we both know."

Gwen's eyes widened and she ticked off a few possible names. Raine shook her head. "No. Not even close. Rider is Jack Harris."

"Who?"

Raine rolled her eyes and leaned forward. "Jack Harris—the IT guy you thought looked like Superman the other day."

"Noooooo!" Gwen whooshed out the word on a breath of disbelief, and sat back in her chair, flabbergasted. "You've got to be kidding! What are the freakin' odds on that? Oh, my God! Raine, I can't believe it. What happened? God, he's gorgeous."

Raine smiled faintly, absentmindedly arranging papers on her desk as she spoke. "Well, we were both pretty disappointed, to put it mildly. We argued a bit, then he… well, he—"

"Yeah? C'mon! What?"

"Well, he kissed me. Major-league kiss."

"Hold the phone. For whatever reason, you weren't happy to see each other, you argued, and he kissed you?"

"Yeah. I know. It doesn't seem to make sense, but it does, when you think about it. I guess we were both so worked up from the anticipation, the time online, we just had to find out. You know, what it would be like." She took a deep breath, blushing furiously. "It ended up being a little more than a kiss. We, um, ended up going back to my place."

Since Gwen looked as if she might fall out of the chair and let out a hoot, Raine jumped up to close the door.

"You slept with him?"

Raine nodded silently and Gwen grinned. "How was it?"

Too many reactions hit Raine at once. She started to speak, but stumbled, and felt her eyes burning. "It was great, but it was awful, you know? I mean, finally I meet someone who can…who could…" Just when she thought her cheeks wouldn't burn any hotter, they did.

Gwen smacked the table. "All right! It's about time, I was keeping my fingers crossed for you. But may I say that you don't look all that thrilled about it."

"Gwen, the guy I slept with Saturday night is not who I thought he would be—it was a fantasy. In real life he is a complete jerk with a horrible attitude who for some unknown reason can't stand me! And I can't stand him either. He's so…rude. And arrogant. And I went to bed with him! How could I have done that?"

She dropped her head to the desk for a moment, and then raised it to look at Gwen with miserable eyes. "When we were in bed, at a, um, critical moment, he called me Nilla instead of Raine, and I don't know—it was like he couldn't think about being with *me*. The real me. He just wanted the fantasy. He wanted Nilla. It was humiliating."

"Oh, Raine, honey, c'mon, people fantasize all the time in bed, and he knows you better as Nilla than Raine. I would think that was completely natural. It's only a name, for goodness' sake. I'm sure he knew exactly whom he was with. And you *are* Nilla, after all. It's not like he was thinking about a different woman."

Raine sucked in a breath and her voice became stiff and prim.

"Maybe so, but Nilla is a creation, she is many things that I am not at all. So, it just underlines the fact that he didn't want to think about who he was *really* with."

"Well, all right. What happened then?"

"He spent the night, and it was...nice. But then in the morning, I knew that it was all wrong, that we'd made a huge mistake. I feel like such a fool. I hate that I had such a lapse in judgment. I have never gotten so caught up in someone before, so swept away..."

Gwen offered only a satisfied smirk. "It's about time, if you ask me. That's what it's *supposed* to be like, Raine. You are supposed to get so caught up you don't care about anything or anyone else. We all wait to be swept away like that. Thank your lucky stars!"

"My lucky stars? Are you crazy? Not only did I sleep with a man who dislikes me, now I also have to think about dealing with him at work. Does it occur to you that this is a little weird?" She got up and paced the office.

"I have to see him here in the office and pretend nothing happened. I had phone sex with him, for God's sake, and was, well, pretty open with him online. It's so embarrassing! I'll thank my lucky stars if he isn't having a good laugh about it downstairs with the staff."

Crossing over to hug Raine, Gwen stroked her hair and

cooed reassuringly. "Raine, this is not a bad thing. Maybe not ideal, but not bad. You guys just have to work it out."

"There is nothing to work out. He was very angry when he left…. I guess I was a little, um, harsh. And that's just as well. Now we just have to get past a few awkward moments here, and as long as he doesn't go telling anyone else, it'll be fine."

Gwen sighed. Raine knew she thought she was too stubborn, and too afraid. But her voice was supportive.

"Hey, you took a chance, and you had a great night, right? So you had a tiff—those things can be smoothed out. Don't make up your mind so fast, just see what happens."

Raine nodded, though she did so only to placate Gwen. She had no doubts that she and Jack were definitely not a possibility. Gwen went on.

"I don't think he is the kiss-and-tell type, anyway. I wouldn't worry too much about that. He just didn't seem to be that way. More like tall, quiet and intense." She shifted gears quickly, sitting up and wiggling in the chair. "So, anyway, let me tell you about the new guy I met. I went down there, and…"

"Down where?"

"Downstairs. Remember we were joking about if there were more cute guys hiding downstairs where Jack works? Well, I decided to find out, and figured even if there weren't, maybe I would run into Jack—not that I would even have so much as a fantasy about him now that I know you two are having a thing—" Raine tried to interject that they were definitely *not* having a thing, but Gwen just rolled on with her story.

"Anyway, you should see it down there. I never knew. It's like something out of a movie. All these small offices circle around the edges of this one big room, and there are *thousands* of computers there. Well, maybe not thousands, but a lot. It's all kinda dimly lit, and romantic in a techno comic-book kind of way."

Raine raised her eyebrows, wondering at Gwen's description of the building basement, but listened as she continued.

"Anyway, I figured I would go down, and just see what or who was there. So, I was poking around looking for Jack's office, and bumped into this guy." Her eyes took on that faraway look that Raine knew well.

"His name is Neal. Don't ya just love that name? It's so, I don't know, down-home." She smiled. "He's kinda cute, not as built as Jack, but cute in that nerdy I-work-on-my-computer-in-the-basement kind of way, you know? And he even had the thick, black-framed glasses."

Raine couldn't quite hold back her amusement when Gwen sighed, but motioned for her to continue. At least this was taking her mind off her own problems.

"Okay, so you met this guy Neal and…"

"He asked me why I was there, and I told him I was looking for Jack, and then we got talking and I asked him out."

"You don't waste time, Gwen."

"Life is short. Anyway, we had a very nice dinner Saturday night, talked a lot, you know, got to know each other a little bit, and then went back to his place and just made out for hours."

"Made out?"

Gwen sighed again. "Just kissing. Kissing and kissing and more kissing. I haven't done that since high school, and it was terrific. Hot, sweaty, got-my-panties-soaked kissing that went on for half the night and then we just said goodnight. We're going out again this Friday." Gwen smiled, and blushed a little, and Raine smiled back.

"Sounds nice. I'm glad for you." And she was. It was

her turn to sigh, though, and she blocked out the images of what she had been doing for hours on Saturday night, and tried not to remember the feel of Jack's mouth on her skin.

"So, are you going to see him again?" Gwen's voice broke through the fog as she headed to the door.

"Hmm? Who?"

"Jack."

Raine screwed up her mouth and shook her head. "Gwen, I told you—"

Gwen put up her hand. "Okay, okay, just want you to be open to the possibilities. You know that's half the battle. If you are open to things happening in life, they tend to work out."

"Yeah, well, you have to be careful what you are open to." She'd been way too open lately, she thought, a wave of embarrassment washing over her.

Gwen made a face. "Pessimist. Focus on the positive, at least you got laid by a gorgeous guy, right?" She grinned. "I'm back to work. Maybe I can break something on my computer so Neal can come up and fix it. I'd like to watch him bending over to get down into all those wires under the desk."

Raine smiled. "In that case, may all your files crash today." Gwen giggled and waved as she left.

RAINE PARKED HER CAR in front of the castlelike building of the Witch Museum and walked across the street to the Salem Common, a large, open-area park where people came to walk their dogs, play and hang out.

It was a place where you could be by yourself but not alone. Exactly what she was looking for. It was too early to go home. She stared up at the looming statue of Salem's first settler, Roger Conant, and felt a shiver run down her spine. The statue always seemed so eerie to her. She turned her back on him and entered the park.

Some intrepid dog walkers were exercising their canine friends, and groups of children were having snowball fights, their shrieks of joy cutting through the crisp air. She started at the closest corner and followed the maze of walkways without paying much attention to which way she was moving. Snowmen in various stages of meltdown stood here and there along the walk, and she smiled as she walked past the form of a snow angel frozen into the snow. The snow lit up the night; she loved the way it looked like diamonds scattered all over the ground.

"Mind if I join you?"

She was startled to see Duane fall into step beside her.

"Um, sure."

"I usually walk through here on my way home, and saw you get out of your car over there. I live just over on Oliver. How about you? You live farther out, right?"

"Yeah, on Chestnut. I just felt like a walk. Long day."

He nodded and they turned the corner near the ornate structure known as the bandshell, a domed stage resembling a very large gazebo. It had stood there since Salem's early days.

"Listen, Raine, I was wondering how the column is going. I know I was a little hard on you about it before, and if you don't want to meet his guy, you don't have to. It was wrong of me to push you. We can work the article without the meeting."

Now she really didn't know what to say. She wasn't ready to let Duane know she had met Jack, and had no idea how to explain what had happened. She tried to sound unconcerned and professional.

"Thanks, Duane. I'll let you know how it works out."

They walked by a group of children in the playground

and Duane bent, picked up a handful of snow and whipped a snowball into the group, smacking a young boy on the arm. Delighted yells followed, and before she knew it, they were running down the walk, being chased and pelted. Duane laughed, and she joined in.

"I forget," he said. "Never instigate a snowball fight when you are outnumbered."

Raine smiled. "I think that is the first one I have been in, so you're the expert."

He was looking at her differently, and she blinked when he raised his hand to brush some snow out of her hair.

"You have a pretty smile. I wish you would show it off more often."

The hairs on her neck stood up in awareness, and she took a step back from his hand. This was not boss-to-employee chat, at least not the kind she was interested in. He put his hands in his pockets, and bent his head down for a moment, and then looked at her, chagrined.

"Sorry, I guess that wasn't too smooth."

"Um, Duane, you know I like you, you're a good boss, but I don't think—" He held his hands up and interrupted her, laughing in a kind of embarrassed way that didn't make her feel any better.

"Listen, I'm sorry. I've just been trying to screw up the courage to ask you out for a while. I know you keep to yourself a lot, and I figured you wouldn't be someone who would get involved with anyone at the office, but I thought, hey, what the heck."

Raine held her breath, thinking of Jack, and felt her stomach sink a little more. Duane continued.

"And then, here I am forcing you to go meet some other guy, and I couldn't believe how stupid that was." He laughed again and kicked some snow, looking at her with intense, blue eyes.

Raine couldn't believe what she was hearing, and had no idea what to do with it.

"Duane, I just don't think going out with you is a good idea—"

He looked down again, and nodded, and she searched for something, anything, intelligent to say.

"I mean, we work together, you are my boss. And I like you, I do, but you know, things like this never work."

"Yeah, you're right. I knew that, but seeing you every day, and then thinking of you going to meet some stranger—well, I figured…hell, I don't know what I figured. But hey, I took my shot, and now we know." He tried to sound offhand, but Raine could hear the strain and felt terrible, though she wasn't quite sure why she should.

"I'm sorry, Duane." It was all she could think to say. She was freezing, her teeth were beginning to chatter, and she couldn't feel any more awkward.

"No, I know, it's okay. Listen, let me walk you back to your car. You're freezing."

She sighed and nodded. They walked across the park to her car in silence, and she was relieved to finally say good-night and watch him walk away. The situation was just surreal. She had never picked up one hint from Duane that he was interested in her—and she had never thought of him that way, not once. He could have his pick of just about any woman in the company, and he was asking her out?

Life was getting too strange.

She drove home with the radio blaring. She just didn't want to think about any of it anymore. She grabbed her mail, surprised to see so much of it, on her way in the door.

She put her coat on the hook, and looked through the stack. Something wasn't right. These all came from the creditors she had just sent checks to. Opening the first envelope, she discovered a thank-you letter for her recent payment, but they had issued a refund check since her account was already paid in full. Another assumed she had overpaid and sent back the check. Raine blinked, and opened the other envelopes—all the same. Every one of the payments she had just made to credit cards, a parking ticket, and even her student loans, was sent back, and she was informed her accounts were paid in full.

How could this be? She slumped against the door. Just what she needed. Now she had to try to figure out this mess, resend all these payments and get this straightened out before her credit was completely destroyed. Just wonderful. She was already behind on her column, she had two men she had to avoid romantic entanglements with at work, and tomorrow she would have to spend half the day on the phone getting this mess fixed. What next?

JACK TOOK AIM at the multicolored dart board about twelve feet away. He rocketed his arm forward, and the red dart flew and just hit the board, barely sticking to the outside edge. He grunted in disgust as a couple of the guys he was out with cheered and slapped him on the back. They were happy because with that crappy shot, the next round was on him. He was off his game, to say the least, but he lost fair and square. Heading to the bar, he put in the order and went back to the table.

"So, Jack, where have you been lately?" Greg, a programmer with a high-profile company in Boston, tilted his head toward the dartboard. "It's been a while since I've seen you play that badly, not that I'm not grateful." Greg, an incorrigible flirt, eyed the waitress appreciatively as she placed a tray with several bottles of beer in the center of the table. Greg watched the young woman walk away, and sighed lustily.

"Now, if you had a pretty thing like that at home, we

could understand why you might not come up for air for a while."

The other men laughed, and tipped their beers, and Jack just shook his head.

"Do you ever get your mind out of the gutter, Greg? No, don't answer, I already know. But if you got laid as much as you talked about it, we'd all be a lot happier."

A howl of laugher went up, and Greg took the jibe in good humor, shrugging and taking a swig of beer before sending one back Jack's way.

"Sounds like maybe I hit a nerve there. Did you get back together with Marley? Or did you meet another honey who dumped you out on your keister—again?"

Jack winced inwardly, Greg's comment hitting the target spot-on, but he wasn't about to share that with these guys. And besides, tonight was not about women, past or present. He was happy to be out with his friends, having his evenings back, playing darts, drinking beer, talking trash.

"Yeah, well, part of why Marley dumped me, as you so eloquently put it, is because, as you know, she hated me spending one minute out with the guys—that would mean you."

They clinked bottles and talked about the usual things, which was good with him. But if he was dead-honest with himself, he felt restless. He was missing Nilla—the nightly conversations, the sense of connection. And he was pissed at Raine. It messed him up to both want and miss and be furious with the one person at the same time. He took another swig of beer, and listened to the voices that surrounded him, trying to enjoy himself.

The nice thing about talking with the guys was that they didn't complicate anything. The conversation rolled over weather, politics, sports, women and work. He finished his beer, and joined in for a bit, but his heart wasn't in it. Standing up, he said his goodbyes, and headed home.

However, he didn't really feel like going home. It was early, and he was too jumpy to be banging around the house alone. Driving into the parking lot near the office, he decided to catch up on a little work. Neal had closed the gap in the security program. The kid had done a good job. But that morning, there were problems again. Jack just couldn't figure it.

He could shut down the computer, and then, when he rebooted, the problem would just show back up again. There appeared to be a simple glitch in the programming, but it wouldn't patch. The bug just kept reappearing. He supposed it was nothing earth-shattering, but it was annoying, and it gave him something to focus on instead of thinking about Raine.

Hours later, his head was aching, and his stomach finally would not be ignored. He had missed lunch, not really wanting to admit that if he went to the second-floor kitchen or to the cafeteria, he might run into Raine. He wasn't hiding, not exactly. He was avoiding. It was a different thing entirely. He grabbed his coat and headed out.

It was late. The building felt hollow as he walked through it to the exit. On his way past the offices on the first floor, he heard a noise over past the desks, and stopped for a moment to listen again. Someone working late? He heard something hit the floor in a solid clunk and decided to take a look.

Rounding the corner of the main desk, he was surprised to find a couple in a passionate clinch, and his eyes narrowed as he thought he recognized the profile of one of his men. It *was* Neal. Wrapped around, as far as he could tell, the woman who had been in Raine's office the day he had been in there. And here he thought Neal was all work and no play.

Trying to retrace his steps and make a quiet exit, he misjudged his step and stumbled over a trash bin, cursing. Too late to be inconspicuous. The two lovebirds heard the clatter and were now looking at him in surprise, while he set the bin upright and tried to look apologetic.

Neal turned red up to his ears, and his friend—Raine's friend—seemed a little less concerned as she grinned, then laughed, tugging down her lacy, skintight shirt. Her voice was full of mischief, and Jack couldn't resist smiling a little.

"Oops, caught in the act, Neal, and by your boss."

Neal did not look as amused, from what Jack could tell, and he tried to put him at ease as much as possible.

"Sorry to interrupt, folks. Just heard a noise and didn't suspect, ah…"

"Sorry, sir, um, Jack." Neal seemed to relax a little when he realized he wasn't going to get chewed out. "I just bumped into Gwen on my way out, and we got talking, and…"

Jack held a hand up. "No need to explain to me, Neal. It's after hours. But you might want to take the party elsewhere."

Gwen grinned and threw her arms around Neal, smiling at Jack. "Thanks."

"Yeah, sure. Neal, find me in the morning, that bug is popping up again."

Neal just nodded as Jack waved and walked away. It wasn't hard to see that the woman, Gwen, would be a handful. Very pretty, and probably more than a little wild—definitely not a woman he would have pegged as Neal's type. But what the heck did he know?

Jack sighed, feeling a little old as he walked out of the

building. It had been a long time since he had felt as carefree and crazy as Neal and Gwen. It seemed that as you got older, there were always more complications, and romance meant something else entirely than it did before. It all became more serious, and so...*adult.*

As he emerged outside, the cold slapped him, and he breathed it in. He liked the cold; it freshened him. Shaking off his mood, he headed down the street to a local café where he knew he could find something decent for dinner. He felt like being around people, even though he suspected that that would not ease the blues that were settling around him.

7

RAINE GOT AN early start, plunging through the bitter cold to get to the office so that she could take care of the problem with her accounting and not get too far behind in her work. Her car didn't have time to heat up, and she still had to walk from the parking lot. She shivered all the way in and wondered why she hadn't requested a transfer to the Miami office.

A few hours later, discouraged and frustrated beyond reason, she hung up the phone from the last call. The story was the same across the board. As far as the records said— their records, not hers—her credit and loan accounts, and her parking ticket, were all paid up, and she was not required to send any more payments. Something was wrong, but no one would believe her. In fact, it was quite clear they all thought she was nuts.

She took pride in keeping her finances together on her own, not overspending and sticking to a budget that she planned. She did not take or ask for one cent of her father's money, and she liked looking after her own affairs. He wasn't really her father anyway, he was just the man who had adopted her. They certainly didn't have anything even resembling a relationship you could call familial.

She heard Gwen's laughter echoing down the hall, and looked up to see her friend in the doorway, attached to a tall, thin, dark-haired and serious-looking young man who blushed furiously though his smile as Gwen squeezed his butt, not realizing Raine was able to see them through her partially open door. Raine cleared her throat, and Gwen turned her head, laughing.

"Oh, Raine, I'd hoped you weren't too busy. I wanted you to meet Neal!" She stepped into the office, dragging Neal behind her. "Neal, this is my good friend Raine Covington, and Raine, this is Neal Scott. Neal works downstairs in the IT department."

Neal smiled at Gwen, and held out his hand to Raine, closing cool, dry fingers over hers.

"Nice to meet you, Ms. Covington."

Raine smiled. "Hi, Neal. Nice to finally meet you."

Gwen looked up at Neal brightly. "Isn't he just adorable, Raine?"

Raine smiled as she watched the color deepen in poor Neal's cheeks. He obviously was not used to being publicly adored. He'd better get used to it fast if he wanted to be with Gwen. So, this was the man who could kiss for hours on end? The contrast between him and Gwen was a stark one, but the opposites-attracted rule held fast. She smiled at him.

"So what do you do, Neal?"

He shifted a little, and disengaged himself from Gwen. "I mostly do C-Sharp application development and Solaris network administration. You know, troubleshooting."

Raine nodded as if she had some idea what he was talking about, though she hadn't a clue.

"Sounds interesting." She smiled pleasantly and turned her attention to Gwen. "Um, Gwen, I wondered if you had a minute sometime today?"

Gwen nodded. "Sure. Neal has to get back down to the Batcave anyway—isn't that a riot, they call it that? So maybe you are Bruce Wayne, eh?"

Neal blushed again and smiled at Gwen, looking just slightly relieved to make his exit. "Uh, okay. I do have to go. Mr. Harris—Jack—has something he needs me to look at."

Raine smiled and nodded, feeling a slight twinge at the mention of Jack. "It was nice to meet you, Neal."

He nodded and left, offering Gwen a fleeting smile. Raine watched him leave, and frowned.

"You could break that boy if you handle him too roughly, Gwen."

Gwen just giggled and sat back. "You'd think so, but there's a lot more there than meets the eye. When he takes off those glasses he is just so yum. And he is very gentle, and shy, and then bam! He's hotter than hot. I mean, he was all over me last night...."

Raine held up her hand. "TMI, Gwen—too much information, that's okay. I'll take your word for it."

Gwen smiled widely. "Ha, no such thing. But, what did you need me for?"

Raine smiled, taking a moment to consider the beautiful and energetic woman sitting on the other side of the desk, before gathering up some papers. Gwen was a bundle of unpredictability. She could probably crook her finger and have any guy she wanted, but she chose Neal. Raine hoped he knew how lucky he was.

"I was hoping I could get some help on editing a few of these freelance articles. I am so behind, and I've just spent hours on the phone trying to straighten out a financial mess that I can't figure out, and now I am even more behind."

Gwen nodded. "Sure, I can do some edits. No problem. What's the financial thing? Do you need to borrow some cash?"

Gwen was just too sweet. Just like that, without so much as a blink, she would help. That made Raine feel more wealthy than her father's millions ever had. She smiled warmly.

"No, just the opposite." She told Gwen about the refunds, and sighed. "I just hope I can get someone to listen and figure out the problem."

"Well, if you can't, bank the money and thank your gift horse."

"It's not that easy, Gwen. There must be a computer glitch somewhere, and when they find it, I could get, well, screwed. I want them to find it now."

Gwen nodded. "Well, at least they didn't mess up in the opposite way. They could be telling you that you owe them millions or something."

Raine smiled and shook her head; leave it to Gwen to always find the upside. She glanced at her computer as it made the little sound that alerted her she had new mail. Looking at the screen, she didn't recognize the email address, and there was no subject line. Opening it, it only said:

You're so beautiful.

And that was that. No signature. Raine spoke almost to herself. "Nice message—too bad the person it was for didn't get it."

"What's that?"

Raine gestured to the computer screen. "Oh, someone just sent a nice note telling someone she's beautiful, but it isn't signed and there isn't an email address I recognize, so it must have gotten misdirected."

"Well, you *are* beautiful."

Raine smiled. "Thanks, but compliments won't get you out of work. Can you take care of these, and send them along later?" She pushed the pile of edits across the desk. Gwen took them and sharply tapped them on the desktop.

"No problem, I have time today. See ya later."

By SEVEN, Raine's concentration was fading, though she had gotten an immense amount of work done. Her new column was all but done and ready to submit for the first round of edits. The internet-relationships column had been a difficult one to handle. There were lots of issues to be dealt with: safety, honesty, and what to do when you meet someone whom you've only known on the internet.

She thought she had kept her objective viewpoint fairly tightly in line. She had created a neat sidebar containing safety tips for romance on the Net, and emphasized that while her brief experience had not worked out, the fact remained that lots of people were finding happiness through online relationships. Regardless of her own experience, it was her job to report the facts for her readers, although now she could supplement them with a healthy bit of informed opinion.

In the current day and age, the Net was just one more place to meet, no more no less. That's how she pitched it. It didn't matter if you met someone on the Net, or at, say, the park. The same relationship issues existed.

Part of the problem, she wrote, was that people developed unrealistic expectations when they met online. Unrealistic expectations were a problem in many kinds of relationships, but the online universe seemed to multiply them. Or maybe relationships in general just never lived up to what we wanted them to be.

She needed to wrap it up, but for the most part, the article was done. It made her feel as if she could lock one more door on that chapter of her life. The chapter where Jack had played a part. She checked her email once more before getting ready to go, and when she did, she was shocked. She had several more messages just like the one she had received earlier. At least fifty of them!

She read through them quickly. There wasn't anything lewd or threatening in them, but Raine felt a tiny shiver run up her spine. It was definitely weird. Maybe one of those funky internet viruses or something.

She was being paranoid, and decided she should probably just email the person back and let them know. So, she hit the reply button, and typed out a neat and impersonal message informing the sender that they had mistakenly sent several personal emails to the wrong address, and that they should probably check their address book.

"There, that should do it." She shut down her computer and stared out the window. It was snowing again. She crossed her arms over herself and hugged. She hated the cold, even more so when she felt so alone. This time of year, the days were getting shorter, but the winter seemed so long. And the nights lasted forever.

She had considered asking Gwen over for supper, but when she had popped back in to say good-night, she was clearly looking forward to seeing Neal at the end of the day. Raine wished it would go well for her. Gwen was exuberant and open, and dated all the time, but Raine couldn't remember the last time she had seen someone as steadily as she was seeing Neal. Maybe it was because they were together in the same office, so it was easier to make plans, harder to avoid each other.

She frowned. Not that Jack had any problems with avoidance. She had not seen him in over a week, since Sunday morning when he left her. She knew he must come in to work, and she caught herself looking for him when she left her office to get coffee, or go to the bathroom. He was never there.

She wondered how it was she could still feel the touch of his hands on her skin, and the heat of his breath mingled with hers. Unconsciously, she squeezed her legs together remembering the pleasure he brought her, and a swirl of heat settled in her core that made her forget the cold outside.

The office was silent, most everyone had left an hour or so ago. Suddenly she felt strange, vulnerable, being there all alone. She stood quickly, grabbed her jacket and briefcase, and headed out. She'd put in a long day and felt edgy and unreasonably agitated. She needed food, a couple glasses of wine and a long soak in a hot bath. Feeling good about that plan, she turned the corner to the exit, and saw him.

Jack.

He had just gone through the door a moment before her, and was walking across the street to the parking lot. She moved closer to the door, placing her hand on the glass, and watched him. He was a graceful man, slow-moving and sexy. Sexy as all hell. Her knees wobbled a bit as she pushed through the door, unable to keep her eyes off him.

Even at a distance, she could see his hair being whipped around by the wind, and she curled her hand into a fist, her nails biting into her palm, as she remembered how it had felt to sink her fingers into those silky, burnished-copper waves.

Then he stopped, and turned, and she felt the heat rush into her face. Suddenly the cold dropped away. She should have turned and left, but it was too late, he saw her, his gaze locking in on her like a hawk on its prey. All the need and unanswered questions tumbled between them, and then he turned away.

She heard the door slam, the engine start. He drove out of the lot and disappeared down the road. Shaken for reasons she couldn't even imagine, she crossed over to the lot as well, finding her own car. She got in, and sat, seriously rattled.

God help her, she wanted him.

THE WINE AND THE BATH had been a very good idea, in theory. Except that as she sank into the relaxing effects of the merlot and hot water, she also sank helplessly into fantasies of Jack that tortured her until she had relied on her own hands, all the while thinking of his mouth on her, to find some release from the tension that was addling her brain.

It hadn't worked, but instead had brought all the memories of their night back to her full force, and she had gone to bed thinking she could detect his scent on the sheets, even though they had been washed days before. After a night of tossing and turning, trying to block erotic images from her mind, when she awoke she was in no mood to think about romance.

But romance was exactly what was blooming all over her desk when she walked into her office. The bouquet of roses was so large that the spray of flowers practically obscured the top of her desk, their crimson petals eerily resembling blood on snow in the stark winter sunlight shining through the window. Raine stopped in her doorway for several minutes, staring at them until Gwen came up behind.

"Looks like you and Jack made up—or at least he wants to! Good for you—oh, aren't they *amazing*—they must have cost a fortune!" She wiggled past Raine, who was still caught in the doorway staring. Gwen fussed over the roses and inhaled deeply.

"Ohhhh. My allergies are going to act up for the rest of the day, but it's worth it, they smell as good as they look. You know, that's how you can tell the quality of flowers, especially roses, they smell so *wonderful*—some of the inexpensive ones, like the ones you see at the grocery store, they don't smell at all, or they have some weird kind of chemical smell, probably from the preservatives, I mean, who knows where they came from, but these are certainly not like that. These are amazing!" She turned to Raine, eyes sparkling, out of breath. "Have you looked at the card yet?"

Raine stepped forward, amazed that Gwen could make it through that entire speech on one breath. She set her coat down on the chair and took the little white card out of the holder. Opening it slowly, she inhaled sharply as she read the simple, male script.

"You're so beautiful." She whispered the words written on the card. There was no other signature, no hint as to the sender, and her heart pounded as she looked at the flowers again, frozen.

Gwen wrinkled her forehead, and took the card, shrugging as she looked at it. "That's kinda weird. Same as that email you got yesterday, huh?"

Raine nodded. It was hard to believe that these were sent to the wrong person—her name was clearly written on the card's envelope. She looked at Gwen. "I have no idea why anyone would be sending me these."

"Well, looks like maybe someone is trying to get on your good side. Maybe it *is* Jack, and he's just trying to soften you up a little before he talks to you in person. I suppose it could be Jerry. Have you been seeing anyone else?"

Raine shook her head. "No, not in months, not really—

just that one date with Jerry, and I haven't heard from him since. Nothing so serious that they would be sending me *these*." She thought of Duane, and closed her eyes. He wouldn't. Would he?

"Except for Jack."

Raine nodded. She hadn't told Gwen about Duane, and didn't intend to. But this was not Jack's style. Intuitively, she knew he would not try to get around her this way. But if not him, who? She had seen Duane daily since their talk in the park, and after he apologized profusely one more time, it was back to business as usual.

She and Jack *had* seen each other last night—he had been too far away for her to make out his expression. Maybe he was trying to reconnect with her. Then why had he driven away? She shook her head and paced the office. No, that didn't make sense. She didn't know him very well, but she sensed that he would be more direct.

But no one else had any reason to send her flowers. There simply was no one else. She looked at Gwen.

"Well, I guess there is only one way to know for sure."

Gwen's eyes widened. "You're going down there? To see him?"

"Yes. I need to get this settled. This doesn't seem like Jack, but if it is, I want to know why. If not him, I want to know who."

Gwen nodded and smiled. "Well, you are going down to see him. Maybe that is the whole point. Very romantic."

Raine pursed her lips. "More like very creepy. I prefer to know who is sending me emails and flowers."

Gwen shook her head on her way to the door. "Raine, you are the only woman I can think of who would think that getting a dozen of these long-stemmed beauties was at all creepy." She sighed dramatically. "Anyway, good luck! I want to know all about it later!"

Raine summoned up the calm she needed to go deal with Jack and this problem. If the person responsible for sending the emails and flowers was him, though her instincts told her it wasn't, she wasn't exactly sure how she felt about it.

Still, she needed to know, for her peace of mind, one way or the other. Raine crossed to her desk, looking up his extension, and dialed the numbers, her fingers tightening on the receiver as his phone rang.

"Jack Harris."

The sound of his voice on the phone threatened another avalanche of erotic memories of the last time she had spoken with him on the phone, and she squelched them ruthlessly, keeping her voice neutral.

"Hi, Jack. It's Raine. I'm in my office, upstairs, and need you to come up when you get a moment." Of course he knew where her office was! God, just hearing his voice had turned her into a babbling idiot.

"Are you having a computer problem again? If you can tell me what the trouble is, I can send someone up to fix it."

His voice was impersonal, as if he was talking to a stranger. She nearly hung up, there was no way Jack had sent these notes and flowers. But she had to make sure before checking out other possibilities.

"Um, no, I just need to ask you about something. It won't take long."

She heard him sigh, and he said he would be up in a few minutes. Foolishly, she nodded, and hated how breathless her voice sounded when she said goodbye. Trying to get a grip, she took a deep breath, and looked at the work stacked on her desk, trying for normalcy while she waited.

JACK HEADED UP the stairs, hating the feeling that he was being "summoned." He had been avoiding her for days, and now was going to have to be in close quarters with her in the office; he would just settle whatever problem she had, and get out as quickly as possible.

Last night, seeing her standing there like a statue in the doorway, he had almost let go of his pride and gone to her. He found himself hungry to have her in his arms again in a way he had never experienced before, not with any other woman. He wanted to crush her to him, and make her want him, regardless of their differences. At this point he wasn't sure he cared about her past or her attitude or what she thought about him; he wanted her body naked and hot underneath his.

He wanted to make her beg for him and for what he could do to her. He had replayed making her come over and over in his mind, and wanted to do it again. He sighed in disgust at the direction of his thoughts. It had been like this ever since he left her, and he didn't like it. Most times he got past bad experiences with women easily.

Opening the door to the main floor, he walked down the hall to her office, his stride more controlled than usual. Rapping a knuckle on her door, he pushed it open a bit, and felt his mouth go dry.

How was a mortal man supposed to deal with this? She was so damn hot, her blond hair spilling over the shoulders of a royal-blue sweater that hugged her breasts in a way that made him ache. She looked a little pale, and there were smudgy shadows under her eyes, which, perversely, only made him want to touch her more. She brought out his protective instincts; he wanted to comfort her. Maybe because doing so brought comfort to him, as well, among other things. Stuffing his hands in his pockets, he spoke first.

"Okay, I'm here. What's the problem?" His voice was gruff and unfriendly, he knew. Good.

She shifted in her seat a little, and motioned him to a chair, which he rejected. "I only have a minute."

She nodded vaguely. "Um, okay. Well, I feel foolish even asking this, but I needed to make sure. Are these from you?"

He stared at her blankly and she pointed to the flowers; he saw them and his eyebrows lifted. Then he felt something twist in his gut—someone had sent her these? Although he had no right to feel one way or the other about the situation, it angered him.

"You think I sent these to you?"

She felt a slight color tinge her cheeks. Was she destined to be humiliated by this man?

"Um, well, I figured it wasn't you, but there was no name on the card, and I couldn't think of anyone else…. I haven't seen anyone for a long time. Except you."

He was at a momentary loss for words, and walked to the roses, which must have cost a mint. They would have put him back a good percentage of his paycheck if he had bought them. He looked at the card, and read it aloud, making her color even more deeply, hearing the words in his voice. He dropped the card carelessly back on the shelf.

"No, it wasn't me. Is that it? Is this all you needed me for?" He raised his eyebrows as she nodded. "Looks like you have a secret admirer, Raine. But it's not me." *How ironic,* he thought.

Her forehead wrinkled and she nodded again. "I didn't really think it was you, but the message on the card matched the one on the email, so—"

"What email?"

"I got a bunch of messages yesterday from the same person, and one of them had the same message as the card. Seeing as you and I met online, I thought, maybe…"

"But you know my email address—we didn't use work addresses, but you would have known what was from me."

"Yes…I know. I didn't think it really was you who sent the notes, but, well, I don't know! This is all so confusing. The last few days all kinds of things have been going crazy. I didn't know what to think of it. I'm sorry I bothered you."

"Do you still have those emails?" She nodded, and he crossed to her desk. "May I see them?"

"Sure…they're all right here." She shifted in her chair, trying to ignore how close he was to her, leaning over her shoulder. She could feel the heat of his skin, and moistened her lips unconsciously, remembering his taste. Hoping her hands didn't tremble, she opened her inbox, the list of messages displayed. And one more. A new one.

She clicked on it, and caught her breath. This message did not seem harmless. It was not overtly threatening, but starkly sexual. The comments about admiring her beauty were still there, but this time the sender was describing, in great detail, what he would like to do with her—what he liked to do for himself while he watched her.

"Watching me?" Her voice had tightened to a harsh whisper, as fear made it hard to breathe. Jack was leaning over her, focused on the screen, his eyes intense.

"Let me sit." She did, rising to pace the office, rubbing her arms with her hands as he took her chair and tapped away madly at the keyboard. She stopped and stared at the roses, unable to tear her eyes away, and startled when Jack's curse cut across the room.

"Bastard! He's using a dummy email account, but it's been bounced around so many locations it will take forever to dig through to the source, and even then, we might not be sure it's real."

He looked up to see Raine standing in the middle of the office, pale and shaken, and was consumed with anger for the jerk who was messing with her. He was still angry with her, but he didn't want to see her harassed and afraid. He tried to reassure her as best he could.

"I won't say you shouldn't worry about this, but chances are that this is just a lot of empty words. This could be international, or whoever is doing it could be far away from here. You are a published personality, after all—anyone could contact you and send things here."

Raine just nodded. He stood, and crossed to where she stood, trying to keep his tone and behavior professional and not take her in his arms, as every voice in his head was screaming at him to do.

"I'll grab those messages and work on trying to trace them downstairs. If I can track down the sender and find the source, we can have his accounts closed, and that should solve the problem." Raine nodded again. He moved to the door, thinking back for a moment, reconsidering. "Raine, what did you mean, things have been crazy all week?"

She took a steadying breath, and told him about the bills, the refunded checks, and felt a knot form in her gut as his eyes darkened, and he came back into the room.

"Sit down before you fall over. You need to calm down and think clearly here—make sure you have given me all the details. Are you sure you didn't make a mistake in your checkbook and double-pay your accounts? It happens."

She looked at him, snapping out of her fugue for the first time since he had come into the office. "Of course I checked. I didn't double-pay anything. There was just an accounting error, and I have to get someone to pay attention and fix it, but I don't see how—"

"Raine, you said it was credit cards, student loans, and what, a parking ticket?"

She nodded.

"How do you suppose the same error happened with all those different creditors? How could the same thing happen at the same time with all of them?"

Raine hadn't considered that—she had been so caught up in trying to straighten out the mess that that simple fact had not occurred to her. Now that he'd pointed it out, she felt so stupid. She looked at him. "What are you thinking, Jack?"

His mouth was set in a grim line. "It means someone probably messed with your accounts." His eyes flashed to the roses and back to her again. "I guess you do have a secret admirer. Someone who knows how to hack into banks, too, by the looks of it. I guess he thought that might have been a nice gesture. And those flowers. He's really trying to impress you, whoever he is."

A chill ran over her skin, and she wrapped her arms tightly around herself. "Someone is doing these things on purpose? Why? What do I do? How do we find him?"

"Well, we should tell the police, and since he has found you at the magazine, you should let Duane know."

She paled, and he gave in. Closing the distance between them, he pulled her a little roughly into his arms and held her close. She smelled so good, felt so right. He knew there were other things they should be doing right now, but the minute she relaxed into his arms, his body went on full-scale alert.

He released her gently, moving back just a bit before she could detect the evidence of his arousal. *Focus, Jack, focus.* But she looked up at him with those passionate green eyes, and he was lost. She wanted him, too, he could see it. She trembled under his hands, and he lowered his mouth to hers, kissing her hungrily. There was no gentleness in it. He wrapped her tightly against him again, releasing all of the pent-up desire he had been holding back.

Then, in a flash of sanity, he pushed away from her, angry with himself that he would take advantage of her at such a time. She was afraid, confused, and he had pounced on her like a wild man. He walked to the other side of the office, his chest heaving as he fought for control. When he had his voice back, he spoke.

"I'm sorry, Raine. I know this isn't exactly the time."

"Let's not talk about it, okay?" Her voice was not much more than a whisper, and he felt even worse.

It wasn't okay, but he nodded. "I'll tell you now, the police probably aren't going to do much about it—this is small stuff to them, and the New England chapter of the hi-tech crime investigation unit is in Boston. They might be interested because he got into your bank accounts. Has anything happened at your home? Any phone calls or strange people hanging around?"

A chill settled at the base of his spine; he knew she could be in real danger.

Raine shook her head. "No. Not since the bills. And he didn't send them, technically."

"So, we'll tell Duane first, and get his take, then let the authorities know."

"We?"

Jack nodded, feeling a little something inside twist as she looked up at him, a slight edge of fear, and then—something else—gratitude?—shining in her eyes. "Yeah, since I'm the security administrator, he'll want my take on the situation."

She nodded, and the light dimmed a little. "Okay."

THE CONVERSATION WITH Duane was tense, and by the end of it, she had a raging headache. He ordered Jack to make sure all the magazine's systems were secure, and while he was concerned about Raine, he was obviously more concerned about a security breach bringing down the magazine's computers. It appeared he was over his little crush.

Raine took the thought back as soon as she thought it—Duane was just doing his job. By protecting the magazine's computers, he was protecting her, too. And it wasn't as though he wasn't concerned about her, there just wasn't much he could do.

They called the police from his office, on conference call, and the detective responded just as Jack said the police would—unless things got more serious, their hands were tied. She could go down to the station and file a report to formally document the incident, just for the sake of having it on record. They could send it on to Boston. She didn't even know whom she was complaining about—she had an email address and that was about it.

Jack insisted on driving her to the police station, though she didn't know why. He just seemed unwilling to leave her alone, which she thought was odd. He was brusque and businesslike, but she admitted to herself that his presence did help. She didn't allow herself to think about the kiss in the office, and what it could have meant. But for one lovely moment she hadn't been cold and afraid.

8

JACK RETURNED TO Raine's office after clearing up some matters before they could leave for the police station, and stood in the door for a second, watching her, fighting off the coil of protective feelings that he'd been struggling with all morning. She was sitting at her desk, her head in her hands. She didn't move, she didn't even look as if she was breathing. Her skin was porcelain, and he remembered its taste. He shook himself and tapped on the open door. She didn't jump, but just looked at him, expressionless.

"Okay, I'm ready." Her voice was quiet, smooth and calm. He wanted to hold her. But he didn't.

"Let's get some food first, you look like you could use something."

"I'm fine, I just want to get this over with."

"You're white as a sheet, and you need to eat. We'll just stop for something quick." His tone of voice told her he had already decided for them both. She grabbed her coat and realized she wasn't going to win this one, and besides, she was a little hungry.

When she picked up the flowers as she left the office, she got a curious look from him.

"I don't want them," she said, "so we can stop by the

hospital on the way and leave them at the desk. They can keep them or give them to someone who will enjoy them."

That annoying feeling itched at him again, the one that made him think maybe he was wrong about her. Or maybe it was a convenient rationalization so that he could be more comfortable with the fact that he wanted her in his bed. Again. Soon. But it still stung how she had turned on him the last time. No guy in his right mind set himself up for something like that twice.

As they drove off, her scent and the fragrance from the roses combined in the most erotic way possible, and he felt himself harden unexpectedly. Shifting in his seat, he adjusted his coat so that she wouldn't notice. She wasn't saying anything, and he felt the need to break the silence.

"Do you like Italian? There is a good little café-deli place down the block."

"Anything is fine."

More silence. He shifted in his seat again, staving off the image of her sprawled naked on a bed covered with rose petals. Hell, forget the rose petals.

"Are you okay?"

The rough concern in his voice made her look at him, and she was able, for the first time, to really appreciate what a gorgeous man he truly was. His profile was sharp, straight nose, full lips. Those intense eyes that seemed to pierce through everything were focused intently ahead on the road. For a moment, she forgot he had just spoken to her.

"Yes, I'm just a little…freaked out, I guess. I've never had anything like this happen."

They pulled up next to the deli and parked. As they entered, Raine felt a shock of pleasure at the flood of warm colors and the spicy smells that had her lifting her hand to her stomach.

"Oh, I am hungry."

"Let's order and sit then. They are pretty quick here. Great soups."

After ordering sandwiches and soup at the counter, they found a small booth in the back, and waited for their food with steaming cups of coffee. She wanted to talk about anything but work, so she tried her hand at small talk.

"Have you always lived in Salem?"

He shook his head. "No, I grew up in Connecticut."

"Huh. Me, too. Where?"

He wanted to avoid this question for now—it would just open a can of worms when things were wormy enough. Instead, he sort of slid around it a little.

"My family owns an inn there. It was just my mom and dad and me."

"No brothers or sisters?"

"Nope. They wanted to have more kids, but I think there were some problems, and they couldn't. Didn't matter, I never felt alone, I had people around me all the time, the guests at the inn, some of the part-time staff."

"Didn't you hate not having a regular home?"

He blinked, as if surprised by her question.

"I never really thought about it as not being a regular home. It was where I lived, it was comfortable, homey. My mom cooked all the food for guests, and there were never more than six or eight at a time. They seemed more like relatives, several people we came to know very well, since they came back each year. There was always work to do, but it was fun."

"Where are your parents now?"

"Still there. I go home for holidays, talk to them all the time. I miss them, even though they are not too far away. They close the inn for half the year now and travel themselves. They're good people."

Stirring her coffee, she smiled slightly. "That sounds wonderful."

"It is." He phrased his next inquiry carefully. "Raine, speaking of families, do you think that this harassment could have something to do with your family?"

She glanced up sharply. "What do you mean?"

"Well, children of wealthy families are often targets for crimes like extortion and kidnapping."

A chill set over the table.

"How would you know about my family's money?"

Jack silently cursed his slip. He should come clean about knowing her when they were younger, but he couldn't. Not yet.

"Someone at the magazine mentioned it. Your father is pretty well-known around New England. Lance Covington Industries seems to own half of Massachusetts and New Hampshire."

She pushed her coffee to the side, and met his eyes squarely. "I am more or less estranged from my family—if you can call it that. It's really only my father, and I haven't seen him for years, since I left for college. I have never really thought of myself as attracting any negative attention because he's wealthy. Most people probably don't even know I exist."

Jack watched her, saying nothing, and thought about that interesting little detail—she had said that her father was wealthy, but had not included herself in that definition. Yet surely she was heiress to her father's fortune? She was the only child, after all. She must have money of her own, a trust fund, or something of that sort. He pushed a little more.

"I'm sure your father would want to know if you were being threatened. He might want to set up some security for you."

At this she laughed out loud, though not happily. It was the first time he had ever seen any kind of hardness about her, though it changed quickly to a deep sense of sadness he could see reflected in her eyes and the tightness around her mouth.

"Hardly. If I was kidnapped, I am not sure he would see it as a smart investment to pay the ransom."

Their food came, and as he dived into his, he watched her play with hers. He wanted to draw her out, to find out more.

"Did you have a falling-out?"

She bit her sandwich, and chewed slowly, waiting to answer, unsure about opening up to him but feeling irrationally compelled to do so. Somehow, she wanted him to know something about her, about who she was. Not Nilla, not the Raine he knew at work, but just her. Her voice was not much more than an edgy whisper.

"No, never that. Nothing as emotional as that. Though he was disappointed that I didn't want to make more out of myself. We didn't argue about it because he wasn't paying for my education. I was on scholarship. So I did what I wanted. He didn't see journalism and sociology as leading to much of anything. He would probably have approved if I owned the magazine rather than just writing for it."

She sipped her soup. It was delicious, but her appetite had gone.

"I don't want to give the wrong impression," she said. "He's not a tyrant or anything. He never hurt me or left me wanting for anything. He made sure I had all the things I needed, clothes, food, education."

"Love?" It escaped his lips before he could stop himself, and he regretted it as soon as the word passed between them. She looked away, staring at her food.

"No. But a home. People to take care of me. A place to be, the things I needed. More than a lot of people have."

"Children need more than things, Raine." He thought of his own home and parents, the happiness they had together and had shared with him. They weren't wealthy, but they had had what they needed materially, and more. He'd never been unhappy, or lonely, even though he had no brothers or sisters. The inn was busy most of the year, and there were always people around, but his mother and father always made him feel loved and valued. He couldn't imagine what she must have grown up with. How could a child deal with that kind of coldness? He quieted his own thoughts, and focused on what she was saying to him.

"Well, it doesn't always work out perfectly for everyone. But I shouldn't complain. He was good to me, in his way. Better than he had to be."

She continued in a matter-of-fact voice, "I mean, after all, I was adopted. So it's not like I am his blood. I never got the whole story, he didn't like to talk about it. But the staff talked, and every now and then I would pick up bits of information. Enough to know my situation. Apparently he and my mother couldn't have children, and she insisted on having a family and they ended up adopting me."

He nodded, sipping his soup, and let his silence encourage her to continue, at the same time he was kicking himself. He had terribly misjudged her.

"She left when I was about two. I don't remember anything specific. He never said anything about her, why she did what she did. There were no pictures around."

Jack was quiet, unsure of what to say. He was very uneasy about how he had treated her in the past. He realized he didn't know her at all. But he wanted to.

Meeting her as Nilla had offered him some small glimmers into who Raine really was, and it had been enough to capture his interest, until his latent adolescent fantasies had gotten him off track. They were silent for several minutes, then Raine smiled, a little too brightly.

"So, that's me. The poor little rich girl."

"Don't." He reached out a hand to grasp hers, and was immediately shocked at the heat the simple touch produced, but he held on and kept his gaze on hers. "Don't make light of it. That was a horrible way to grow up."

She relaxed, and nodded at him. Pushing her food aside, she sounded resigned. "Yes. You're right. But don't feel sorry for me. I like my life."

Her voice was stronger now, and she sighed. "Anyway, I wouldn't ask my father for money for protection or for anything else. I make a nice living at the magazine, but not enough to afford something like personal security. I'll just have to deal with the situation the way most people would, through the police, or on my own."

Jack squeezed her hand again.

"Thanks for telling me, Raine."

She just shrugged. After a moment, they stood and gathered their plates, setting them back on the counter, and headed back out into the cold. To the police station. Jack hoped that the stalking situation wouldn't get worse; she had been through enough already. But whatever happened, he planned on being there.

DURING THE AFTERNOON, Jack got to know a very different side of Raine. At the hospital, she dropped off the roses and suggested that the nurses save a few for themselves at the nurses' station, and split up the bouquet to bring a rose to patients who needed the lift. She had taken an ugly gesture and had turned it into a giving one. To say he was impressed seemed shallow; he was deeply moved.

On the way up the stairs of the police station, he found

himself reaching to clasp her hand, enjoying the way it felt small but strong in his, and noted that she didn't pull away. Anyone looking at them would have thought they had been together for years.

He glanced at her as they walked down the hallway, and she looked like a woman with a purpose, her stride strong, her eyes direct. She didn't look frightened, and he added admiration to the list of new feelings he seemed to be quickly accumulating for this woman. At the main desk they asked for the detective they'd talked to on the phone, then took a seat, waiting for him to come down.

Raine looked around, feeling very much out of her element, but intrigued all the same. She had never been in a police station before. It looked pretty much like any office building, but had a different sense about it. There was something in the air; the weighty presence of authority, the stale smell of coffee, and a weird sort of tension.

Normally at this time of day she would be working on an article, wrapping up a meeting or tracking down research. But her life continued to veer far away from normal. She felt a draft of cold air wash by her, and watched two policewomen walk through the doors she and Jack had just entered.

They were average-looking women, but they had an aura of power around them. One was slight, with brown hair and ebony skin, and the other thin and muscular, with long, auburn hair pulled back tightly under a cop's hat. The auburn-haired one glanced at Jack as they passed by, and Raine detected her glint of appreciation before they continued on and disappeared down the other end of the hallway on the other side of the desk.

The smaller woman had been wearing a wedding ring— married—would she have children? Raine made a mental note—this was her next article pitch. She wanted to know about these women, their personal and professional lives and relationships, how they made it all work. She wanted her readers to think about women who put themselves at risk daily to help others. Her mind turned to the nurses at the hospital—maybe she would broaden it out to writing about women in emergency services....

Her line of thought was cut short by a booming voice saying a hearty hello to yet another cop that was passing by, and she looked up to see a man walking toward them.

Raine felt a smile tilt up as he walked over and extended his hand. There was no way you could not smile at him. He was at least six feet tall, probably in his late forties, she thought absently. And he was like a huge...leprechaun. Not fat, but muscular and wide. His green eyes twinkled at hers, under a thick shock of hair that was a riotous mass of salt-and-pepper curls surrounding a full, friendly face. He was a handsome man and he sure filled up the room.

She eyed his gun and holster and felt as if she was in a movie. His huge hand wrapped around hers, squeezing in a friendly way; then he shook Jack's hand as well, a little more firmly.

"Hello, hello.... Just follow me right back here where we can talk. I'm Detective Delaney. I'm glad you found time to come down. Like I told you on the phone, there isn't much we can do except take a statement, but if things heat up, that could come in handy down the line. It's wise to have everything documented."

The thought brought her back to the moment, and she felt the weight of why they were there return. Following the detective down the hallway and into a small office, Raine sat in the one chair he pulled out from under a pile of papers and boxes, while Jack stood beside her.

Jack met the detective's eyes briefly. He knew he was being sized up. Crazy boyfriend? Jack knew his posture

clearly declared: "Mine." Detective Delaney nodded, more
to himself than to Jack, smiled and turned to Raine, his
voice professional and friendly.

"So, Ms. Covington, it appears you have a bit of a situation at work?"

She nodded and reached into her briefcase, pulling out a
sheaf of papers, and handed them to the detective. "These
are all the emails—the last one is the worst—and the card
from the flowers."

He took them, and looked them over, not showing any
reaction until he read the most recent email, his mouth
turning down disapprovingly.

"And you said you suspect the person who sent you
these has also intruded into your bank accounts?"

Raine explained about the returned checks, again. She
was tiring of the story, but went over it detail by detail,
and had written down the dates, and creditors, handing
him that piece of paper too. He sighed and looked at Jack.

"Do you have any proof these things are related, the
flowers, and the bank accounts—any sort of computer
evidence you could find?"

Jack shook his head. "Nothing from the emails—it's a
dummy account, impossible to trace back to the original
source. But it's the same guy."

Delaney sighed and nodded. "Well, that would seem
logical, though we need proof for us to take any action.
We'll get your statement down formally, have you sign it,
and keep the papers you gave us here. Then it will just be
a matter of wait and see."

Raine sat forward, placing her hands on the edge of the
desk. "What can I do? I need to do something. I can't just
sit around waiting to see what happens next."

Delaney sat back and gave her a serious look. "Well,
waiting isn't really a choice—the ball's in his court. But

you might consider living somewhere else for a while, changing your email accounts, notifying your creditors and banks. Basically, you have to make it difficult for him to get at you, if he tries again."

Jack knew that made sense, but he couldn't stand watching how pale she got as the detective spoke. "Why don't you just do your best to scare the life out of her, Detective?"

The cop's eyes narrowed, and he nodded.

"Sometimes these folks get bored and move on, sometimes not. Fear can be your best friend now—makes you pay attention to things. Warn your workplace to be very cautious about deliveries of any sort. Don't work alone late at night, walk to your car with someone, check it before you get in. It pays to be careful."

At their silence, he continued. "So, let's put this down in a formal statement, and then you can get out of here and go enjoy the rest of your day, or what's left of it."

Raine answered his questions, and it didn't take too long to finish the report. They needed copies of all her bills, and then she just had to wait. Relief flooded over her when it was done. They all shook hands again, and parted ways.

It was dark outside now, and a burst of frigid wind met them when they opened the door. She disengaged her arm from Jack's hand, not liking how he was pushing her along. He let his hand fall without comment, but slowed his stride slightly.

His jaw was set, and she had no idea why he was in a mood. Maybe he was just tired of dealing with her problems. She didn't blame him, she was sick of it, too. But a little thread of hurt wrapped itself around her heart at his sudden coolness, though she tried to school her face and voice not to show it.

"If you want to take me back to the office, there is some work I have to do. Nothing got done today, obviously."

"Fine."

In the car, he didn't say a word. He was afraid for her and the only way he knew how to handle it was to get angry as hell. He knew he shouldn't be taking this out on her, and tried to get a grip. He took a deep breath, willing his mind to calm.

"I have some things I want to check," he said. "I can bring my laptop up and work from your office."

"That's not necessary."

"It is—don't argue. As the good detective pointed out, you shouldn't work alone at night. So you're not going to."

Raine raised her eyebrows at the peremptory tone of his voice, and while she knew he was right, she didn't like anyone bossing her around. She was tired, and just wanted to get to the end of this very long day. She didn't have the energy to put up with Jack's domineering attitude tonight. Her voice was clipped.

"Listen, I appreciate you going through all this with me, and I know it has cut into your day as well. I can wait to catch up on work tomorrow, so you can just drop me at my car and we can both get home early tonight."

He pulled to the side of the street, and put the car in park, gripping the wheel tightly, trying not to be so incredibly pissed at the woman sitting beside him. That queen-bee attitude just pushed him over the edge he was trying to hang on to.

When he looked at her, she drew back, shocked by the sharpness of his eyes.

"No—*you* listen." He leaned in. "I don't like someone breaking into my networks, I don't like them harassing you or anyone else, I don't like that the cops can't do crap about it, I don't like the way that cop looked at you, and I don't like that prissy little tone you always use when you think you are calling all the shots."

Unsure of how to respond to his litany of complaints, she tried to control the fact that she felt a little breathless, and went for the easy one.

"I do not have a prissy tone."

He narrowed his eyes. "Oh yes, you do, princess. And you use it whenever someone steps on your pretty little toes, or gets closer than you want them to. Like now. Like the morning we woke up together. Remember that, Raine? Remember how we made love, how hot it was? Do you remember how I felt inside you, how I made you come?" He gripped the steering wheel a little harder. "God knows I think about it every day. Every night."

He watched her lips part as she caught a breath and simply stared at him. He liked reminding her of what they had shared, didn't want it leaving her thoughts any more than it had left his. She wasn't so cool and prissy now, he thought.

He turned and reached out, cupped her cheek in his palm, rubbing his thumb over her silky skin. She flushed and went hot under his hands. He saw the flash of desire in her eyes, and knew that she remembered every detail, just as he did. He smiled, satisfied, and gentled his tone.

"We'll go back and work together for a while, okay? I want to help, Raine. Let me."

She nodded, and turned her face into his palm, rubbing her mouth against his skin. When he drew his hand away, she could see that it wasn't steady, and she smiled.

9

SPICY SCENTS OF GARLIC and ginger filled the office, and little white Chinese food containers were scattered everywhere. Raine had not had Chinese food in a very long time; they'd practically bought half the take-out menu, and had been quietly working and eating for the last several hours. Stopping her research for a moment, she picked up a container and scraped out the last of the lo mein noodles at the bottom, feeling sated and relaxed for the first time in over twelve hours.

It was almost nine-thirty at night. Time to leave, she supposed. She watched Jack, lost in deep concentration as he tapped away on the keyboard of his laptop, occasionally grunting or cursing to himself. She hated to interrupt him, to break the easiness they had fallen into. She enjoyed the happy hum of work that had settled over the office.

She never really worked with anyone around and had thought she would find it distracting, but they were enveloped in a companionable silence that was not the least inhibiting. In fact, there was something about working together that helped her get into a better groove. She wondered if it would be that way with anyone, or if it was just that way with Jack.

Jack heard Raine shove away from the desk, and out of the corner of his eye could see her beginning to pack up. He had mostly been puttering, contacting some friends about his quandaries about the network break-in and cleaning up some bugs in a program he was testing. After checking over the entire network, he couldn't find anything wrong—not even the little oddity he had been struggling with before.

"Here, let me help with that." He got up and helped her fit all the small containers into one larger bag for disposal. Raising an eyebrow, he surveyed the desktop. "Wow. We actually ate all that? No leftovers. Damn."

"Why? Are you still hungry?"

"God, no, I just like Chinese leftovers—good snack at three in the morning."

"Or for breakfast."

He nodded, grinning at her. "Oh, well, maybe next time."

Raine felt a little squeeze in her chest—did he mean next time *they* ordered Chinese? Next time *he* ordered Chinese? Or next time they had midnight snacks or breakfast together? Although technically they had never had snacks or breakfast. She took a breath and stopped the whirl of overthinking—bad habit, analyzing everything. It had probably just been a meaningless comment. She was a little overwrought.

Out in the parking lot, Jack chucked the garbage into a Dumpster and then walked to his car, reaching in to start it, before closing the door and turning back to her, snow-brush in hand. A light layer of snow had fallen, and everything around them sparkled.

"I'll follow you."

"Hmm?" She had been too busy watching his lazy, sexy walk to pay attention to what he was saying.

"Home. I'll follow you home. We can check your place, make sure everything is okay, and then I'll head home."

Raine started to protest, then realized she wasn't really completely comfortable going back to her dark house alone, and felt relieved he'd offered. She took a deep breath, hating the situation. She had never been afraid to go home. Her little house was her sanctuary, and now she had to be paranoid about walking in the door. Hopefully, it would be over soon.

"Okay. So you remember where it is, in case we get separated?"

"Yes. But we won't."

She looked at him from underneath soft lashes, her eyes a mix of emotions. "Thanks, Jack—you are being way beyond nice to me. But I am thankful. It would be hard to go back there alone at this time of night."

Jack nodded, considering.

"Maybe you should take Delaney's advice and move out for a while."

She shook her head definitively. "No, it may be a little creepy to think I have to watch my every step for a while, or be careful about things I take for granted, but I am not being driven out of my house by some lunatic who may or may not even be around here."

She wrapped her arms around herself, looking around them into the cold, stark night. "Besides, where would I go?"

"You are friends with Gwen, right? Good enough friends to stay with her?"

"Oh, yes—Gwen is one in a million. She would probably sleep on the floor and give me the bed. But she has a small apartment, just one bedroom. And she is, you know, involved right now."

"Yeah, I saw that, with Neal Scott." He smiled at her

surprise that he knew. "I caught them in a, um, clinch in the office a few nights ago."

Raine smiled. "Yeah, Gwen is crazy about him. Though I never would have thought of them as each other's type. Considering the circumstances, my staying there would be a painful inconvenience for her, and I don't think the situation really merits it."

His eyes turned very serious. "Raine, until we know exactly what the situation is, you should just be extremely careful. I'm sure if Gwen and Neal want to fool around, they can go to his place. They didn't seem to care about using the office floor the other night." He smiled, but saw she wasn't going to bite.

Her voice brooked no argument. "No, I want to be home. In my home. I am not going to let this situation get to me any more than I already have. It's already disrupted my work life, and I am not going to let it make a shambles of my home life."

Jack grimaced, but understood and admired her resolve. Still, he wished she wouldn't be quite so independent at the moment.

"Then I guess you will have to get used to me dogging you home every night. And if I can't, I'll make sure someone can."

Raine observed the stubborn set of his chin, the glint in his eyes that was just short of begging her to argue with him, but she decided to take a different route this time.

"Okay. I think I can handle that—if you will let me make dinner for you one night when you—how did you put it?—dog me home." She grinned, feeling absurdly happy, given the discussion and the situation.

Jack felt everything inside him melt as she looked up at him with a smile that he couldn't have imagined in his dreams—she was like pure sunshine, and, for that moment, standing here in the bitter cold, he was warmed.

As she looked up at him, her features softened and her eyes became pools of clear green. He didn't know if she leaned into him, or if he pulled her close, he only knew he couldn't wait another minute for her. He leaned forward, offering a soft kiss, licking the spicy taste of dinner from her lips. Then he covered her lips more fully with his, gently at first, but when she sighed into his mouth, he plunged as deeply as he could. He'd forgotten how passionate she was—no, not forgotten, heaven knew—but his memory had not quite served the reality justice.

When she dragged the tip of her tongue along his lower lip, he pressed her closer, and she felt him, hard and ready, rubbing against her hip. Her body responded, and she felt her lower abdomen tighten and ache. They stood in a fog of heat and car exhaust that was piping out into the cold air, oblivious to everything but each other.

She buried her hands in his hair, forgetting reasons and reasonableness, wanting only to lose herself in him. The man had a mouth like none she had ever known, and he knew how to use it. She felt her knees quiver when he nipped her lightly.

He burrowed into her neck, biting a tender spot, then moving on to another. Raine swallowed, her breathing ragged. She knew she wanted him, but she didn't know what else she wanted from him.

She wanted to be safe—and right now, Jack was safe. She wasn't sure how much of one was combined with the other. He had been so good to her all day, so helpful, and she was, when she thought about it too much, frightened. It was easy to misunderstand one need for another under these circumstances.

"Jack, we shouldn't—"

He inhaled the scent of her hair and perfume and knew he wasn't backing off—not this time. He wanted her in his bed, and maybe in his life. The unbidden thought shook him, but he pushed it aside. For now, bed would suffice— or the backseat of his car, as luck would have it.

"Raine, just be quiet."

He didn't wait for a response but kissed her again and wound her arms tightly around his neck as he reached to the side and opened up the back door. To be honest, he felt a little thrill but also a little apprehension—it had been many, many years since he had had a woman in the backseat of his car. He hoped he was up to the challenge.

He disengaged from her slightly, and met her bemused stare as he began to unbutton her coat. Her eyes widened. He finished unbuttoning the coat, unwound her scarf and pushed them both from her shoulders.

"Get in before you get cold."

Shivering once, she slid into the car, but eyed him warily.

"Jack, seriously…"

His own coat was off and thrown down on the seat, and he was glad to find the car toasty warm. They were alone in the parking lot, and the windows were nicely fogged. Perfect.

"No, Raine…absolutely no seriousness. Let loose a little—remember online you told me you have never had sex in the backseat of a car before, and wondered what it would be like? Let me show you."

"But…"

He somehow slid his hands under her butt and pulled her up next to him, then shifted and settled her over his lap, where she could feel the hard ridge of his cock pressing against some very sensitive places. She wriggled a little to get comfortable, and he moaned and lifted his hips up.

His kiss was so hot she started to break into a slight sweat. He murmured against her lips, words no one had ever said to her before. Things he had only written on the screen of a computer were now coming to passionate life.

"I'm so ready for you, Raine. I've missed this so much... how hot you are..."

She replied with a vague sort of "me, too," but he didn't seem to care much what was coming out of her mouth, he was too busy doing other things.

Her head swam, and she lost track of exactly what it was she was going to say. As she tried to remember, his hand was slithering up inside her sweater, and closed over the warm skin of her breast, kneading and pinching until she couldn't think at all.

Sighing in pleasure, she gave in and slid her hands up inside his sweater as well, hungry fingers remembering the shape of his body. She put her hand over his heart, and felt it pumping madly.

"That's better, baby—just let go."

His voice was rough with need, and she joined him in frantic touching, kissing and biting. They laughed as they fumbled in the confined space, pushing her skirt up, his jeans lower, until his hot, velvet shaft sprang free and jutted against her.

He closed his mouth tightly over her nipple, drawing hard as he worked one hand between them, rubbing and stroking her sex quickly with his able fingers, applying just the right pressure, knowing just where her most sensitive spots were, hardly letting her take a breath as she rocked into his touch and she shuddered against him with one of the fastest, sweetest orgasms she had ever known. He continued to stroke, his hand hot and wet next to her skin, probing and stretching her tender nether lips.

She felt his hand move away, and looked down to see

him closing it over his huge erection, rubbing her glistening juices over himself. She felt her insides liquefy as he touched himself, and she licked her lips, meeting his hungry, dark eyes with hers.

"Raine, I need you, I can't wait...."

She didn't want to wait, either, but couldn't form the words. Straddling him, she moved up close, steadying her hands on the backseat, and took him inside in one smooth move. He groaned, lifting up underneath her sharply until he was buried to the hilt, and she dug her fingers into the material of the backseat as her body found a seductive rhythm of its own. His hands gripped her ass firmly, squeezing and guiding her as she rode him hard and fast.

His head was thrown back on the seat as he gave himself over to her, and she felt a swift rush of power she had not experienced before. She was still sensitive and shivering from her own climax as he slid in and out. She wanted to give him as much as he had given her, and focused on how she could make this as good for him as he had made it for her. He was panting, his head was thrown to the side, and she smiled, loving how it felt to have this hot, needy man underneath her.

She ran her hands over him lightly, teasing, and took his mouth in a wide-open, wet kiss as she thrust against him, taking him whole each time, squeezing tight. Suddenly he cried out her name and his entire body stiffened underneath her. She didn't let up, but adjusted to his body's movements, sliding her body along his as he trembled with release. He stroked her back, emptying himself utterly, until he simply sighed and let his head fall forward, his face buried in the hollow of her neck.

His voice was muffled when he spoke.

"Okay, you killed me. Call nine-one-one."

She smiled again and kissed his temple, and he lifted his

face to see her looking at him with satisfied, happy eyes. It was a look he could get used to. He felt himself go flaccid, leaving the warmth of her body, and hugged her close.

"They would have to bring two stretchers. One for each of us. I'm not sure I can move—they could find us here in the morning."

He smiled and laughed lightly, not wanting to let the moment pass, not knowing what to expect when it did. Would she just dismiss him, the way she did before? Would he be even more addicted to her now, had he gotten himself in too deep? As if he had a choice. She was all he could think about—all he had been able to think about for months. She was everything he wanted—fantasy and reality all rolled up into one. Now all he had to do was convince her of that. His heart sank a little, as she was the one to disengage first, her voice light.

"I guess I'll have a hard time explaining this skirt to the dry cleaners."

She was tugging her clothes back into place, smoothing her hair, making a light joke. He did the same, pulling up his jeans, searching the front seat for his jacket. She smiled at him, looking shy. He touched her face, and kissed her, not saying anything. Maybe things were best left unsaid for the moment. This was better, he knew, than last time, when she had kicked him out—but still, it was less than he wanted—not that he could define what that was.

"You stay here, let me get your car warmed up, then I'll follow you home." It was on the edge of his tongue to ask if he could stay when they got there, but he bit down. Too much too soon, and he wasn't even sure how she was going to react to this once it set in.

Heading out into the cold, his body was still so hot from their lovemaking that he barely needed his coat. It was snowing harder now, and it took him a few minutes, but he found her car and started it. When he opened the driver's door, she was there, waiting.

"You're all set."

She nodded, and stepped forward, seeming awkward and unsure. He marveled—this woman who had just ridden him with such confidence and intention that he had almost spontaneously combusted underneath her was now uncertain about what to do next? He met her halfway, and slipped his arms around her, pulling her close, and sighed a deep breath of relief when hers went around him as well. They stood like that for a quiet moment, and then she pulled away gently, and gave him a warm look before getting into her car. He went to his, and followed her out of the lot.

Neither of them noticed that by the corner of the magazine's office building, a figure in a long dark coat stood watching, deftly sliding into the shadows as they drove by.

THE NEXT MORNING, any hopes Raine might have had about the stalker going away were leveled. There was a message on her desk to come down to Duane's office immediately, and without so much as turning on her own computer, she headed straight there.

The news was not great. She had not been able to deal with her reader correspondence for more than a week, due to the chaos in her life, and had been planning on taking care of it that very day. But apparently the stalker decided to take care of it for her. Raine sat in shocked silence as Duane explained.

"Somehow, he got into your email, and got hold of all your reader notes—and responded to them. The responses were insulting or sarcastic. He used every offensive word in the book, Raine. I've had phone calls and emails flooding in nonstop complaints, demands to cancel subscriptions, and we've been explaining that there's a problem and giving the readers an extra year for free to convince them not to cancel."

He looked down, shook his head.

"We can't afford this, we are still a relatively new publication, you know that. I think readers would believe it wasn't you who wrote the replies, and we plan on printing an immediate explanation and apology on the website and in the next issue. But this is a real mess, Raine. I know it's not your fault, but it's not good."

Raine nodded, barely containing her fury that someone had interfered with her work this way, and had tried to tarnish her reputation with her readers.

"I know, Duane. I don't know how he could have gotten in. Jack told me that he had sealed up the network, and there was no way he could have gotten in again."

She unwrapped her fingers that had been gripping the chair arm like a vise, stood, and squared her shoulders. "I'll send personal thanks and apologies to each of the readers affected. Can you tell me their names?"

Duane looked stressed, and paced around to the back of his desk, staring out the window for a moment, and then looking back at Raine. She felt the hairs on the back of her neck stand up, not knowing what that look meant, but she knew she wasn't going to like it. He sighed, and looked her in the eye, clearly ill at ease.

"Sure, you can do that, I will get you the names. It will probably help. But until this thing is over, the publisher wants you to take a break."

He held up a hand, staying her immediate objection.

"Raine, listen—I went to bat for you, and you know I want you here. But right now, they feel you are indirectly making the magazine a potential target, and if this guy would go this far, then he may be willing to do a lot more damage, and we can't risk it. Neither can you. A few weeks off—paid—is not so bad, right? Maybe he will lose interest, maybe he'll do something stupid and the police will catch him. Either way, you can still work independently."

Raine sat again, miserable. "How are you supposed to explain that I'm not here? Why I'm not at meetings?" she said, her voice reflecting the numbness she was feeling.

Duane nodded. "Well, if anyone asks, you are taking part of your vacation, sick, working from home, whatever. It's just until this thing blows over, Raine—then you are back here, no problem."

She raised her eyes to his. "What if it doesn't blow over? What am I supposed to do? The police said they can't help, the magazine wants me out…." Her voice started hitting a hysterical pitch, though she hated it, she couldn't control it. Duane was around the desk, his hands firm on her shoulders.

"No, we don't want you out—you aren't losing your job, okay?—I promise. Get it out of your head that you are in trouble here. But try to see the situation from our perspective, Raine. This may ultimately be safer for you, too—it's obviously too easy for him to get at you here. Just take a few weeks to let it settle down. Then if it continues when you come back, we will have to find some way to get the authorities more aggressively involved."

"But right now you don't see the point in doing that? I know, the publisher doesn't want the bad press. You know, he may come looking for me even if I am not here." She chilled at the thought.

Duane sighed, and nodded. "I will talk to the police again, and see if we can get them to move on anything. Until then, maybe you should take a real vacation, get away from here, visit home or something. Go to the beach somewhere warm. Get out of the target zone. Don't worry about the next issue. We can expand Gwen's section to fill the space for one month."

Raine didn't—couldn't—respond. Now he was cutting her articles? She wouldn't be in the next issue. Her heart sunk. Her readers would probably think she was fired.

She would be damned if she would go on a *vacation* when her life was falling apart. She was going to find out who—and why—starting with how someone could have accessed her computer after Jack had said it was safe. Anger flowed through her veins, replacing numbness, and she stood, and left his office without a word, heading straight for the basement.

10

"JACK." RAINE STOOD in the doorway of the small, softly lit office. She was surprised, it was nothing like she would have expected. The way Gwen had described the basement made it seem like something out of a sci-fi thriller, but while there were many, many computers humming, it was basically just another floor of offices.

Jack's office was particularly nice. Twice the size of her own. He had eschewed the fluorescent lights for lamps that sat on the desk and a wooden bookcase, and several plants appeared to be thriving in spite of the artificial light.

He was bent over his desk, angled away from the door, set back in a corner. Not the typical power-position office design. This office design stated: "Don't bug me if it's not important."

Well, this was important, and he apparently hadn't heard her the first time. She stepped into the room—something smelled very nice—and walked up directly behind him. "Jack."

He looked up calmly. He had been so focused she had expected him to jump, or at least startle, or scowl. Instead, he smiled. It was a warm—no, hot—smile that made awareness skitter over her skin as time stopped for a second and she remembered every moment of the night before. God, she had been so riled by the meeting with Duane, she had forgotten when she'd stepped into his office that just a little more than twelve hours before, they'd had wild sex in the backseat of his car. She was completely knocked back. Wow. That was one killer smile. And it was for her.

"What?" he said.

"Hmm?"

He raised an eyebrow at her. "Um, you said, 'Jack'— twice—and I said, 'What?'"

She frowned. "If you heard me the first time why didn't you answer?"

"I'm sorry, I was just finishing a thought on this report. Someone fried my mind last night—more than my mind, actually—and I am having a little trouble concentrating today."

"Oh." There was that smile again. He got up and walked to her, standing so close she just wanted to fall against him and forget it all.

"So, what can I do for you?"

Raine raised an eyebrow now, not sure if she'd heard a suggestive inflection in this simple question. Her anger was dissolved by the smile and the comforting atmosphere of the office, and she walked over and slumped into a chair, closed her eyes, raising her hands to her head.

"He got into my email."

"Tell me."

All jokes aside now, he turned his full attention to her. She relayed the details of the break-in, and what the stalker had done to her readers. Jack's eyes went to ice, then fire, as he listened.

"Jack, I guess these things aren't infallible, but how could he have done this, and not have left a trace? I thought you said it was impossible. That things were locked up."

Jack nodded. "They are. I scanned the network this morning for any intrusions in the last twenty-four hours, and there were none. I changed your email login last week. But there are a lot of ways still that he could have gotten your address book—a single-purpose virus, or a trojan attached to one of those earlier emails—not all of this stuff is easily detectable, or detectable at all—it depends on how good this guy is, and how determined. But I'm sorry, Raine. What did Duane say?"

Raine tried to follow the explanation. Trojans? What the heck? She shook her head, and made a note to ask what those things were—insofar as computers were concerned—later.

"He said the publisher wants me to take a 'vacation.'" She spat the word out derisively. "They think I am indirectly making the magazine a target, and that if I go away for a while, the problem will, too."

She looked up, and was shocked. Jack was at the boiling point. She had never seen him so angry, not even with her. But his voice was calm—in the way a frozen lake was calm.

"I'll talk to him. You shouldn't be punished for this. The publisher is an ass."

He started to leave the office, and she stood quickly, catching his elbow. "Jack, please don't. I mean, thanks, but it's not Duane's fault. He did what he could. He says if the guy is still out there when I come back, they will try to get the police to do something more aggressive."

Jack glowered. "Well, that's just dandy. How noble of them to be willing to put you out there to take bullets for the magazine."

When she paled, he shook his head, and put his hand over hers and squeezed.

"Not literally, Raine, I'm sorry—bad phrasing. But it's

much safer for you to be here all day with all these people around, than home, or anywhere else, alone. They are just worried about their precious bottom line instead of thinking about your safety first. Their attitude is inexcusable, and I intend to talk with Duane about it."

She nodded, seeing he was committed to the cause. And it wouldn't hurt, having someone in her corner. In fact, it felt pretty damn good.

"How did you find out about this? Was there anything in your email today?"

Raine blinked. "Duane left a note on my desk that he had to talk to me—that's how I found out. I haven't even checked my email, I completely forgot."

Jack nodded, and guided her to the seat. "Do it now, let's see if there are any more nasty little surprises there."

Raine nodded, sitting at the laptop and tapping in her login information. She swallowed hard when she saw the long list of emails pop up, all from a strange-looking account, all with the same subject heading:

Whore!

The word streamed down the screen in an endless parade of slurs, hundreds of lines all the same, filling screen after screen after screen.

She heard Jack swear, and he leaned over her shoulder, opening one of the emails, and found no message. Tapping away at the keys, and cursing mightily, he finally slammed the laptop shut.

"There's no trace. At least at this level. I'm going to have to dig deeper. This slime won't keep breaking in, I can guarantee you that."

"Well, it doesn't really matter anymore, does it?" Her voice was hushed, as she felt the crushing wave of blues set in. "I won't be here. And I am not going to send one single email from home. I am not even going to hook up at all. No more internet for me."

Jack rubbed her shoulders, digging his fingers into her neck, where the muscles were so tense they were hard as a rock. He wanted to comfort—he wanted to *do* something—this whole situation was making him feel ineffectual, and now he couldn't even make sure she was okay here at work. With him. He inhaled the scent of her hair, and continued massaging until he felt her loosen up.

"Feel better?"

"My neck does. Thanks. You probably just helped me avoid a killer headache."

Although his hands on her had inspired aches in other regions of her body, which surprised her, given the circumstances. Suddenly the softly lit office seemed close and intimate, and she realized his hands hadn't left her shoulders, but rested there, rubbing the hollows of her shoulder blades. Funny, she had never before thought of that as such an erotic spot. But it was now.

"Raine."

"Hmm?" His hands were melting her stress into a light buzz.

"Why do you think the sudden change in attitude? This guy seemed to want to impress you, sent you expensive roses, cleared up your bills—he wants you to know how skillful he is, how much control he has, how much he likes you—but he seemed to be trying to do good things for you, perverse as they were. But now, well, now he sounds pissed off."

Raine nodded slowly. "Well, it's not exactly a stable person who does this kind of thing in the first place. Maybe he is angry that I haven't acknowledged his gifts, or that you changed my email login."

Jack nodded. Possible. There was another possibility, too. That he had seen them. Perhaps last night, in the parking lot. Perhaps earlier in the day, holding hands at the police station, when Jack had followed her home, or when they had been talking in the café. This guy could be watching. He could be jealous. Jack didn't want to let Raine know that—she had enough to deal with; he didn't want to scare her with suppositions, but he had a bad feeling.

The stalker had somehow figured out that she had a man—him—in her life. He was angry. That made him dangerous. And for Jack, it made it even more personal. He couldn't share this with anyone, not when it was just speculation, and not when he had to send her home, alone. He felt anger rise again, bitter in his mouth; oh, he would be talking to Duane about this. The magazine wasn't just going to abandon her. And neither was he.

Raine wasn't looking at him but felt his hands go still on her shoulders, and she could almost feel him thinking. She wondered about what.

"Raine. I want you to move out of your house, and maybe move in with Gwen."

"I already told you, Jack, I am not going to do that…."

"Listen, I don't think sex with Neal is so all-consuming to her that she would put you at risk. It's nice of you to be thoughtful, but you need to consider the idea more carefully."

"No. I'm not letting this maniac drive me out of my home or endanger my friends."

"Then move in with me."

He said it so calmly, so matter-of-factly, that she almost thought she'd imagined it.

She stood, facing him. "I can't do that, Jack. I am not leaving my house. It's bad enough I'm being booted out of here."

Jack's eyes sparked, and he realized hers did, too, her jaw set as stubbornly as his own.

"Then we'll talk to Duane and have the magazine pick up the expense of some sort of protection. The cheap bastards are going to do something."

Raine nodded, not opposed to that idea, and feeling a little disconcerted that she had won that argument so easily. And a little disappointed—did this mean that Jack was opting out?

She had gotten used to the idea of him being her self-appointed protector, but she guessed she couldn't just expect him to go on being her bodyguard. He had work to do, and he had been spending a lot of time watching over her. Without really thinking too much about it, she had let herself get a bit dependent on him, and that wasn't like her at all. Usually she just depended on herself. But he had insinuated himself into her life. He was her…well, her lover. Or maybe it was just those two times? She felt a sinking sense of loss, and the issue added even more confusion to everything she was already feeling.

Jack watched the emotions play over her face. She didn't realize what an open book those green eyes were. Surprise, fear, anger, sadness and something else—despair? Loss?

He was struggling with his own demons. This situation allowed him to see her differently, to look a little deeper than he had before. He was losing emotional ground, and fast. While he didn't want her in this dangerous position, he had to admit a certain male pull of satisfaction at being her protector.

There was the beginning of something between them. He had felt it with her online, as Rider and Nilla, and at her house that one passionate night, and last night. God, though they hadn't spoken of it, last night she'd blown him away. He didn't know what was next.

He needed to know she was safe, and now he wouldn't be able to have any control over that. He was sure he could push the magazine into anteing up for some protection. After all, all he had to do was mention a lawsuit if something happened to her and they would be held responsible. But even if they got the best protection in the country, he wouldn't sleep easy with it. Not unless it was him. Because he was starting to care. And that meant he had more investment in protecting her than some stranger being paid a high fee.

But he wasn't exactly in a position to do too much for her now. He eyed the computer; perhaps the best way he could really be of help would be to track down this psycho. Then they could just forget it. Having focused on this purpose, he felt more steady.

Raine had been lost in her own thoughts, and as if someone flipped a switch, they both came back to the present, and found they had been staring wordlessly at each other. Fire caught in her cheeks, and she looked away. She must be losing it, she had never behaved this way with any man; Jack was definitely a different experience for her. And he had been great, there was no denying it. But now she was on her own. She sucked up a breath.

"Well, I have some stuff to do here, and I guess I will head home. On my *vacation*." She drew out the word, ended on a sigh, and Jack reached out to touch her hair lightly with his fingers.

"Hey, not a bad deal if you can get it, having extra time off and getting paid for it. Make good use of the time."

She shrugged. "I suppose. I can get ahead on some story ideas and work for when I get back, get ahead of the game."

"Relax a little, Raine. This has been a tough week." He kept his hand in her hair. "Would you mind if I dropped by?"

Her heart skipped a little and she smiled. "That would be great. I don't think I have all that much on my calendar."

He smiled at the light comment, and felt his own tension ease as he backed away and nodded.

"Good, then don't be surprised to see me on your doorstep. Probably in a few hours."

She nodded, and turned to leave, stopping by the door for a moment to turn and look at him again. He wanted to go with her, to hold her, to make things easier, but instead his eyes sent her a silent promise that she wouldn't be facing this alone.

RAINE SAT IN HER CAR out in front of her home. In the backseat she had a briefcase full of work and a box of papers she had brought from her file cabinet. A few people had wondered why she was clearing out, and she had managed to smile blithely and keep her voice normal as she chatted briefly about taking a working vacation, and listened to comments about her luck and how they wished they could have it.

Yeah, right.

She couldn't seem to get out of the car. She should feel free, right? Unfettered. All this spare time, paid leave, she could get work done, sleep, exercise, read and clean her house. She had plenty to do, and now she was free to do it. But she didn't feel free. She felt…exposed. Abandoned.

She grabbed the handle and opened the door, forcing herself to move and haul her work up the walk and into the house, finally getting it all inside and put away where she wanted it.

She had to keep moving, to keep busy, and not let herself mope or dwell on the situation. Hopefully, Duane was right and whoever was bothering her would just go away. Maybe he would figure she had been fired from the magazine and be satisfied after his mischief with the reader emails. Maybe it was someone trying to get back at her for something, though she couldn't imagine what.

She sat down at her desk and spent a few hours writing out personal letters to each reader who had been affected, letting them know that there had been a problem on the computer network, and that she had not sent the emails they had received. She dearly hoped they would accept her apologies and continue to read the magazine and her column.

When she was finished, she decided to walk to the mailbox to stretch her stiff legs. The sun was still up. It had been a bright winter day, and there was no biting cold at the moment—a perfect time for a walk. Closing the door behind her, she felt more cheerful, and set out down the steps.

HE COULDN'T CONCENTRATE. He wondered what Raine was doing, if she was okay. He had hacked open those emails that were sent to her as far as he could, and he couldn't trace anything. Everything led back to dummy accounts piled on to more dummy accounts, and finally he realized it was just useless.

They weren't going to find this guy electronically. He was either going to disappear, or they would find him when he tried something more aggressive. He hoped it was the former, but something in his gut told him it wouldn't go away that easily. He looked at the clock. He could still get some work done, but his heart wasn't in it.

He wanted to see her; it was as simple as that.

He couldn't remember any other time he had missed a woman after just a few hours, or anyone he had worried about as much, except for his own family. But he would let her be for now, let her settle in, get used to the situation before he went knocking at her door. After all, it had only been a few hours. For now, he would go home, and try to relax and get Raine off his mind for a little while. *Good luck,* he thought as he grabbed his jacket and left for home.

RAINE HAD RELAXED considerably by the end of the day. The walk had been pleasant, and she had come back and made herself a delicious salad and pasta, taking her time and making herself the kind of dinner she rarely had the chance to enjoy during the week. She called Gwen and filled her in on the recent happenings, and then spent a half hour convincing her friend that she was okay on her own, for now. It was nice to know that Gwen wanted her to come stay, but she didn't intend to lead danger—if there was any real danger—to her friend's door.

Now she was stretched out on the sofa with a blanket, a glass of wine and a novel. The novel may not have been the best choice—a hot romance, the kind she secretly read and had boxfuls of in her attic.

Ever since she was young, she'd loved escaping into romances for hours at a time, losing herself in the world of emotions and experiences she never had. She enjoyed seeing the heroines and heroes grow over the years as she herself had grown; the story lines became more daring, the women more independent, the men more sexy and complex.

How was it that the men in these novels were so amazingly clued-in to the needs and feelings of the heroines? She smiled to herself—because women created them, of course. But maybe there were one or two out there who really were like that in real life. Or maybe just one.

She averted her thoughts, took a sip of wine, her eyes glued back to the page as the hero seduced the heroine for the first time, and she felt her own blood heat as the two lovers experienced the ultimate pleasure together.

She smiled, squirming a little on the sofa, feeling a tickle down low.

For once in her life, she could relate—she knew what a man could do for a woman—thanks to Jack. It seemed like aeons ago that they had made love, even though it was just last night, but her body remembered every single sensation vividly.

She felt heat move up her face; she was incredibly warm from the book, the wine and the blanket. Fanning her face with the book, she decided it was time for a break, or sleep would not come easy tonight. Apparently, she couldn't keep Jack out of her head for more than five minutes, though she had to admit that her reading material wasn't helping matters.

She looked at the phone. It was late, but he would be home. She could call. But what would she say? Their relationship was changing, but maybe not so much that she could feel comfortable calling him at this time of the evening. She had no idea how to handle these things.

She wished she was brazen enough to call him as she had done that first time, to hear his voice on the phone, to seduce him with her words.

But that was Nilla—it wasn't really her. Was it? Her body was humming, she missed him, and she felt very alone in the house. It was late, but it wasn't *that* late. Maybe she could just call to let him know she was okay, and they could talk, and that was all.

Jack's number. Where had she left it? Yes—the nightstand—she'd put it there. Running to the bedroom, she let out a small cry of dismay when she didn't see the paper on the table, and got down on her hands and knees to find it. There it was! It had gotten knocked down under the bed. Thank God she hadn't sucked it up in the vacuum, though in her mood, she might have gone digging through the dusty bag to find it.

She reached for the phone, her hands trembling slightly. It was just a phone call, for goodness' sake. She shook herself mentally, and grabbed the receiver, lifting it to her ear, and heard nothing. She dialed the number, but there was no sound. Her phone was dead.

She clicked the hook a few times, held the phone back to her ear, and nothing happened. But she'd paid her bill.... She set the receiver back down in the cradle, and fear seeped through her, chilling her to the bone.

Had someone messed with her phone? She felt panic skitter down her spine, and she tried to control her breathing. It was late, and she was afraid. She had her cell phone.... Frantically, she ran to her desk and dug through her bag, finding the small phone she only used for work. She had almost forgotten that she had it.

Hands shaking, she dialed the number. She only got his office message. Dammit! Damn! She felt tears squeeze against the back of her eyes; this was his cell phone number, too, not his home number. She sat on the floor, wedged tightly to the wall, and tried to calm down.

She called back, and left a message. Hopefully he would check. She willed herself to think. She could call the police, but if her phone was just dead and her lines not actually cut, she would look like a fool. What if this was another billing mess-up?

She needed to take control. Running into her bedroom, she pulled on jeans and a sweater, put on her jacket and headed for the kitchen door. She grabbed a flashlight, keys and a sharp nail file. She would go see if her lines were cut herself, and if they were, she would call the police from the safety of her car—she wouldn't go back in the house, just in case. All the women in the movies always went back in the house; it was always a mistake.

Armed with her plan, she went out the back door, and kept the flashlight off until she got to the side where she knew the phone hookup was. She kept close to the house, looking all around her. The snow made it almost as light as day outside, and she took comfort from the fact that she could see clearly that no one was there but her. Her neighbor's windows, only a few yards away, were lit. There was help nearby if she called out.

She turned the flashlight on and searched the side of the house, and saw the phone connection—the wire was indeed cut. Swallowing down her fear, she forced herself to follow her plan—she walked quickly to the front of the house, her breath coming raggedly. In a wave of panic she realized that she had left her cell phone on the bed. *Stupid!*

Now she would have to go back in. She turned around and headed for the door, when she felt a hand grab her from behind. She screamed, reaching for the nail file in her pocket and spinning around, struggling away from whoever had hold of her arm, flailing the file in front of her.

"Raine! Stop it! It's me, Jack—you're okay.... *Stop!*"

Jack managed to get hold of both wrists, and held them tight, as her eyes, wide and blank with fear, finally focused in on him. Her face was deathly white, and he saw recognition dawn; she let the nail file fall from her fingers. It glittered in the light as it fell to the ground.

Her teeth were chattering, and she stood, frozen, staring at him wordlessly. He released her wrists from his tight grip and pulled her close, walking her to the door. "It's okay. I was on my way home and got your message. I tried to call back, but no one answered. Scared the hell out of me, Raine. Where's your cell?"

She tried to talk through great gulps of panic and shiver-

ing. "The...phone l-line...is cut.... I checked.... I left my...
c-cell in the bedroom.... I f-forgot..."

Inside the door, he spun her around to face him. "You
did what?"

"I...I...l-left my...phone on the b-bed...." She was shaking from head to toe now, and he pulled her to the couch,
warming her hands between his.

"Raine, you went out to check if the phone line was
cut? Are you nuts? Someone could have been out there."

She shook her head.

"I looked around, it was bright.... I h-had the file.... I
couldn't ca-call the cops if the phone was just dead...and
I didn't know where you were...."

Tears were starting to flood her eyes now, and he took
her shoulders. "Okay, I'm sorry, baby. Hold it together, just
for a while, okay? It's okay. We're getting you out of here."

She nodded faintly.

"You get clothes together, I'll call the cops. Go pack
what you need. Don't pack light—we don't know how
long this will be for."

She nodded and stood on trembling legs, unsure of exactly where he thought she would be going, but she knew
she couldn't stay home alone and feel safe. She went to
pack, hearing him in the distance, calling the police.

It didn't seem like very long before she heard voices in
the living room, and she came out. Jack was talking with
two uniformed officers, and they were taking notes. She
joined them, feeling steadier but no less afraid.

"Evening, ma'am. Mr. Harris reported that you had
some trouble here?"

She nodded. "Someone cut my phone line."

"The phone is dead?"

"Yes. Someone cut the line into the house—I checked."

The officer raised his eyebrow, but didn't say a word

for a moment. "Okay, we're going to go out and check the premises. Just sit tight for a few minutes."

Jack thanked the officers and took in Raine's face. She was still ghostly pale, but the trembling seemed to have stopped, and she was calmer.

"All packed?"

"Yes. I just need to get some work together. I suppose that I could see if the inn down the street is open, but it's late…"

She felt the sharpness in his voice cut through her fog. "Inn? You aren't going to a damn inn, Raine—what the hell are you thinking? You are going home with me. You can stay at my place."

She blinked at him. "Your place? I can't stay with you."

He stared at her. "Yes, you can, and you are. You said yourself you don't want to go to Gwen's, and this way, you have built-in security—me."

"But—"

"Listen, I have enough room, and two beds, if that is what's worrying you."

She felt heat invade her face, and her throat tightened. "No, that's very kind of you, I don't want to intrude. This isn't your problem."

His voice was cooler now, his eyes glittering as they bored into hers.

"Don't do that, Raine. Don't do it, not now. Not this time."

She just nodded, went quiet under his hard stare. He relaxed, and backed off as the officers came to the door, looking serious.

"Yep, the phone line is cut. We can look for prints but I don't imagine we'll find anything. There are a lot of footsteps in the snow, but some of those will be yours, from what you've said. You're going to have to have your car taken care of. All four tires were cut. Maybe you scared off whoever did it when you went outside, but it isn't safe for you to stay here alone."

Jack's arm came around her shoulders, holding her fast. She couldn't say anything, but she heard Jack tell them that they had already filed one complaint with Detective Delaney about a stalker, and that this was probably connected to that incident. The uniformed officers nodded, and looked at Raine.

"The detective may want to talk with you again, ma'am. Do you know a place you can stay for the night?"

Raine looked at them mutely, and Jack stepped in, giving them his address and number. Grabbing her bags, and shutting off the lights, they left the premises with the police officers, and went to Jack's car.

Raine looked at her car sitting lopsidedly in the driveway, and felt the panic surge up again. Who would want to do this to her? She had never hurt anyone. She kept to herself. She hardly even *knew* anyone.

She felt Jack guide her into the passenger's seat, and she let her head fall back against the headrest, closing her eyes, feeling a massive headache coming on. The car rolled forward, and everything dimmed to gray.

11

THE NEXT THING she knew, she was being shaken gently, and she startled upright, not exactly sure where she was. It was dark, there were comforting smells of spice and— Jack. They were in his car, he was leaning over, his hand on her shoulder; she must have fallen asleep. His voice was quiet, gentle.

"There you are—I didn't realize why you were so quiet for a while, you had me worried. I was talking to you and there was only silence. I didn't realize you had fallen asleep, but I'm glad you got some rest." He was smiling at her, but his eyes looked tired.

She yawned, still groggy with sleep. "I'm kind of surprised, too. I guess it was just being in the car, warm, and I relaxed a little." With you, she added silently.

He nodded. "Well, we're here. My place. If you want to go in, I can get your things." He held his keys out.

She blinked hard.

"No, I can help."

She opened the door before he could argue, and felt the cold blast of air hit her in the face, waking her. She stepped out, and looked at the beach cottage in front of her. It was dark, but she could see the house was not a new construction, not one of the parade of characterless condos that had sprung up along the shoreline, but an old, square, two-story stone house, with a cobbled chimney.

Brambly beach-plum hedges poked gnarly branches up from underneath a light layer of icy snow and little wooden tents stood duty under the windows, protecting the bushes from the weather. The place, glistening and shadowed under the moon, looked magical. It was set far back from the shoreline, but she could still hear the waves crashing behind the house, and salt hung in the air.

The winds were frigid, and she shivered, turning to the car. Jack had already pulled her bags out from the trunk, and she grabbed one of the heavier ones and walked toward the charming wooden, cathedral door with a heavy brass knocker. The single, wide step was a large stone slab, and she felt the crunching under her boots where Jack had salted the slippery walk. A bright porch light in the shape of a lantern helped her see clearly as Jack slid the key in the lock and pushed open the door.

As she walked in, she was enveloped in the scent that she had come to associate with the man himself, a heady aroma of wood, cloves and sea. She set her bags down and looked around the small entry that was simply decorated with some antique naval items on the walls and a straight-backed Shaker bench where she sat to remove her boots. The floors were all hardwood and gleaming, and colorful Persian rugs were scattered everywhere. Everything about the house seemed sturdy and square, but it was inviting as well. *Cozy,* she supposed, was a weak word.

Secure. Solid. *Safe.*

Jack's voice interrupted her observations.

"It's a little chilly in here. It gets that way if I let the fire go out for a long time. Let me get it going, and I'll show you your room. You can look around wherever you want." He pointed down a narrow hallway. "The bathroom is down that hall, up the stairs to the left, if you need it."

She nodded, and stood up, feeling strange. The whole evening had been surreal, and here she stood now, in Jack's house, feeling both incredibly at home and yet like a complete stranger. She just stood in that spot, and he walked up to her, placing his hands on her shoulders.

"Raine, I want you to feel comfortable here. You're safe. No one except my closest friends and family have this address, and it's not even listed in my name. I have lived here for a long time, but it is actually my grandparents' property. I use a post-office box in town. No one can trace us here. No one could possibly know you are here."

She nodded and felt the warmth from his hands on her shoulders move across her skin, and she thought she might be safe from the stalker and even from Jack, but she wasn't too sure about herself. Some of her thoughts must have shown in her eyes, since his eyes snapped in recognition as passion ignited between them.

But he let his hands drop to his sides, smiling slightly as he turned and walked into another room. Raine went to find the bathroom, pleased but not surprised to find it very modern, offering every convenience including a large set-in tub with massage jets that made her purr with anticipation of a hot bath. She ran her hand along the edge of the cool, granite-textured porcelain. Tension had made her ache from head to toe, and she felt like a piece of raw meat.

Pursing her lips, she walked back down the hall, where she was treated to a very nice view of Jack's backside as he bent over, stoking a fire. The central room with the fireplace was as beautiful as the rest of the house, but she wasn't really paying attention to the details at that very moment.

"Um, Jack?"

"Yeah?" He looked over his shoulder and smiled. "Almost done, this will warm the place up fast."

"Oh, it's fine, I love it. I was just wondering, I know it's very late, but…"

He stood and looked at her, and she was mesmerized, watching him. He almost seemed to glow as the flames started to leap up in the background, and she licked her lips.

"I am feeling pretty achy, and was wondering…"

He shot her a huge grin.

"Ah, the bath. Absolutely. No one ever resists that for long once they've seen it. Help yourself. I'm serious, Raine, that I want you to treat this place as you would your own home. You want something, you don't need to ask."

She nodded, still staring at him standing in the firelight, and felt her insides melt, and she wasn't thinking about the tub now.

"But you may want to get in there now, before you get too tired. I'll show you your room so you can just hit the sheets if you want. You've had a tough night."

She nodded, then followed him into the foyer again and grabbed her bags, walking behind him up the stairs and past the magnificent bathroom to a room at the end of the hall. He opened the door, and turned on the light.

"I'm afraid it is the smaller of the two bedrooms, but I hope it will be comfortable. It has a nice view in the daylight."

Raine caught her breath. The room was smaller than hers at home, but the high four-poster bed covered in white and blue linens looked like something out of a dream.

Jack walked to the window and gazed out.

"Actually, the moon is so full tonight you still have a nice view—the snow makes it so bright."

She joined him by the six-over-six, square-paned window that looked out over wind-bent trees and dunes. The corners were edged with snow, like something out of a postcard. The room had the same homey feel as the rest of the house.

Someone cared very much about this old place. A lovely old waterfall-style dresser and full-length mirror filled one corner of the room by a closet and a quilt stand. The walls were a pale green, and ink drawings of seabirds and flowers were on every wall. She sighed, turning back to the room.

"You may never get me to leave."

He smiled, wondering why that thought caused his breath to come up short for a moment, and walked back to the doorway.

"It's yours for as long as you want it, Rainey. I'll be downstairs. Enjoy your bath."

And he was gone. Raine sat on the bed, which she practically needed a stepstool to crawl up onto, and tested its mattress. It was just right. Of course. She gathered up her bath necessities and headed back to the bathroom, her thoughts on the tub and her aching muscles.

JACK SAT BY THE FIRE, exhausted but unable to sleep. He had been badly shaken when he had received that message, Raine's voice, tight and panicked, telling him her phone was dead and pleading with him to please call back on her cell. He ran a hand over his face, reminding himself that he had her here now, with him, safe and sound. He wouldn't let his imagination torture him with what ifs.

He barely remembered the mad drive from the highway back to her house. He was glad he was still so close by. After leaving work, he was too restless to go home alone, and had stopped for some food, then for a few drinks. A pretty brunette had flirted with him at the bar; she had re-

ceived his polite but clear "not interested" message quickly
and left him alone.

His mind was consumed with thoughts of a particular blonde. Who was upstairs naked in his tub right now.
Who would be sleeping just yards away from him tonight.
He felt his body react to the thought and tried to stem his
desire. That wasn't what Raine needed right now. She'd
had a nasty day followed by a nastier night, and though
his mind swam with images of what could happen between them here in his house for an undetermined length
of time, he primarily wanted to make sure she was safe
and taken care of.

But he also knew that he had not mistaken the flash of
desire in her eyes when she had looked at him in the entry
hall. That had spoken to him loud and clear. He stared at
the fire for a long while, sipping a cognac and sinking
into his dreams.

RAINE PADDED DOWN the stairs; the house was amazingly
silent. She had sat in the bath until the water had turned
tepid and she was in danger of drowning by falling asleep.
But then when she had gone and crawled into the huge,
soft bed, she'd laid there wide maddeningly awake. So she
went in search of some reading material to try to take her
mind off things.

When she went into the den, she was surprised to find
Jack stretched out on the huge burgundy sofa, slumped
down in a half sitting position that didn't look very comfortable, but he was sleeping deeply nonetheless. She sat
carefully on the opposite edge, in front of the fire, watching him sleep.

He was an incredibly beautiful man, something she
hadn't fully appreciated before. His face was softened by
sleep, and she longed to reach out and touch him. Instead,

she curled her feet up underneath herself, and opened the book she'd chosen from the bookcase against the far wall.

Jack was awakened by the familiar scent of citrus and flowers filling the room. He opened his eyes slightly, looking around, and saw Raine sitting on the sofa, legs curled beneath her, staring at a book. The flickering light played off her face, and he took in her long hair, damp and curling, pulled up on the back of her head, exposing the graceful length of her neck.

She was dressed in flannels—green, blue and white check, and white, fuzzy socks. Baggy pants and a button top, cinched modestly. It should have been more cute than sexy, but he remembered her telling him about her flannels once before, and he felt himself go hard.

"Raine." His voice was barely a whisper.

She lowered the book and looked at him, her face freshly scrubbed, glowing in the firelight, eyes sleepy.

"Oh, I'm sorry, I didn't want to wake you, but I just didn't…well, I couldn't sleep. I came downstairs and saw you sitting here, and thought I would just sit with you, and…"

She was babbling and couldn't stop. He was looking at her, sleepy, relaxed, and with undisguised desire in his eyes.

"Come here."

His command was simple, and quietly spoken, and she never in a million years would have thought of not following it. Sliding over, she placed the book on the table, and sat on the edge of the sofa, in front of him, snuggled between the heat of the fire and the heat of his body. He reached up and slid his hand over her cheek, traced a finger down her neck, and she shivered, but not with cold.

He drew her to him, sliding his mouth gently over hers. Then, he drew back, muttered something into her mouth, and kissed her again. Heaving himself fully up onto the long, lush sofa, he settled back against the pillows. His look invited her to join him. She did so, bringing her legs up and stretching out along the length of him, nestling her head in the crook of his shoulder.

A wave of heat washed over her skin when she felt the hardness of him against her hip. He kissed her hair, and made soft comforting sounds, drawing her more intimately against him.

She worked her arms around him as well, and nestled in closer. Slowly, she heard his breathing even, and felt her own eyelids fall. She fell into dreamless sleep, more safe and secure than she ever remembered feeling in her entire life.

THE FIRE HAD DIED DOWN a bit and the room was cool but not uncomfortable. She had no idea what time it was. Feeling relaxed for the first time in ages, she didn't care. She could feel Jack's breath stirring against her cheek, and smiled. He slept like a rock. That bit of knowledge felt…intimate. She saw springy chest hair curling in the V where he'd loosened the buttons of his shirt; he was still fully dressed.

Sliding her fingers out from under his arm, she touched the spot tentatively. She was curious about his tastes and textures, wanted to memorize the geography of his body, learn what he liked, what he wanted.

She was surprised at her thoughts, but he was sleeping, they were alone. Her thoughts and desires were hers, and she wanted to indulge in them.

Tilting her head backward she memorized the sinewy muscles of his neck, the angle of his jaw, and marveled at his skin. It was manly, a bit tanned even in winter, and just rough enough. He had the beginning of a beard that had miraculously appeared overnight. Running a finger over the stubble lightly, she wanted to know how it would feel scraping over her skin.

Her finger continued its journey along the shallows of his throat. She pushed herself up slightly and, holding her breath, turned her face into his neck, and let the tip of her tongue just touch him, ever so lightly, delighting in his salty, manly flavor.

Jack was having a difficult time keeping his eyes shut and body still. He had buoyed quickly into consciousness when she'd been touching his chest, and every part of him was becoming fully aware and awake more quickly than he had control over.

Finally, he gave up the pretense of sleep when she nipped the sensitive skin beneath his ear. He released a long groan, gathering her more fully against him and burying his face in her fragrant hair, which had somehow come loose in the night. His voice was gruff, and he felt surprise in her body as she realized he was awake.

"Morning—don't stop on my account."

Raine pulled back a little. He was wide-awake now, and ready to go, from what she could feel as he rubbed an impressive morning erection against her leg. He turned his face to slide his tongue along her ear. She caught her breath, feeling the zing from the subtle kiss travel straight down and land deep in her belly, the sharp bite of pleasure soaking her panties. She wished he would promise to never stop tracing his tongue over her skin—oh, yes... just like that.

Moving her legs apart, she rubbed the crux of her sex along his hard-on and moaned with need, seeking and finding his mouth with hers. She licked his lips into a wet kiss, wanting to lose herself in it. He slid his hands down and grabbed her derriere firmly, settling her against him, smiling into her mouth when she whimpered and strained, bunching her fingers in his shirt.

"We're both overdressed for this." She nodded and slowly, reluctantly, pushed away, standing by the side of the couch. Smiling at him, feeling free and bold, she slowly unbuttoned her top, and dropped it to the floor. She felt a blush steal up her cheeks when she saw him swallow deeply and clench his hands at his sides.

Sliding her hands down over her full breasts, across small, rosy nipples, and down her stomach, she eased her thumbs under the waistband of her pajama bottoms, lowering them slowly, until she stood before him wearing only a pair of scant, pink silk panties. He reached out, but she backed away, out of his reach, her voice coy.

"Uh-uh…your turn."

Though he appreciated her show, he was impatient, and lost his own clothing quickly, tossing them on the floor behind the couch. He stood up next to her, drawing her against him, taking her mouth in a bruising kiss. Slipping his hands down her back, knotting his hands in the scrap of silk she wore, he pulled the crotch up tight, evoking a cry from her as he tugged the soaked fabric tight—and released—then did it again.

Biting his bottom lip, Raine absorbed the growl of his response, and pressed her thighs together tightly around his steel-hard erection, loving the feel of him rubbing against her skin. She dropped her head back and bent into him like a bow when he cupped both breasts in his hands.

He squeezed her aroused nipples sharply, but when he shifted, prodding against the barrier of thin silk, seeking entry, she made a sound of slight protest, and put her hands on his stomach, pushing lightly. He blinked, unsure of what she was doing.

He smiled, reaching his hand up to touch her face tenderly but still with a quizzical look in his eyes. She slid her hands from his stomach to chest to shoulders, and pressed him back to the couch, shushing his questions with her lips.

Her eyes were hazy with desire, but clear with purpose. His heart missed a beat when she smiled against his lips and whispered, "This time, for you."

Then she was trailing kisses down his body, licking her hot little tongue across his stomach, and creating a ball of need so tight in his groin that he thought he would explode without her even touching him. When she bit the inside of his thigh, he had to protest, loudly; he was going to lose it before she went much further. She just smiled, and leaned back for a moment.

"Jack?"

"Hmm?"

"Move up on the sofa a little. I want you to watch."

His limbs went so weak he didn't think he would be able to lift himself, but somehow, he did. His chest was heaving with effort and anticipation as she tormented him by trailing her fingers lightly up his leg, and she made sure he had a clear view as she drew her luscious, pink tongue up the rock-hard length of him, and then back down again. She cupped his balls in her hand, stroking gently, her fingers finding the spot down between his legs that she knew would push him to near the edge. His head dropped back in ecstasy, and she scolded gently.

"No, Jack, look at me…look at me."

God help him, he watched her descend again, wrapping her lips tightly around him and taking him to the hilt. Her eyes never left his. His head spun with pleasure, and he couldn't have controlled the noises he was making if he'd tried. She sucked and nipped at him, lolling her tongue around him until he was crazed. Just as he reached the edge, she drew back, always making sure his eyes were on her. Sucking the pulsing head of his throbbing cock hard and sharp, she watched him lose control, his eyes blind with passion, but glued to hers. His breath heaved, he arched up under her, and he choked out a single plea that taught her a new kind of pleasure.

She sighed, taking him deep, gladly giving him what he needed. Sucking him hard, she gloried in his harsh cries of release but didn't see the pleasure contort his face, focused on draining the last drop of pleasure from him as she tasted the hot, salty evidence of his ejaculation at the back of her throat.

He called out to her, but she kept him inside her until he softened, and lapped him clean, nestling her face into his stomach when she was done. Sliding up his body, and wrapping herself against him, she buried her face in his throat. She was very aroused, but also oddly satisfied.

His breathing calmed and he kissed her hair, holding her. He didn't remember ever having such a wildly strong orgasm in his life; every muscle in his body felt like jelly. He wasn't sure his arms worked, but he wanted to touch her. He could feel the heat coming off her body, and stroked her back.

"Rainey...you are, well...nothing I can say..."

She smiled and rubbed her cheek against him like a cat. "I liked it, too. I never...um, did that before, with anyone. I wanted to with you."

His eyes became soft and dark; he was deeply touched that she wanted to give to him so deeply, and he stroked her hair. She kissed him lightly, trying to calm her own arousal. This had been perfect. She had gotten more from pleasuring him than she ever would have expected, and it was enough.

He shifted himself a little more solidly beneath her, bringing her fully on top of him, and buried his face in her neck, light kisses sending flares of desire racing across her skin. His hands stroked her back, moved down over the gentle curves of her bottom, pressing her against his thigh, and then moved back up over and over until she felt her heart pounding.

"Jack, it's okay…. I'm okay…." Her breath hitched as he wrapped his hands over the tender flesh of her rib cage, under her arms, and stroked the sides of her breasts. She raised her head to look at him. He was smiling, his eyes glinting with something like mischief, and she gazed at him warily. "What are you doing?"

His grin split wider.

"You know what I'm doing…. You don't like it?"

He licked a hot trail from her collarbone to her mouth. She pressed against him, her body leaving her brain behind and acting of its own accord. He pushed his knee up, positioning her on his hard thigh, urging her to ride him.

She shook her head. "No…" Her voice squeaked a little as she panicked.

"Yes." He pressed her down, whispering lovely hot things as he felt her melt over him, and bit her ear. She relaxed and pressed against him shyly, reluctantly, and made those soft kittenish sounds he loved. After a few minutes he felt her starting to lose control, grinding herself against him without his help, her breasts pressing hotly against his chest as she moved.

"There you go…. Yeah…that's it…. Let it go, sweetheart…. Take what you need." He planted wet kisses on her ear as her thighs squeezed him and she cried out, her fingers digging into his shoulders. He felt the release of tension in her body as the orgasm rippled through her, smiled when he felt the flood of warmth on his leg. Slowly, he lowered her, holding her close. He stroked her back and felt her body shaking slightly.

He reached up and slid his fingers under her chin, lifting her face, worrying he would find tears, and instead saw her eyes alight with laughter, her neck and face flushed with pleasure. She shook her head, burying it in his neck once more. She spoke, her voice muffled.

"I can't believe you made me do that."

"What? Come? I *like* making you do that."

She laughed, and sounded shy; it made him smile. Her voice squeaked, "Like that though—I mean…geez…Jack."

"Hey, it's about whatever works, *Rainey*. We have all these parts, it's a shame not to experiment with them, wouldn't you say?"

She nodded against his chest, and sighed deeply.

They stayed there for a while, lost in the warmth of each other, and Jack felt that he could stay in this position, wrapped around her naked body for a long, long time. He felt good. What they had shared had been even more intense than the last time, and he wouldn't have thought that was possible.

But even though it had been damn near perfect, he missed being inside her, and was already wanting her again. He couldn't escape the unceasing, and somewhat annoying, urge to connect with this woman in every way possible, and he needed time to think about that. He wanted more. He wanted it all. He sighed and rubbed her back, enjoying the feeling of her nestled against him, but forced his thoughts back to the day.

"It's got to be halfway through the morning. The troops are going to wonder where I am."

"Hmm?" She lifted her head, looking at him.

"Work. Some people may be on extended vacation, but we poor working stiffs still have to go out and earn a dollar."

He tweaked her chin, and smiled, shifting them both

up and feeling the cool air of the room sneak in between them when she lifted herself.

She was looking around for her pajamas, standing there completely naked in his den, her hair in complete, gorgeous disarray, skin rosy, nipples hard from the coolness of the air. He felt himself go semi-erect again, and was abashed enough to feel a little heat rise in his face as she stared at his erection, and then smiled up into his face, her eyes playful.

"You must really like your job."

He snorted, swatting her on the butt as she reached for her pajamas on the floor.

"I do, but I like your job better." She turned a rosy shade of pink, and he chuckled. Standing, pulling his pants on loosely as she dressed, he smiled and reached out, bringing her back to him for a moment.

"I like it when you look like that—satisfied and happy. We haven't had too much of that together, really, have we?"

She felt unsure of how to respond, unable to handle the intimacy he obviously wanted to share with her.

"I, um…" She just squeezed him back and stepped away, brushing off the front of her pajamas absently and turning around. "Oh, look, it is almost ten. Are you going in?"

Jack stared at her, more curious than upset about her obvious discomfort. He pursed his lips. "No, I can telecommute today."

Then he crossed his arms over his chest and leveled her a serious look.

"Raine, why are you doing this?"

Pulling on a sock, she looked at him. "My feet get cold."

He sat back down on the sofa, still warm from their bodies, and reached up and tugged at her elbow for her to sit down with him. She looked away but sat, putting her hands in her lap when she couldn't figure out what to do with them. He moved closer, took them in his and held them steady.

"No, not that. Why, after we have sex, do you withdraw emotionally? The first time we were together, you did it—you backed off so fast I could feel the ice forming. I didn't even think there would be a next time. In the car, you did the same thing, and now again. But it's especially confusing at this moment, Raine, because we share more now, we knew this was going to happen between us. I figured we both wanted it."

Raine grimaced, looked out the window and then back at Jack. Unable to sit, she got up, paced, and looked back at him.

"I'm sorry. I didn't realize I was being so…rude." When his eyes narrowed to annoyed slits, she realized her mistake, made a frustrated sound and came back to the couch, faced him, tried to speak normally.

"Jack, I don't know how to make you understand. I didn't have family, didn't have many friends. I don't know how to handle these moments that seem to come so easily to everyone else. I'm not always sure what to say. I didn't have boyfriends until college, but that was nothing like this, that's for sure. Nothing has ever been like this."

He liked hearing her admit that, and saw more in her eyes than he thought she probably knew showed there. He nodded, took her fidgety hands back in his as she went on.

"And then there is the fact that we really don't know each other, not really. I don't know much about you, really, except your job, the bits and pieces I picked up online, and what you have told me since I've been here, which really hasn't been much."

He frowned at that; she was right. They hadn't spent much time talking about their lives, they were too busy reacting to circumstances. They hadn't really dated, there was nothing traditional about their relationship. Her voice lowered, but she continued.

"And I…I do want you. I have never felt like this before—physically—with anyone. But I don't know what else we have, and if it is just the circumstances, you know…"

He angled his head, prompting her to continue, and she took a deep breath, plunging forth.

"Just our situation. I mean, it's human—you're human. You have been so good to help me, but it's like we are in a movie—this isn't real, an evil stalker and a handsome hero who saves the damsel in distress—it's like playing a game."

He shook his head adamantly.

"I'm not playing games with you, Raine—not now—and what we just shared was very, very real. It's all been real."

"Well, yes, in one sense…"

"No, in *every* sense. I agree with you that we met under odd circumstances, and that we haven't had time to get to know each other like couples usually do. But that doesn't mean that what we have isn't real. It's real, Rainey. Trust me."

She stood up again, her uncertainty wrapping around her like an old robe. It was familiar, and kept her safe. It kept her from risking too much.

"I do trust you, in a way—but how can I know what will happen next, if you will still feel this way once the danger and drama are over with? Or how can you know that anything you feel is more than that? You may just feel sorry for me…now that you know about my background, and my problems in bed." The color in her face burned and she looked away, trying to hide from the heavy burden of self-consciousness that she carried. He stood, crossing the distance between them quickly, turning her to him.

"Are you crazy? You turn me inside out with a touch, with a look—how can you think you are bad in bed? We just finished with each other and I could pull you back down on that couch right now and do it all over again." He took a deep breath.

"As for the orgasm issue, Raine, you just need to explore what works and what doesn't—that doesn't make it boring, hell, it's the exact opposite! I get worked up just thinking about ways to make you come. And I've been thinking about it a lot. I like it. You're incredible in bed."

She shook her head, started to interrupt, but he wasn't finished yet.

"As for the rest, I'd like to think at this point of my life I'm grounded enough not to just get caught up in circumstances, though I'll admit that I do feel protective toward you, and the situation has emphasized that. I'll even admit to using it a bit to get you here with me."

She gave him a shocked look, and he smiled, touching her face.

"I wanted you here with me so I knew you were safe, yes, but selfishly I wanted to have more time with you."

He stepped in, pulled her closer, the heat from his still-bare chest burning through the flannel of her top.

"As for feeling sorry for you, I hate it that you were unhappy, but that's the past. I do feel sorry for the child you were. I hate even thinking about how you grew up. But you aren't a child anymore. There isn't much room for pity in what I feel for you. Desire, interest, admiration… hope. But not pity."

He stroked her back in that way he knew she liked and felt her ease against him. Her face on his shoulder, Raine sighed. He had neatly dissolved each one of her doubts as if they were snowflakes melting on his tongue. Though she believed the things he said, she still had reservations, she just couldn't help it.

He made it all sound so logical, so easy, but it wasn't as easy for her. He rubbed his cheek against her hair.

"Just one promise?"

"Hmm?"

"You'll stop withdrawing from me emotionally and be open to seeing what we have here."

She smiled slightly. "That's two promises." But she nodded, and he smiled.

"Okay, I'm going to grab a shower—you can join me if you like." The wicked grin drew one from her in return.

"My stomach is growling." She made the excuse, but didn't tell him what his offer caused other parts of her anatomy to do. "But thanks for the offer."

"Anytime. Like I said, feel free to help yourself to anything you want."

With that suggestive offer, he left her there, staring after him. She shook her head, feeling as if her life was being turned upside down in more ways than one. But some of it wasn't so bad.

12

THE NEW ENGLAND BLUES and whites of the small kitchen made it appear bright and charming. She particularly admired an impressive collection of yellow-ware bowls displayed on an antique walnut stand. Like the rest of the house, the kitchen was compact and old-fashioned, but well equipped. Except for the refrigerator. She found one egg, a near-empty quart of milk long past the expiration date and some English muffins that had seen better days.

She found supplies for coffee and grabbed a banana from the counter. She would go shopping. She could feel useful and thank Jack for his generosity by stocking the kitchen and making dinner. She looked out the window, toward the shore, and felt an itch to take a long walk by the sea, which she rarely did in the winter months.

She liked being here in the cozy house with Jack—maybe too much—but this wasn't a permanent arrangement. The sooner she could get back in her own house, with her life back on track, the better. As for where that would leave her and Jack, she was willing to wait and see, and maybe hope a little. It was all she could manage at the moment.

She heard the shower running and decided to go get dressed. Walking by the bathroom, she inhaled the scent of musky soap that drifted into the hallway. She stood outside the door for a moment, contemplating, and then shook her head, and walked down to her room, firmly shutting the door.

Quickly brushing her hair and tying it back in a long, thick braid, she put on a well-worn pair of low-rider jeans and a boxy dark blue sweatshirt, the edge of which just skimmed the top of her jeans. She heard the shower stop, and she grabbed her small cosmetics kit. Opening her door, she stepped gingerly out into the hall and almost collided with Jack in the narrow hallway.

His hair was wet and tousled and water gleamed off his skin; he wore only a white towel, and even that, loosely. His stomach was muscular and lean, the five-o'clock shadow was gone, and the eyes she met as she finished her long survey of his body were laughing. He reached out, tugging on the braid that lay over one shoulder.

"Hey there, Heidi. Wanna come out to play?"

She raised an eyebrow, resisted grinning, and stuck her nose primly in the air. "That's Swiss Miss to you."

He stepped to the left to let her pass, and she did so, but didn't take her eyes off him, not trusting the glint in his eye. She had just made it to the bathroom door when… *thwack!* She felt the sharp sting on her butt and jumped, hollering in surprise.

She spun around, and could only stare with her eyes wide. Words stuck in her throat as she watched him saunter down the hall away from her, his fabulous bare buttocks in full view as he twirled the damp white towel victoriously in circles at his side. She could have sworn he chuckled as he disappeared into his room.

SHE SIPPED COFFEE and looked out the window, then back to the pad of paper on the counter, jotting down some things on her list.

"What'd'ya got there?" She hadn't even heard him come in, and glanced up with a start; he was all dry now, and she noted how his amber hair curled where it was still damp, just around the edges, and settled in waves across his forehead. He picked up the steaming cup of black coffee and repeated his question.

"Oh, sorry. Shopping list. You have no food."

He grimaced. "Yeah, I eat out a lot."

"No problem. I'll go to the store. I want to make you dinner, and it will give me something to do."

"I'd like that a lot—haven't had anything made at home in a while."

"Great! I won't be too long."

She went to grab her coat and make her escape. She needed to get out for a while, to think. Or to not think. As she passed by, he snagged her elbow and yanked her up against him, sealing a kiss to her mouth, then abruptly letting her go.

She lifted her hand to her mouth, her eyes dazed. When she looked up at him he had a lazy kind of self-satisfied look on his face that made her blink, and before she thought about it too much, she flung her forearm around the back of his neck and pulled him down to her, kissing him back and running her tongue sensuously over his bottom lip for good measure. Now *he* was dazed. She smiled, and headed out.

RAINE LOVED the town of Gloucester. She had been here a few times in summer, but it was glorious in winter. She wandered around for a long while, visiting the Fisherman's Memorial, which always tugged at her heart. In the stark cold it seemed an even more brutal reminder of what had happened to those that had "gone down to the sea in ships." How many of them had loved and been lost—or worse, had not loved at all before sailing out to their deaths? Running her gloved fingers over some of the names, she sighed and turned away.

She wandered the streets a little more, gazing out over the harbor, before eventually strolling into a small specialty-food store. Grabbing a basket, she went up and down the aisles, making choices carefully, and thinking about what Jack had said.

She did want to thank him for being so good to her, and cooking was one way she could do that, but she didn't mean it in a distant, formal way. In fact, this would be the only time she had ever shopped and cooked for a man in his own house. It was an interesting feeling.

It wasn't long before the basket was full. She had even decided to try to make some bread. How hard could it be? She read the recipe on the back of a bag of flour, and thought it looked fairly straightforward. Why not?

Happily, she unloaded her goods on the single counter by the cashier—they must not get too much of a rush around here, she thought, smiling. Her groceries rung up and bagged, the young girl turned to her, obviously uncomfortable.

"Um, miss, your card didn't go through."

Raine stared at her. "What? There must be a mistake."

The girl shook her head. "I'll try it again, but the machine says it was refused."

The cashier slid her card through again, and her face was tense as she turned back to Raine. "I'm sorry...."

"No, that can't be right! There isn't even a balance on this card."

"Would you like to try another one?"

Raine nodded, and slid the only other credit card she had with her across the counter. A heavy weight sat in her gut and she knew something was wrong. A few moments later, the same story; that card didn't work, either.

"Do you have an ATM?"

The cashier nodded and pointed to the machine by the door, and Raine went to it, slid her card in and paled, feeling her knees go wobbly when not only did the screen tell her that she had a zero balance, but it wouldn't return her card. The cashier was calling her, someone else was in line waiting.

"Miss? Miss? Are you taking these groceries?"

Raine stared at her and shook her head, turned abruptly and fled out the door, making her way on shaking legs back to the car. She drove back to the house caught somewhere between fear and rage, trying to concentrate on driving down the winter highway, dealing with the winding road and the thoughts jamming in her head. By the time she parked, she was numb with anger.

As she went up the walk, she saw the door open, and Jack appeared on the step, handsome and smiling.

"Need help? What—" He stopped, looked at her once and raced down the walk. "Raine…what is it? What happened?"

She was so angry—she had never been this angry— she could barely form thoughts. He put his hands on her shoulders, looked into her stormy eyes filling with tears, and he noticed she was shaking. He put his arm around her and guided her inside.

"Tell me."

She told him what happened at the store and felt his hand tighten on hers, his eyes darkening with fury and concern. She fell back against the sofa.

"So, I have no money, I have no credit, and I have no

food. I don't know what to do. I can't go to my house, I can't go to work, I can't use my car. He is stripping my life away bit by bit. It has to stop. We have to do something, if no one else will. I can't just sit around taking this. I won't."

Jack was glad that she wanted to fight back. He had been thinking along similar lines while she was gone, but didn't know if she would feel inclined to try to trap her harasser.

"Yeah, he's ticked—he knows you have moved by now, but he doesn't know where. He's probably checked the magazine somehow, noted no use of your email. He may be trying to flush you out."

He took her hand in his and played with her fingers. "He won't give up and go away, Rainey, so maybe the next best thing is to lure him in. Let him find us."

She nodded, feeling scared, exhilarated, and without a clue as to exactly how they were supposed to do that.

"Yes, I want to do that—but how?" She paced around the coffee table. "I have to call the police—this should be reported, anyway, not that they can do anything."

Jack nodded. "Do that now. I might have a plan. We'll talk about it after you get off the phone."

She nodded, went to the phone and called Detective Delaney. Luckily, he was in.

When she got off the phone, her mouth was set in a grim line, and she wondered what Jack's plan was—they weren't going to wait for this guy to slip up—they would *make* him slip up. She wanted her life back.

Jack came to sit with her on the sofa and she told him about the phone call.

"What did Delaney say?"

"Still not much he could do personally, but he was going to contact someone in Boston at their computer crime unit to come down and talk to me, said he would let me know when."

"Good, at least he's doing something."

She rubbed her hands over her eyes. Someone must have a voodoo doll and they were jabbing a pin right between her eyes that very moment, because that's what her head felt like. He peeled her hands down, and pulled her up off the couch.

"C'mon."

"Where?"

"We're going to run by your house, get your credit card statements so tomorrow we can make some calls, try to do some damage control. Then I'll tell you my plan."

13

LATER THAT EVENING they sat in the corner of an out-of-the-way seafood restaurant, munching on fried clams and spicy French fries, and drinking glasses of a fairly decent chardonnay. Raine hadn't realized how hungry she was—her stomach was in such knots from stress that she'd forgotten she'd only eaten a banana all day, and Jack had not even had that much.

They went to her house, which felt strange—it was her home, and yet it felt unsafe to be there. She found her recent statements, took a few more things she needed and called a truck to come take her car to a local garage. Having it sitting in the driveway with its wheels all flat was a depressing sight. The garage said it would be a few days until they could get to it, but she felt lifted by the idea of having one normal thing accomplished.

She looked out the window into the darkness. "So, you said you had thought of a plan?"

He nodded. "Yeah, well, I have some information." He paused as her eyes went wide and focused on him intently. "I was messing with those emails that were sent to you before, and seeing if I couldn't trace something more in them, and I did manage to trace some of them."

"And?"

Jack sighed. "Well, I don't have an ID, but I have narrowed down the field. I think it's someone at the magazine."

Her voice dropped to a whisper, and he could see she went pale even in the warm light of the restaurant.

"How do you know?"

"The email was traced back to the office. Whoever sent it sent it from inside. That's why I couldn't find any break-ins. I've been working on this for a few days, and wanted to be sure before I said anything, and even then, it's a little vague—I know where the emails came from but not from whom."

"How do you know?" Her voice and eyes burned into him insistently.

"After the first bunch of emails, I placed a monitor behind the firewall—we call it a sniffer—no one would see it if they didn't know to look, or where to look. It tells me about all the internet traffic going in and out of the magazine. The weird thing is, the bunch of emails sent to you first—the ones before the roses—came from outside, and were anonymous. The second ones, the reader responses, were also anonymous, but they came from inside—no traffic left the network. A little more work, and I could tell that some of them—the ones that went to subscribers—came from your own machine. He sent them directly from your office, Rainey. Sat in your chair and answered your email for you. Ballsy bastard."

"So what now?" She felt slightly queasy and pushed her food away—the person who did this worked at the magazine. She could have stood by him at the coffeemaker, passed by him in the hallway. He had been in her office—at her desk. Her stomach turned, but then the anger kicked back in. The idea that someone she possibly knew, even slightly, had done this was reprehensible.

"Whatever it is, I want to do it. I don't care what—anything is preferable to sitting and waiting."

"Okay, but we have to move fast, capitalize on the credit card thing that happened today. I figure you can send him an email and tell him that we know this much, and soon we'll know more. You can say you don't want more trouble, but you will make it if he doesn't come to meet you."

Raine frowned. "He might know that's a trap. Kind of obvious, don't you think?"

"Yeah. I thought of that, but I also figure he's running out of options. He's lost the ability to contact you, he's done everything he can do for the moment, and may just be cornered enough to bite. And we can add the pressure that we are going to the cops and the magazine with what we know if he doesn't show. Then we can just see who shows up."

Raine nodded. "That's good—it might work, but I am going with you. I'm not just sitting home and waiting while you go save the world. Let's do it. We'll send the email when we get home tonight. I want this done with."

Jack grinned and stroked her fingers where her hand lay on the table. "Wow, you're sexy when you're tough."

Raine grinned back. Their dinner plates were empty, and though she was full, she was actually considering dessert. Her appetite surged back; she figured trapping a bad guy took a lot of energy.

"Share a dessert with me?"

Jack lowered his voice. "Maybe we can take one home and find some...*creative* use for it."

Raine raised her eyebrows and remembered getting that same offer from Jerry, which seemed as if it had happened a million years ago. But then it hadn't been nearly as appealing as Jack made it sound now.

Jack watched the movements of her eyes and wondered what she was thinking. He imagined licking hot fudge off her breasts, and shifted in his seat, suddenly a little uncomfortable.

"We should have bought some goodies when we were at the store."

Her voice was husky and sexy as hell, and he definitely couldn't stand up now without embarrassing himself completely. He cleared his throat, and smiled.

"I think I could manage a piece of pie, if we share. And as for the goodies, we'll definitely add them to the next grocery list. I'm thinking hot fudge."

Raine felt her heart pound a little harder at the thought of it, drifting away until the voice of the waitress shook her from her erotic reverie. She glanced at the pretty young girl, but forgot what she wanted to say—what was she supposed to be doing right now? She flushed as Jack's fingers squeezed hers, and he smiled at her knowingly as he ordered them a piece of cherry pie and coffees. Raine licked her lips.

"You are full of surprises, Jack. I don't think I have ever been so distracted by thinking about a trip to the grocery store."

"I don't think it was the grocery shopping that had you distracted." He laughed in a low, sexy way that made her skin tingle, then he became more serious. "So, we are going through with this?"

She nodded. "Yes—let's do it."

ON THE WAY HOME, Raine thought she already felt lighter just because she was finally taking some action, doing something rather than just sitting around waiting for the situation to resolve itself. It felt good.

She had a gut feeling this plan would work, that she

could get her life back, and the thought gave her new energy and focus.

Jack responded to the change in her, perhaps feeling better himself. They bantered and chatted all the way back to the house, enjoying the ride and each other's company.

Jack grabbed the few bags of things they had picked up at the town grocery, and headed to the door. His hands full, he dropped the keys into Raine's hand and asked if she could get the door and the mail. She did, checking the box, and picked up a small package wrapped in brown paper. They got through the door, hands full and anxious to get their plan started.

Jack took the bags directly into the kitchen, and Raine set the stack of envelopes and the package on the table, noting that several of the pieces of mail had come in cheerfully colored red or green envelopes with snowman stamps. She had almost forgotten. Christmas was only a few weeks away.

She hadn't intended to look at Jack's mail, but her eyes slid across the address on a large sticker attached to the package, and she frowned when she took a closer look. The return address was from the town she had grown up in—in fact, she knew the street quite well, as she had gone to piano lessons there—and the name on the return was Harris. She was standing, staring at the package when Jack called to her.

"Hey, what was that package—can you bring it in here?"

She glanced toward the kitchen guiltily. Hanging her coat on the rack, she picked up the package and brought it into the kitchen. She set it on the table and looked at him. He cocked his head, curious about what had put that odd look on her face. Then, crossing, he looked at the package, and it hit him—she'd noticed the return address. Oh, boy. Okay.

"Ah, a Christmas package from my parents."

"Your parents? They live in Essex?"

"Um, yeah."

"I lived in Essex."

He hesitated. "I know."

Jack pursed his lips, choosing his words carefully. It was best to deal with this before they got deeper into their relationship. He was already more than half in love with her, and before he fell the rest of the way, she had to know the whole story. He braced himself for how she would react.

"We lived in the same town. Growing up."

She looked up at him, her forehead creased.

"What do you mean?"

They stopped and faced each other, and Raine stared at him.... He was making her a little nervous now, as he looked at his feet, then out over the water, then, finally at her.

"You and I grew up near each other. We lived in the same town, Essex. Went to the same school, Eaton Marsh. I recognized you immediately when I saw you at the magazine."

She looked at him quizzically. "That can't be. Maybe you just thought you knew me, it may have been someone else...."

He bristled. "No, Raine—I'm not mistaking you for someone else. Is it so hard to believe I went to Eaton? I may not have been one of the upper crust, but my parents worked hard to send me to that school. They own the Arbor Inn—perhaps you know it?" He saw the recognition dawn, and continued. "I was there with you, whether you find that believable or not."

Raine blinked. She had offended him, and hadn't meant

to. She just found this so hard to process, and wondered why he had kept such a thing to himself.

"But why didn't you say something? When I thought I recognized you in the office, you said we had never met before...."

"We never did. Not really." He looked her in the eye now, and felt more than a little uncomfortable. He grimaced, and kicked at the rug with his toe.

"I had a crush on you, but you were way out of my reach. I tried to talk to you once, but you didn't say anything back. I figured you thought I was not exactly your type."

"And what did you think my type was?" she whispered. She hadn't had a type back then. She hadn't had anything.

"Someone with a lot more money and position than me. It was intimidating as hell."

Raine stood back, still shocked. He had known her? He had known her all this time, and had never said anything? And he had *liked* her? Had a crush? On her? Had been intimidated by *her?* That was ridiculous! She thought he must be joking, and it showed in her face. As she fought to come up with words, he read meaning into her silence that wasn't there. She stared at him, and started to speak, but he interrupted, sounding defensive and even a little hurt.

"I should have said something about it sooner, I know. But obviously you don't remember me at all. No problem. I knew that. Why would you have? Even at the office, for months, you would look at me and it was like I wasn't even there. Let's just chalk it up."

He went back to finish putting the groceries away, and she stood for a moment, sorting it all out, then strode over to him, taking his elbow and tugging him back around to face her.

"Jack, I'm just surprised, that's all. You have always seemed a little familiar to me, so that's why."

She stepped in front of him, looking up into his face. The lights played softly in his russet hair, but his jaw was tense. She discovered that she didn't like it, the loss of connection with him, and she wanted to get it back. She lifted her hand to his cheek, stroked him with the back of her fingers, and spoke gently.

"I wish I remembered. I'm sorry. I was so alone and screwed up back then.... I knew the other students didn't like me, that they thought I was strange—and I didn't know how to make them like me. It was hard, I didn't fit in anywhere. I didn't belong at home, I certainly didn't belong at Eaton. If you spoke to me, I wouldn't have even known how to respond. If I didn't see you, it wasn't because of who you were, it was because of who I was."

She smiled slightly. "As for the office, I was so busy thinking of Rider, I wasn't paying attention to any other men. No one seemed to be able to measure up to him— and you were so pissy all the time. I figured you found me annoying."

He smiled a little. "I did."

She stared at him, and laughed. "You had a crush on me? An actual crush?"

He absorbed her words—he hadn't been seriously offended, just slightly peeved, and quickly melted when her hand touched his face. He turned his mouth into her palm, covered her hand with his and pressed her soft skin to his lips.

When he smiled at her, she felt everything lighten.

"Yeah, I couldn't sleep for thinking about you. You were so untouchably beautiful. You *are* beautiful...even more now than then. I guess I still have a crush on you."

She smiled, and loved how the world zoomed down to

the two of them. It all made her feel daring, and so she spoke her heart.

"Yeah? Show me." She moved closer to him, looked into his eyes fearlessly. "I can see you pretty clearly now. I like what I see."

His eyes sparkled with heat. She lost her breath in one whoosh when he grabbed her and pulled her flush against him. His mouth came down on hers in a branding kiss, a meeting of the lips meant to claim her and be claimed by her.

He wound his hands in her hair, tugging her head back and urging her to open for him even more as he tenderly explored every sweet curve and crevice of her mouth. She strained against him, moaning into his mouth, dragging her tongue across his teeth, tickling the roof of his mouth. He didn't take his lips completely away from hers when he spoke, his voice guttural and full of undisguised need.

"Come to bed with me, Rainey."

Her breath came in short gasps and she could only nod, letting him lead her from the kitchen, but they stopped in the hallway. Unable to wait, he pushed her up against the wall, finding her mouth again. Tearing at each other's clothes, then underwear, they stood naked in the entry hall, hands and mouths all over each other. Raine caught their reflection in the hallway mirror on the wall across from them and laughed breathlessly.

"We're never going to make it up to the bedroom, are we?"

Effortlessly, he lifted her, thrilling in the feel of her skin against his, and started up the stairs. She lifted her head from his shoulder and looked at him, snaking her arms around his neck as they climbed the narrow stairwell.

He smiled, and squeezed her to him, walking down the hallway past her room to his. Nudging the door open with his foot, he carried her in, and stood for a moment, holding her by the bed. The room was lit by a small lamp on the dresser, but even in the low light she could see the emotion in his face, and it overwhelmed her. He spoke, nuzzling her cheek, his face close to hers.

"This time is special, Rainey. I want you in my bed. I want to be able to roll over at night and touch you, to catch your scent off the pillow, hear you breathing. I want to make love to you in every way I possibly can."

He set her gently down on the huge bed, and stood looking at her, risking more of his heart than she could imagine.

"I need to know you want that, too. That you want to be with me like that, as well. And not just for tonight." He could barely keep his feelings for her from spilling over; it was time to risk it all. She extended her hand to him, her answer in her eyes. He smiled, relief and lust coursing through his body, chased along by something deeper. Lowering himself to the bed, he took her in his arms and held her—just held her—for a moment, as if she were the most precious thing on earth.

Raine listened to the drum of his heartbeat under her cheek, her body tense with anticipation, but easing as he held her, his breath fanning her cheek, his foot moving slowly up and down her calf. She was stunned to notice how even those parts of them, the curve of his instep along her leg, fit so perfectly. She'd never been held before, not like this—so close and so long that it was a source of pleasure unto itself. She slipped her arms around him, too, reveling in the sensation of closeness she had had so little of in her life. It was addictive.

Their bodies warmed, and his hands stroked the curve of her back and hip, his fingers moving lightly down her thigh, then back again. She answered his call, raining small kisses along his collarbone and fluttering her hand lightly over his back. With every touch he cherished her, and she basked in it. Once again, she felt what it was like to truly connect with someone, and the emotion made her giddy with desire. The fingers that lightly teased her skin began leaving trails of fire behind, and her nipples beaded against his chest in response.

Still on his side, holding her close, he reached down, lifting her leg up over his hip, opening her to a fuller exploration. When his hand found its way between her legs, seeking her through the damp, hot folds of skin, she moaned, and brought her mouth to his, sighing as she surrendered to his touches.

She let her body follow his lead, let herself be carried away on a wave of sensation that peaked when he slid a finger into her, and flicked her to a quick, soft climax that only increased her need for something more intense. Eyes dazed with passion, she looked up into his. He stared at her with such need, and such emotion, she thought she wouldn't be able to breathe.

Moving a finger across his lips, she teased her fingers across his chest, experimentally pinching a nipple, heard him gasp, and was encouraged to continue. His fingers played with her sex absently, stroking her and creating wonderful sensations that urged her on.

Snaking her hands lower, she wrapped her fingers around his velvety, hard penis and stroked lightly, down to the base, then back. When she reached down a little farther, running her nails lightly over his balls, he groaned and removed his hand from her, pushing her back onto the mattress, and slid down her body, burying his face between her legs. She writhed on the bed as he brought her to the edge and left her there, tortured with wanting him.

"Jack…make me come…please…"

With a growl, and a promise to himself that he would

stay in control for as long as he needed to, regardless of
the fact that his body was taut as a wire, he brought himself up over her and slid the entire hard length of himself
into her. Leaning down close to her, he kissed her deeply,
rubbing his cheek, slick from her sex, over her face, and
then licked it from her cheek with hungry kisses. His voice
was hot and commanding next to her ear.

"Oh, you will come, Rainey. Hard and long…and with
me inside you…."

She squeezed her eyes shut, feeling the panic and doubt
starting to rise. The expectation chilled her. "I…I can't…
you know…"

He brought his hands up to her breasts, kneaded them,
pinching the nipples sharply, causing just enough pain to
draw her attention away from her negative thoughts.

"Look at me, Raine."

She opened her eyes and he kissed her, staring into her
eyes, hypnotizing her. He weighted her down almost flat
to the mattress, his legs spread out flat as he lay between
hers, and moved up, pushing himself into her in such a
way that his hard pelvic bone pushed insistently against
her swollen sex. His voice was rough, the effort of holding himself back warring with the powerful urge to let go
and drive himself to completion.

"Focus on how it feels, Raine…. Feel me, every bit of
me filling every bit of you…."

Opening her legs wide, letting them fall to each side,
almost flush to the mattress, she rocked back against him
and moaned, learning quickly how to maneuver in this position that touched all the parts of her she needed touched
at once.

He said sweet, hot things to her, his voice becoming
her world. He didn't allow her thoughts to slip even for
a second to any other subject but the two of them bound

together. She kissed him deeply, her eyes never moving away from his as he cradled her head in his hands, thrusting into her in deep, sure movements that maintained the pressure in all the right spots.

She began to feel a sweet pressure that she wanted to let build, yet wanted to release as well, and she moaned, begging him to help her.

His breath was ragged, and she felt him swelling even larger inside her, knowing he was close to climaxing, and the knowledge pushed her even higher. He was beyond words now, murmuring unintelligible sounds. He buried his face in her neck, his hands wound in her hair so tight it should have hurt, but it didn't. Tensing, he rocked into her harder, faster. She cried out when the burst of heat exploded from her loins and spread down her legs, curling up her back and twisting through her with the most wonderful sense of pleasure she had ever known. She pushed back against him fast and hard, seeking every last drop of it.

Jack moaned when he felt her contracting around him, felt her hot, wet muscles shudder and clench, and he buried himself in her as deep as he could, letting her climax take him the rest of the way. He came furiously, chanting her name, his body unable to stop thrusting even after the orgasm passed, he laid on her, quivering with the sheer intensity of it.

She was slack and panting beneath him, and he waited a few moments before rolling to the side, knowing he must be heavy, but smiling when she whimpered an objection as his softening cock slipped from her body.

He gathered her close to him, kissing her hair and yanking the blankets up to fend off the chill of the room on their hot skin. It was dark now, and the room was quiet except for the sounds of their gradually calming breathing. Kissing her hair, and feeling her curled up close against him, Jack took the reckless leap into love.

14

LIFE WAS GETTING more complex, but she didn't have too much time to sit around and think about it. After making love, they'd gotten back up, dressed quietly, touching and murmuring as lovers do as they walked back down to the kitchen. They got some wine and went to the office. It wasn't the most romantic follow-up to an evening of passion, but it had to be done. The trap had to be set.

Raine's hands were cold as she sat in front of the laptop trying to ignore the words on the screen. She hit the reply button and sat staring, then looked at Jack.

After a few moments she focused on the screen and typed experimentally:

We know you work at the magazine. It's only a matter of time before we find out exactly who you are. If you agree to meet me, and tell me why you have done what you did, and make things right, I might not report you to the police. If you don't meet me, I will absolutely report you as soon as we track your identity. This is not a bluff—we have proof that some of your emails were sent from computers in the magazine's offices. At the very least, we will inform the magazine of recent activities, and advise them to launch an inside investigation. Make it easy on yourself, and meet me at the Main Street Coffee Shop at one, tomorrow. RC

Jack nodded—that should get his shorts in a twist—but looking at the words on the screen, he felt a sudden flash of trepidation and wondered if this was such a smart idea. She hit the send button before he could say anything else, and heaved a sigh.

"Well, I guess now we just wait and see what happens tomorrow. Maybe he isn't even checking email."

Jack rubbed her shoulders through the soft material of her sweatshirt.

"Let's hope he takes the bait."

She nodded and looked at him. "I want to wait for him—alone."

"No." He squeezed her shoulders once and walked to the other side of the office. She spun the chair around, aggravated at the tone of his voice, and her own cooled.

"Listen, he may be watching before he comes in. He may sense it's a trap. If he sees me there, he will be more inclined to think it's not a setup. And you can still follow him, get a picture, proof—"

"Raine, the plan stays the way it is. This guy is plainly dangerous. You don't want to meet him face-to-face. Anything could happen, too quickly for anyone to help."

"It's a busy coffee shop. There are lots of people there all the time, nothing can happen—"

"No, I can't let you do it."

She frosted over and looked at him, arching one eyebrow in a way that had him shaking his head and muttering to himself as he crossed the room toward her.

"It's too dangerous. We should keep it simple. I can sit

at the counter and see who comes in that we know, and then follow him out, and everyone is safe."

"What if it is someone we don't know?" She closed her eyes.

"Jack, it could be anyone—a janitor, a secretary. Do you honestly think you can recognize everyone? Remember, over two hundred employees work for the magazine. I don't know half the people in my department, and you rarely come out of the basement."

He swore. She had a point. He scowled, and paced the office behind her.

"I don't want you in there, at least not separate from me. We don't know what he might do, especially since you threatened him."

Raine shivered a little, but pressed on.

"True—but I won't lift my butt out of that chair to so much as go to the ladies' room, and you will be there, along with dozens of other people. I'm sure if things get out of hand, the cops would be there before we knew it. And that is if he even shows up—though I hope he does. I want my life back. I want this nightmare over with. A little risk seems like a small price to pay."

Jack watched her, and felt love and fear and admiration well up together in his chest. He wanted to take care of this for her, he wanted to keep her protected, but he saw strength in her eyes that he had never seen until just this moment, and he couldn't deny that she had a right to be involved.

"Okay. Okay. But you will not go anywhere alone, where I can't see you, no matter what happens. And if anything hits you wrong, you make noise, and lots of it."

She nodded and smiled.

"Thanks. For understanding that I need to be part of this. I need to get the control back."

He nodded, and drew her next to him, wrapping his arms around her and resting his cheek against hers. She moved her hands soothingly up and down his strong back and smiled. This was nice. For a moment, she believed everything was going to be okay.

THE NEXT DAY SHE didn't feel so sure of the plan as they drove into Salem. Nerves skittered along under her skin, giving her goose bumps and making her hands freezing cold, even under her wool sweater and jacket. She looked at the holly and garland on the lampposts, the colorful lights on the houses and businesses, the Santas ringing bells collecting coins in black pots. The world was a very odd place indeed.

So many happy and sad things always going on at once, you only had to look in one direction or the other to see someone sad or happy, ugly or beautiful, and if you were wondering if things would change, all you had to do was wait a minute. Here she was, herself, going to meet a criminal who had been terrorizing her life, while simultaneously thinking that she needed to look for a Christmas present for Gwen.

She had almost completely forgotten about the holiday. It had never meant much to her, as she'd never had anyone to celebrate it with. With Gwen, she had celebrated her first holidays, and had bought—and received—her first real Christmas gifts. She looked forward to it, but this year she almost had completely forgotten.

And Jack—should she be thinking of something for him, too? What was to become of them once this was finished? He had told her the night before that he wanted her in his bed, in his life, for more than one night. She wasn't completely sure what that meant.

Jack drove into a parking space quite a distance away

rom the coffee shop so that they could split up and go
head separately. They had about a half hour, and he hated
o admit that he was edgy enough to turn the car around
nd head back to the house. He looked over at Raine. She
eemed cool enough, gazing out the window at Christmas
lecorations, lost in her own thoughts. He hoped that he
vas included in them.

"Okay—you have the tape recorder in your purse? It
vill only pick up forty-five minutes, so hopefully it won't
ake more than that—hit it before anyone comes in." He
urned in the seat, grabbed her hand and pulled her over
o him. "I'll be nearby, and I won't take my eyes off you."

He pressed his lips to her cheek, letting them drift to
ier mouth, where he kissed her with such tenderness it
ased the anxiety that had taken hold of her. She sighed
igainst his mouth, kissing him back, then set her fore-
iead against his.

"It's going to be just fine. I'll be fine."

He nodded. "Okay, let's go get this over with."

She moved away from him, then checked the recorder
n her purse. Stepping out of the car, she started down the
valk by herself, confident that Jack was not too far be-
iind her. She saw the coffee shop and felt her stomach tie
nto a knot, but she kept walking, across the street, in the
loor, to a table in the back that, thankfully, was free. She
at, shrugging off her coat, and looked around. The door
himed again, and she looked up, saw Jack come in, and
ie looked away, heading for the counter directly across
rom her but facing her direction. His back was to the door.

Raine took a deep breath. It was shortly before one, so
he turned on her recorder, and left her bag lying half-
pen on the table.

A waitress came over to her table, took her order for a
offee, black, and Raine sat back and waited, pretending to

be involved in reading the local newspaper. Minutes ticked
by slowly, and she looked up at Jack; his gaze burnt into
hers for a moment, and then he lowered his eyes.

He isn't coming. Raine felt a sense of despair drift over
her—she had so hoped this plan would work. But fifteen
minutes passed and all she had on her tape recorder was
the sound of her drinking coffee and rustling a newspaper
she'd already looked over three times. Her head popped up
when the door chimed, and her eyes went wide.

Jack saw, and pivoted swiftly to see what had caused
her alarm, and groaned inwardly—*great—just freakin'
great.* He saw Raine's friend Gwen, on the arm of his
employee Neal, hustling in the door, laughing and talking, their heads close together, until Gwen saw Jack and
squealed in delight.

"Jack! Neal—it's Jack!"

Raine got up from the table and headed to the counter,
and when Gwen saw her, another shout went up. Raine
tried to smile, but was frustrated beyond reason when
Gwen's arms came around her in a big hug.

Even so, how could she be mad when Gwen was telling
her how worried she had been and how much she missed
her? Dammit! They were busted. Even if the stalker did
come in now, there was nothing they could do. Worse, he
might think she was trying to set him up by having her
friends there. Terrific. She caught Jack's eye, and knew
he shared her thoughts. "Hi, Gwen. Neal."

Gwen slid right over the tension in the air, not even appearing to notice it. "Raine—I hate being at work without
you—it's so *boring* there. Except for Neal, of course. But
I miss coming by your office for girl talk. I called you at
home and no one was there. What's up? You had me worried sick! Ask Neal, it's all I could talk about yesterday."

Neal smiled in agreement, then sent a knowing look at

ack. "She did. She is very worried about you, Ms. Covington. Jack, you are working from home?"

Jack nodded, but Gwen jumped in before he could say
nything else. "Raine, where have you been? You called
1e the other day when you left the office, but I haven't
eard from you since then. I was worried—I called your
ouse and there was no answer, and your car was gone."

Raine felt color edge up in her cheeks, and she stumbled
minute, but Jack interrupted this time.

"She's staying with me, Gwen, at my place up near
loucester."

Gwen's eyes widened; she stared at Jack, then at Raine,
vhen a huge smile overcame her face and she nodded at
oth of them in a very knowing way. "Oh, that's terrific!
knew you two had something going on. I knew it!"

Raine tried to interject, wanting badly to change the
ubject, but Gwen pressed on.

"We're on lunch—do you guys want to get something
o eat with us?"

Raine shook her head. "Oh, I don't think so, but—"

"But why don't you both join us for dinner tonight.
'ou can come out to the house." Jack's invitation was
mooth and quick, and he ignored Raine staring at him,
er eyes slits.

"I know Raine has missed you, too, Gwen, and it's been
ind of a crazy few days, so we can catch up. Neal, we can
alk shop." He grabbed a napkin from the counter, took a
encil the waitress had left there, and scratched out direc-
ions. "Here—how about seven?"

Gwen hugged him and accepted for them both. Say-
ng some quick see ya laters, Raine and Jack headed back
o the car. The plan had failed, they hadn't accomplished
nything. He had dearly hoped that by this time today they
vould have something solid, something to help wrap this

mess up. He bent his head to Raine's ear, his voice low and sympathetic.

"I know. It's too late for us to do anything now. We'll have to send another message maybe, since this got blown out of the water. Could be that he never even got the email—or chose to ignore it."

Nodding, she got into the car, feeling bad-tempered and frustrated.

"He won't come back. He could have been there and seen the whole thing. If he knew we were trying to set him up this time, he'll be especially cautious, and probably livid—God knows what he'll try to do this time. Maybe burn my house down."

Jack glared at her. "Don't even joke, Raine. We just have to play the hand we've got. Anyway, we can keep working on it—I know this came from inside. I want you to tell me about anyone you have had a hard time with, anyone who was passed up for a promotion that you got, someone you refused a date with—anything. We'll start there, and I am going to get into the files and find whatever leads I can and we'll still keep trying to flush him out."

She felt a little less disgruntled at the idea. At least they could keep working at it.

"But how are you going to get into people's files?"

"You don't want to know."

His eyes had taken on the glimmer of the hunt, and Raine felt heat curl through her body, responding unexpectedly to the bad-boy appeal he emitted. She was coursing with emotion from the afternoon, switching back and forth between anxiety, despair, and excitement so quickly she was on overload. She felt as if she had just downed about ten coffees. Though she'd barely finished one.

Raine reached over and laid her hand on Jack's thigh, felt him tense. He looked over at her, his eyes hot, and she squeezed, sliding her hand up a little higher, and felt powerful when she heard him catch his breath. He sent her a sidelong glance.

"If a little illegal hacking gets you all worked up, I'll willingly turn to a life of crime, Rainey."

She laughed, and leaned over, stretching the seat belt as far as she could, and traced the tip of her tongue along his ear, then dipped it inside and felt him shudder. Fortunately, they were close to the house, and he managed to concentrate on the road as her hands explored other, more interesting places and her mouth worked magic on his skin.

By the time they parked in the driveway, he seriously considered tumbling her into the backseat again and just taking her there, fast and hard. Turning off the ignition, he hauled her across the middle and into his arms, covering her mouth with his in an insistent kiss, but his hands were frustrated by the thick material of her jacket, and he growled.

But his jacket was unzipped, and the next thing he knew, she shifted over and was unbuttoning his jeans; he grabbed her hand, protesting. Then he looked into her eyes, saw the fire there and let his hand fall away from hers.

She reached down, fitting her hand around him beneath the material of his jeans. Her lips and tongue were all over his face, in his mouth, down the side of his neck, while her soft, delicate fingers massaged and caressed him. He gave himself over to her, dropping his head back as she stroked him and feeling the quick throb of pleasure take him over right there in the driver's seat, in his own driveway.

Raine felt wild and female and daring. It was one of the best feelings she had ever had, seducing him right there on the spot, knowing that he would let her have him, however she wanted, when she wanted. She fondled him, whispered to him gently, covered his mouth with hers, the kiss tender but rife with female satisfaction. She slid her hand up and grabbed a tissue from the dash while he blew out a breath and buttoned up his pants. He looked at her, she at him, and they both smiled. The windows were fogged, and his eyes were deep and soft.

"I'm loving this car thing. You can count on getting yours later."

She wiggled her eyebrows at him and popped the door open. "I hope so."

LATER, THE FOUR OF THEM sat over plates of spaghetti and meatballs that Jack and Raine had made together. It was both entirely natural and totally weird to be entertaining friends as if this were her home; they had cooked together, showered together, and now sat with good friends eating and chatting as though this was an old habit. While the sauce was simmering, Jack had made good on his earlier promise to "give her hers"—right on the kitchen floor. Raine smiled to herself, having acquired a new appreciation for hard surfaces.

She watched Gwen leaning into Neal, who had been quiet most of the evening. He did, however, seem to complement her friend's effervescent personality. Gwen was really, really happy. She was going on now about something that had happened at her Reiki session, and both men listened with rapt attention, though Raine felt Jack's foot on hers, his toes scratching at her ankle, and she smiled at him openly now.

"And you guys can stop playing footsie under the table for a minute and listen to my new idea."

Surprised, Raine looked at Gwen, and her friend laughed. "Well, I'd like to say I knew that psychically, but you can always tell when people are fooling around under the table, can't you, Neal?" Suddenly Neal jumped a little in his seat, and his face went quite red. Gwen laughed, leaning over to plant a kiss on his cheek.

"So anyway, I was thinking when I finish my Reiki lessons maybe I can volunteer at the local animal shelters and do some healing for the animals there—if they are more peaceful and happy maybe people will adopt them faster. Or I can at least help them feel happier and like someone cares about them."

Raine frowned when she thought she saw Neal almost roll his eyes, but then saw him squeeze Gwen's hand. Jack, stacking more pasta onto his plate, appeared completely serious and interested, and Raine could have kissed him for that alone.

"So what is this you do, exactly, Gwen?" Jack asked.

Gwen smiled, and leaned toward him.

"Reiki is an ancient form of healing. It works with the natural energy forces that flows through our bodies and spirits, and helps us to manage them. Reiki can help us to figure out where energy is being channeled incorrectly, or where problems are, and can bring a more peaceful, balanced kind of energy to a person through specialized touch. I think it can work for animals, too. Poor babies, after being given up, or even abused, they need lots of good touching."

Jack nodded, and Raine just looked on.

"My mother used to massage our dog. The dog had arthritis, but also Mom thought if you touched in a very particular way, it helped the dog relax and feel happier. It always seemed to work."

Raine smiled. "Like sex."

The entire table was dead quiet for a moment, and she felt the heat move up into her cheeks as she realized she had spoken out loud. Then everyone roared with laughter, which would have been mortifying, but Jack pulled her over and kissed her, looking delighted, so she smiled, too, and shook her head. Gwen, still bubbling over, nodded.

"It's true—there are lots of ways it can work. Usually touching, the right kind of touching, is key. When people go without being touched, or are touched in bad ways, it can really mess your energy up—and making love is a great way to touch." She sent a particularly glowing look Neal's way, then turned her gaze back to Raine and Jack.

"There are lots of studies connecting touching and sex with emotional and physical health. Reiki just adds a spiritual dimension."

After dinner, Gwen and Raine sat chatting on the sofa while Neal and Jack got involved in some technical issue in Jack's office.

"So you and Neal look like you are doing well."

"Oh, yeah—we haven't, you know, said anything too much yet, he's very quiet, and I think he would be very careful about telling someone he loved them, but..."

"You love him?" Raine whispered, holding her hand to her heart as she gazed at her friend.

Gwen's doubts were evident in her eyes.

"I'm not sure. God knows, when we have sex, it's like heaven, and he is so sweet—he is so, I dunno—attentive, I guess. Not in front of people, then he is shy, but when we are alone, he's completely different, and well, I know I like him—a lot. But sometimes I think I don't know him, like there are layers there, things I don't know. I have tried to see in the cards, but they don't seem right."

"Gwen, do you really think you should be looking at your tarot cards for relationship advice?"

"Well, it's not like hard-and-fast advice. The cards are good reflective tools. They help me see things I may not otherwise, just by making me think about it."

"And so what are you thinking?"

"That I want to wait and see, but that this could definitely be going somewhere."

Raine smiled. "Then I hope it goes well."

Gwen grinned back. "Yeah, and who would've thought you'd be living here with Jack?"

Raine winced. "We're not living together—we weren't even dating—but all these things happened at once and coming here seemed to be the best thing. But yeah, it's good. Really good."

Gwen bounced up and down on the sofa cushion, and Raine continued. "But we are not living together. This is a temporary arrangement just until this stalker mess is figured out."

Gwen sobered. "Yeah—what's the word on that? I didn't want to bring it up at dinner. Buzz kill."

"Not much. We thought we had a plan to move things along, but it didn't pan out." She didn't go into detail, not wanting Gwen to feel responsible for messing up their trap. "But Jack has a plan, he is tracking down a lead, and so maybe we can find something there."

"It completely sucks that the police can't help. What the heck are they there for?"

"There is an internet crime expert Jack has been talking with in Boston, but no word yet." Raine sighed.

"The guy was at your house, for Pete's sake."

Raine nodded, feeling as if that took place a million years ago, when it had only been less than a week. "Yeah, but he didn't leave any traces behind. Hopefully something will shake loose soon."

She thought of the list of names that Jack had started working on earlier. As soon as Neal and Gwen left, he would be back at the computer, she knew, trying to pry out whatever information he could on magazine employees, which she found kind of exciting, in an illicit way.

On that thought, the guys came back in the room, and Raine smiled when Jack squeezed down on the couch beside her and planted a kiss on her lips. Raine caught Gwen's knowing look and blushed, but Gwen's eyes just danced as she leaned back against Neal, who was sitting on the opposite arm. It was late, and the fire was burning low. Neal stood up, yawning.

"This was great—thanks for inviting us—but I think we should leave."

Jack stood as well. "You're welcome to stay if you want—we have an extra room."

Neal shook his head. "No, thanks. I have to get in early. Ready, Gwen?"

She nodded, and crossed over to hug Raine, and then Jack. "I missed you—I hope this mess is straightened out soon."

Jack nodded, placing his hand possessively back on Raine's shoulder. "We do, too. He'll make a mistake at some point. And we'll be ready."

Gwen nodded, and Neal made the move to end the evening, shaking Jack's hand, then Raine's, and guided Gwen out the door. As they stepped out into the night, Jack shook his head.

"I still have a hard time seeing those two together. She is like a ball of fire, and it's like pulling teeth to get Neal to say anything unless it is about computers."

Raine shrugged. "Well, she says he is different in private. She's nuts about him—I hope he knows—it's kinda hard to tell."

Jack smiled, linking his arms loosely around her waist. "Do you think people notice that I am crazy about you?"

She smiled, and felt herself melt a little. "You are a lot more obvious about it than Neal."

"Is that bad? Does it bother you?"

Raine considered, then shook her head. "No. I like it."

He smiled, grateful for her answer, and pressed a kiss to her forehead. "Good. Because I want to yell it from the rooftops."

Raine hugged him back, and buried her face in his neck. She knew she was feeling something for him—definitely more than friendship—certainly more than simple lust. But she didn't completely understand it yet, and didn't trust how things would be when life went back to normal. She had led a pretty normal, even boring life. Would that be as interesting to Jack as playing hero to her damsel in distress?

"I want to go do more work on those names—see what I can find. I have to figure out how to, um, get past some particularly tricky obstacles."

She nodded, wondering what the obstacles might be. "Okay, me, too."

"Why don't you go up to bed. It's late, and I'll probably be a while."

"No, that's okay, anyway I won't be able to sleep wi—" She stopped short, her words stuck in her throat. *Without you. I won't be able to sleep without you* is what she almost said. The truth of it stunned her, froze her in her tracks. "Um, with having just eaten dessert. Indigestion. Can I keep you company for a while? Maybe I can help."

He looked at her intently, wondering what caused the quick flash of dismay in her eyes, but he nodded, and grabbed her hand, walking with her into the office.

RAINE AWOKE to see Jack still staring intently at the computer, tapping keys, and taking notes, just as he had been hours ago when she had nodded off. Crossing over to him, she wrapped her arms around his shoulders from behind, snuggling into his warmth.

"What time is it?"

"A little after two."

"Time for bed, huh? Did you find anything?"

He grunted. "Nothing notable. Maybe this wasn't the best strategy."

She squeezed his shoulders, and shivered. "It's the best idea we have right now. And I appreciate you doing all this detective work while I fell asleep in the chair."

He craned his head back, and kissed her softly.

"You cold?"

"It's gotten a little chilly in here."

He moved forward, disentangling himself, and stood. "The fire must have died down—I need to go out and get more wood. It will only take a few minutes to get it warmed up in here, then we can go to bed."

Heat leaped between them as he uttered those completely mundane but deeply intimate words. He found that love made everything, even the slightest moment, richer and more meaningful. He walked to the door, shrugging on a jacket and sending her a warm look.

"Back in a minute."

15

IT WAS BITTER COLD outside, and Jack grabbed his work gloves as he walked out back toward a large stack of split wood. It was a crisp, moonless night, and he stood for a moment, taking a deep, refreshing breath.

The snow from the recent storm lay like a sparkling blanket on the landscape. He was exhausted—but he was happy, and warm with anticipation of going back to the house to spend the night with the woman he loved. *The woman I love. I love Raine Covington.*

He laughed to himself, feeling a little giddy, like the teenager who'd had a crush on her so many years ago, but this time he wasn't just watching her from afar. She was his now; he wanted it to stay that way.

He leaned over to grab some firewood, and tumbled forward, plunging hard into the dark, snowy corner when something cracked him on the head. He lay there, collapsed against the woodpile, fighting the darkness creeping over his consciousness.

His attacker, just a shadow skulking in the dim light, strode quickly back to the house.

IN THE DEN, Raine lost the battle and dozed off. She smiled when she felt a caressing hand on her cheek awaken her.

She raised her hands, put them on shoulders that were close to hers and registered immediately that something was wrong. Her hands knew Jack's body intimately, and she knew the broad feel of his chest and shoulders—and this wasn't it.

Too slight. Too narrow.

Alarmed, she cried out, pushing wildly at the shadow in front of her, striking out with her legs and catching him unexpectedly, toppling him over the coffee table.

She heard the resulting crash and a string of vile curses as she bolted over the side of the sofa and ran toward the door. *Jack. Where was Jack?* She screamed his name. Just making it to the door, she reached out to open it, but was tugged back rudely by the hair, her scalp screaming with the force of it. Pain shot up her arm when she smashed her elbow into the wall as she was dragged backward almost off her feet.

"Sit down, dammit!" The voice that yelled at her was high and almost whiny, and she felt herself shoved down into the couch cushions, where she sat and tried to focus on the face across from her. The fire was gone now, and light entered the den dimly from the office down the hall, so it was hard to make out details.

The figure paced back and forth in front of her, grumbling to himself, and she felt a prick of familiarity at the back of her mind—the stature, something in the voice—and she struggled through her fear to place it.

Neal.

It was Neal, though he looked different. Not the quiet, reserved young man who had sat across the table from her earlier in the evening; his hair was tossed about, and his face deathly pale except for the red splotches on his cheeks.

For a moment, she was too shocked to think about her situation—Neal was the one who had been harassing her?

He was staring at her now, staring through her as if he was trying to read her thoughts, and she looked away, a new wave of terror overcoming her. She leaped up from the couch, which had him crossing the room, and she spun on him, screaming at him.

"Where's Jack? What have you done with Jack?"

He walked up and grabbed her by the neck, yanking her close to him, and she fought, flailing, but he was surprisingly strong and dug his fingers painfully into the soft skin behind her ear to keep her still.

"Lover boy? Oh, I took care of him. I took care of him but good. I wouldn't be counting on any help from your precious Jack." He grinned, and Raine felt the coldness of it down to her bones. "Besides, what do you need him for? You have me now."

She fought again, not caring about the pain of his fingers in her skin, and finally he drew his hand back and the strong slap against her cheek tumbled her back on the sofa. She felt tears sting her eyes, and looked up at him. He was standing over her, his voice shaking.

"I didn't want to do that! I don't hit women, don't like to hit them—why do you keep making me do these things?" He looked at her, his face contorted with rage. "Bitch. You're all bitches. Every last one of you. I thought *you* might be nicer, different, but you aren't. A whore, just like all of them."

Raine felt weak with fear. "Why, Neal? Why would you do this? I don't even know you—"

His face momentarily softened, then contorted with anger again. "You didn't want to know me. You met me before him—I watched you at work, I tried to get to know you, and you all but ignored me. Vague pleasantries—that's all you ever offered. The things people say when they really want you to leave them alone. But then you found *him,* and you didn't tell him to leave you alone, did you? Sluts—you're all sluts."

He turned on her, spitting mad.

"But you were mine first. He had no right—neither did you. I knew you were meant to be mine. And you would have been if he hadn't interfered. I just needed more time. Now we have the time."

Raine raised her hand to where the side of her face was stinging, and tried to comprehend what he was saying. It didn't seem right—Neal? She thought back to the times she'd dealt with him at work, but she couldn't remember any of their encounters clearly.

"I tried to do nice things, tried to get to know you—the only way I could get around you, or get any information about you was with Gwen—"

Raine's eyes flew open, and she sat forward. "No—you haven't hurt her, Neal, please say you haven't."

He made a disgusted face. "Hardly. I just gave her a little something so she would sleep really sound tonight. She thinks she's in love with me—so stupid. But she was convenient—she liked to talk about you, and she was an easy lay. I figured it was practice until I could get the real thing. I'm good, you know—very good. Gwen even said so." His smile was sly. Raine felt her skin crawl, but made her voice sound as calm as she could.

"You can't get away with this, Neal. Gwen will know. Everyone will know."

"No one knows anything! I'm taking you out of here with me tonight, and no one will know anything." He smiled again, moving closer. "As for your former boy-friend, I figure he'll die of exposure. Sad, but necessary. I can't afford to have him around. They'll just think he fell down getting some wood, smashed his head on a log and died from being out in the cold too long. That's how I planned it."

Raine felt her stomach twist and her whole body began to shake as she realized that Jack was hurt, maybe dying, and she was trapped in here with Neal. She had to do something—had to figure out a way to get to Jack.

She looked up at Neal, the change in his voice alerting her to something dangerous, and she felt shivers run down her back. He was standing closer now, and he looked at her almost—gently? He made a clucking noise and stepped closer to her.

"Oh, I've upset you—don't be upset about him, you have me now. I can take care of you. All I want to do, all I have wanted to do is be with you, take care of you." He reached out to touch her face. "Touch you." She pulled back, and saw the flash of anger in his face, and stopped herself. Swallowing her fear and the vile repulsion that surged through her, she made herself smile as she looked up at him.

"I'm sorry, Neal. I don't want to hurt you—please don't hurt me."

He leaned down over her, and she felt the tears choke her. She only had one shot to save Jack and herself. Neal was focused on her now, stretching out to touch her again, and speaking to her in that nasal-thin, quavering voice.

"I don't want to hurt you—I love you." He strummed his fingers down her arm, and she tried to hold herself steady, not giving in to the repulsion that followed the path of his cold, clammy touch. He braced his knee on the edge of the sofa, his hot breath suffocating her as he leaned even closer, pressing his moist mouth to her temple.

Focusing—focusing hard—she placed her hands on his shoulders, turning her face to his, and he sighed, obviously pleased, and kissed her. Mustering all her will to kiss him back so that she could keep him distracted, she blanked her mind of the urge to throw up.

She shifted a little farther under him as a groan of desire rattled from Neal's chest. She thought she heard a noise behind her—*Jack*. It had to be Jack! She twisted underneath Neal's groping hands, at once pushing down on his shoulders and bringing her knee up into his crotch—hard. As he sucked in a sharp breath, she dug her fingers into his shoulders and brought her knee up again, for good measure.

"Raine!" Jack staggered into the doorway just in time to see Neal doubled up over Raine and keening in pain. Jack tried to make his body move faster, but the crushing pain in his head was holding him back. When he stepped forward the room spun; he had to stop and grab on to the door frame and catch his breath.

He saw Raine stand, and tried to focus his blurred vision—Neal—it was *Neal?*—Jesus. It *was* Neal. He watched in disbelief as Raine jumped up from the sofa, pushing hard at Neal, causing him to fall backward over the coffee table, his head hitting the floor with a thud. He stayed there, curled up and making strangled sounds. Jack blinked, trying to comprehend what was happening, and steadied himself.

"Rainey…"

"Jack! Oh, my God." She rushed to him, and he felt the welcome relief of her hands on him, and her lips touching his face, her wet cheeks against his.

"Raine—God, did he… Are you…okay?"

Raine looked back at Neal, lying helplessly on the floor.

"He's not getting up for a while. I'm okay." She felt another wave of nausea as the memory of Neal's hands and lips washed over her. Needing to erase it, she got closer and kissed Jack, and set her forehead to his, trying to catch her breath. Then she stepped away, and picked up a poker from the fireplace, handing it to him, just in case. "Stay here—I'm calling the police."

Jack nodded, his vision cleared again—it seemed to come and go. He had barely found his way back to the house, feared he might have just as easily ended up in the water as he struggled through the dark. His face felt raw from where he had fallen face-first into the woodpile, and his head was spinning, but he kept his eye on Neal, holding the poker firmly in his hand.

Raine came back, took the poker from him and urged him forward to the sofa. Neal was curled up on the floor, whimpering now, mumbling unintelligible things. Jack looked at him and wished they were both standing so he could kick his sorry ass, but then Raine had already done a pretty good job of that. He turned, only to find her gone again, and panicked for a second, until he saw her return, with a wet rag and an ice pack.

"The police will be here very shortly."

She steadied his head so she could wash some of the blood from the cuts on his face, and felt her stomach clench when her fingers felt the stickiness on the back of his head. He winced, going pale. She pulled her hand away and saw blood on her palm, Jack's blood, and choked.

"Oh, no, Jack…"

He reached out to hold her, but his voice slurred and she felt her skin turn to ice, unsure of what to do. "S'okay Rainey…. He hit me with something…. I'm sure it's not that bad…. Don't worry."

At that moment Raine saw the flashing lights in the window, and managed to get up on her wobbly legs, rushing to the door to let the officers in.

"I need an ambulance, he's hurt! Please, hurry…." She pointed to Jack.

Over the radio, they called an ambulance, and crossed the room to where Jack lay on the sofa.

"Ma'am, can you tell us what happened here?"

She rattled through what happened and pointed to Neal. She suggested they contact Detective Delaney.

"Do you have any proof this is the man who has been harassing you?"

Jack's voice interrupted, a bare croak, but there. "Except for the fact that he just tried to kill us?"

Raine shot the officer a look, and went to Jack, sitting down next to him as two other officers attended to Neal.

"He told me—he told me it was him, and why."

The cop nodded. "Okay, you both need to go to the hospital, we're going to investigate the scene, and we'll contact Delaney—we'll need your statement as soon as you can give it."

Jack nodded, and Raine pushed him gently back against the sofa, murmuring to him as she heard sirens from the ambulances coming up the road. The cops were handcuffing Neal, and reading him his rights even as he lay there on the floor still moaning. Suddenly she started to shake.

She heard the door open again, and she was very cold. It must be from all the frigid air coming in from the door, she figured. There was a lot of noise, and she couldn't seem to stop her teeth from chattering, no matter how hard she tried.

She watched them lift Neal onto a stretcher, blinking. It didn't seem quite real. Someone was kneeling by her and saying something, but she just gazed at him blankly. Somehow understanding that it was over, she let herself slide into the relief of oblivion.

IT WAS A FULL WEEK later when Raine was helping Jack back to his house. She had only been kept overnight in the hospital for observation, but he had sustained some serious head injuries and had been hospitalized for a week. Gwen had also been admitted overnight, after she told the police that Neal had drugged her—fortunately, it hadn't been a lethal dose. It was over now, and they could relax.

It was all cut-and-dried, according to the prosecutors, with the abundance of evidence implicating Neal that the police had uncovered while going through his home and computers. He apparently had a long but previously undetected habit of email harassment and internet theft. His most serious charge—attempted murder—would send him away for a good long time.

Jack mulled it all over as they pulled in to his driveway, flexing his fist and wishing he could have a go at Neal's face now that he was fully recovered. But it was over and it was time to move on. He looked at Raine and smiled—move on to better things. Yeah.

"Well, let me get your case and we'll go inside—"

"Raine, I'm not an invalid. I'm able to carry my own case. I feel as good as new."

The worry was still apparent in her eyes, and she stubbornly took the case from the backseat, reaching up to slide her hand gently over the back of his head, over the stubbly spot where the doctor had shaved his gorgeous hair and stitched up his wound.

"Yeah, you're a real tough guy. Just let me take it, okay?"

He decided maybe it wasn't so bad to be taken care of, after all, and grasped her hand as they walked up the steps. The house was cool, but it felt good to be home. As soon as the door was closed, Jack showed Raine just exactly how recovered he was feeling. Sliding his arms around her, he pinned her firmly against the door, fitting his mouth over hers before she could so much as take a breath. She melted into him, heat flaring as he moved his mouth across her cheek, nuzzling her.

"Maybe I will need a little help, you know, getting my clothes off...."

She laughed and squirmed in his hold. "Jack, we just got in, you should sit down...."

He growled against her ear. "I'll sit down if you sit on my lap...."

She giggled, and didn't believe it—she never giggled. Realizing that made her giggle more as he kissed her face, and she playfully shoved him away.

His expression was passionate, but amused, and he backed up, holding her hand. As they stepped into the foyer, he looked into the den, and remembered the last time he had come through this door. Clinging to the door frame, barely able to stand, he'd seen Neal leaning over Raine, watched her fighting him off, feeling sick with helplessness. He shook his head in disgust at the memory.

"Ouch." Raine tugged her hand from his. "You're squeezing too hard."

"Oh, hell. I'm sorry, baby. I just..."

She touched his face. "It's okay. I know, the memory of it hits you when you walk back in. Me, too. I almost couldn't stay here alone the first night, but it wears off soon. Get some food, a fire, and the house feels better."

He pulled her close again. "The house feels better with you in it."

Kissing her soundly, he picked up his case. "I'm gonna take this up and change—wanna help me?"

She grinned. "Later—maybe after I get you some lunch."

"Toasted cheese? And tomato soup?" he angled, figuring if she was in the mood to baby him, he wasn't going to pass it up.

"Sure."

He grinned and kissed her again, and went upstairs. Raine busied herself in the kitchen, and didn't even hear him when he came quietly back into the kitchen.

"Raine?"

She turned from stirring the soup, and smiled. "Hey. Almost done here. Maybe you should get a fire going, it's going to be a cold night."

"Where are your things?"

She turned, wrinkling her forehead. "What?"

"Your stuff—your clothes, paperwork, your briefcase—nothing is here."

She felt her muscles tense in response to the edge in his voice, and she kept her voice light and even.

"I took my things home. I stayed here for a day or so, but I was spending most of my time at the hospital with you, and I figured it was safe to go back—"

"You left? Why?"

Truly puzzled now, she turned the burner under the soup off and shrugged. "It was over, time for me to go home. There wasn't any point in me staying here after things were settled."

"Over? No point in you being here? How about the fact that we are together now, Raine? This is where you are supposed to be." The words really grated as he said them, causing her anger to flare.

"Where I am *supposed* to be? What the hell does that mean? Yes, we are together, but I have my own house, my own life, and I needed to get back to it. We are still together. I don't know what you are so upset about."

"I told you I wanted you with me, every day, every night—in my bed. Not in another house, another town."

She felt the blood drain from her face. "What are you

saying? You expected me to live here? With you? Permanently?"

He was so angry she nearly flinched just from the expression on his face. She'd seen him angry before, but this was different. Something else was layered over the anger—hurt? She felt terrible when she realized what he had expected.

"Jack, be reasonable—we have only been together a few weeks, and under stressful circumstances. It was nice for you to let me stay here, and we obviously are together, but—" She paused, hearing the strain in her voice.

"Nice? You think I was *nice* to let you stay here? You want me to be *reasonable?*"

"Stop repeating everything I say."

Crossing the kitchen in a few long steps, he backed her up against the sink, pressing into her, his face close.

"I don't feel like being reasonable, Raine. I can't believe you would pull away from me like this, just…up and leave. What do you want, Raine? How do you feel about me? What do you think this thing is between us?"

His eyes searched her face, and she stammered under the scrutiny, not able to form a reply before he continued.

"Because I'll tell you, my ideas about us didn't include you moving out and going happily on with your life— where did I fit into your plan, Raine? Am I in it?"

His eyes glittered, and she gazed back at him. "Yes, God, Jack, yes! I didn't leave *you,* I just returned to my own home. I assumed we would keep seeing each other, see what it is we have, what we really feel…"

She couldn't finish as he leaned even closer into her. "What we *really feel?* What do you really feel, Raine?"

"I…I— I'm not sure. It has all gone so fast, and there has been so much—how can we know for sure…?"

"I'll tell you what I know for sure. I love you. I love

you and I want you here with me, living with me, sleeping with me, sharing everything with me. I don't want to date you, Raine—we crossed that line a long time ago."

She couldn't breathe—he *loved* her? He thought she was just going to live with him, to stay there and never go home? A feeling of uncertainty suddenly overwhelmed her, and she wiggled her way out of his tight hold. She crossed the kitchen, then whirled, turning on him, confused, angry and a million other things.

"You love me? And what does that mean? That you get to make all the decisions, that you decide what this relationship will be and I am supposed to just go along? I don't think that is how you show you love someone."

"Oh, and you didn't do exactly the same thing, just moving out of here, and never mentioning a word of it? Why didn't you say anything, Raine? You have spent every day with me, but never mentioned a word about going back home."

"I…I guess I just didn't figure it was a big deal."

She felt his chill across the room, and realized she'd put that badly, but refused to back off now, and lifted her chin stubbornly. He walked to her, slowly, and looked at her deeply

"What exactly do you feel for me, Raine? You want me to ask, so I am asking."

She squirmed. He wasn't touching her, only standing there, looking right through her, and she could only find weak words, started to lift her hand to touch him, but dropped it back to her side.

"I…well, I want you. I care for you—a lot. You know that."

His eyes veiled, and he didn't say anything, just nodded. "You care for me."

She nodded, and felt lost. Small. Sad.

He walked to the window, and leaned on the counter, looking out. "And do you believe I love you?"

She took a breath, trying to find something right to say.

"I know you care about me, too—I don't know about love, Jack—I haven't had any experience with it. And we have been in this horrible situation, so maybe it has made us feel things that we normally wouldn't have—"

He turned, cutting her off. "Please, Raine. We've been down this road. I am a grown man, and I am in love with you. At least accept that much."

She felt sick, and wanted to go to him, but didn't know how to break down the wall that was growing between them.

"I just need some time—we can still be together, still see each other."

"Why? So you can decide if you really feel anything for me or not?"

"No! Stop twisting things. You know I have feelings for you, I just don't know how to handle them, I don't know what they are. I need to figure things out."

His shoulders slumped, and he ran his hand over his face.

"Fine. Okay." He came back to her, placed his hands on her shoulders, pain evident in his eyes.

"I guess that's it, then. I guess we'll just see where it goes. But right now, I need you to go. I want to be alone."

Raine felt the hurt cut through her, and nearly wept. She wanted to say something, but the words weren't there, she didn't know what they were, where to find them. So she nodded as his hands fell away, and she whispered, "Okay," and went back to the hall to get her jacket.

Walking away from the house, she felt her heart break with each step she took, but for reasons even she couldn't understand, she kept walking.

16

HERE SHE WAS. Home. It was what she wanted. The fight with Jack had left her miserable and frustrated—why couldn't he understand? He had had no right to make the assumptions he had. He had no right to be angry at her. She was sure of it.

So why did she feel so awful? So lonely? A knock on the door startled her out of her muddled thoughts.

"Just a second."

A shiver of paranoia ran down her spine, and she breathed in and out slowly, reminding herself there was no one stalking her now: she was safe. She opened the door.

"Gwen!" She smiled with joy at seeing her friend, but the joy faded when she took in Gwen's pale features and sad eyes. She wasn't sparkly the way she usually was, and she was dressed in jeans and a plain gray T-shirt, which was definitely *not* Gwen's style.

Raine slid her arm around her friend's slim shoulders and drew her inside. She had talked to Gwen the morning after everything had happened, offered to be there when the police wanted to talk with her, but Gwen had insisted she was fine and needed time alone. Raine knew she was embarrassed, humiliated and hurt.

"Here, sit down, and let me make us some tea."

Gwen nodded. "Yeah, put something stiff in it if you have anything."

"Sorry, all I have is some good old Earl Grey."

Raine stopped halfway to the kitchen and watched Gwen bury her face in her hands. The tea could wait. She went back to the couch, surprised at how tightly her own heart twisted when Gwen raised her tear-filled eyes to her and spoke raggedly through sobs that seemed to be threatening to take over.

"I...thought...he was it, Raine. I...slept with him.... He said things, made me feel so special. I went to the jail to see him—yesterday...."

"Oh, no—you should have called me, Gwen. You shouldn't have done that alone."

Gwen nodded. "I couldn't process it. I needed to hear it from him. And boy did I hear it. He said I was just a slut he was using till he could get what he really wanted. You." The last word came out on a wail, and she fell against Raine, wracked in sobs. Raine followed her instincts and hugged her.

Eventually, Gwen's sobbing ceased, and they just sat there, two friends, comforted by having each other. Raine hadn't known until this moment how much she cherished their bond. Rarely in her life had she felt that kind of connection with anyone.

"I feel so stupid. How could I have thought I was in love with that insane *jerk?*"

Raine sat back, and took both Gwen's hands in hers, and squeezed.

"You were not stupid. Not ever, not for a moment. He was more than a jerk, he was evil, Gwen, and you can't be expected to have known that. He fooled you, and used you in the worst possible way. He fooled all of us. It's not your fault."

Gwen didn't quite nod, and Raine didn't know what else to say, so remained silent.

"I told him things, about us, being friends, about you— just general stuff, but he might have used the information to hurt you, I didn't know. If you had gotten hurt, I never could have forgiven myself."

Gwen was on the edge of tears again, and Raine put her hands on either side of Gwen's face, and spoke firmly. "Nothing that happened here is anyone's fault but Neal's. He's sick. I am so sorry you are paying so dearly for this, Gwen. You don't deserve it. You just don't deserve it, hon."

Gwen nodded, sighed, and sat back against the couch.

"I thought you were getting wine."

Raine smiled. "Tea, Gwen. It's only one in the afternoon."

"So?"

"I don't have any wine, but I might have some chocolate chip cookies in here somewhere."

Gwen smiled, the first real smile Raine had seen. They went into the kitchen to sit.

"So how are things with you and Jack? I'm so glad he was okay. I would have come to see him in the hospital, but…"

"He understands completely." She sat, sighed. "Things kind of…blew up the other day. He was mad that I wanted to come home."

"Why would he be mad about that?"

Raine looked sheepishly at Gwen. "Well, I guess I didn't go about it very well. I moved back home while he was in the hospital, and didn't let him know."

"Ouch. Raine, sheesh."

"Well, c'mon! It's not like we were really living together, not like I ever agreed to that. We never even discussed it, he never asked me what I wanted."

"What *do* you want?"

Raine stared out the window.

"I don't know. I guess we'll have to wait and see if what we had was real or just part of the situation. I don't know how to trust what he feels...what I feel."

"What *do* you feel?"

Raine couldn't answer. Words jammed in her throat, feelings in her heart. Gwen smiled again.

"Raine, it's pretty clear that you love him."

"I do?"

"Yeah. And he is nuts about you, too—has he told you?"

"Yeah."

Gwen prompted her eagerly. "And you said...?"

"Um, well, I wasn't sure—how can he be sure he loves me? I care about him, and I want to be with him, I told him that—"

Gwen collapsed back in her chair. "So he spilled his guts to you, and you told him thanks, I care about you? Oh, God, poor Jack. That is the worst."

"What do you mean, poor Jack?" It came out in a squeal, and had her up and stomping to the sink again, then back to the table. "He shouldn't have assumed so much, he just had it all so neatly planned, and without talking to me about it at all."

"You didn't tell him you had moved out, either."

"That's different—I never moved in on a permanent basis. He should have known."

"C'mon, Raine—the guy basically laid his life at your feet, and you stomped on it."

Gwen got up to go get the tea, and came back to the table. "Listen, I know you are afraid, and that it's a risk.

Believe me, I know what it feels like to fall down on the wrong side of a risk."

Raine started to speak, but Gwen was on a roll, and continued. "But there's no gain without risk. I jumped too quickly with Neal, didn't know enough about him. But as much as my ego has taken a bruising, losing Neal was not a fatal blow. We didn't have what I see when I look at you and Jack—that connection, that passion—I *wanted* us to have it, maybe so much I missed the signals. If you let go of what you have with Jack, Raine, I think it will be one of your biggest regrets. He's one of the good ones."

Raine absorbed the words, unsure what to say. Her mind was going a mile a minute.

"Raine, stop thinking—just feel—how does he make you *feel?*"

She sighed, fidgeted with her cup. "Safe. Cared for. Special."

"Desired? Passionate? Happy?"

Raine nodded, feeling uncomfortable. "Yeah. I know it's not just sex, it's more. I just don't know how much more. I don't know how I am supposed to know. How can anyone know?"

"Well, you just have to trust your heart. And his. Think of how you felt when you knew he was seriously hurt, about the time you spent together at the house, and how you felt when you went to stay with him in that hospital room—every day."

Gwen leaned across the table, squeezed Raine's hand and looked at her intently. "I know I didn't deserve what happened to me with Neal—neither did you. But you *do* deserve Jack. You have to go for it, Raine—admit how you feel to yourself, and then let him know. It could be the only good that comes out of this mess, aside from putting that asshole in prison."

Raine nodded, and sipped her tea, and knew Gwen was right. Overthinking things wasn't going to make them clearer. She had hurt him. She was so caught up in her own baggage that she hadn't put it down long enough to think about how her actions were affecting him. She had to stop hiding behind her wounds.

She missed Jack—it was the plain truth. The truth she had been struggling with since she had left him. She had hated walking away from that house with every step she took. She had felt empty every second since. She hadn't ever really known love, but she thought, maybe, she was knowing it now. And, at the moment, it hurt.

"I think Jack's due back in town today. I guess I have some Christmas shopping to do."

Gwen smiled, and the old sparkle came back into her eyes for a moment. "Attagirl. Go get him. And remember, I'll want all the details."

They laughed, and Raine felt more alive than she had in her whole life. She knew exactly what to give Jack for Christmas.

HER NERVOUSNESS was all-consuming. She had never done anything like this in her life. Obviously. If she had done things like this before, she would not be so nervous now. She would be cool and calm and ready to go like she always imagined she would be, like when she had thought this was a good idea, and in the shops when she had gotten this entire deal together—*stop!* God, she was rambling in her own head. Silence. Relax.

This may not have been a good idea, but it was all set to go now, no backing out, and she had to see it through. God help her.

She'd bought a Christmas tree, decorations and candles. She had decorated it in Jack's bedroom. She then put one brightly wrapped box underneath. She took the pretty quilt from the bed and laid it out on the floor beside the tree.

She looked at the clock and hoped he would come home before she completely lost her nerve, but not before she was completely ready.

She had called him, left a message on his cell that she wanted to see him and would wait for him at his house, so he knew. Ducking into the shower, she soaped and shaved and shampooed with the fragrant accessories she had bought herself, ignoring the totals that had added up on her credit card. It was Christmas, after all. Time to splurge.

She dried off, applying the exotic lotion she'd bought, and slipped on the bright-red, lace flyaway baby doll she had purchased that afternoon. She looked in the mirror and her eyes nearly popped out—it sure didn't hide much. But she was done with hiding, so she took a deep breath and turned, examining herself in the mirror. Not half-bad, really.

The top barely contained her breasts, and parted at the middle to show off her trim waist and inny belly button. The small, triangular scrap of lace that lay over her abdomen made her feel sultry and sexy. Daring, even.

She slipped on a furry white garter and felt a sense of anticipation flow over her. She fluffed and dried her hair, applied a deep red tint to her lips. She didn't need any other makeup, her cheeks were flushed enough with anticipation. She had never seduced a man before. Furthermore, she had never seduced a man she loved before.

It was five minutes to seven. God, she hoped he was still coming home tonight.

Taking a deep breath, she went into the living room and checked the champagne she had bought, lit the candles she had placed on each stair leading up to the bedroom. She lowered the lights and, finally, put on the satin Santa hat she had bought, just for fun. Then she returned to the bedroom to wait. It was just past seven. She hoped he wouldn't be very late. She had called him at four. Not that he would come running just because she called.

BUT HE HAD. Pulling up to the house, he saw her car, and had no idea what was going on, or why Raine had left the vague message on his phone. But he had listened to it twice, just to hear her voice more than anything else. It had only been a day, but he missed her like hell. He frowned; why didn't she answer the door? Pushing the door open, he only heard silence, and apprehension clutched at him as he turned the knob.

"Raine…where are you?"

He stopped for a moment, surprised, and then caught his breath and grinned like only a man can when he realized what was going on. Lowered lights, candles, champagne—*oh, yeah.* He locked the door securely behind him and followed the candle-lit path up the stairs to his room, where the door was partially open, and soft lights blinked out into the hall.

He stopped dead in the doorway, losing his breath completely in the wash of stunned desire that swept over him when he saw her. She was laid out on a green blanket under a Christmas tree. The scrap of red lace that barely covered her gorgeous body turned his mouth dry in seconds. The room was dark except for the blinking tree lights that played over her skin. She tilted her head provocatively, bending one leg up at the knee, tempting his eyes to follow the movement, and smiled at him.

He moved into the room, staring at her, his eyes dark with desire, his voice choked.

"Raine…what…? You look…amazing. But…"

"I'm your Christmas present—I hope you like it. I know it's a few days early, but I couldn't wait to…give it to you."

Jack stood over her, felt himself go hard in a flash, and regarded her silently, unsure of what to say. So he just lowered himself to the floor next to her, leaned over and touched his mouth to hers.

He had so much to say, was feeling too much, it all logjammed in his chest. He'd been furious with hurt, but that quickly melted away into desire. He'd meant just to give her a hello kiss, but his soul caught fire just from the scent of her, and the kiss became more demanding. She pulled away, and he groaned, almost falling over to follow her, needing more.

"Uh-uh—you have to open your present first."

"But you are my present."

She smiled, all nervousness gone as she read the pleasure in his eyes, and she let herself absorb the peculiar but wonderful sensation of female control and power. She pushed herself up slowly onto hands and knees, letting him have a full view of her breasts and behind as she leaned over to reach for the box under the tree.

She handed him the box, smiling seductively when she noticed his erection straining against his pants; reaching down, touching him there for just a moment, lightly, her eyes lit with need and mirth.

"Wow, and you don't even know what's in the box yet."

He growled and reached for her, wanting only to tear off her wrapping and enjoy the gift of her hot, sweet body, but she leaned back, and gestured to the box.

"You have to open this first. I have to see if you like it. Then we'll go from there."

Jack's hands trembled as he took the box and ripped through the wrapping paper, thinking only that he knew he would love whatever it was—a watch, a tie, *socks,* for

God's sake—anything—he didn't care as long as when he was done he could go play with Raine under the tree.

His body was aching for hers—it had been so long. He lifted the top and wrinkled his forehead as he found the box empty except for a small piece of red stationery in the bottom. He reached down, lifting the paper and unfolding it. He read it to himself, and found emotions clogging in his throat. For moments on end, all he could do was stare at the paper.

This gift entitles the recipient to all the love I have to give. There's more than I could fit in this box, as there is more than I could ever fit in my heart. I love you, Jack.
Merry Christmas,
Raine

Raine thought she would die a thousand more deaths if he didn't say something soon: he was still, staring at the note, and she felt as if she would pass out if he didn't just say *something*. Then he looked up, and her breath caught. His eyes glowed with raw emotion, and he set the box and the note carefully aside.

Getting up on his knees, bringing them face-to-face, he drew her into a long, deep, drugging kiss. Pulling back, he looked into her eyes, and felt his world fall into place.

"Rainey—I love you…. This is the best gift I have ever had, the best I will ever have. Tell me, though, I want to hear you say it."

She wasn't embarrassed when her eyes swam with tears, and she hugged him tightly to her, telling him over and over and over, until they were both laughing with sheer joy. She drew back, her face glowing with happiness as she looked into his.

"But that isn't all of it."

His eyes went opaque with desire, and he looked at her hungrily.

"I was hoping not."

"Let's get you out of these."

Enjoying her new sense of confidence and control, he let her undress him, only helping minimally, until he sat completely nude and aroused before her. Her breath was shallow, and he raised his hand to cover her breast and pinch her distended nipple through the lace, tugging her down next to him when she moaned.

Love made need multiply exponentially, and Raine gasped when she heard the lace rip. His hands raced hungrily over her skin, touching her everywhere, his mouth capturing hers, kissing her deeply, plundering her while his fingers did the same. She came suddenly in helpless waves as she wrenched against him, moaning into his mouth. She was his, and she gave herself freely. Her hand stroked his cock as she recovered, and he gently pushed her back to the blanket, beginning to position himself over her, when she planted a hand on his chest.

"Let me love you, Jack. Let me take you."

Jack sat back, praying to the universe for control beyond what a mortal man could possibly be expected to have. He laid back on the blanket, and watched her, smiling, her eyes hot and confident, her lush body flushed with the pleasure he had just given her. And wanted to again.

He heard himself curse hotly, not quite believing his own eyes as he watched her standing over him, her legs parted. She dipped a finger into the shadowy crevice between her legs and then trailed it up the firm flatness of her stomach, massaging the wetness from her sex on one nipple, then repeating the process on the other. He licked his lips, his body hard as a rock and frozen still, his fists digging into the blanket.

She looked down at him, wearing only the satin hat, drunk on power and pleasure, her sultry voice every man's erotic fantasy.

"Santa thinks Jack has been a very good boy."

He could barely talk, but tried, his breath heaving. "I have been very good, Santa. I can be even better if you come down here."

She laughed, and the husky sound nearly drove him over the edge. She lowered slowly to one knee, and then to the other, leaning over him, letting her breasts fall forward, swaying in front of his mouth. She trembled with sensation as she ran her wet, hot sex along his erection, teasing them both.

Her own vision blurred when he moved up and drew one breast, salty and delicious with her own taste, into his mouth. He suckled one, then the other as she slid over him, until he lost track of where she started and he ended.

Needing him more than she had ever needed anything, anyone, she took him deep inside of her, glorying in the guttural cry that broke from him with the contact. She smiled, and almost lost herself again when he arched upward, driving himself into her. But she held on, no—not yet. Her breath came out in pants, and she smiled at him, pushing him back, moving her hips slowly. Taking charge.

She watched him, his skin taut, his head arched back, mouth moving in gasps of shock every time she ground against him. She knew what she wanted, what she wanted to give him most of all, and she knew it was within reach, recognizing the hot pleasure building in her.

She gave him everything—all of her passion, all of her trust, all of her love. She looked down into his eyes, and saw that he was offering her the same, and her heart burst as she lost control, loving him with all that she had.

He brought his hands up, grabbed her hips tightly and moved wildly under her. With him supporting her, she met his rhythm and rode him hard, arching her back as her orgasm consumed her. As the waves of it traveled through her, she declared her love for him when she felt him shudder underneath her, the heat of his climax shooting inside of her. Their voices blended, faded to murmurs; their bodies continued mating, until she fell against him, their hearts pounding, exhausted.

She lifted her head and kissed him tenderly.

"I do love you, Jack. I haven't ever loved anyone, haven't ever been loved. But I want to discover what it all means with you."

He slipped his arms around her, holding her close, cherishing her words.

"I want to share it all with you, too, Rainey, but I have to say, I think we have one problem."

She frowned against his shoulder. "What?"

He laughed softly, burying his face in her hair, inhaling the scent, and feeling—incredibly—his passion stirring again.

"This is only our first Christmas together, and I am not sure you can ever top this gift, sweetheart."

She laughed, too, feeling happiness deep down into her bones.

"Well, I'll just have to keep on trying." She wiggled against him in a way that made his blood catch fire. "But I don't think we are quite done here yet."

"Me, neither. And by the way, don't ever, *ever* lose that hat."

Laughing and loving, Raine lowered her lips to his, and made that promise to him. And many more.

* * * * *